An interview with legendary American fantasy writer Raymond E Feist inspired Duncan Lay to try his hand at fantasy writing. He writes on the train, while commuting from his Central Coast home to his other job as Masthead Chief of *The Sunday Telegraph*. This is his second fantasy trilogy.

Connect with Duncan Lay at:
duncanlay.blogspot.com
facebook.com/duncan.lay
Twitter @DuncanLay

BOOKS BY
DUNCAN LAY

THE DRAGON SWORD HISTORIES

*The Wounded Guardian* (1)
*The Risen Queen* (2)
*The Radiant Child* (3)


EMPIRE OF BONES

*Bridge of Swords* (1)

EMPIRE OF BONES
ONE

# BRIDGE OF SWORDS

## DUNCAN LAY

HARPER Voyager
*An Imprint of HarperCollinsPublishers*

**Harper***Voyager*
An imprint of HarperCollins*Publishers*

First published in Australia in 2012
by HarperCollins*Publishers* Australia Pty Limited
ABN 36 009 913 517
www.harpercollins.com.au

Copyright © Duncan Lay 2012

The right of Duncan Lay to be identified as the author of this
work has been asserted by him under the *Copyright Amendment
(Moral Rights) Act 2000.*

This work is copyright. Apart from any use as permitted under the
*Copyright Act 1968*, no part may be reproduced, copied, scanned, stored
in a retrieval system, recorded, or transmitted, in any form or by any
means, without the prior written permission of the publisher.

**HarperCollins***Publishers*
Level 13, 201 Elizabeth Street, Sydney NSW 2000, Australia
31 View Road, Glenfield, Auckland 0627, New Zealand
A 53, Sector 57, Noida, UP, India
77–85 Fulham Palace Road, London W6 8JB, United Kingdom
2 Bloor Street East, 20th floor, Toronto, Ontario M4W 1A8, Canada
10 East 53rd Street, New York NY 10022, USA

National Library of Australia Cataloguing-in-Publication entry:

Lay, Duncan.
  Bridge of swords / Duncan Lay.
  ISBN 978 0 7322 9418 2 (pbk).
  Lay, Duncan. Empire of bones ; 1.
  Fantasy fiction.
A823.4

Cover design by Darren Holt, HarperCollins Design Studio
Cover images by shutterstock.com
Map by Darren Holt, HarperCollins Design Studio
Author photograph by Anthony Reginato
Typeset in 11/15pt Sabon by Kirby Jones

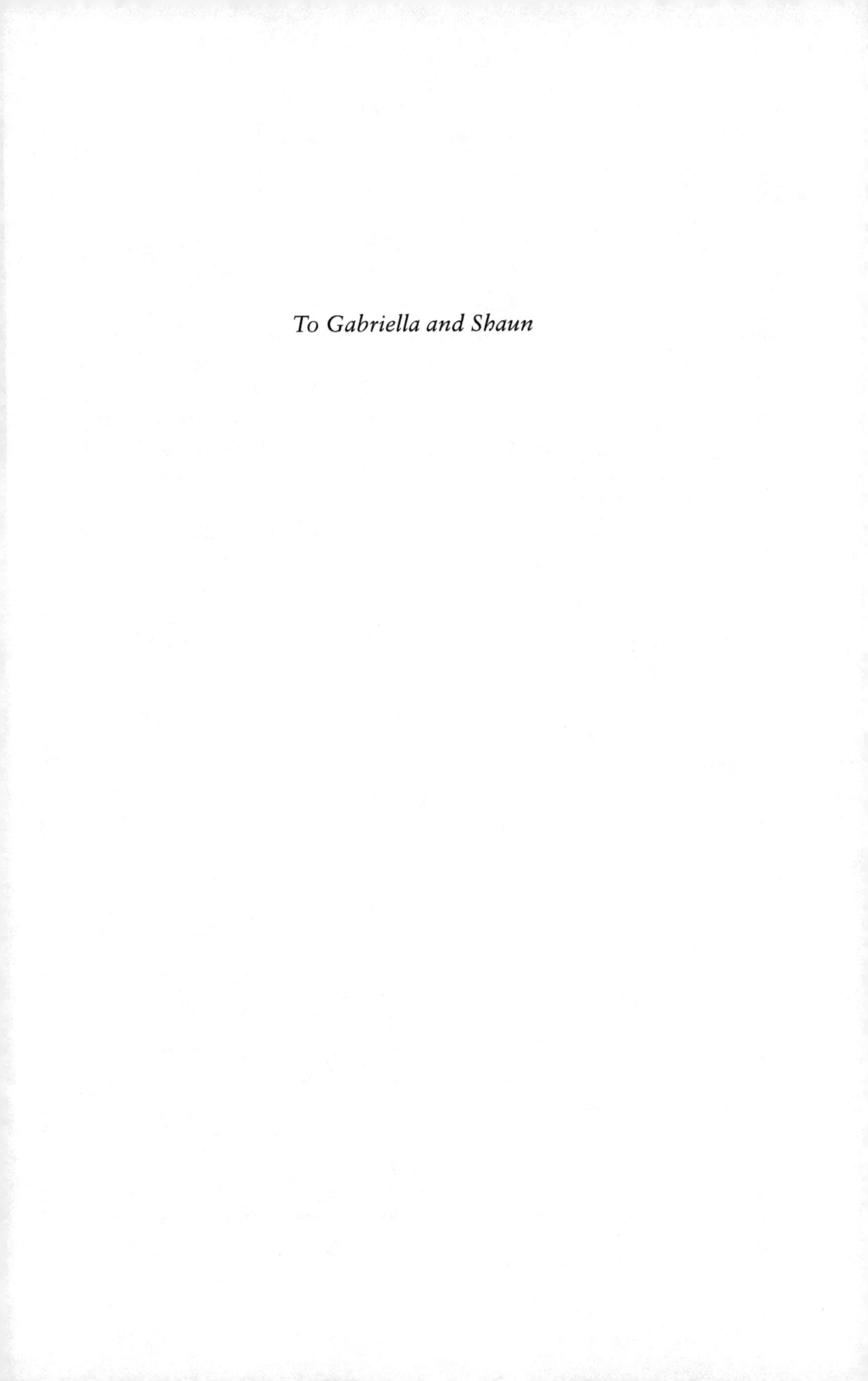

*To Gabriella and Shaun*

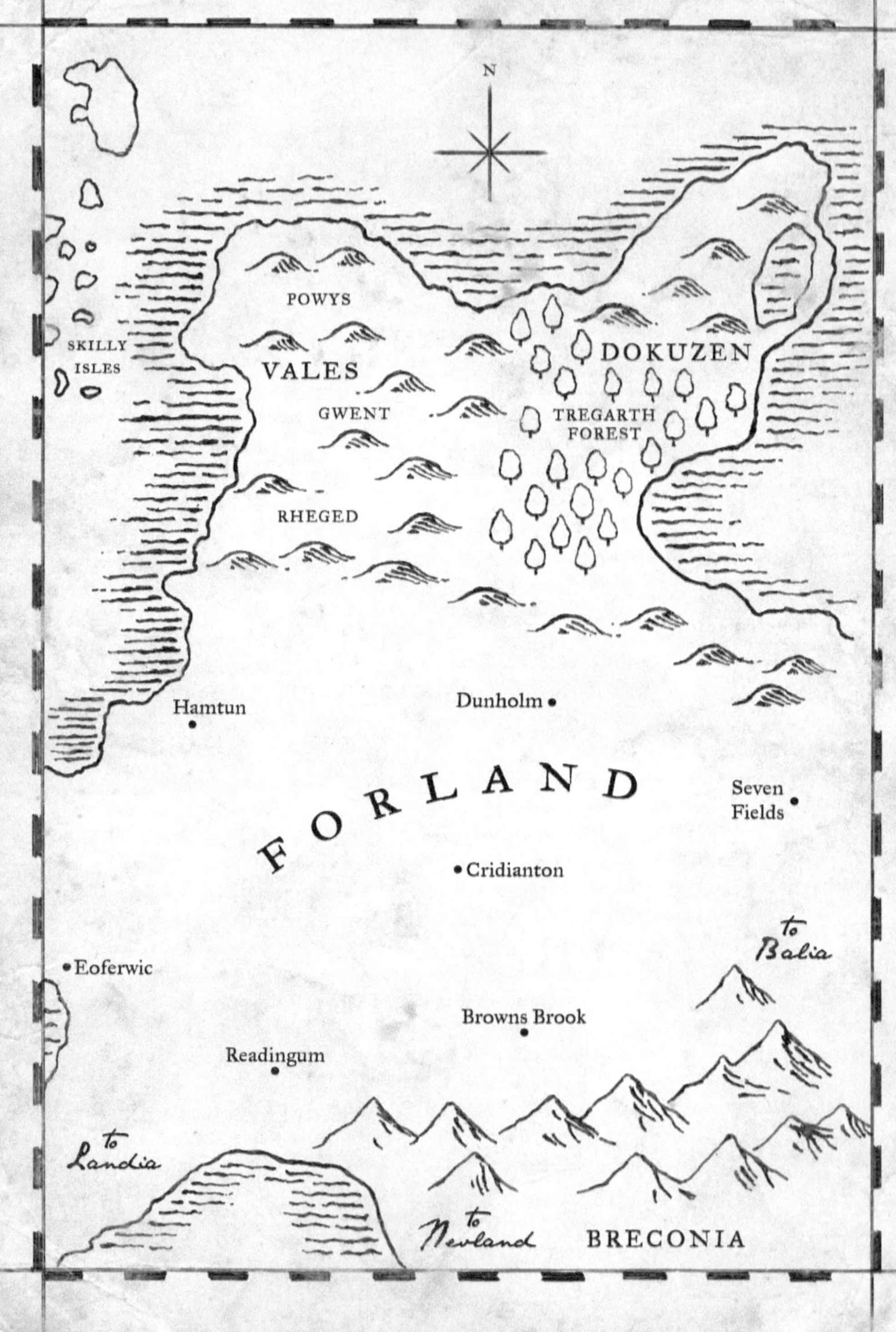

N
SKILLY ISLES
POWYS
VALES
GWENT
RHEGED
DOKUZEN
TREGARTH FOREST
Hamtun
Dunholm
FORLAND
Seven Fields
Cridianton
to Balia
Eoferwic
Browns Brook
Readingum
to Landia
to Newland
BRECONIA

# PROLOGUE

*I am writing this so you may learn the truth after I have been murdered by my people, by those I once loved and some I still love. My name will be forgotten, wiped clear from history. I have lost everything I hold dear and tomorrow I shall lose my life as well. But I shall write my own history and, perhaps, the truth will be known. It is an ugly truth. Even my own clan hates me because it is easier to believe a lie than face the fact we are not elves, we are humans — there is no difference. But they would rather kill me than admit they are not the only ones with magic, not creatures of legend but flesh and blood men.*

*Magic — it has been the saviour and the bane of us.*

*Once we were a race of men known as Elfarans, called to serve the dragons. My ancestor and his friends left the dragons' service, took a gift of long life and passed down to their children a legacy of magic. We thought it wondrous but it is a double-edged sword.*

*No land wants to welcome a people who can all use magic, ruled by a group of immortals. At first they are happy enough but then the fears grow. No wonder, when some of my kin think themselves above all other humans, call themselves elves, not Elfarans. They even pretend they are creatures of song and saga. Perhaps it was harmless at the start — but it is deadly serious now.*

*My ancestor and his fellow forefathers were worried enough to make us seal ourselves away from the other human lands, where we can do no harm. But, before they could finish, they disappeared, crumbled to dust, as though the weight of history caught up with them.*

*While some of us mourned them, others planned to take control. It is they who will kill me tomorrow, along with every human they can find who has magic, or knows about us. I shall hide this book, hope one day it shall be found and history can right itself.*

*My name is Sendatsu. It means a guide or pioneer in our old language. I had hoped to lead my people to a life of peace but instead I have been led to my own doom. I can only pray one of my children, or even their children's children, can be a better Sendatsu for my people than I.*

# 1

Sendatsu burst out of the tree as if running for his life. One moment the old oak stood alone atop the hill, as it had for a hundred years. Next moment an oaken staff appeared out of the mossy heart of the tree, making a strange shadow dance across the surface of the rough trunk, the image of a perfect garden. A heartbeat later, Sendatsu rushed through, falling to the ground in his haste.

By the time he had rolled over, the staff had retracted into the trunk, the shadow of the garden faded and there was no sign anything had ever happened — except for the sight and sound of Sendatsu as he lay, panting, on the ground. He ran his hands across himself, to reassure he was not just alive but whole, then sprang to his feet and pressed desperately against the rough bark of the oak — but it was once again solid, once again ordinary. There was no way back.

'But I never got the chance to say goodbye,' he whispered, holding the tree.

The tears came then, sobs ripping their way out of his chest, and he slumped down to the ground, against the tree that had saved him and yet cursed him at the same time. His body was safe but his heart was torn and bleeding. It could never be whole until he returned home — and he might never be able to return home.

What would happen tonight? What would they tell his children?

Mai. She could not get to sleep unless he brushed her hair and sang her the special goodnight song. Nobody else knew it but the two of them.

Cheijun. His mother had died giving birth to him. Sendatsu had put him to bed every night of his young life and, even then, he often crept beside Sendatsu in the early hours of the morning, saying he had been dreaming of gaijin monsters.

They were safe enough, at least for now, for they had been visiting their grandparents. But for how long? What would his father tell them? Would they think him dead? Would his enemies come for them? The thought terrified him and he beat his hands against the trunk.

'Let me come back! I am sorry — I swear I shall forget all I know, never speak of it again, just let me hold them one more time!' he screamed the words into the wood, knowing as he did so that nobody could hear and nobody could help. His only choice was to go on, to find the answers — and hope that might somehow get him home.

He fumbled in the pouch on his belt. They were in there, they were both in there. His father refused to have such things in his house, thought it made the children soft. He despised Sendatsu for letting his children have them. No matter that Mai was just five, Cheijun barely three. Sendatsu had never been allowed such things, for his father believed they made one weak. Mai's little doll, Cheijun's small bear. Together they fitted inside his hand.

He wrapped his fingers around them, prayed with all his heart, sending everything he had out to them. *Keep them safe. Let them know they are loved.* One day he would return and they would be together again. He opened eyes blurred with tears and tucked the toys safely back into the pouch. They were crude, woollen things but they smelled of home, of love. He would give them back as soon as he returned.

*If you return*, a tiny voice in the back of his head said.

He wiped his face clean and took a deep breath. How had it come to this? Just a few days ago he had been, if not entirely happy, then certainly content. Now he was an exile, hunted by his own kind — worse, the first elf to travel to the human lands for centuries. All because of an old scroll ...

The day had begun like many others. As the son of a clan leader — one of the twelve who made up the Elven Council and ruled Dokuzen — work was for other people. The lower classes had to take fishing boats to sea, work in the huge rice paddies, dig for coal and iron or labour in one of the trades. But not the nobility. Sendatsu had served in the Border Patrol — elves dedicated to protecting Dokuzen — for a couple of years, because it was expected of the upper classes. They could then settle into a life of leisure, parties and pleasure, content in the knowledge they had done their part for elven society.

Even that token effort had come to a halt when Sendatsu's marriage had been arranged. While life as the son of a clan leader brought with it many privileges, it also had a price. For as long as he could remember, Sendatsu had been in love with Asami, the daughter of one of his father's most loyal supporters. But such a match would bring no benefit to clan Tadayoshi. Instead Sendatsu was forced to marry Kayiko, a daughter of the leader of clan Chenjaku. Such a union brought clan Chenjaku firmly under the sway of clan Tadayoshi, and enhanced both his father Jaken's power and Jaken's position on the Council.

That neither Kayiko nor Sendatsu wanted such a match was immaterial. Worse, he had been forced to watch Asami marry Gaibun, a friend but also the son of Jaken's only rival for leadership of clan Tadayoshi. Another union that was more for Jaken than for the young couple.

This was the last straw for Sendatsu. His father often used him to further his own ambitions. He had driven Sendatsu mercilessly to excel with the bow and the sword, for the son of Jaken had to be the best. Failure brought a furious tirade at best — more usually a beating. At first Sendatsu had done everything his father demanded. But then he had begun to question why he had to devote himself to his father's ambition. As he grew older he chafed at what he was forced to do, although he dared not rebel completely, for his father's rage was terrifying and all the extra training in the world did not allow him to match Jaken.

Sendatsu had never loved Kayiko but moving into his own home had at least removed him from the baleful influence of his father. Better yet, he had been instantly smitten when Mai was born. Love at last entered their home. He thought nothing could be as perfect — until Cheijun also arrived in his life.

The price was high — it cost Kayiko her life — and although Sendatsu had not loved her, he still mourned. With nothing else, he threw himself into his children, living his life through theirs.

Everything he had not received, he wanted to give them. He tried to fill their childhood with all his had lacked. He had only seen his father when he had done something wrong, or when he was being 'taught a lesson'. Painful as those were, strangely he had found himself looking forward to another session with practice blades, even though it left him bloodied and bruised. It was still time with his father.

He was determined his children would have more of him than that.

Better yet, his children gave him the strength to defy Jaken. Usually he arrived at his father's house full of defiance and strong words, only to have them vanish like the morning mist under the blaze of his father's anger. Yet when Jaken ordered him to leave the children and spend his days working to advance clan Tadayoshi, he refused to back down, vowing he would look after Mai and Cheijun at least until they were ready to begin their schooling.

Even more surprisingly, his father had eventually agreed, when it became obvious that no amount of shouting would change Sendatsu's mind. He had walked away with Jaken's words, that he would 'regret' his actions, ringing in his ears.

They had seemed like nonsense. He could never regret time with his children. And yet it had led him here ...

It had begun simply enough. Mai had been asking questions about elven history. Unlike his father, he did not shout at her, or ignore her. Instead he took them both out to the tombs of the forefathers, the twelve elves who had brought them to this land, created the clans and founded Dokuzen. Of course Cheijun was too young to understand but he enjoyed looking at the strange armour and weapons.

Few elves travelled out to the tombs of the forefathers, a dark, gloomy building on the outskirts of Dokuzen, once an oasis of peace, surrounded by space and gardens, now overgrown and returning to the woods. They had been the only ones there that day.

'Why doesn't anybody come here?' Mai asked as they wandered around the tombs, looking at the carved stone figures.

Sendatsu did not answer straight away, as he was busy chasing a giggling Cheijun around one of the stone slabs.

'I don't know,' he finally admitted. 'It is not forbidden but neither is it encouraged. It is like an unwritten law.'

'Will we get in trouble for being here?'

Sendatsu smiled. 'Of course not. Your grandfather is a clan leader. That means we can do almost anything we want.'

'So I can stay up late and eat as many plums as I can?'

He laughed. 'Nice try, little one. But that is not what I meant.'

'Why don't the forefathers look like us? Their ears are the same but their faces are different.' She changed the subject swiftly, as she always did.

'I don't know,' he admitted again. 'Perhaps the sculptor wasn't very good,' he offered.

'And what is this?' She pointed to a carved stone list beside each tomb.

'Well, this is a list of the wives and children they had,' Sendatsu said, pleased to have an answer for her this time.

'Why so many?'

'Well, if one of them died, then they married again,' he replied, then cursed himself.

'Like Mother?' Mai asked softly. 'Will you marry again?'

Sendatsu opened his arms and she hugged him. 'I could not love anyone else as much as you.'

'Good.'

But they could only stay like that for a few moments before Cheijun was tugging on Sendatsu's arm.

'Swords!'

Mai gave her father a smile and wandered off around the tombs, while Sendatsu held up Cheijun so he could look inside a cabinet of strange armour and weapons. Despite his age, he was already fascinated with such things and loved to watch Sendatsu train each day with sword and bow.

'Look, those are straight. Not like my sword.' Sendatsu pointed out the difference between the gently curved blade he had at his hip and the straight piece of metal in the wooden cabinet. And next to it some sort of strange crossbow, nothing like the longbows Sendatsu had spent the past twenty years learning to use.

'Mai! Mai!' Cheijun's shouts brought Mai wandering over, but she had little interest in the weapons.

That would change soon — it had to. When she was seven she would have to begin to learn how to use a bow, at ten she would begin sword-training as well. Every elf had to be ready, in case the gaijin, the humans, ever came.

'These are boring,' she announced. 'Papa, there are books over there. Can you show me?'

As always he was happy to, although Cheijun was less than impressed to be taken away from the weapons.

'Back! Swords!' he insisted, but Sendatsu tucked him under an arm and tickled him until he forgot about them.

'What are in the books?' Mai wanted to know. 'Why are they here?'

Books were both valuable and rare in Dokuzen — and treated with the greatest of respect. Anything in them was regarded with the same reverence as a sermon from the High Priest of Aroaril. If you were going to make the effort to write something down, it had to be information of the highest value. Only the very rich could have books. Sendatsu had a dozen, while his father's shelves groaned under them.

'The forefathers must have brought them here, like the swords and armour.' Sendatsu was fascinated by the books as well. He had been here as a boy, along with Asami and Gaibun — but he could not remember the books from that visit.

'Can we see one? Can we?'

The cabinet was locked but they were the only people there. Besides, he would put them back afterwards. Nobody would be the wiser. Sendatsu was not very good at magic — he had barely scraped through his Test of magic — but impressing his children was a powerful motivator. He reached into the magic and warmed the metal inside the lock until it sprang open.

'Magic!' Cheijun cheered. 'More!'

'Hush, Cheijun, Papa will get into trouble,' Mai told him loftily.

Sendatsu felt the tiredness that always came after using magic, even for something as trivial as opening the lock. But he did not show it, instead reaching in and pulling out a book at random, sniffing a little at the smell of must and dust.

'We have to be very careful,' he told them and opened it reverently.

Together, the three of them stared at the writing.

'I can't understand any of it. It's just swirls,' Mai complained.

Sendatsu said nothing — for he could not read it either.

'It must be in another language,' he muttered, replaced it and selected another.

But this one was also unreadable, although in a different script again.

'What does it say?' Mai insisted.

He searched through the books rapidly, no longer handling them as carefully but desperate to find something he understood.

'Can we go now?' Mai asked.

Cheijun had wandered off again, and was trying to look in the weapons cabinet.

Sendatsu grabbed one final book — and stopped. Inside were more unintelligible words but also, nestled into a space cut into the pages, a scroll. He unrolled it and read it easily, even though it was faded with age. This alone he could understand. It was a letter written to him. Well, not exactly him, for while this Sendatsu had the same clan name, Tadayoshi, he did not have the same family name of Moratsune.

Stranger still, it had been signed by all the clan leaders. And not just any clan leaders — the original forefathers of Dokuzen, the elves who had left the dragons' service. Although his children had long since lost interest and were wandering around, Sendatsu felt this was too important a find to leave there. He had a cloth bag over his shoulder and, on impulse, he slipped the scroll in before returning the book and hurriedly locking the cabinet again. If anyone said something, well, his father was a clan leader. Besides, it was not as if people came here all the time.

Only later did he realise what he had done.

The children had been put to bed, the night song sung, and he had stalked around Cheijun's room warning any gaijin or monsters they would die a thousand deaths if they dared invade his son's dreams. It never really worked but there was always the hope this night would be undisturbed. The servants had been dismissed after cooking the evening meal and he was alone. Beside a pair of lamps, Sendatsu brought out the scroll and started to read — and his world changed.

It began simply enough: a request to carry out the wishes of the forefathers. He nearly put it down and went to sleep himself. Then he read one more passage and his son's nightmare, which he dismissed every night, came alive. Every line was shocking. Sendatsu had been told, as every elf in Dokuzen had been told, that the elves had sealed themselves away from the world to protect them from the hordes of gaijin outside. A magic barrier kept the gaijin at bay but all had to learn the sword and bow, just in case the humans ever came.

Yet this implied the opposite. Sendatsu could read the words but struggled to understand them. The forefathers spoke of the elves being a danger to humans, of needing to protect the humans from elves. They claimed the elves had stolen from the humans and could not be trusted. To protect the humans, the elves needed to be locked away. Yet, bizarrely, it never said elves. It referred to his people not as elves but as Elfarans.

His first instinct was to roll it back up and hurl it on the fire. Surely this had to be a fake. But it was signed by the forefathers, using their official seals, still used today by clan leaders such as his father, Jaken. That alone made it very valuable. Besides, he had been taught from birth that anything written was true. And it had come from the tombs of the forefathers. He could not destroy it. His next thought was to take it back tomorrow and never think of it again … then something seemed to leap off the page. A passage written in a larger script and circled in ink.

*The magic does not come from within us, but is a legacy of our service to the dragons and their long exposure to magic. It is not our birthright, as some claim now. This lie will be exposed, for the magic will fade with each passing generation. Not all Elfarans will be able to perform magic and, eventually, no more of us shall be able to use the magic than any other race of humans. As the magic decays within us, the barrier around Dokuzen will decay. It will fade, disappear, and our people will be able to make a home for themselves among the other humans.*

Sendatsu felt sick with horror at the thought. For an instant he was a small child again, being told the gaijin were coming to get him. For the magic was failing now. Sendatsu had learned to fight with sword, bow and bare hands with one class of elves, all his own age — and he had also learned magic with them. Of all, only one had gone on to become a Magic-weaver. Asami. None of the others showed much ability with magic. Many, like Sendatsu, had scraped through their Test of magic and few used magic in their ordinary lives.

It was something the Council had been debating for years. There was talk of increasing the time to learn magic from two years to three years — perhaps even five years. There was even talk of working more closely with the Magic-weavers, an order distrusted and ignored for centuries. The latter, however, was fiercely opposed by Jaken and his supporters. They preferred an approach of warning students they had to devote themselves to study — and threatening anyone who failed the Test of magic would be instantly banished from Dokuzen — no matter how high-ranking their family.

If the fading magic was linked to the magic barrier around Dokuzen, the thing that protected them from the hordes of barbarian humans outside, then it was a matter of life and death. This scroll could change every elf's life. He had to show it to the Council, had to act now, before it was too late.

Except, after watching his father devote himself to the politics of Dokuzen, Sendatsu wanted nothing to do with it. His father had tried to push responsibilities and duties on him from a young age until he rebelled against them. Since his wife died he had stepped even further back. Friends and former classmates came to him with problems and requests for help — he ignored or refused them all. But, much as he might want to, he could not forget about this. Every elf was taught how important the barrier was. It protected them from the humans. Cheijun's nightmare was a common one. Elven parents regularly told their children to be good or the gaijin would come to get them. This warning from the past could not be ignored. That thought, on top of the writers' names and the power of the written words, settled in his gut. He had spent years running away from such things but now one had caught him, he could not let it go. What was it doing hidden in the tombs of the forefathers? If only he had not taken it ... if it was true, it could change everything in Dokuzen. He shuddered at the thought. Words from the forefathers themselves. Instructions they wanted carried out. And then there was the implication that clan Tadayoshi once ruled Dokuzen, for this other Sendatsu had been the Elder Elf. His father needed to see that, while the whole Council needed to hear the warning about the barrier.

For a moment he thought about addressing them himself, but decided it would be far better to hand it to his father. Then he had yet another thought. His father was a master of scorn — and he never missed an opportunity to tell Sendatsu he was wasting his gifts, ruining his life and spoiling his children. If this was all a child's tale, or some sort of humour, his father would be furious.

Perhaps he should speak to a Magic-weaver first, see what they thought. The fact it gave him a chance to speak to Asami had nothing to do with it.

The nobility of Dokuzen loved to throw parties. For them, life in Dokuzen was simple. Every person knew their place, their role in society, an order created and enforced by the Elven Council. Your clan's position within the Council and your family's position within your clan determined how your life would be lived. If you were at the top, your only duty was enjoyment. Sendatsu rarely attended these parties, preferring the company of his children to his peers. He knew they were speaking about him behind his back. So many of them longed to wield the power and influence he refused to use. And as for a warrior looking after children — it was unheard of. He knew what they said. Why had he not married again? He was not handsome — he was of average height for an elf, but seemed shorter because of his huge arms, shoulders and chest, the legacy of years of work with the bow. His hair was cropped short, while his jaw always seemed dark with the trace of a beard, his nose was too long, his ears too big. But his position made him very attractive and only his open love for Asami had kept the daughters of high-ranking elves away from him before his marriage.

Still, while being at a party was unpleasant, it gave him a reason to see Asami. Like many arranged marriages in Dokuzen, her and Gaibun's was a union in name only. Unlike others in the same situation, who managed to keep up some form of public pretence with their marriage, they lived lives apart under the same roof. He served in the Border Patrol, she worked as a Magic-weaver. Friends with both, he saw them separately but never together. There was some secret, some darkness at the heart of this, but although he was close to them both, neither would say a word about it. And, of course, once joined before Aroaril there was no way out of this unhappiness.

So he knew Gaibun would not be there when he arrived. That was lucky for, as always, Asami took his breath away when he saw her.

She stood in the atrium, greeting her guests, as the host should. That day she wore a glorious red robe, and her long black hair was pinned up carefully, showing off her swanlike neck and accentuating her high cheekbones and pert nose. But when he stepped in front of her, Mai and Cheijun holding hands just behind, her studied mask of politeness cracked.

'Sendatsu!'

He took her hand and could almost feel the heat between them. For a long, long moment they stared at each other and he had to hold himself back from sweeping her into his arms. For a heartbeat he thought she might leap into his, then they both became aware that all conversation had stopped and everyone was staring at them.

'Come, bring your children through to the garden,' she said hastily. Not letting go of his hand for an instant, she rushed him past the other guests, down a corridor and out into the air.

'You shouldn't have come, not after last time,' she hissed, glancing around the garden to see who was watching, but her glowing eyes contradicted those words. He thought she was going to kiss him but then a pair of servants discreetly stepped onto the terrace, out of earshot but clearly within sight.

'Are they there on your orders, or on Gaibun's?' Sendatsu nodded towards them.

'Mine,' she said with a half-smile. 'I am afraid I cannot trust myself around you. Why did you come today? I thought you hated these parties?'

'I have something of great importance to say ...'

'Wait!' She let go of his hand. 'My guests might come out here before the entertainment starts.'

So they stood and talked about nothing, while Mai and Cheijun chased butterflies. It should have been awkward but they had never had any problem finding something to say. They could always make each other laugh as well. It was as if they had seen each other yesterday, not a whole moon ago.

Sendatsu always loved this. Talking to her, with Mai and Cheijun playing nearby, he could imagine they were a real family.

'You know, perhaps you should come back to my villa,' he blurted.

Asami chuckled, then stared at him. 'You would risk everything for me? Be prepared to have Gaibun challenge you?'

Sendatsu hesitated, his silence saying it all, then the music began and the spell was broken. From deep inside the house the strings echoed out to the garden, as did the applause and gentle cheers of the guests.

'What was so important you needed to come here? Was it to torment me with false hope or did you just wish to create more gossip?' She sighed.

Still Sendatsu hesitated, then reluctantly reached into his pouch and produced the scroll.

'Read this.' He handed her the scroll and watched as she unrolled and scanned the words. He read her face as she read the scroll, seeing surprise turn to amazement and then close up. He felt his heart beat faster. Something was going on behind her eyes ...

'Where did you get this knowledge?' Asami breathed.

'In the tombs of our forefathers. But it seems so ridiculous, except for the passage about the fading magic and the threat to the magical barrier. Can it really be true, that the barrier is here to keep us in, not the humans out?'

'I think it is all true — and the evidence we have been looking for,' Asami said slowly.

Sendatsu laughed at Cheijun's antics and was slow to reply. 'What? Do you mean to say you believe it?'

'My sensei, Sumiko, has had me testing the barrier these past few moons. It stands but it is not what it once was. You can now approach right up to the edge of it safely — and may well be able to travel through it, as long as you have magic. And as for the magic decaying within us — we all know it to be true. Sumiko has been warning the Council of it for the past few years. She would love to see this. It is real evidence of what we have been trying to tell the Council for years — the elves do not understand magic and take it for granted. They have been able to ignore it so far but this evidence about the barrier will force them to take notice. Give it to me and I'll take it to Sumiko.'

'Wait — I only talked to you so my father would not shout at me for wasting his time. I don't want to be handing stolen scrolls to the Magic-weavers,' Sendatsu said, alarmed. He knew how much Jaken despised the Magic-weavers in general and Sumiko, their leader, in particular. Then there was the tantalising news about clan Tadayoshi ruling the elves, as Jaken longed to do. If Jaken found out Sendatsu had handed something so valuable, let alone dangerous, to the Magic-weavers rather than bring it to him ...

'This could change Dokuzen, might even bring down the Council itself. Why did you even come here, if not to do something about it?' Asami kept a light smile on her face but her voice had turned cold and scathing. 'Do you merely seek to hand the problem to someone else and then run back to your children, hide under the bed with them?'

'I wanted to see you, have you tell me it was nothing to worry about,' Sendatsu admitted miserably.

Asami shook her head. 'Sometimes I wonder about you, Sendatsu. Perhaps one day you shall find the courage to live up to your name.'

'What do you mean? None can match me with bow, sword or even bare hands. The only elf to ever score higher than I in the Tests was my father ...'

'There is a big difference between sword-courage and real courage,' she told him. 'If only you had learned that, then perhaps we would be together even now.'

'That is unfair! My father forbade our union and forced me to marry Kayiko ...'

'You could have walked away. We could have both walked away from Dokuzen, gone and lived up north, found a small farm or fishing shack ...'

'Left Dokuzen? Left our lives behind, turned our backs on our birthright, clan and class, become nothing more than esemono and grub in the dirt? What would our families think of us then? We might sooner go and live among the gaijin!'

'You are too proud of what you are, not who you are,' Asami said coldly. 'Calling those who work for us esemono is too much like your father. And since your wife died, you still haven't found the courage to be with me. I always hope the next time will be different but it never is.'

'We have to be careful. A scandal could destroy our families, tear apart the clan ...'

'And what does your clan and family think of you now?' Asami continued remorselessly. 'Is your father proud of the way you spend every day with your children, rather than working for him?'

Again, Sendatsu said nothing.

Asami sighed. 'We would have been together. We could have found a way. We are no longer children — we've seen twenty-seven summers together, yet we are still apart. Don't we deserve to be happy?'

Sendatsu looked around, but the servants were behind him. He reached out and took her hand, hiding it from them.

'You know I wish for that. I just couldn't go against my father. He probably would have sent guards to drag me back home.'

Asami smiled briefly, but also slipped her hand out of his. 'I am sorry too. At least you have your children from your marriage. I have nothing from mine. I see you, I think of what could have been, I dare to dream and then you break it once again. Gaibun and I cannot even talk without fighting these days. Half of those inside my home have taken great delight in telling me Gaibun has another lover. It is not so much that I begrudge him a little love in his life, for seeking what I cannot give him, but I hate it when others gloat behind my back.'

'Perhaps one day things might change ...'

'You have been saying that for many years — and I am yet to see action.'

'I dream as well!' Sendatsu declared. 'You know that I long for the day when we can be together. But Gaibun has always been there for me, stood by me when other elves turned their backs, when my father drove all others away. We cannot be together without humiliating him ...'

She reached out and brushed her fingers across his cheek but he was too fast, turning his head to kiss her hand.

'Things can only change if you let me take that scroll and do something with it!' she told him.

'But what can a scroll do?'

'You know what the people think about words. If they are written, they must be true. Besides, instructions from the ancestor elves themselves, written from beyond the grave, advice about the magic fading and the barrier decaying! Who could not take notice of them? You are the most trusting person I know, blindly following your father, but even you were disturbed by it. Imagine what the rest of Dokuzen will think,' Asami said simply. 'Let me take the scroll to Sumiko. Life here has gone on unchanged for the last three hundred years. The barrier seals us away from the human world and blocks out anything new at the same time. Everything about our life is so formal, so restricted. And the Council makes sure nothing ever changes. Your life is mapped out from the moment you are born. There are brilliant elves forced to labour in the mines, while fools sit in my reception room, contributing nothing but enjoying everything. Some are free to marry for love while others, like us, have to marry who we are told. I know you hate this as much as I do! The Magic-weavers may be separate to the rest of society but they are also the only ones with the power to challenge the Council. Imagine it — life without the Council controlling every aspect — who does what, who gets what — and who marries who.'

Sendatsu felt the temptation. He wanted to say yes. But it would mean setting himself against his father, against the Council. It would mean taking sides and taking a stand. The thought made him feel sick. As always, he sought a way out. He did not want to do anything that would risk his children. That made his decision easy and he told himself it was the right thing to do.

'I shall show it to my father first. I have to give him a chance to act. But if he does not take me seriously, then you can have it, I swear.'

Asami shook her head.

'I don't know why I expect more of you, but I always do,' she said softly.

He leaned in, but not too close. For the thousandth time he looked into her eyes and dearly wanted to smooth a stray lock of hair back across her ear.

'I don't have a choice.'

'There is always a choice,' she told him sadly. 'But you seem able to pick the one where you do nothing and let others decide for you.'

'Asami …'

'Go! Just go!'

'I will be back if my father does not take this seriously,' he promised.

Asami turned away. 'My guests will be wondering where I am. I need to get back to them. If you leave now, I can tell them I had enough of your bad manners and unruly children. Then it will not get back to Gaibun.'

'Asami, wait …'

But she swept away, leaving him frustrated. His father had been making noises about another marriage — there were always daughters of clan leaders and important elves desperate for alliance to clan Tadayoshi. But the thought of being married off to another who was not Asami … the last time he had said the words before a priest of Aroaril, he thought they would choke him.

'Mai! Cheijun!' he called and they came running.

'Look at this flower!' Mai held up a trophy for him to admire.

'Wonderful,' he enthused, but his heart was not in it.

He picked them both up, one in each arm, and forced a laugh as Cheijun tried to tickle him with a stalk of grass.

'Where are we going?' Mai asked.

Sendatsu took a deep breath. He dearly wanted to go home, pretend none of this had happened — or slip back to the tombs, return the scroll and forget all about it. But the truth was, he could not forget. It was too mysterious.

'How would you like to see grandmother Noriko?' He smiled.

* * *

'Your mother spoils those children of yours. Nearly as much as you do.'

'I am pleased to see you also, Father,' Sendatsu said stiffly.

He had bathed and dressed the children carefully, made sure they were wearing their best clothes, that Cheijun had his tiny wooden sword tucked into his belt and he had Mai's doll and Cheijun's toy bear in his pouch before they arrived at his father's villa. He told himself this was only prudent and it would make it easier on the children. His mother had been happy to see him but far happier to see the children, and had the servants take them through to the garden while Sendatsu stepped into his father's study. This had always been a place of punishment and terror when he had been a boy and it was hard not to be haunted by the same feelings now.

'What is the purpose of your visit? Surely not to tell me you have woken up and decided to accept your responsibilities.'

'I am not ready to work for you, Father. The children are still so young and they need me ...'

'They need to be fed, clothed and disciplined. Nothing more! They lost a father when Kayiko died, not a mother. You might as well wear a robe rather than a hakama, get a job as a nursemaid to some esemono family for all the good you do this family and your clan! You should be my strong right hand, not a burden and a bitter disappointment.'

Sendatsu felt the usual flare of anger at his father's words but had many years of practice at hiding it.

'I did not come here to talk about me, Father — but rather a matter of importance to the Council,' he said, trying to keep his voice level.

'See what I mean?' Jaken pushed himself back in his chair, which was as hard and unyielding as its owner, Sendatsu thought as he shifted in his own.

'What, Father?'

'A true son of mine would have fought back against my words. But you, you just sit there and accept it. I tried to harden you up as a child but I can see that failed. You have too much of your mother in you. I am very busy — in part because you do not help me — but I could make time to train your boy. Aroaril knows he can't be learning how to be a man from his own father ...'

'You will never touch Cheijun,' Sendatsu swore, his voice cracking. 'He does not need your training.'

'It worked on you, did it not? You were useless as a boy but, by the time of the Tests, you were almost as good as I,' Jaken mused.

Sendatsu had to bite his tongue to say nothing. Jaken was determined Sendatsu would live up to his reputation. This meant extra training and a beating if Sendatsu failed, which for his father meant not finishing first. He still bore the scars and the thought of his father doing the same to Cheijun ... he would rather die first.

'Still, that seems to have you showing a bit of fire at last,' Jaken continued. 'Perhaps there is hope for you. Perhaps I just need to find the right lever to move you ...'

Sendatsu stood. 'I can see coming here was a mistake,' he said stiffly. 'I apologise for wasting your time, Father ...'

'Sit down!'

Sendatsu sat before he could even think of refusing, and before the whip-crack echo of his father's voice had died away.

'What is it you wanted to tell me?'

Sendatsu pulled his thoughts together and explained about the tombs, taking the scroll home and what he had found inside.

'I know it was written down and I know it claims to be instructions from our forefathers but still I found it hard to believe. The idea that the barrier was put there to protect the humans from us, not the other way around, that the magic is fading ...'

'The Magic-weavers have been spouting this sort of nonsense about the fading magic for many years,' Jaken dismissed. 'The Council had to forbid them from speaking of it two centuries ago. The idea of elves without magic — the idea is laughable!'

'But Father, what about the passage where it describes how we will lose magic with each passing generation? Two centuries ago the magic was much stronger. Now there are few who use it in their ordinary lives and fewer still who have the power to become Magic-weavers. You cannot argue against that. And if that is correct then it means the barrier is also fading, will soon be gone. What will happen then?'

'It is all nonsense,' his father still dismissed.

'I did think that,' Sendatsu lied. 'After all, there was also a passage about clan Tadayoshi ruling the elves ...'

He held his breath, expecting to have his head taken off with a torrent of derision but, for once, Jaken looked interested in what he had to say.

'Where is this scroll?' he asked.

'At my home. Safe.'

'You must get it and bring it back here, at once. I shall have a squad of Council Guards meet us here. Once the Council has it under safekeeping, you must never speak of it again.'

Jaken grabbed a piece of parchment and began furiously scribbling something.

'Well, what are you waiting for?' he snapped.

Sendatsu still sat. 'It is true, isn't it?' he said softly. 'It is all true and you seek to hide it.'

Jaken surged to his feet and loomed over Sendatsu.

'Listen to me, boy,' he snarled.

Sendatsu gritted his teeth as he prepared for another lecture. That term always infuriated him. One day he might even tell his father that.

'There is so much you do not understand, that you have chosen to ignore. Dokuzen is balanced on a knife-edge. Only the authority of the Council and the habit of people's obedience are keeping us from falling apart. If it was to get out that the magic was dying within us and that soon there will be elves born with no more magic in them than a gaijin baby — how would the people react? And most of them think all that stands between their children and hordes of ravening gaijin is the magical barrier around Dokuzen. If they knew that was fading, the people would panic. The barrier is the one constant in every elf's life. Without it, Dokuzen will fall apart. And what would the Magic-weavers do with this knowledge? They have long lusted for power, sought to overthrow the Council and rule themselves. Why do you think every elf must learn the sword and bow? It is not just to protect us from humans. It allows the clan leaders to summon an army of elves, means the Magic-weavers cannot take power by force. But if the people refuse to obey the orders of the clan leaders, there is nothing to stand between the Magic-weavers and absolute power.' Jaken paused and looked sternly at Sendatsu. 'But you don't want to know all that, do you? You don't want to think about your every action, try and anticipate what your enemies are doing. You don't want the responsibility for the safety of an entire people. You would rather play with your children and let your brain rot away.'

'I ...'

'We don't have time for this. Go and get me that scroll, then take your children, go home and forget all about this day. At least you had the sense to come and see me first ...'

Sendatsu tried to compose his face but he was horribly aware he had never been good at creating what the elves called a mask of inscrutability, not letting others read your thoughts on your face.

'You have told another,' Jaken breathed. 'Please tell me it was not Asami ...'

Sendatsu thought about lying but knew it was pointless.

'I thought it a children's tale, or similar. I wanted to know if the passages about magic and the barrier were worth bothering you ...'

'You mean you wanted to impress her,' Jaken spat. 'And what did she say?'

'That the Magic-weavers would believe it true and she wanted to give it to Sumiko ...'

'Sweet Aroaril, boy! If brains were fire, you wouldn't have enough to light tinder! This scroll must never fall into the hands of the Magic-weavers! The Council thought all those things had been destroyed and what were left in the tombs of our forefathers were relics in different languages. I can see I shall have to take care of what is in there myself ...'

'But if it is true, then we cannot hide it away,' Sendatsu argued. 'It should be brought to the attention of the full Council. The people need to know — you cannot hide something like this forever.'

'Have you not been listening to me, boy? This does not have to be forever, just long enough for me to gain control of the Council and see clan Tadayoshi rule supreme. Until then not a word of it can get out. Too much is at stake. That knowledge could destroy us all. Now go and get that scroll — I shall have the Council Guards meet you there.'

'But ...'

'This is not something for you to worry about. Go now! Your children are waiting.'

Sendatsu reluctantly stood. As ever, he was leaving his father's study feeling sick to the stomach. This was nearly as bad as the time when Jaken had informed him he would not be allowed to marry Asami.

'Move, boy!'

Jaken hustled him out of the office and towards the front door.

'I'll just tell Mai and Cheijun where I am going.' Sendatsu took a pace back to where he could hear their voices.

'You will be back within a turn of the hourglass. They will not even miss you. Go!' Jaken propelled him onwards.

Sendatsu tried to set his feet. The voices were closer, he wanted to wait for a few more moments and he was sure he could see their faces. As ever, after talking to his father, he needed a way to lift the darkness inside him and his children were the only way he knew to do that. But while he trained with sword and bow every day, his father was just as strong — and twice as determined.

'Hurry back.' Jaken pushed him out of the door.

Sendatsu, looking back, thought he almost saw his children; he could hear them clearly — then the door shut and they were lost to him.

Heart still heavy, he turned and hurried back home.

# 2

*When we arrived in this land, we found the people warm and welcoming. The north-east, where we landed, was either hilly or covered in forest and few people were living there. They were happy to let us settle. Here we were able to use magic and our knowledge to turn the land to our advantage. We were a curious mix. We still retained some of the building and masonry habits and culture of our Elfaran forefathers, yet our food, farming and fighting techniques came from the Nipponese, the people among whom the Elfarans had first found a home.*

*This was a golden time when we exchanged information with the people we found here. Yet already we were splitting. Some of us wanted to live among the people here, while others built a magnificent city for us. It wasn't clear at the time, but already we had reached a dangerous fork in the road.*

When Sendatsu arrived home, he raced into the main reception room. In most elven villas this was a large, airy room, with a scatter of couches and the place where noble elves would receive guests. Here, it was filled with Mai and Cheijun's toys, clothes and a scatter of dirty plates the servants had missed beneath the children's mess. Beside a couch, on a small wooden table, was the scroll, just as he left it.

Sendatsu lifted it, then hesitated. He had promised to bring it to Asami if his father failed to take it seriously. Perhaps he should do something with this knowledge, show his father that he could not be pushed around. The only time he had stood up to Jaken was over the children. Instead of leaving them with servants, or his mother, to run errands for Jaken and supervise his many landholdings, mines and fishing vessels, he had declared he would look after Mai and Cheijun. But the thought of being at the front of this political battle terrified him. This would tear apart Dokuzen and he would be at the heart of it. That was too much to ask him to do. Not even for Asami. No, he would hurry back to his father's villa, deliver the scroll, pick up the children and forget all about it. Much safer.

'Is that the scroll?' Asami asked.

Sendatsu nearly dropped it in his surprise, as Asami and Sumiko walked into the room. Sumiko, the head of the Magic-weavers, had taught them both magic, years ago. For the son of Jaken, who was hated by the Magic-weavers, it had not been a pleasant experience.

'Just give us the scroll, Sendatsu, and we shall make everything else happen. You need not bother yourself with it any more,' Sumiko said brightly, stepping forwards.

'I can't — there are Council Guards on the way here. My father knows about it — if he does not receive it …'

'It is even more important than we thought,' Sumiko breathed. 'Council Guards? We don't have much time. Give us the scroll and we'll make it look as though your home was robbed and ransacked.' She glanced around the room. 'It won't take much effort.'

Sendatsu held onto the scroll.

'What will you do with it?' he demanded.

'Save the elves. Protect Dokuzen. Make a better life for everyone,' Sumiko said enticingly.

'Everyone? Or just you?' Sendatsu's memory of her classes made his voice harsh.

'Don't be a fool. This is far beyond you. Leave the big decisions to those who are able to make them,' Sumiko insisted.

'No.' Sendatsu clutched the scroll to his chest.

'Sendatsu — please?' Asami asked softly. 'Do you want to see your father rule Dokuzen as Elder Elf? Who will you be forced to marry then? And what of your children — what control will he have over their lives? Little Mai, the granddaughter of the Elder Elf. He will want to sell her to the highest bidder ...'

Sendatsu tightened his grip. 'I will never allow that to happen,' he swore.

'Sendatsu? Where are you?' another voice called, and the tramp of booted feet on tiles reached into the room.

'The Council Guards — quick, give us the scroll!' Sumiko snapped.

But handing it over would forever set him against his father. Sendatsu froze at the thought. Far easier to do nothing and let others solve the problem for him.

'What is going on here? Why are these Magic-weavers here?' The squad of Council Guards strode in, making even the airy room seem crowded.

Sendatsu had served with the Border Patrol, who watched the magic barrier around Dokuzen, but he had little to do with the Council Guards — a small group who existed to do the Council's bidding and exercise its authority. They were the ones to knock on doors in the middle of the night if you failed to pay taxes or obey Council orders or, worse, challenged your place in society. This squad was ten-strong, and they all looked as though they would be happy to use the swords at their belts. All wore leather armour over red hakama and short kimono.

'I am Tadayoshi Chikata Hanto. My clan leader has ordered me to get a scroll from this house,' their officer declared. 'All three of you will accompany me to the house of Tadayoshi Moratsune Jaken for questioning.'

'There is no need for that. These guests were just leaving,' Sendatsu said hurriedly.

Hanto swivelled to face Sendatsu and unrolled a piece of parchment. 'They are not going anywhere. My orders,' and here he flourished the parchment, 'are clear. All in this house must come with me. One way or another.'

'This is an insult. Do you not know who I am?' Sumiko swelled indignantly.

'You are a Magic-weaver and must obey my orders. Now.' Hanto pointed and his squad spread out.

'Lay hands on me and you will regret it,' Sumiko threatened. 'I will not be bullied by a Council thug!'

Hanto drew his sword, followed by his soldiers. 'This is your last chance,' he said stolidly.

'Put up your swords! I am Jaken's son and this is my house! I will not have swords drawn in here — I shall speak to my father ...'

'Enough — take those two.' Hanto waved and his men flooded forwards. 'I'll deal with this one.'

Sumiko drew herself up and Sendatsu felt her reach into the magic. For a moment he thought she was going to turn this room into a battleground, but then she subsided.

'We shall accompany you, but I shall have words with Jaken when we get there,' she hissed.

All had felt her prepare to use the magic, so the nearest guards let her walk past them. But the threat of the magic seemed to have infuriated Hanto.

'Grab hold of the other one!' Hanto snarled. 'Quick!'

The nearest pair shrugged then grabbed and twisted Asami's arms behind her back.

'Let her go!' Sendatsu stormed forwards as Asami cried in pain. 'This is outrageous ...'

'Keep out of this!' Hanto intercepted Sendatsu and swung his free hand in a backhand blow aimed to snap Sendatsu's head back and stop his progress.

Only it never landed.

Reacting instinctively, Sendatsu dropped the scroll and instead blocked Hanto's blow. His years of training, beaten into him by Jaken, took hold and without thinking he twisted the arm, locking the joint, and then struck with his free hand just above the elbow, breaking Hanto's arm with a crack that echoed around the room.

Everyone looked in surprise and horror as Hanto fell to the floor screaming in pain. For a long, long moment nobody did anything, then Hanto rolled to his knees, cradling his misshapen arm, agony etched into his face.

'What are you waiting for? Get them!' he screamed.

The nearest guard raced at Sendatsu, sword raised. Again, instinct took over and Sendatsu swooped on Hanto's fallen sword. The guard swung in the classic thunder-strike, designed to split him in half, but Sendatsu blocked easily and cut back with a reverse side stroke that bit deep into the guard's neck. The guard's sword fell from a nerveless hand as blood spurted across the nearest couch and the guard collapsed, choking out his last.

All watched him fall, then all eyes went to Sendatsu as he stood, perfectly balanced, blood-spattered and bloody sword in hand. Most remembered then he had scored second only to his father in the Test of swords.

'You know what is at stake — we are all dead if we do not return with that scroll!' Hanto shouted and they rushed forwards, hoping to swamp Sendatsu from all directions.

Then a table lifted up and flew into the three nearest guards, sending them flying.

'That's it, Sendatsu, use magic on them as well!' Sumiko cried.

Sendatsu paused for a moment, wondering what she was going on about — then realised she was going to help him without seeming to.

While all eyes focused on Sendatsu he pointed at Asami. She closed her eyes for a heartbeat and a couch lifted up and swept away the pair holding her arms. The guards fell back at the magical assault, thinking it came from Sendatsu when he had nothing to do with it, then Sendatsu waded forwards, sword already moving.

He was not thinking about his children, he was not thinking about his father; his mind was clear, thinking only of the next threat. He had learned to lose himself in the blade after many hard lessons at his father's hand.

His speed was dazzling and, although the Council Guards were chosen for their ability and strength, they could not match him. He used the double-strike style on the first one, tearing great wounds in his chest and belly, then switched to the floating cloud to despatch a second. The floor was sticky with blood, littered with all sorts of wooden toys and rubbish, but he stepped forwards, always in balance, blocked a pair of attackers, got them tangled up in each other's way and then went under a wild blow, rolling forwards and using the dragon-tail cut to take off a leg below the knee, yet still had the time to parry, regain his feet and take an arm with a massive tiger-claw stroke.

Around him, the air filled with furniture and flying guards as Sumiko and Asami wielded their magic, while pretending to cower against a wall. A last guard made a break for the door but Mai's wooden horse flew across the room and struck him in the head, sending him tumbling limply to the floor.

'Is that all?' Sendatsu was covered in blood, none of it his own.

They looked around wildly, at the screaming wounded, the silent dead and the merely unconscious.

'Hanto! Where is he?' Asami cried.

'And the scroll — where is it?' Sumiko shouted.

Sendatsu looked around quickly, could see neither — and realised Hanto must have taken it and run out the back. The knowledge of what he had just done slammed into him and he almost fell to the ground and vomited. What had he been thinking? He had not been thinking — thanks to his father's training he had reacted instinctively, dealing with every threat and offering no mercy. All his life he had trained — never had he drawn his sword for real. Now he had used it, he was horrified by what he had done. Horrified ... and yet exultant. He had been unstoppable, triumphant! Part of him wanted to roar that to the skies. But the greater part was shocked and afraid. Now not even his father might be able to get him out of this ... and then he remembered Hanto's words about his orders and wondered what his father had planned. His father already thought him a disappointment. Had he intended to remove Sendatsu and focus his attention on Cheijun?

The room stank of blood and dead men's bowels — now Sendatsu could also smell fear. His own.

'Come on, we have to get out of here, before they send more,' Asami cried.

'Hanto — should we not chase him? He only has one arm he can use ...'

The sound of a galloping horse in the street outside told them it was too late.

'Go to your house. Take Sendatsu, wait for my instructions. We can still find a way out of this,' Sumiko ordered.

'But surely they will come for us there ...' Asami began.

'I should go to my father, blame it all on Hanto, say he exceeded his orders and sent his men to attack me, forcing me to defend myself,' Sendatsu interrupted.

Sumiko bent over and picked up Hanto's parchment, dropped when Sendatsu had broken his arm.

'It may be too late for that,' she said as she scanned it.

'Why? What does it say?' They hurried to her side.

'Bring me the scroll. Let nothing stop you. Use whatever force necessary,' Sumiko read sadly. 'I don't think your father will believe Hanto overstepped his orders.'

'I did not mean this to happen,' Sendatsu mumbled, trying not to look at the elves bleeding to death where his children had been playing only a few turns of the hourglass ago. 'What am I going to do? How can I explain this? To kill a Council Guard is a sentence of death!' he groaned.

'You should clean up while we think,' Asami suggested.

Sendatsu hurriedly washed, his mind in a whirl, and changed, naturally strapping on his sword. After a moment he picked up his bow and a bag of arrows, just in case. He splashed water on his face, forced himself to think of a way out of this.

'I have decided what to do,' he announced as he strode back into the room. 'I shall throw myself on my father's mercy, do whatever he wants, even if it means spending my days threatening fishermen and farmers, bullying officials to bring him more power and wealth ...'

'You can't do that,' Asami said firmly. 'It would destroy you.'

'It is the only way,' he insisted, then realised they were alone. 'Where is Sumiko?'

'She had to leave — it was too risky for her to be seen with you. The Magic-weavers must be protected. Come, we have to get you away from here. They will be back here any time. We should go to my house.'

'Why have you not joined Sumiko and left?'

'Because there are some things that are more important.' She grabbed his arm and hustled him out of the door and down to the next corner.

'I need to send a message to my father,' he began, but she pulled him into a doorway.

'That'll have to wait — look!'

He peered out to see a force of Border Patrol and Council Guards galloping towards his villa — swords in hands.

'I don't think they will listen to reason. We have to get away. Sumiko will help us. She told me she has a plan. We'll get to my house and wait for her instructions.'

'But I thought you said they'd look for me there?'

'We must trust my sensei. Now hurry, for Aroaril's sake!'

They raced through the streets, keeping to the shadows and forced to dodge the armed elves riding around. Anyone the guards saw was immediately questioned and even beaten.

'They look like they are ready to strike first and ask questions afterwards,' Asami muttered as they crept behind bushes, watching a trio of guards screaming at a young elf.

Sendatsu said nothing but there was still one ray of hope among the fear. His father could sort out anything. He just had to pay his father's price.

Finally they reached Asami's house.

'Where is Gaibun?'

'He has probably been summoned, along with other Border Patrol.' Asami opened the door and waved him inside.

'Curse it! He would be the best one to take a message to my father. That is the only way out of this mess,' Sendatsu decided.

'Well, sit down and write your message, while I try and find Gaibun.'

Sendatsu grabbed parchment and pen but found time to smile at her.

'Asami, thank you. I can't tell you how much it means to have you here at this time.'

'I thought you would be angry with me — if I had not brought Sumiko to your house then none of this would have happened.' She smiled.

Sendatsu sighed. 'The fault was not yours. I agreed to give you the scroll if my father refused to act on it. And then my father gave Hanto outrageous orders — and he exceeded even those. There are many people to blame but you are not one of them.'

For a moment it looked as though she would say something more, then she ducked out of Gaibun's office, leaving Sendatsu to stare at the blank parchment and wonder what he could say to his father. It was hard to talk to him at the best of times — and this was certainly not the best of times.

Then Asami burst back through the door.

'Gaibun is here!'

'I haven't written my message yet ...'

'He's at the head of a hundred soldiers — including that Hanto!'

Sendatsu surged to his feet but before he could reach her side, someone beat on the front door.

'Sendatsu! It is Gaibun! Open up!'

Sendatsu's childhood friend, and Asami's husband, was a tall elf with a burning gaze and a long moustache. Like Sendatsu, he had powerful arms and chest, a legacy of so much work with the bow but, with his extra height, he seemed to carry it better. Normally he was smiling but his face was grim, his eyes sad as he embraced Sendatsu.

'My friend, I told them I was coming to persuade you to surrender without more bloodshed. But I am here to tell you to flee,' he said urgently.

'Flee? What do you mean?'

'Your father received your message ...'

'I haven't sent him my message yet!'

Gaibun looked taken aback. 'He received something that drove him mad. I have never seen him like that. He was raving that you threatened not just him but Dokuzen when you declared you would reveal your secrets if taken to trial.'

'What?' Sendatsu spat. The right to trial was only available to elves of noble birth, of course. The lower classes had to accept whatever justice the Council was prepared to give. But elves such as Sendatsu could have their case heard before the full Council, with anyone able to go along to watch.

'Apparently you have threatened to bring down the Council and destroy Dokuzen with some great secret if you are taken to trial,' Gaibun insisted.

'I would never say that!'

'Well, your father believes you did. And the fact you slaughtered a squad of Council Guards is hardly in your favour. Everyone is screaming for your head and your father has signed orders saying you are to be killed.'

'No! That cannot be true!'

'I have seen it myself. Hanto has been telling everyone how you murdered his men with sword and magic — that you have gone mad and will not stop until every last elf is dead.'

'Gaibun, I need you to take a message to my father, a real message, which will explain everything,' Sendatsu said urgently.

Gaibun reached out and grasped his shoulder. 'Of course I would do that for you, my friend — but I fear it will do nothing. Words will not stop the desire for your head. You need to flee somewhere, let all this die down and then perhaps you can try again.'

'Flee? Where? I don't know anyone outside Dokuzen! Should I try and hide in some fishing shack up north? I would stand out like a fire in the night. Besides, if I run, they think me guilty. Take a message to my father. That is the only way out of this mess.'

'Of course, brother. I will do anything — but I warn you to be ready to flee. Asami can send you somewhere north, somewhere safe. I ordered my warriors to wait for my return but your father could get here at any moment and send them swarming over the walls.'

Sendatsu grabbed quill and ink and wrote feverishly, gabbling out a declaration of innocence, a plea to solve this without further bloodshed and a promise to do whatever necessary to make amends.

'I shall take this to your father. But be prepared for warriors to attack if I come out without you,' Gaibun warned.

'I will take that chance. It is the best one ...'

A noise outside the room made them all turn, made Sendatsu reach for his sword — but it was not a Council Guard.

'No, there is another choice,' Sumiko announced as she walked in.

'Sensei — how did you get here?' Asami gasped.

'I opened a gateway through the oak tree in your garden. I have told you, many times, to put a ward of warning around it,' the Magic-weaver said crisply. 'Sendatsu, you cannot negotiate from weakness. Go out there and you will be lucky to escape with your life. The best you can hope for is to lose your children to your father.'

'I will not let that happen!'

'You have no choice. Your father will do whatever he wants. But there is a better way. The knowledge in that scroll terrifies him, as it will all of the Council. Use that knowledge to get what you want.'

'But I don't have the scroll — Hanto took it!' Sendatsu protested.

'Yes, but we don't need the scroll. The knowledge within it is just lying out there, ready to be picked up.'

'What?' Sendatsu's head was spinning at this.

'The human world. Out there is all you need. The truth about why the elves sealed themselves away into Dokuzen — everything. Get the living proof of what is in that scroll and I swear the Magic-weavers will protect you and give you back the peaceful life with your children that you want,' Sumiko said with a smile.

'Go into the human world? Are you mad?' Sendatsu goggled at her. 'No elf has been through the barrier in three centuries! It would kill me!'

'No — it is but a shadow of what it was. An elf strong in magic can get through it now. Asami's studies have proved that.'

Sendatsu knew it was possible to travel great distances, using oak trees, but he had no idea how, nor anything like the magical ability necessary. 'I don't have the power!'

'No, but Asami does. She can send you through,' Sumiko said complacently.

'I can? Are you sure it is safe, sensei? Should we not try it on an animal or something first?'

'I have already done so. It is perfectly safe. And it need not be for long. The alternative is either to flee north into the fishing villages of the coast, or fight here and die.'

'No,' Sendatsu declared. 'Gaibun, take that message to my father. That is still the best way ...'

'I think you need to flee. Sumiko may be right. Perhaps the human world is the best place for you,' Gaibun offered.

'Please — the message?' Sendatsu pleaded.

Gaibun nodded, embraced Sendatsu one more time. 'If you do go, then know both Asami and I will be doing everything we can to help you get back home, my brother,' he whispered.

Sendatsu hugged him back, feeling tears prick his eyes at the thought of having such a good friend. Gaibun left, with a nod to Asami, the first time either had acknowledged each other.

'Put your trust in the Magic-weavers. Get us the evidence we need to show the Council is lying to the people and can no longer be trusted to protect Dokuzen, and everything will go back to the way it was,' Sumiko promised.

Sendatsu took Asami's arm and guided her out into the garden.

'What do you think?' he asked softly.

Asami looked torn. 'I do not love Gaibun but I trust his words. If he says your message will not stop those guards outside, then it must be true. But to go into the human world ... you'd have to find evidence the Magic-weavers can use to turn the people against the Council. You need to find humans who know what happened three hundred years ago, why the elves sealed themselves away.'

'But, even then, can Sumiko overthrow the Council and give me my life back?'

'Of course. If the people know the barrier is failing and the Council cannot stop it, naturally they will turn to the Magic-weavers to save them. And things will be different with Sumiko in charge. The Magic-weavers are sick of the way the Council rules Dokuzen for the benefit of the nobles, grinding the lower classes down. We would make a better Dokuzen, one where your skills and character are more important than your clan and family. I believe that with all my heart.'

'Can I trust Sumiko to give me my life back?' he insisted.

'You can trust me,' Asami promised. 'Get what we need and I will get you back here, get your children and life back.'

Sendatsu felt torn. Even if his father intervened and saved him, life would never be the same. He would be working for his father, doing everything he hated and missing his children. Jaken would use them against him every day. The thought was revolting. But to risk everything on going out into the human world ... Sendatsu had never liked making decisions and his mind rebelled at the size of this one.

Unthinking, he reached out and held Asami's hand, just as he would hold Mai's and Cheijun's hands when they were upset or scared. The tension was too much to bear.

'Where has Gaibun got to?' he asked the question that was twisting his insides around.

Then Gaibun burst into the garden, waving his arms. 'Sendatsu! Run! They are coming!' His bellow confirmed Sendatsu's worst fears.

It had barely finished echoing around the garden when the first of the guards began dropping over the walls, swords in hands.

'Wait!' Sendatsu cried, holding up his hands — but arrows flickered close to his head, forcing him to duck. There was nowhere out of here — he was surrounded.

'Asami! Get him away!' Sumiko called.

'She's right, you have no choice, you have to go!' Asami cried, dragging him across to the oak tree in the centre of her garden.

'But how do I get back?'

'The moon. The tree you come out, return there at each phase of the moon and I shall open a gateway at midday and midnight.' Asami grabbed the oaken staff that Sumiko had left against the tree, closed her eyes and thrust the staff deep into the trunk.

'Is it safe? Are you through?' Sendatsu worried.

'I am through the barrier!' she exclaimed, then opened her eyes. 'It is even weaker than we thought. But you must hurry. Hold onto the staff until you are through.'

Sendatsu could see the guards closing in and, although he did not want to go, did not know what else could be done.

'Hold!' Gaibun waved down the archers who had drawn their bows again. 'My wife is there, he is holding her prisoner! Nobody loose an arrow!'

'Help me get back. Look after my children,' he pleaded.

Asami reached up and kissed him, hard, oblivious to her husband just yards away. 'Come back, for all of us,' she whispered.

An arrow flew then, just missing his head. Grabbing the staff, Sendatsu raced into the tree like a man running for his life — and Dokuzen vanished behind him.

That was how he left Dokuzen. He did not know when he could return but, finally, his tears dried and he stood up. His children were lost to him but crying would not get them back. He knew what he had to do — find out if humans could do magic, discover what had really happened when the elves had withdrawn into Dokuzen. It was his only chance. He did not want to overthrow the Council but, if that was the price of getting them back, he would destroy his father and the other clan leaders and anyone who got in his way.

He could feel a new determination within him, a grim desire that would not be stopped by anything. He would turn the human and elven worlds on their heads to hold Mai and Cheijun again.

Down the hill there was a human village, smoke from its fires staining the afternoon sky. It was a place to start. He began to walk towards the village.

# 3

*Lies will kill me. But the truth must live on. My enemies will find what I have already written and they will either destroy it or lock it away where none can find it. My instructions from the forefathers are written on a scroll, hidden inside an old book. That might survive — or might be burned. But not this. I shall hide it too well — and it will be in the last place they expect to look. I pray the one who finds it can use my tale to change Dokuzen for the better, make it a place where the truth is more valued than lies.*

*I hate lies. And yet they are so much more powerful than truth, so much easier to believe. The people think we built the magical barrier around Dokuzen to keep the humans out. No, the barrier was built to keep us away from the humans. For our magic was too strong. Elves might have used it wisely, done things to improve the lives of all. But we are human, we just pretend we are elves. We would have used it to rule the other human tribes, turn them into our slaves.*

*The Elfarans, our forefathers, realised this. They had a plan to give the humans back their future, the future we took away from them. I was the one chosen to make it happen. For a while I dared to dream of success — but then I was betrayed by those I trusted. Friends who I thought protected my back in fact stood behind me because it was easier to plunge the knife home. My dearest friend, who called me brother to my face and held me close, was the one to bring me down. The leader of the Magic-weavers, who I thought my ally, plotted for herself. So many had their own motives that I stood no chance of success.*

*Yet I was not a complete failure. I saved the humans from us — for now, at least. We took so much from the human lands we found here. Death would be too bitter for me if I knew we had also taken their freedom. I hope they learn and develop, away from us, so that when we finally meet again, it can be as equals. I hope for many things — but then, hope is all I have in the little time left to me.*

Rhiannon screamed.

Huw jumped out of his chair, heart racing, not knowing where he was or what was going on for a moment. He had drifted off to sleep and been in the middle of a dream, where King Ward's soldiers had been chasing him. In the dream, he had been unable to run away fast enough, his feet seemingly churning through the thickest mud while Ward's men raced lightly across the ground after him, wicked swords thirsting for his flesh. He had been trying to scream himself when Rhiannon screamed for him.

He looked around, the dream's fears still holding him, but the room was empty, the door still locked and a chair braced under the handle.

He spun to where Rhiannon was sitting up in bed.

'What is it?' he asked, trying to blink open eyes still gritty with sleep.

'I keep having nightmares about King Ward killing my father,' she said in a small, choked voice.

She had gone to bed while he had been downstairs seeing to the horses and now he saw she had also taken the time to change into her nightgown. It was impossible to ignore the fact it was far more flimsy than it had seemed to be when he had stuffed it into a bag for her, along with a handful of other clothes.

He reached out to hold her — then hesitated. Firstly, although he had sworn on the stars above they were just friends and he would never take advantage of her, he had been desperately in love with her since the first time he saw her in King Ward's court. Secondly, he had lied and tricked to get her away from Cridianton. Her father was not only alive, but he and Ward were probably plotting a hideous vengeance on Huw right now. Luckily he had also lied to them, so they were probably searching for him hundreds of miles away. They thought he was one of them, a Forlishman. Instead he came from Vales. Ward would certainly never let a Velshman into his court, even a bard as talented as Huw. He had lied to them, said his name was Hugh of Browns Brook so he could make his dream of being a bard come true. He had lied to Rhiannon to save her from King Ward. One lie was already coming back to haunt him. He could only hope the other lie would protect him long enough to make up for it.

'I too am having bad dreams about escaping from the king's castle,' he said softly, sitting on the very edge of her bed and holding her hand. Friends would do that, he told himself. Just try to look at her eyes, not lower down …

'Just before I open my eyes, I think I will wake up in the king's palace and imagine that everything is as it was, everyone is waiting for me to sing and dance, so they can cheer for me. Then I remember what really happened …' She stopped there, tears overtaking her.

'It's all right.' Huw leaned in and she clung to him, crying into his shoulder. He patted her back and tried not to think about how sweet her hair smelled, or how smooth her back was, or how good it felt to hold her. Every night he had been in Ward's castle, he had dreamed of having her in his arms. But now she was here, he could do nothing. Not until he had admitted the truth, at least.

He told himself he had done the right thing. He had been about to leave anyway, for he had discovered King Ward was planning to bring Vales under his rule. The Forlish had spent the last twenty years slowly crushing every southern country. Vales, to the north, had been no threat, for it had no army and no leaders. But now, with almost nobody to oppose him, Ward was turning his attention north, to complete his conquest of the human lands. Only he was not sending his unstoppable armies north, for they were still finishing off the Balians and Landish. No, he had a much worse plan for the Velsh. A plan nearly as revolting as the one Ward and Rhiannon's father, Hector, had for Rhiannon.

He had overheard them discussing the transaction as if Rhiannon had been a favourite horse. The whole court had been captivated by Rhiannon. The way she sang and especially the way she danced would have been enough in themselves. But she was also tall, willowy, with glorious red hair and a face that made every man's head turn. It was currently snuffling into his shoulder now, blotched and running, but she had sparkling green eyes, a slightly upturned nose, bow-shaped lips and a light dusting of freckles across high cheekbones. In a world where faces were covered in dirt, where hard work and illness ate into every line of your face, she stood out like a star at night.

Everyone coveted her — but her father was always there, always protecting. Until the day Huw had heard him sell Rhiannon to the king, auction her off as if she was some creature. Even without his own desperate love for her, he could not leave her to that fate. To be the plaything of a cruel king, abused and then discarded ... it was monstrous. Yet he knew she would never believe the truth, at least until it was too late. So he lied, pretended her father had been killed defending her from Ward, and smuggled her out of the castle and come north. She was the beautiful maiden and he had sung enough legends and sagas to know he had to rescue her. And yet, by doing this, he was lying to her and tormenting her. She would forever have this distorted view of her father as a hero who had laid down his life to save her, when in reality Hector had wanted to lay her down to enrich his own pockets.

Huw made a deal with himself to prove he had really snatched her from Cridianton, her father and all she knew for her own good, not because he was filled with impossible dreams about her. He would be no more than a friend to her until he told the truth. That way she could still make her own decisions. The fact she would only learn the truth when she was alone, in Vales, miles from anything and everyone she knew, was a sticking point, but he was able to ignore that. It had seemed like the perfect plan in Cridianton, only they were now in Vales, and he still could not bring himself to explain everything to her. It would be more sensible to wait until they were at his village of Patcham, he decided. His conscience protested a little but he was able to push it aside. After all, he had spent the last few moons ignoring it. He had taken on a false name, pretended he was not even Velsh and looked the other way when fresh slaves arrived in the capital, victims of the southern wars. The vicious way Ward and his nobles treated servants, the filth, hunger and despair in the backstreets of Cridianton and the cruelty of slavery, people ripped from their homes and loved ones and made to work and suffer for the glory of the brutal king — he managed to pretend they were not happening. He even stayed in Cridianton for almost half a moon after discovering Ward's plan for the Velsh, when he should have rushed home immediately, because he had befriended Rhiannon and cherished the mad hope she would want to leave her dream and come home with him. By then his conscience, which had been loud and strident when he left home with his father's blessing, was but a whisper. Keeping up the lie to Rhiannon seemed easy in comparison.

He realised, with a start, her tears were drying up.

'The first few days are the hardest. But the pain will always be there. It is difficult but it is also a fitting reminder of your father,' he said soothingly.

'I don't know what I would do without you. You are a true friend,' she sniffed, sitting up again.

Huw tried to smile, guilt and lust warring within him. 'Whatever I can do to help,' he said, trying not to look at the way her nightgown clung to her breasts.

'I am sorry for falling asleep like that but I am so tired ...'

'Don't worry. Do you want something to eat?'

'I'm not really hungry.'

'But you should eat something, especially as we are going to perform here tonight.'

'What? Perform? Why?'

Huw smiled carefully. 'We spoke about this before. We have to let the people know the Forlish are coming. We have to warn them. And this is the best way to do that.'

'Should we be drawing attention to ourselves by performing? Shouldn't we just try to hide? After all, King Ward is still after us. If there are any Forlish in the audience tonight, then we can expect to be dragged back to our deaths. Or worse!'

'Ward's men might be after us but this is Vales and he does not rule here — yet. We have to warn these people. We both heard what he plans, saw the men he will be sending north. These villages won't stand a chance unless they know what they are facing.'

'But what can they do to stop them?'

Huw hesitated. He did not really have an idea, beyond knowing he had to do something. His whole plan was based on going home, telling his father and handing the problem to him. Ward was sending hundreds of his soldiers north, into Vales, disguised as bandits. There they would wreak havoc across the hamlets and villages and isolated farms, until the Velsh begged Ward to come and save them. Even now, thinking about it made his blood boil. Ward wanted the Velsh tin and iron and coal and food to feed his war machine but didn't want to go to the trouble of another war. And he didn't really need to. The Velsh had no army, no organisation. Villages traded with each other on occasion but the three Velsh districts of Rheged, Gwent and Powys had little to do with each other. Men could hunt and farm and mine but there were few proper weapons and none trained in their use. This was beyond him. They didn't need a young bard — they needed a hero.

'I don't know what they can do — but we have to give them a chance,' Huw admitted.

'Should we not perform under different names, at least?' Rhiannon pressed.

Huw bit his lip. It seemed like a sensible idea but he had always dreamed of being famous, of having people across Vales point him out when he walked past. It was why he had gone to King

Ward's court. True, he had pretended to be a Forlishman while he was there but there was no need to mention that and to throw his glory away now seemed unfair. Besides, Ward was not going to hear what was being said in a small Velsh hall. He was looking down south.

'It will be safe enough. The people here are not going to run south and tell everyone that we are here,' he dismissed her concern airily.

'Well, how exactly are we going to perform when my clothes are soaked through, and I have no powders or makeup?' she demanded.

'We'll stick one of your dresses before the fire and then just get out there. When people hear you sing, see you dance, they'll listen,' Huw promised. 'It doesn't matter how you look, they will all be captivated by you.'

Rhiannon was not so sure. Her father had said it to her again and again: 'Men are only interested in you if you look good. Talent can only get you so far.' And she had always listened to him.

He was the centre of her world. She lived to make him smile, to win his approval. Since her mother had died giving birth to her, Hector had devoted himself to her. He explained how he had sacrificed his own skills to help her, how not one father in ten thousand would do all he had for a small girl. He patiently pointed out how lucky she was to have him and how grateful she needed to be for all he was doing.

'Make your mother's death mean something!' he always told her.

With those words in her ears, she threw all her energies into training, working from dawn to dusk.

She had no time for friends, for anything but what he said she must do. As she grew older, she begged him to take her to Cridianton, give her a chance to honour him.

'When you are ready,' was all he ever said. 'If you work harder and listen to what I say.'

And she had. She worked until the sweat poured off her, obeyed not just his every command but his every suggestion as well — until the moment when he turned around and declared she was ready.

Now he was gone, she had fled Cridianton and her life was in ruins. But she had to cling to something.

'I'll dance and sing with you but I have to look the part,' she insisted.

So Huw spent the best part of a turn of the hourglass going through the village, buying chalk powder and jars of crushed berries to stain her lips and highlight her cheeks.

She was dressed when he returned and happily accepted his trophies. While she peered into a small bronze mirror and tried to do something with her hair, he thought she looked better than she had for days.

'You're wearing that ring?' Huw pointed to the chunky gold ring that sat on her thumb, looking out of place against her slim hand.

Rhiannon twisted it around, so the seal was uppermost. 'I shall always wear it,' she said sadly. 'It is all I have to remember my father by.'

Huw nodded solemnly, trying to keep his thoughts from his face. It was the thing he had used to convince Rhiannon her father was dead — and evidence of his lies. He would have been far happier never to see it again.

'As long as it doesn't fall off when you dance,' he managed to say.

'It won't,' she promised. 'I wonder who will be the audience tonight?' she continued, dabbing her lips with the berry juice.

'No one of interest,' he assured her.


Sendatsu hurried down the hill towards the village. He doubted he would find the answers he sought at the first village he found but, for the sake of Mai and Cheijun, he hoped he might find something. The rain swept in then, a thick curtain of it, dropping down from the skies with a vengeance. The path he took, already muddy, turned treacherous in the downpour. His boots were tall, of rich leather and bearskin, but he had to work hard not to become bogged, dragging them out of the clinging muck, and doubly hard to avoid slipping and falling.

Grunting with the effort, he made it to the bottom of the small hill and began to walk into the village. To someone used to the stone precision and beauty of Dokuzen, it was horrifying. The rain seemed to have brought out the worst of its smell, although it looked just as bad; crude wooden circular huts, plastered with mud, their roofs thatched but the thatch covered in a bedraggled mass of grass and moss. They were built low, the roofs sweeping down almost to the ground, while dung heaps were stacked against side walls, almost reaching to the roof, their stink making the gorge rise in his throat. It was hard to tell the difference between one and the other. Dogs tried to shelter from the rain, while the people stayed hidden. A few dogs barked half-heartedly but quietened when someone yelled at them.

Smoke curled despondently out of the very top of these roofs, as well as from the doorways, but not from a chimney. None had anything so fancy. And none had a window. The walls were blank, featureless, unless chunks of missing mud, showing the rough wattle walls beneath, counted as decoration.

Even with the rain, he found it hard not to stare. How could they live like this? Even the esemono, the lowest of the low classes, lived better than this in Dokuzen. There they had brick homes, proper chimneys, proper food. He began to fear he would find no answers at all.

He walked towards the nearest house, but the rank smell coming out of its open doorway made him turn away. Unwashed humans, wet animals, thick smoke and dung. Nothing that smelled that bad could hold anything useful.

He squelched down the middle of the road through the village until he came to a building that was different to all the rest. He stood in the middle of the crude street, heedless of the rain, and stared at it, hope rising in his heart.

It was elven — had to be elven. It looked nothing like the crude huts he had walked past. Two storeys high, made of stone and

48

with a tiled roof, it towered above the rest of the village. His heart beat faster. Perhaps in there he would find answers.

He slopped over until he could step onto the crude flat rock that served as the door stone. He kicked it with his boots, but the mud and dung that clung to the soles were reluctant to leave.

'Get inside! No day to be outside and there's just as much mud in here as out there!' someone boomed from within the smoke wafting out the door.

He scraped his boots once more, this time almost revealing the rich brown leather, then stepped inside.

It took a few moments for his eyes to adjust to the smoke that filled the room. While his eyes were adjusting, he did not think his nose would ever get used to the assault. The smoke from the fire was actually a help, disguising unwashed bodies and clothes, dung, animals and cooking food, which seemed to coat the back of his throat. A dog snarled at him and he looked down to see a large, hairy animal crouched on the floor, eating what looked like a pile of vomit. It certainly smelled like it.

Revolted, he blinked and looked around. This was not what he expected to find. How far had these humans regressed? Back home, a place like this would have a series of low couches, as well as statues and other artwork, beautiful rugs on the tiled floor and either tapestries or gorgeous murals on the plastered walls. A handful of elves would be talking politely, perhaps one would be playing a musical instrument or singing.

Here, humans filled most of the room, jostled each other around a long table that was stacked high with barrels, crude mugs and horns, as well as a strange assortment of goods, from chickens to clothes to a small goat in a cage.

The floor was filthy rushes, the walls bare yet stained with things he did not want to think about. The noise, the smells, were overwhelming. If not for Mai and Cheijun and, admittedly, the rain, he would have walked away.

The closest humans stared at him with a mixture of curiosity and animosity. All wore crude tunics and trews, some of them bright in colour but uniformly stained with mud and worse. They had long, dark hair and matching beards, although several of the older ones were going bald.

'Welcome to my hall,' a voice boomed, the same voice that had invited him in. This man, who had a huge beard, stood behind the table, from where he and a young woman handed out mugs of strange-looking drink and plates of stranger-looking food to other humans.

He pushed his way across to them. Time was wasting. 'Where am I?' he asked.

'Why, you're in Pontypridd, the most easterly village in the whole of Vales, the most southerly in Gwent — and one of the finest!' The man grinned, showing blackened teeth through his thick beard. 'I am Vernin, headman of the village.'

The words washed over him, meaning nothing. Instead he found himself staring at Vernin's face, fascinated by the man's long nose and large eyes, as well as his reddened ears that stuck out proudly either side of his beard.

Vernin carefully wiped out one of the wooden tankards with a grubby cloth then filled it with a brown liquid from a large barrel.

'Try this. My finest ale. It'll drive out the cold,' Vernin offered.

He inspected the filthy tankard doubtfully. 'Thank you. I am not thirsty,' he said carefully. 'Instead, I have questions for you ...'

Vernin chuckled. 'Questions? I don't have time for questions! I have two performers, all the way from the court of King Ward of Forland himself, and a huge crowd wanting food and drink! How about that, eh? No wonder people from all over have come here, wearing their best clothes.'

Sendatsu looked around at the humans. Most had long tunics and some sort of woollen leggings. Everything seemed ill-fitting and baggy. There were colours but they were patchy and faded, while mud seemed to have stained everything. He hoped it was mud. He pulled the cloak around him a little tighter, to hide the fine dark blue cotton hakama trousers and kimono top he was wearing.

'But I need to talk to anyone around here who knows about elves and magic ...'

'Listen to the show — I reckon you'll hear all you need to then,' Vernin promised.

Relief flooded through Sendatsu. This was perfect! With any luck, he could be back home before he even knew it.

'Where are they?'

'Oh, they'll be out soon,' Vernin said. 'Show me the colour of your coin and you can eat and drink while you wait.'

Sendatsu would normally have refused — he could not imagine anything cooked in this place would give him anything other than the need to vomit. But the thought of finishing his quest so quickly made him want to indulge this strange human. He felt in his belt pouch — below the toys was a handful of coins and he slapped one on the table.

'Gold!' Vernin whispered reverentially. 'Haven't seen that in a year! You can have something special for that!'

He hurried away, going through a rough curtain into a back room.

'Where are you from?' a human with just two fingers on his left hand asked.

Sendatsu thought it would be best not to mention he was an elf. After all, these humans had not seen one for centuries.

'Nowhere you've been,' he said evasively.

'I asked an honest question. The least you can do is give me an answer,' the man growled, straightening up from where he leaned on the table.

'Now that's enough — I want no fighting in my hall, especially not this night!' Vernin bustled back, bearing a small barrel and a plate of strange-smelling food.

'What is this?' Sendatsu asked as the two-fingered man subsided back into his drink.

'This is the finest honey mead, all the way from Powys.' Vernin poured some into a horn.

Sendatsu had no idea what mead was, or where Powys was. But it felt like everyone was watching and the height of bad manners not to drink. Besides, the liquid smelled sweet; his nose recognised honey, which was the first familiar thing. He took a sip. It tasted like honeyed water but, when he swallowed, it first tingled his tongue, burned down his throat and then sent warmth to his stomach and out beyond. He tried it again, amazed at the effect, and felt the tension slip away from his muscles, while his head felt light and even the smell seemed to lessen.

'Good, eh?' Vernin grinned and he found himself smiling in return, holding out the horn for more.

'Try this. Bacon, fattened on acorns in the woods, and eggs laid this morning.'

The eggs, golden and mostly white, he instantly recognised but the thin slices of something pink and brown were a mystery.

'Bacon? What is that? I've never heard of a fish like that.' Sendatsu was intrigued. Where was the rice? Where were the vegetables? Was bacon perhaps the human word for some sort of shellfish? Surely it was not octopus. He picked up a strip, heedless of the heat and bit into it. The sensation on his tongue, the initial crunch, then the chewiness, the salty-sweetness and smoky flavour, burst into his mouth and he almost gasped aloud.

'Is bacon a fish? Skies above, where are you from? Bacon comes from pigs!' Vernin chuckled.

Sendatsu choked on his mouthful. 'Pigs? Like wild boar? You mean I am eating their flesh?' he gasped.

Vernin roared with laughter. 'Stranger, surely you are having sport with me! Of course it is from pigs! Would you prefer some roast mutton? I have half a sheep on the spit ...'

'I think I'm going to spit.' Sendatsu took a huge mouthful of the mead to wash his mouth out and then coughed as it burned the back of his throat.

'Easy there — you'll be face-down in the rushes before the show starts if you keep drinking like that.' Vernin smiled.

Sendatsu looked in the horn. 'So what's in this?' he asked, dreading to think of the answer.

'Well, that's just fermented honey, to make you feel good.'

'Fermented ... this is alcohol?' Sendatsu gulped. He knew the esemono drank a rice wine to dull their aches after a hard day of labour but none of the nobility would dream of befuddling their senses with alcohol, nor devouring the flesh of a beast. His head felt like it was spinning, while his stomach was heaving.

'Do you want more?' Vernin offered.

'No, I've never drunk alcohol before, nor eaten animal flesh,' he admitted.

'No meat?' Vernin's eyebrows seemed to disappear into his hair. 'What do you live on then?'

'Rice and vegetables mainly, with fish,' Sendatsu said weakly.

'Skies above! I've never heard anything so revolting!' Vernin gasped. 'And what in the name of the night stars is rice?'

Sendatsu did not think he could explain without vomiting. 'Can I have some water and a plate of vegetables?' he asked faintly.

Vernin and the two-fingered man exchanged horrified looks. 'Well, we have some turnips out the back that the pigs eat. Or I could put some pease pudding in the pot. It'll be ready soon,' Vernin offered.

'Whatever. Just give me some water and let me sit down,' Sendatsu groaned.

'Go sit by the fire — they'll be out soon,' Vernin said.

Sendatsu staggered through the crowd of humans until he found an empty wooden stool — just a sawn-off chunk of trunk really — close to the fire but, best of all, away from the main crush of humans. His head was spinning and he breathed deeply — then wished he hadn't. A young woman pushed her way through the crowd towards him, holding a plate and wooden cup. She was wearing a purple, sack-like dress, tied at the shoulders, while her dark hair was braided and hung over her shoulder.

'Here you go. Fresh turnips and water,' she said flatly.

Sendatsu looked at the wooden platter. She had placed two raw turnips on it, still with mud crusted on them. He hoped it was mud, for it looked like one of the pigs had taken a bite out of it already.

'Just the water, thank you,' he said, taking a deep draught. This would settle his stomach.

'Are you sure this is water?' he spat a moment later.

'Fresh out of the well. There was a frog in the bucket ...'

'A frog?' he croaked.

'You are a strange one. Would you rather eat the frog? I hear the Breconians like such things ...'

'I shall just sit here,' Sendatsu said hastily.

'Suit yourself.' The young woman walked away, leaving Sendatsu to lean back against the wall and groan. He hoped the show would begin soon and he could find the answers he sought. The less time he spent here, in this mad human world, the better.

# 4

*How did I come to be chosen by my forefathers? Why was I chosen by my forefathers? These are questions I have pondered many times in the past few moons — and none more so than now. What did they see in me that was missing in others? Unfortunately it was my own fault that I came to be chosen. I could see the forefathers were distracted, unaware of much that was going on in these lands. After all, when you are an immortal, the everyday happenings of rice production, of mine tallies, seemed unimportant. I was the one who suggested we have a Council, one from each of the twelve clans, who could supervise and then report back to the forefathers, as necessary.*

*They thought it a wonderful idea — and then made me head of this new Council. My old friend Naibun jokingly referred to me as the Elder Elf because of this. It was a jest — but strangely I found the name stuck. I had a title but their respect was something else.*

'Do I look ready?' Rhiannon asked, twirling around.

Huw could not think of words suitable enough. Back in Ward's castle, the king's dressmakers had laboured night and day to create new dresses for Rhiannon. Most had been both impractical to wear and impossible to pack, so he had grabbed a handful at random. Rhiannon had chosen this one, a glorious strip of green linen, which stretched only to her knees and was split in a dozen places along the hem, so she could dance freely — but every time she moved, it revealed more of her legs. She had used the powders and berry stains to accent her lips and cheeks and eyes, and Huw could only gaze in admiration. Once again he was torn. She was so beautiful and yet he knew she just thought of him as a friend. In the first few days after they left Cridianton, she had been in such a mess, he could have persuaded her to do anything. So he had done nothing. He had tricked her out of Cridianton, he would not trick her into bed. He would not try anything until he could tell her the truth — although skies above knew when that would be.

The whole thing seemed almost like one of the sagas he would sing. If it had not happened to him, he would have barely believed it.

He had left his home in Vales, travelled south to the court of King Ward in far-off Cridianton and persuaded them he was a Forlishman called Hugh of Browns Brook and won the right to perform for the king. That was exciting enough but then he had fallen, head over heels, for a fellow performer, the beautiful but remote Rhiannon of Hamtun. Her father tried to keep her away from the rest of the court but Huw had been able to first perform with her, then talk with her — and finally sneak her out of the castle to see the city. He had learned there was a network of servants' passages that guards and nobles never used and he had found his way through them.

Then all had come crashing down when he discovered Ward was looking to enslave his people. He wanted to rush home but Rhiannon persuaded him to stay, just a little longer. He had, willingly, under her spell. Until the day he had sneaked into her room, found it empty — and overheard how she was to be sold off to the king. She would not believe it if he told her now. He barely believed it all himself. So it was easy to put off the day when he was forced to explain everything. Better yet, it allowed him to hope, and put off the day when he suspected she would simply reject him. After all, he knew he was not a worthy companion for her. He was only average height, with the typical Velsh dark hair and pale skin, a dark beard that would grow thick and curly if he let it, but kept it shaved in the Forlish way, using oil and a short blade to scrape the whiskers off each morning. It was a losing battle, for he always had a dark shadow about his jaw, but at least it stopped him from looking as though he was wearing a small bush beneath his face, like every other Velshman. His father, Earwen, had always told him he was handsome but the lack of interest from the Velsh girls made him think that was a lie. Of course, that could have also been because they all thought him a fool for dreaming to be a bard, not working to be a farmer. Still, he had a strong smile, with good teeth that he took care of every day — for his mouth would be his fortune. That meant avoiding bread, which often had scraps of rock inside from the grinding stones used to make flour. He also brushed them with green twigs and even salt, when he could get it. And his brown eyes could melt a room while he was singing, even if they did not melt the clothes off the village girls the way he daydreamed they might. He was slim, beneath the wide shoulders he had inherited from his father, for years of playing the lyre, rather than slaving away on the farm, had not added muscle to his frame. No, he was not the man Rhiannon deserved. The way she looked, she needed a hero, someone from one of his legends or saga stories, not the son of a farmer. But he could say none of that.

'They will love you,' he promised.

Rhiannon smiled and nodded. 'Then I am ready.'

Huw stepped out first and stroked his lyre, a pure and high note that effectively silenced the room, people nudging each other to be quiet.

'Ladies and gentlemen! Direct from the court of King Ward himself! I present to you, Rhiannon of Hamtun!' he bellowed. His voice made them all look, for it was a true Velsh voice, as rich and rolling as the hills themselves — even stranger because it came out of such an ordinary-looking man.

Sendatsu sat up at the introduction. He even forgot the way his stomach was complaining. The voice was rich, powerful and smooth. This was what he had come here for. The young man walked among the crowd, playing a tune that was both familiar and strange to Sendatsu. It had echoes of songs he had heard before but, over the top, was something different, as if he was hearing two songs, not one — or perhaps half of each.

The humans pushed back, creating space for the bard — and then all eyes switched from him to a young woman who sprang into the open area, spinning as she did so. Tall, lithe, dressed in a green linen dress that shone in the smoky hall — and showed off her long legs — she began to sing with the man, while her dancing ...

Sendatsu could not take his eyes off her. It transported him back to Dokuzen. The dancing was an imitation of the elven dances he had seen more times than he could remember. The human girl lacked proper techniques, did not flow properly from one step to another, but she was a head taller than any elven girl he had seen, and the way she could extend her legs, could hold the poses, sing as well ... surely these two would hold the answers he sought. He watched, entranced.


Huw was both delighted and horrified to see every eye in the place fixed on Rhiannon as she danced. It was exactly the reception he had hoped. Although his eyes kept being drawn to a man by the wall to the left. There was something strange about him, the way he sat, the way he held himself — and the thin staff leaning next to him was also weird. His face was shadowed by a hood but the light from the fire kept flickering across his face and there was something about his eyes, a hunger in his expression, which sent a shiver down Huw's spine.

Finally the dance was over, and the hall erupted with cheers and applause. Huw let Rhiannon take the bows, then began to play again, traditional Velsh tunes all knew, everything from lullabies to tales of Velsh heroes past. He had taught several of these to Rhiannon in the afternoon, so she often joined in — as did many of the audience, although, as Huw watched, not the strange man to their left.

Finally he finished, letting the last note trail off into the distance.

'Men and women of Vales,' he began. 'I have an important story to tell.'

The drinking had died down and while a few were still more interested in Rhiannon's legs than what he was saying, he was confident he had the room in the palm of his hand.

'As I said, we have come direct from the court of King Ward, where I, Huw of Patcham, was the first Velshman to play for the Forlish king!' he could not resist saying.

He paused and the expected applause came.

'But I have returned home because of what I learned there ... the Forlish king seeks to conquer Vales. He looks at our freedom, at the way we live our lives, and he wants to rule us. But he is not sending his armies north — because they are too busy down south, trying to destroy the other countries there. No, instead he plans something far worse. He will send several hundred of his most vicious soldiers here, to raid, to burn, to rape and to kill. He thinks to terrify us, to force us to bend the knee to him. He thinks we shall happily exchange our freedom for his tyranny, in order to save our wives and children ...'

Huw could see his words were hitting home, while he also saw, out of the corner of his eye, the mysterious man in the shadows shifting around in his seat.

'After he has raided and murdered, he will send emissaries to us, promising Forlish soldiers to protect us. Protect us from his own men! By this he thinks we shall accept the yoke of Forlish rule, allow ourselves to give away our real fortune, our freedom, in exchange for Forlish taxes and laws and a cruel king's rule!'

'When will these raiders arrive?' someone shouted.

'I do not know,' Huw admitted. 'Some could be here now. They could be scouting out villages, ready to launch an attack whenever they sense a weakness. We need to be vigilant. I know we have never had guards or foresters on duty but we need to keep a watch out ...'

'And what do we do if we see them?' Vernin called.

Huw stopped then. He had not thought this through, he realised. Knowing you were about to be attacked was one thing — stopping such an attack was another thing altogether. Every village had men who liked to hunt, who could use slings to bring down birds, or spears to kill boars. But they had few, if any swords.

'Aye — and what if we do turn some bandits back? Will they not just return in greater numbers?' Vernin continued.

Again Huw was stuck. He had thought to issue his warning, be acclaimed as a hero and then move on, his job done. He sensed the room was turning against him — and asking Rhiannon to dance again was not going to save the situation. He glanced to his left, where the man sat in the shadows, and inspiration came to him.

'We have to watch out for strangers, people who do not fit in, for they could be Ward's men.'

He was staring straight at the man as he spoke, and could feel the focus of the room switch from him to the man. What if this really was one of Ward's men? What if he could catch one of the spies, find out how to stop them — he really would be a hero then!

Sendatsu had listened to the tale with growing horror. It seemed the humans were not without their own troubles. He had no wish to be around if there was a war about to erupt in this area. It added yet more urgency to his quest. It was also disturbing to hear the plan these Forlish had come up with. It was something his father might have done, and seemed to indicate a subtlety far beyond what elven lore said could be expected of any humans.

'Does anyone know that man?'

Sendatsu heard the change in the bard's voice, looked up to see the bard pointing at him, every eye on him — and they all seemed unfriendly. There was plenty of muttering going on around the room. He hurriedly tried to think what had been said and what he had missed.

'He walked in not one turn of the hourglass ago and he is the strangest stranger I have ever seen,' Vernin announced. 'He slapped gold on my table and had never tried mead before!'

Instantly the muttering doubled.

'Aye, and he did not know what a pig was, is scared of sheep and eats only raw turnips!' the two-fingered man roared.

Sendatsu opened his mouth to protest but was drowned in a wave of debate.

'Maybe he's from Rheged. I hear they eat turnips over there,' someone suggested.

'My father was from Rheged and I've never eaten turnip before!' another snarled.

'I hear over in Clayhill they like to sleep with their sheep,' someone called.

'I heard that! And it was only in that really cold winter!'

'Tell us, traveller,' the bard's voice boomed over the small arguments breaking out all over the room, 'are you a servant of King Ward? Are you from Forland?'

'I don't even know where Forland is!' Sendatsu protested.

Instantly the atmosphere changed subtly, becoming darker and more threatening. He glanced around at the unfriendly faces and cursed. This was not going well. While he was not afraid of these humans, neither did he want to hurt them. Better to walk away and come back later to speak to the bard and dancer.

'I know nothing about your King Ward. But I know when I am not welcome. I shall leave you in peace.' He stood, grabbing his bowstave from where it rested against the wall, and headed for the door. None moved to stop him, although all watched.

'Stop him! He's a Forlish spy!' the bard shouted.

A handful of men moved across the doorway.

'Let me leave. I do not want to hurt you,' Sendatsu warned.

'You won't leave until you answer to us,' the bard declared.

Sendatsu sighed. He did not want to reveal himself to everyone but it looked like there was no choice.

'There is a simple explanation for this,' he began, placing his bowstave against a wall and preparing to reveal himself.

'Aye — you're here to betray us!' Two-fingers grabbed at Sendatsu's arm.

Instinct took over and he moved smoothly into a fighting stance, freed his arm and flipped Two-fingers across and into a table of drinkers. Humans, food and drink went in every direction. The rest of the hall watched in shock as Two-fingers slowly got to his feet.

'Get him!' the bard yelled.

'Aye — get the Rheged traitor!'

'Stop the Clayhill bastard!'

Instantly a dozen fights began, all across the hall, between all different people, while women screamed and children shrieked and men shouted. Sendatsu took a pace back, to protect his back, but the initial rush was not at him but at each other. Then a bellow of anger made him turn.

Time seemed to slow, and Sendatsu became aware of tiny details, inconsequential things, as Two-fingers charged at him. Sendatsu slapped an arm aside then thrust out his own hand, slamming the rigid edge between thumb and forefinger into Two-fingers' throat. The man's feet shot out from under him and he flipped over backwards, choking and gasping in the muddy rushes.

Then a whole crowd was rushing at Sendatsu. If they had all come together, he would have had no chance but these humans fought each other, or got tangled up in chairs and tables. For an instant he thought about drawing his sword and threatening them — but remembered the carnage he had wrought among the Council Guards. He could not risk that again.

But he was not defenceless. He had learned to fight with his hands and feet — against his peers and against his father. In contrast, the humans that attacked him seemed to move so slow, most of them obviously affected by what they had been drinking. As he had been taught, he merely emptied his mind and dealt with anything that came near him. The answers he sought, upsetting the humans, revealing himself — those worries vanished.

Two men converged on him as he waited, completely calm. He saw a punch coming from his left long before it was dangerous. It was just like being back on the training mats. The moves he had practised a thousand times, until they were second nature, they just flowed now. His left hand curled up, deflecting the punch away, and he stepped smoothly into a second block to avoid a blow from his right, this time catching and holding the man's arm. His left leg snapped out as he shouted, an explosion of sound to concentrate power and focus himself.

He dropped the first man with a kick to the head, then used a double punch, an uppercut followed by a reverse fist to the nose, to send the second man crashing to the floor.

Another roundhouse punch — how slow did they arrive! — came at his head from the right and it was easy to flick the fist harmlessly over his shoulder and then drive the stiffened fingers of his left hand into the balding man's gut. As Baldy folded over, groaning, he grabbed Baldy's shoulders and swung the man into the path of a kick launched by a man whose face was disfigured by huge boils. Baldy went flying, felled by his friend, and before Boils could recover, Sendatsu stepped closer, always in perfect balance, to deliver a punch and a kick in the same instant; the double blow sending Boils reeling away, to where he almost landed in the fire.

A pair of them, son and father, had seized one of the long benches and now ran at Sendatsu, using the bench as a shield, either to strike him or drive him into a corner, where he would be easy prey.

Instead he ran forwards then, at the last moment, slid under the bench, skidding on the damp rushes and deliberately not thinking what he might be sliding through. He reached up as the rough wood scythed over his head and allowed himself to be carried along for an instant, before swinging his legs out to the left, to where the son was carrying the bench.

He trapped one of Son's ankles between his feet, then jerked it to the right and let go of the bench in the same moment. The son went flying, tumbling over the front of the bench, while the father on the other end was sent cartwheeling across the floor.

As more men converged, he flipped to his feet and grabbed the bench, bringing it up like a shield. A grey-haired man punched it and then howled in pain. He kicked Grey-hair between the legs and the man's howl of pain turned into a scream as he folded over.

A man with only one eye dived at him but he shifted his weight and used One-eye's momentum to hurl him onto the serving table, which went down with a crash, scattering goods, drink and chickens into the confusion.

It was time to go, before someone got really hurt. The path to the door seemed clear and he prepared to make a run for it.

Huw watched the hooded stranger in amazement then glanced at Rhiannon, who was also gazing open-mouthed at the man.

Dropping his lyre, he ran at the man, launching himself from the back. Even as he did so, part of him said this was a big mistake. But he arrived from an unexpected direction, and threw his arms around the man.

Instantly Huw realised the man was hugely muscled. But that was not the only realisation. When he flicked his head around, his cowl slipped back and Huw found himself just a couple of inches away from the man's ear. Seeing it was such a shock that he almost let go — and then the man simply shrugged Huw off, sending him flying backwards, tumbling across the floor.

Huw lay there for a moment, winded, as well as trying to understand what he had just seen.

'Are you all right?' Rhiannon asked, rushing to help him sit up.

Huw turned to her. 'He's not a spy for Ward — he's an elf,' he managed to say.

'What? An elf? Are you sure?'

'I saw his skin, his eyes — and his ears! I have heard enough stories about them to know one when they are right in front of me!'

'So what do we do?'

'We have to stop this — we have to help him. Who knows why he is here but an elf! In Vales! He could be the difference if we are to stop Ward. Help me up!'

* * *

Sendatsu cursed himself. He had lost focus for but a moment and that stupid bard had grabbed him. It had only slowed him down for a few heartbeats but the clear path to the door was gone. Instead, Two-fingers and three others stood there, looking grim. There was still a chance to escape through the window — but that meant leaving his bowstave behind. And he needed that bow. There might be nothing for it, he would have to draw his sword. Regrets could come later. Then he saw Two-fingers whip out a knife and realised he was out of choices. Next moment they were all charging at him and he tensed himself for an explosion of blood and violence.

With Rhiannon's help, Huw staggered to his feet and ran at the men rushing the elf. Heedless of their size, numbers and the knife the leader carried, his only thought was to help the elf.

'Stop this! Leave him alone!' he bellowed.

But things had gone too far. Desperately, Huw leaped over a table, hurling himself into the four of them, and bringing everyone down in a huge pile.

Gasping, he bounced clear of them and found himself on his back, looking up into the startled face of the elf.

'Quick! Go! While you can!' Huw cried.

Sendatsu understood the chance being offered — for the moment nobody was trying to attack him, so he jumped across the fallen bodies, grabbed his bowstave and raced out into the rain. He did not stop until he was clear of the village, and under the poor shelter of some trees. There he paused, panting — but there seemed to be no pursuit.

Sendatsu cursed. Next time he went into a human village, he would have to be more careful. The answers were there. He just had to find them.

The rain slowed, dried to a drizzle and then petered out, although heavy drips still fell from the trees. He could not imagine waiting out here. He had to find somewhere else. Propelled by a sense of looming desperation, he hurried west, hoping to find another village quickly.

# 5

*I remember what the forefathers told me about how we came to this land. I do not know if it is true but I believe it is more likely than some of the tales I have heard my people tell the humans. We did not arrive on gull-wing ships, nor on strange craft pulled by dragons. We came in old boats, which leaked, and rotted away on the shoreline not long after we landed.*

*My ancestor and his eleven companions had tried to find a home among the Nipponese. But while they were happy there, for a century, the rulers of Nippon finally drove them out, frightened of these Elfarans, who did not die and instead kept marrying, creating bigger and bigger families, all of them able to do magic. By then there were hundreds of us, and our numbers were growing all the time. Even with the dozens of half-brothers and -sisters among each clan, our Elfaran forefathers were worried about interbreeding and, as leader of each clan, had the final decision on who could marry. Not all were happy with this, but all accepted their judgement. They also created a separate order, the Magic-weavers, the most gifted mages among us. Even then they saw magic could be used as a weapon, and wanted to have it under their control. Although, ironically, they were the only ones among us who couldn't actually use any magic.*

*Every decision they made was for the good. Their intentions were always honourable. But they did not see what was coming.*

*Our arrogance blinded us, we came to believe in our own superiority. Some of us tried to work with the human tribes already here — but not enough, nowhere near enough. The rest despised the humans and used them to make themselves rich. The only solution was to lock ourselves away from them, until the magic within us had faded, until we were like other humans. My forefathers chose me to make this plan happen, and I worked with the Magic-weavers to make it so. I knew there would be danger in this. But I did not realise from which direction it would come.*

'You'll pay for that, you bastard!'

Huw tried to sit up but the two-fingered man grabbed him and loomed above, knife in hand.

'Wait! Stop!' Huw tried to shout — but the man's face was twisted in anger and the knife began to descend ... then his face went blank as a chair smashed across the back of his head and the two-fingered man fell beside the terrified Huw.

Huw — and the man's three companions — glanced up to see Rhiannon there, looking a little surprised, and holding the remains of a chair.

'What was that for?' a man asked.

Rhiannon glared at him. 'My mother was from Rheged!' she lied defiantly.

The three men looked at each other, then one shrugged. 'Fair enough then.'

All around them, the fights were ending and men were helping each other to their feet, comparing wounds and offering to buy each other drinks.

'Shouldn't we go after that spy?' Vernin emerged from under the wreckage of his table.

'No! Leave him!' Huw got back to his feet, using his trained voice to drown out any protests. 'He's not one of Ward's men — he's not even a man at all, he's an elf!'

That silenced the room — even men who had been lying on the floor rolled over to look at Huw.

'What?' Vernin spat.

'I saw his ears — he's an elf. I don't know what he was doing here but ...'

'Never mind him — what have you been doing here? First you tell us Ward and his Forlish are about to descend on us all, then you say there're spies sitting among us, telling them which houses to rob and which wives to steal, then he starts a fight and you try to stop it!' Vernin advanced on Huw, his face reddening with anger, an alarming number of other men behind him.

'Keep back!' Rhiannon warned them. 'I have a chair and I'm not afraid to use it!'

The ridiculousness of her threat, as much as the fire in her eyes — and the fact her dress was revealing almost all of one thigh — brought them to a halt.

'I am sorry,' Huw apologised. 'I made a terrible mistake. Please, let me pay for it.'

Vernin paused then. 'You would have earned a fair bit at Ward's court then?' he asked cautiously.

'Shall we say two gold pieces?' Huw offered, knowing it would leave him with a much lighter purse. 'And then drinks for all?'

Vernin beamed, while even those men nursing broken noses or missing teeth brightened considerably. And so they should, Huw reflected bitterly, fearing for his purse's contents.

It took plenty of ale, as well as more songs and several dances from Rhiannon, before all was forgiven. Even Two-fingers was happy enough, with four more tankards of ale in him, to tell everyone the story of how a beautiful woman had hit him with a chair.

'Go back to your room — I'll try and find the elf,' Huw whispered to Rhiannon.

'Did he see me dance?' Rhiannon asked.

That stopped Huw in his tracks. 'Yes, he did. He couldn't take his eyes off you,' he admitted quietly.

Rhiannon's imagination had also been fired by the thought of an elf. Her dream had been to dance with the elves — if one had already seen her … perhaps he would ask her to return to mysterious Dokuzen, to perform there!

'Let's find him first,' Huw suggested, not liking this particular development much but the thought of finding an elf wandering around Vales was too exciting to dampen his enthusiasm completely.

'Of course!' Rhiannon twirled off towards their room and Huw felt another stirring of unease. He had enjoyed having Rhiannon to himself.

His disquiet grew as he stepped outside. The rain had died and it was not a cold night, but there were plenty of clouds out and almost no light, beyond that thrown from the fires in the village huts. He was also horribly aware he had no tracking skills to speak of, and the chance of finding an elf, in the dark, in the woods, was roughly the same as King Ward giving up the crown and deciding to spend the rest of his life handing out food to the poor. But what an elf could do for his people was too important to just give up.

Beyond the lights of the village it was almost pitch-black, and he edged forwards, tripping and slipping almost every pace, calling out for the elf and knowing he must look like the world's biggest fool to anyone watching. But he had been called fool before, many times, by his fellow villagers and he refused to let that stop him.

He did not know how long he spent out there, splashing through muddy puddles, searching desperately and calling hopefully. The elf did not answer. He tripped and fell yet again and tiredly got to his feet. The lights of the village were faint behind him and he had to accept he was not going to find the elf. He thumped the trunk of a nearby tree in anger. He had been so close! An elf could have been the answer. Wearily he turned back to the village, feeling the bitter pang of despair more than the aches and pains of stubbed toes and battered elbows and knees.

In the morning they would travel back to his father's village, as planned. His father would know what to do. It would have been wonderful to get elven help, for Vales really needed a hero. But this was a mystery that would never be answered.

* * *

King Ward of Forland looked out across Cridianton and took a breath of sweet morning air. Watching the city come alive in the morning, seeing what he had created, made everything feel right with the world. It was the perfect way to begin the day. The kings of Forland, even his own grandfather, had been happy enough to let things go on as they had for hundreds of years, content to occupy themselves with hunting and whoring and drinking. Ward's father had disliked hunting and, while drinking had some appeal and whoring was always diverting, needed something more from the crown.

He was a keen student of history and had read every book on the shelf in Cridianton's library and he encouraged his son, Ward, to do the same. Both came to the same conclusion — men had fallen and needed to rise once more.

The elves had brought civilisation, culture and grace to these human lands but, when they shut themselves away, humans had regressed. Knowledge that had once been commonplace among the human lands was forgotten, or diminished. But there were pockets of learning, places where skills were kept alive, passed down from father to son and guarded jealously. Somehow they needed to bring those together. If men were to rise, they needed to seek out knowledge and learning, needed to pool their ideas.

Ward's father, Avery, had begun. He hired stonemasons from Balia to build the walls and the castle of Cridianton, invited thinkers and planners and healers from Landia, sent emissaries to all lands with questions about building, medicine, farming and myriad other subjects that could change men's lives.

But, after early success, he found his approaches rebuffed and other countries refusing to share their nuggets of knowledge. Many feared Forland, the largest country by far, amassing such a treasure-trove of ideas. Avery had died disappointed, his dream unrealised.

Ward had taken the throne determined to see his father's vision come true — in a different way. If countries would not share their knowledge in a spirit of brotherhood, he would take it from them. Only together could men rise — under one ruler. It was for their own good — they were just too foolish to see it. All men would thank him, one day.

Besides, history showed him that great advances could be made in war. It brought fresh thinking and new ideas — all the things he wanted. So he trained and worked his armies — and then sent them out to bring the knowledge to him, by force. It was a long process, and the other countries were stubborn. But they could not stand against the Forlish armies.

Breconia, with its skills of woodworking, was his within two years. Nevland, with its farming machines and knowledge of crops and agriculture, was the next to follow. But it was not enough. On he pushed, into Balia and Landia, while already planning for a seaborne invasion of the Skilly Isles to his west.

Of course this did not come without some hardship, and higher taxes at home. Rumblings of dissent at these necessary measures to fund the wars were swiftly stamped out.

But he was not deaf and blind to the unrest. So he decided to show his people the benefits this new enlightenment would provide. He built bathhouses in the city, along the lines of the Balian ones, hosted plays and created statues, like the Landish. The entertainers who kept his court amused were the perfect example of what life would eventually be like. The elves had given mankind a legacy of ideas, but had left them scattered across the continent. He would concentrate them in the one place and then all could benefit. He was sure of it. It would be a better world, under his rule. Certainly there had to be sacrifices made. He had not wanted to enslave other nations but such an ambitious program of empire building needed cheap labour and what was cheaper than slaves? They may not thank him but their sons and daughters would, when they saw what they had built.

He looked down, seeing yet another stone building taking shape in the town below. The walls were covered in a fine tracery of wooden scaffolding, like a spider's web, and, even at this early hour, men were thick on its walls, carrying stones to raise the walls. They would die and vanish into history but the stone building they were making would live on. Just like the name of the king who ordered it built, Ward thought with satisfaction.

Nothing great came without effort, without struggle, but he was feeling the size of the problems facing him. He looked north, to an annoyance that was spoiling his grand vision. He had never bothered with Vales before, for it was no threat to him. But his hand was being forced. He would have to deal with the Velsh, for the good of all mankind. They would also thank him for it, one day.

And as for the elves … that was his real dream. He had tried to study the elven histories as best he could. Not the tales that amused the children but the real story of what happened when the elves left the world and withdrew behind their magical barrier. There were few details and surprisingly little he trusted. And certainly no contact since that day. Any humans who had tried to enter the forests around Dokuzen had never returned, until the tales grew to the point where none were willing to take the risk.

Except Ward was not planning to ride there with a few drunken friends. When he rode north it would be at the head of his army, to take for himself what legend said was their greatest secret — immortality. He had read about it in an obscure scroll from Breconia. Elves living an endless life, still young when the grandchildren of the first humans who had met them were bowed with age. That was the real goal. No wonder they had hidden themselves away, rather than risk the humans finding such a prize. But he would not find it — he would take it.

Not only would his name live forever, he would live forever!

It was a seed that had grown within him, was beginning to consume him. He had ruled for many years and could feel the sands running out of his life's glass. Every night he had to get up every few turns of the hourglass to have a piss. No matter how many young women came to his bed, he could not stop the thought he was somehow becoming less than a man.

And who would carry on his life's work if he died? His two sons were fools, caring only for conquest and slaughter. They could not see how he planned to rebuild. They longed only to destroy. Sometimes he feared that only through Dokuzen could his vision come true.

'Sire?' A nervous voice interrupted his thoughts.

He turned and his sense of peace and impending triumph faded instantly.

'Where is she?' Ward asked softly, ominously.

'I do not know, sire,' Hector admitted, trying not to show his fear. 'The room was locked from the inside and, when we broke the door down, a bag of clothes was missing, as was my ring.'

'So what are you saying? An elf magically made her disappear?' Ward asked sardonically.

'No, sire. Someone has kidnapped her, forced her to go with them ...'

'Who?'

Hector gulped. 'A search of the castle has revealed one other performer is missing. Hugh of Browns Brook.'

'So they were having an affair and have disappeared together, eh?' Ward's only outward show of emotion was a clenched fist, but Hector could feel cold sweat trickling down his back. Fear and anger were warring within him. He had worked so hard, sacrificed so much, to get himself to this position. Now, at the moment of his triumph, a foolish boy and his idiotic daughter might have ruined everything for him.

'No, sire! This Hugh has tricked her somehow — with your permission, I will take a squad of men and get her back. They cannot have much of a lead and anyway, we know where they are going. We can be at Browns Brook right behind them,' Hector promised. 'She will be unspoilt still, for I have told her never to lie with a man unless I give permission.'

Ward did not move for what seemed like an age, before nodding his approval.

'I have many other things on my mind but, for your daughter, I am willing to go to a little effort. Talk to my castellan. He shall give you a squad of men. Travel to Browns Brook and bring her back. As for the lovesick Hugh, I want him back here as well.

Although you don't have to be too gentle about it, I want him alive — so he can understand what I am going to do to him.'

'At once, sire!' Hector bowed low.

The chamber of the Elven Council was a glorious confection of marble, a testament to the finest work of the best craftsmen in Dokuzen. Soaring arched windows revealed wonderful views of the city and the wooded hills beyond. Tall wooden doors, intricately carved, pointed the way to an enormous wooden table, around which thirteen seats were arrayed. Beyond that were simple, yet carved and decorated benches, where more than a hundred elves could sit and watch and listen to the wisdom of the Elven Council. But for now the galleries were empty; there were just two figures in the whole of the huge, echoing chamber.

Jaken, leader of the Tadayoshi clan, took his seat carefully. He had devoted his whole life to one goal — attaining power for himself and his clan. Clan Kaneoki had held the position of Elder Elf for the last three centuries. Thanks to his work, that dominance was finally under threat. Now he faced a difficult choice. He could explain everything, throw himself on the mercy of his fellow councillors and their leader, the Elder Elf, and almost certainly keep control of his clan. But the price would be steep. His power and influence would be broken and clan Tadayoshi, rather than being the main challenger for the position of Elder Elf, would instead become beholden to the Elder Elf. No more could he push to ensure his supporters were officers in the Council Guard and Border Patrol, no more would he arrange for those he trusted to be chosen for important posts such as tax collectors and mine overseers. Instead he would have to beg for scraps from the Elder Elf and be pathetically grateful for anything that came his way. His clan would take generations to recover fortune and position.

Or he could gamble for it all. Tell the Elder Elf only part of the story, use the rest of the information for his own ends and make a play for complete control of the Council. Of course, if it failed, he would lose everything. There was every chance his clan would be expelled from the Council, forced to become esemono or worse.

After what he had read, it was no choice. At stake would be not just the power and glory of Dokuzen but dominion over every land. Much of the scroll his son had found was obviously lies but he had found fascinating nuggets of truth. The first was that Tadayoshi had once ruled the elves and been approved by the forefathers themselves. That meant he had every right to act now. Secondly, the barrier was meant to keep the elves in Dokuzen, not the humans out of Dokuzen. And they would be right to fear an elven army with Jaken at its head! He found it ironic such a truth had come from a forgotten elf called Sendatsu, the same name as his son. This Sendatsu had certainly proved more use than his idiot boy.

He blamed Noriko, his wife, for making Sendatsu soft. No matter what he had tried to do to the child, he had never become the ruthless warrior Jaken needed. Certainly he had shown ability with blade, bow and bare hands but never the spine to go with it. Devoting himself to children — what honour was there in such a life? The two brats were at his home now, wailing their eyes out, despite Noriko's best efforts to keep them happy. Another distraction he did not need. But they would have their uses. He would see they were raised properly.

'A sad day, Lord Jaken.' Daichi, the Elder Elf, the leader of the Elven Council and the nominal head of the elven people, took his seat with equal care. 'I assume you have called me here to announce you shall withdraw from the Council and your position as clan leader due to the shame brought on you by your son's actions ...'

'Not at all!' Jaken said harshly. 'My duty to my clan and to the Council takes precedence. Without me, disaster will befall our people. That is what I am here to talk about.'

Daichi had not achieved his position by letting his face betray his thoughts. But even his years of practice could not help him here. He had never been close to the head of the Tadayoshi and he knew full well Jaken's ambition to be the next Elder Elf — a position Daichi planned to keep within his own clan. But he respected Jaken's single-minded determination. The elven people needed such strength. 'But Sendatsu, your son and heir, attacked and killed Council Guards and has, from all reports, broken through the magic barrier and is in the human world! Despite the best efforts of the Council, all are talking about it!'

'That is what it looks like,' Jaken agreed. 'But that is not what really happened. If we concentrate on Sendatsu's actions, then we shall miss the true plot. The first you will know of it is when the Council is overthrown and you are dragged away to your death.'

He saw the flicker of disquiet on Daichi's face but then the Elder Elf recovered. Jaken knew he would never show weakness.

'I know you have many ears across the city and I thank you for the warning. But I fail to see how the actions of one elf can mean anything. Our authority is absolute. Nobody would challenge the Council, obedience is ingrained into the lower classes. This sounds like an attempt to save your clan's position. I am afraid it will not work. If you want to stay on as clan leader, then I require you to submit to me ...'

'The Magic-weavers,' Jaken interrupted. 'Sumiko was behind the whole thing.'

Daichi paused. 'How can that be possible? It has been centuries since they challenged the power of the Council. They have no power base other than their own magic. And there are too few of them to do anything. They know that the twelve clans, together, would destroy them.'

'They are dangerous,' Jaken warned. 'They are like the snake that hides under the bed, waiting for us to sleep so they can strike. In chaos they see their chance. You think time has tamed them, that they have forgotten they once dreamed of ruling the elves. But we must watch them, now more than ever.'

'Come, my friend, surely you see dangers where there are none ...'

'They tried once before to rule Dokuzen,' Jaken interrupted coldly. 'They think magic makes them better than us, try to tell people they are the only ones who keep us safe from the gaijin humans. Now they have proof the barrier has weakened enough to pass through. Already they are out there, dripping their poison into every ear. All know the power of the barrier — it is what allows many of the people to sleep sound at night. Now all are hearing how elves can pass through it, so how long before humans can invade? They play on doubts and fears, say the Magic-weavers must take control if they are to save the barrier and protect the people. We keep our position because the lower classes think that is the way of things. We only have a handful of Council Guards and Border Patrol. We keep order because of fear, discipline and habit. But if they believe we are lying to them, if they think the barrier is failing and the Magic-weavers will give them a better life, then we are in trouble. For we will have no army to stop the Magic-weavers. Worse, the esemono have all been trained with the sword and bow. If they were to decide to overthrow us, there is nothing we could do to stop them.'

'You disturb me, old friend,' Daichi muttered, and Jaken smiled inwardly at the phrase. It was expected that the Council should call each other such things, even though both knew it was a lie — they had never been friends. 'But while all that is true, you are drawing a long bow indeed from something that might happen to something that will happen. The lower classes may not be content with their lot but they believe Aroaril ordained it this way — and they do not trust the Magic-weavers either.'

'Sumiko was the one to attack the Council Guards with magic — not my son,' Jaken said harshly. 'My son did not have that kind of magic. He barely had the power to make a flower bloom! And then I received a message, supposedly from my son, threatening to use his trial to spread lies to the people unless I gave the scroll to the Magic-weavers for safekeeping. Old friend, they are up to their necks in this. They did not send Sendatsu out into the human world to protect him. They wanted to show the weakness of the barrier — and they want him to return with human help, to allow them to seize control.'

'Surely not!'

'They are the ones who keep the magic barrier in place. Who better to open it to our enemies?'

'What do you suggest?'

'Act as if you suspect nothing. Pretend it was all the action of one mad elf. Publicly dismiss my suspicions. That way the Magic-weavers will gain the confidence to put their plans into motion. Meanwhile, I shall be moving to stop them. As soon as they give themselves away, I shall pounce!'

Daichi thought swiftly. If there was to be trouble, if the Magic-weavers were really trying something, it would be better to have a scapegoat in case things went wrong. Far better for blame to be attached to the Tadayoshi clan than to himself. 'Will you take care of this for the Council? Will you watch them for me — for us all?'

'It will be my pleasure. Sumiko is to blame for all of this. I have no proof but I feel it, deep inside. I shall bring her down if it is the last thing I do,' Jaken said vengefully but, inside, his heart sang. He had presented Daichi with an irresistible opportunity and the Elder Elf had snapped at it, as he'd known he would. From great adversity came great opportunity. Yes, he had placed everything at risk but better to gamble and try to win it all than play safely and lose.

'We shall do as you suggest,' Daichi agreed.

'A wise decision, Elder Elf.' Jaken bowed his head, masking his triumph with the ease of long practice.


The garden of Sumiko, High Magic-weaver of the elves, was rightly famed throughout Dokuzen. Twice the size of the usual villa garden, Sumiko refused to have it tended by gardeners, as was the habit of the rich. But then she did not need to. Plants bloomed or shrivelled at a moment's thought, no matter the weather or the season. She liked it to reflect her mood, could make it do anything she wished. Here she had the ultimate power, here her decisions were obeyed instantly — unlike elsewhere in Dokuzen, where she was forced to grovel before the power of the Council, as all Magic-weavers had done since they had shut themselves away from the humans.

Now, as she walked the garden accompanied only by her two trusted deputies, it was a riot of colour and movement. Her deputies, talented Magic-weavers in their own right, stepped carefully as plants writhed around them.

'This is our chance,' Sumiko said joyfully. For centuries the Magic-weavers had kept to their lowly station in life, bided their time and nursed their grievances. It had fallen to her to right ancient wrongs and restore her order to glory. The relief she felt meant the flowers were exploding into colour around her.

'Sensei?' the senior deputy, Oroku, a powerful elf now running to fat, ventured to ask.

'The people are whispering, fear is loosening the grip of the Council. Our time is coming. Finally we will have our revenge. For the first time in centuries, we have proved the barrier that separates us from the humans can be passed. Events are in motion and the truth will at last be told.'

'Proved, sensei?'

'I didn't know it would work. Obviously I hoped.' Sumiko shrugged. 'Luckily Asami was up to the task. Her strength is amazing but, now it has been done once, it will be much easier next time.'

'So you didn't know Sendatsu would survive when you had her send him through?'

'Of course not! The barrier has stood strong for centuries! But now we have proved it is decaying, and should gain the rest of the information we need from Sendatsu, and the humans.'

'What will that mean for the humans?'

'Who cares about the humans? It will mean the Magic-weavers will rule the elves. I shall be triumphant, and those evil bastards Jaken and Daichi will bow at my feet.'

Oroku and the second deputy, Jimai, stepped back as plants writhed across the pathway in front of them, waving vines menacingly. She shivered as she imagined it. In elven society, there were many different classes, and all were acutely aware of where they stood in its hierarchy. Except the Magic-weavers. By all rights they should be admired, hailed above all others. Magic was difficult and dangerous. It was a natural part of the world, an energy that flowed through everyone and everything. If you were an elf or, better yet, a Magic-weaver, you could sense that energy and draw on it, use it. But anything you took had to be replaced by your own energy. Try to do too much and you would die. But for the careful Magic-weaver, strong and well trained, the magic could be used to do all sorts of things. Anything you found in nature could be replicated — but also changed. The power that allowed a tree root to crack solid rock over ten years could be taken and compressed into a heartbeat. Those able to wield it deserved to be raised high. Instead they were despised, treated like outcasts, not to be trusted. It stung Sumiko, like a thorn under her foot. It seemed a small thing but bear it for too long and it would drive you mad.

'And how will the incident with Sendatsu achieve that?' Jimai, lean where Oroku was plump, ventured.

'Patience,' Sumiko counselled herself, as much as the others. The plants shrank back, allowing the pathway to open once more. 'Sendatsu is a means to an end. If he had given me the scroll, then we would already be triumphant ... but in confusion comes opportunity. Sendatsu is concerned about one thing only — his two brats. It is almost impossible to believe an elf, especially the son of the brute Jaken, would be like that. But then this life is full of mystery. Anyway, he will be the perfect tool for us. He knows he cannot return unless he has some evidence to back up what he read in that scroll. Who knows what he will find — but if there is anyone who can return with what we need, it will be him. Meanwhile, we need to prepare the way. I need everyone to be out talking to the people, let their fears grow about fading magic. Say two things — first, the thought their children could fail their Test of magic and be banished from Dokuzen, and second, the magical barrier is fading and will soon be gone. They ignore us usually but, when there is fear of magic, who do they turn to? The Magic-weavers, the guardians of the magic. We must get everything ready so when Sendatsu does return, we can rise and the Council will fall,' Sumiko said with relish.

'And what of Asami?' Oroku asked.

'Leave her to me. She loves that fool Sendatsu and needs to be handled carefully. She could be the final piece of the puzzle for us.' Sumiko smiled and more plants exploded into flower, red as blood. 'But her first loyalty is to him, not to me. If we are not careful, she might tear a hole in our plans. We must use them for as long as possible and judge perfectly the time to cut them both loose.'

'And what of Jaken?' Jimai asked.

'We have to act quickly,' Sumiko admitted, 'while Jaken is off balance. His standing would have been hurt by his son's actions. Most clan leaders would resign in disgrace after that. But not him. We will have little time. He is utterly ruthless and we cannot underestimate him. Truly, seeing him grovel at my feet will be a day to remember, as I pay him back for a hundred insults.'

Behind her the plants shuddered, petals flying away.

'We shall begin immediately,' Oroku promised.


'Lord, are we sure he has gone into the human world and the barrier did not kill him?' Gaibun asked respectfully.

'I have had it confirmed. I have a spy inside the Magic-weavers,' Jaken said.

'So the barrier is really fading?'

'It has been fading for years. But there is life enough in it for us to complete our plans,' Jaken dismissed. 'Of more concern is what he might find out there and who he might be speaking to.'

'There is nothing to worry about, my lord. Even if he survives there, he cannot do any harm. Nobody cares what those gaijin humans think — if they can even think!' Gaibun tried a little joke.

Jaken did not smile.

'He cannot be allowed to escape justice. What he did to me and my soldiers must be punished!' Hanto snarled. His arm had been healed but his pride was bleeding.

'Did I ask you to speak?' Jaken said coldly.

'My apologies, my lord. I meant no offence.' Hanto bowed immediately, his face going from flushed to white in an instant.

'We have two tasks before us. The first is the most pressing. The Magic-weavers were behind much of what went on with Sendatsu. They will seek to exploit the situation. I expect them to make a play for the remaining books in the tombs of the forefathers. We must be ready for that. We have to know what they plan. Gaibun, I need you to gain your wife's trust and use that for information. Asami will be the key here. The Magic-weavers will try to use her, while she is Sendatsu's link with Dokuzen. All will revolve around her. Succeed in this and there will be glory aplenty to share around. I shall be the next Elder Elf; Gaibun shall take the position of clan leader for our clan; and Hanto, you shall become commander of the Council Guard.'

'You honour us, lord.' Hanto bowed, Gaibun a heartbeat behind him.

'You shall earn it,' Jaken warned. 'Hanto, I need you to take your best two men and go and find Sendatsu, in the human world.'

'Go ... into the human world? Through the barrier?' Hanto croaked, his face going white again.

'I told you. I have a spy inside the Magic-weavers. They will send you through. Now the barrier has been breached once, it will be even easier. It is quite safe.'

'We shall return with his head by the next full moon,' Hanto promised.

'Did I say that?' Jaken hissed. 'I ordered you to return with Sendatsu! Alive! I do not want him out in the human world and I definitely don't want him finding anything that can be used against us later. I want him safe, under guard, ready to be produced when necessary as evidence of the Magic-weavers' treachery. He will be the lever we shall use to overthrow Daichi.'

'I understand, lord.'

'No mistakes. He is no good to me dead. I would rather you kept him alive and he returned through Asami than he died out there. His return will be our signal to move. I want him to come back at a time of my choosing, under my control — but at the very least I must know when he is to return.'

'You can rely on me, lord.'

'I already am. Your revenge can come afterwards. Fail, and you will beg me to end your suffering.'

'Your will, lord!'

'You have your tasks. Go to them.'

# 6

*This would never have happened had our forefather Elfarans still been alive. They were immortals — or so we thought. While they did not have magic, they had the wisdom of centuries, and the stories of the dragons. They were also, literally, the fathers of us all. We all respected them, would never dream of going against their wishes. We put them on a pedestal, thought they could do no wrong ... but, like all fathers, they were flawed.*

*Once we saw they were only human, we had a choice to make. Some of us, like myself, loved them more for it. Others lost all respect, came to believe that everything about them was a lie, all because of that chink in their armour.*

*If they could have explained this to us, things might have been different. But that was impossible. For these immortals, these one, unchanging part of our lives, these invincible fathers, were dead.*

Sendatsu stumped through the trees miserably. Where was he going to find a place to sleep tonight? Even when he had camped out in the woods with his friends, Jaken had ensured a servant had come along to help them make a shelter and cook food. He was horribly aware he had little idea how to do either, yet his stomach was growling and he felt dizzy with tiredness.

He trudged onwards, wishing he had somewhere warm and comfortable to sleep and wishing with everything he was back home in Dokuzen with Mai and Cheijun. Then he spotted a light through the trees. It seemed to be coming from a large building, surrounded by a series of low hillocks. It was strange but he went over anyway — anything had to be better than trying to sleep in the open.

To his shock and surprise, this proved not to be a wattle and daub cottage, like he had seen back in that human village, nor the brick homes he was used to in Dokuzen. This was built of stones, shaped and placed together.

Torches burning inside proved someone still lived here, although their light showed some of it had fallen down, littering the ground with its blocks of stone, while the roof, thatch over wooden beams, was half falling in.

'Hello?' he called.

A curse from inside the building was followed by the appearance of a pair of scruffy humans, both holding torches in one hand, crude swords in the other.

'Who are you?' one grunted.

'My name is Sendatsu and I am an elf ...'

'And I'm the queen of Forland,' the man interrupted.

Sendatsu paused. This ugly, smelly man was almost certainly not the queen of anything. It sounded like something his father might say. But everything he had been told about humans said they weren't capable of such thinking. So why had he said he was? He had no desire to try to work out more of these human eccentricities. Even a warm night was not worth that. Besides, these two were hardly friendly, even if they did claim to be royalty ...

'Apologies for disturbing you. I shall leave you in peace.' He bowed slightly.

'Oh, you're not going anywhere. Not until you hand over your money and your sword,' the man rasped, the pair of them advancing threateningly, swords pointed at him.

Sendatsu nodded. Whatever they said they were, these two were obviously thieves or bandits. He had no wish for violence but knew it was the only language men such as these spoke.

He dropped his bow and drew his sword.

'If you want to live, I would advise you not to do this,' he warned.

'Oh, we're going to enjoy this,' the man declared.

'No, you're not,' Sendatsu told him.

The two bandits raced at him. Sendatsu only hesitated a moment before exploding into movement.

The leader drew his sword back over his right shoulder, ready to bring it around in a huge swing — but Sendatsu was much faster, locking his elbow and wrist and lunging his sword forwards. It sank deep into the man's chest, exploding out of his back in a bloody spray. He twisted it to break the flesh's suction and ripped it clear, the man howling as his life was torn away with it. The bandit had not even hit the ground when Sendatsu took one more step and sliced across to his right in the classic thunder-strike stroke, ripping open the second man's belly as he raised his sword in a hopeless attempt at defending himself. The man blundered on for a few more steps, his intestines spilling out of the massive wound, then Sendatsu took two paces and cut at the back of the neck almost delicately, finishing him before he could barely begin screaming.

Sendatsu wiped his sword clean. The pair of them had no more skill than the average sheep — and smelled even worse. Still, he felt he should offer them some respect.

'My apologies, your majesty,' he told the dead leader.

He found himself wishing there were more, that they had been more of a challenge. The power it gave him, the thrill of using his sword on these humans, of putting into reality all the practice ... it was dangerously seductive. He never felt more alive than when his life was in the balance. He sheathed his sword determinedly. He must not give in to this strange bloodlust.

He picked up one of their fallen torches and decided to explore the structure. Perhaps he could return the stolen property to its owners. Aroaril knew the humans had little enough anyway.

The pair had been living down one end, where the fire that had attracted him flickered and something simmered in a pot. As to the rest of it, much was wrecked and, even though it had been a long time ago, he could tell it had been burned from the black marks on the remaining stone walls.

Something caught his eye beneath the dirt of years and he brushed at it to reveal a design etched into a large stone. He stared at it in shock, for it was unmistakeable — the stylised sunburst he instantly recognised as the mark of Aroaril. It made no sense. He had never heard of humans worshipping Aroaril — he remembered his father declaring Aroaril could only reveal himself to the elves. It was another sign of their superiority and, besides, the God Aroaril would never offer his magic power to mere humans. The last village had certainly showed no sign of worshipping Aroaril. So why had this church been built by humans — for it was no elven building — why were only a couple of bandits living here and, more importantly, why had it been burned? From the overgrowth and general state of the old church, this had happened many, many years ago, perhaps even centuries. He pressed on the Aroaril stone — and it grated a little. Curious, he tried again and felt it move, while those surrounding it stayed still. Years of dust and dirt fought him but he eased the stone out, to reveal a dark space behind it. Thinking it might be the bandits' treasure store, he reached in — to pull out a metal box, again with the mark of Aroaril still visible on the lid. Inside was a strange book, bound in leather but with pages made from animal skin. It was seemingly undamaged by its long storage but he still handled it carefully. There was only one reason a book like this had not rotted away to nothing during the uncounted years it had sat there — it had been preserved through magic. Cautiously he opened it. But the pages he looked at he could not read. The writing was clear but the language was nothing he recognised. It reminded him of the tombs of the forefathers and the books he had found there.

He noticed his hands were shaking a little. Was this the evidence he sought? Did this mean elves had tried to teach humans the worship of Aroaril? And, if so, who had destroyed this place and put a stop to it?

If only he could find a way to read this book! Instinctively he felt this was his way back home. All he needed was to find a human who could read it. It had to be an old human language — there was no other answer. He was not sure if his magic might help but he would do whatever it took to get the answers out of this book.

The fire was warm, while there was food in a pot. But the real warmth came from the book.

Sendatsu sat with his back against a stone wall, the book on his lap, and took out his children's toys from the pouch. Carefully he kissed each one goodnight, sang Mai her special song and then tucked them tenderly back.

'I will be home soon,' he promised them.

Broyle of Readingum was a proud man. He had served his king and country for more than ten years, using ruthlessness and single-minded determination to destroy the enemies of Forland. His one dream was to be rewarded by the king, to be given his own command. And it was coming true!

He basked in the warm glow of that as he rode through Vales at the head of his own miniature army, on a mission from the king himself. He cast his mind back to the beginning of his good fortune.

He had taken command of a company of men after his lieutenant had been killed, driven off a Balian attack and saved a supply column. It had just been another day for him but his captain, Edmund, had brought him back to Cridianton, where he joined a score of other sergeants, as well as their war captains, in kneeling before the king.

'Welcome, my friends,' the king had greeted them. 'Let us begin.'

The captains had sat around a huge table, while Broyle and the other sergeants stood behind, awed, as maps were displayed and weighed down swiftly, small clay and metal markers showing Forlish and enemy forces.

It was a memory Broyle treasured. He could close his eyes and imagine he was back there. One at a time, the war captains leaned forwards and reported villages burned, towns sacked and cities under siege, casualties inflicted, slaves taken and progress made. Ward listened carefully and often interrupted.

'I want that city taken. Spare no effort to break those walls, for it is disrupting our supply routes,' he snarled. 'What is the problem? Are your men cowards?'

'They are trying everything, sire,' the captain, his bald head scarred by a livid cut, ventured nervously.

'There is no try,' Ward snapped. 'There is doing and there is failing. Get me that city by the next full moon or I shall have your head.'

'Yes, sire.' The captain bowed.

'Ostia is the second city of Balia, sire,' another captain cleared his throat to say. 'The walls are said to be even stronger there than at the capital.'

'I am more concerned with its aqueducts and how it has designed a sewer system that is the envy of all others. I want its engineers and its experts. Tell the city fathers to surrender them now, and I shall spare them. But if they continue to defy me I will have every man and every second woman killed, and every child sold into slavery,' Ward said warningly. 'I want every city in Forland to have such things and I don't care about the cost!'

Broyle and the others bowed their heads.

'This is a world of chaos. Since the elves left us, we men have been divided, ragged, clawing our way from hand to mouth, struggling to survive. My dream is to bring order out of this mess. If these countries will not share with us, we shall take their knowledge. Once we have it, then all shall rise.'

The next captain up, a tall man with a flowing moustache and only one ear, began apprehensively.

'Some of the men are asking when they can come home. The Landish campaign drags on, sire.'

'They come home when they cannot fight, or when I say. Tell them to finish those Landish off if they want to see their families again. What is the matter with them? Not taking enough women prisoners?'

'It has been eight years, sire,' the captain suggested.

Ward thumped the arm of his chair. 'The Landish know more about herbs, healing and curing the human body of ailments than anyone else. I want that knowledge. We shall burn their villages and sack their towns until they tell us. This is almost more important than a good sewer system. Imagine being able to live as long as the elves! That is what they are fighting for. Tell them that. If that does not work, find the ringleaders in your regiments and have them impaled. That will stop any muttering.'

Then it was Edmund's turn, and Broyle listened with pleasure as he recounted their successes, and the king nodded in approval.

Broyle found himself daydreaming he would one day sit around that table, have the king nod in approval at his victories, reward him for expanding the Forlish empire.

'Thank you, my friends!'

The king's declaration jerked Broyle's head up and made him realise the reports were over. Ward even seemed happy with the progress that had been made on the maps, where the Forlish markers had been advanced in all directions.

'Mostly pleasing. We are progressing well in our great crusade to bring civilisation to an ignorant world. I have brought you all here to discuss our next campaign. But first I have something of the great benefits Forland has to offer for you to see — one of my new performers!'

Broyle watched a young bard begin to play — and then, like every other man, his attention turned to a beautiful dancer in a revealing costume, a confection of silver and green linen that hugged her body and had Broyle staring hungrily. He devoured her with his eyes as she danced for them, spinning and turning, seeming to hang in the air with her every leap. One day he would see all of her, he promised himself.

Finally she slid to a halt, performing a manoeuvre none had seen before, where she had one leg flat on the floor ahead of her, the other flat on the floor behind her, with the splits in her skirt revealing her legs to the upper thighs. Broyle was first to lead the roars of approval. He would never forget that body — or the face. One day she would hail him as a Forlish hero, he swore.

'Truly, this Forlish maiden is the perfect example of why this is the greatest country in the world!' Ward declared. 'That has to be the equal of anything the elves could have accomplished. Now, to the real reason you are here,' the king boomed and Broyle leaned forwards expectantly.

'As you know, we have more men under my flag than ever before. And this has meant the countries who resist us are trying to raise larger and larger armies. While they cannot hope to match the Forlish fighting man on the battlefield, they all have deep pockets. It has driven up the price of iron ore three-fold in the past year. And keeping our armies supplied, even with slave labour, has seen food prices double also. It has led to some unrest. While I can, and will crush any dissent, some of my nobles are reporting slaves and serfs are leaving the land, trying to escape — and heading north. That is a bigger concern. Our northern border has always been lightly defended, for there is little up there to concern us — just the elven lands and Vales.'

'We are to invade the Velsh, sire?' the captain with the moustache asked.

Ward leaned back and chuckled, a genuine laugh. 'War with the Velsh! How ridiculous! No, we shall not go to war with the Velsh. It would be pointless. There is no ruler, just a ragged collection of piss-poor villages and sheep. It would take thousands of men to suppress them, and it would gain us almost nothing. But I need to deal with them, nonetheless.'

Broyle glanced across towards the dancer and saw her with the bard — who looked as though he had seen a ghost. Intrigued, Broyle marked his face, before hurriedly switching his attention back to the king.

'First, they have knowledge we need. They know more about mining than anyone else — and also sell their iron and coal to the Balians and Landish to turn into weapons. Second, they grow enough food to help solve our shortages. And lastly, Vales provides a perfect place for escaped slaves and fleeing serfs to find refuge. As long as they work, and have most of their own teeth, they are quite the catch in Vales!'

Broyle led the laughter.

'Rather than an expensive war, I have the perfect plan to bring Vales under my control. You sergeants are here to be my strong right hand in this.'

Broyle stiffened to attention, as did every other sergeant in the room.

'I want you to all lead a small company, a dozen or two of men, no more. They shall not wear uniform, shall not march beneath the proud banner of Forland but instead pretend to be bandits. Almost every Velsh village is undefended, and easy prey for our men. A few months of terrorising the Velsh, robbing, burning and raping, and they shall beg for my protection and Vales will come under the flag of Forland. They will give up their knowledge, their iron, tin and coal, their food and their independence in exchange for my help in ridding their lands of these terrible bandits. And of course I shall only be too glad to help them!'

'Brilliant, sire!' one captain shouted, then they were all bellowing approval, Broyle included. His heart was singing. This was the chance he had been waiting for!

'Succeed and you shall return to your own, full, companies.'

'All hail King Ward! All hail Forland!' Broyle stepped forwards and shouted, the others a heartbeat behind, but he was the one rewarded with a smile from the king.

That warmed him now as he rode through the Velsh rain. He had gathered two dozen of his toughest, most ruthless men, all of them eager for this chance to get rich and return to rewards and promotion.

They rode swiftly, wanting to get there first and lay claim to the best areas. It felt strange to be riding without their uniforms, and not to get cheered by the Forlish people as they went through villages and towns. Stranger still, guards often tried to bar their progress and it took some talking — as well as threatening — for the way to open. But getting over the border and into Vales was ridiculously easy — there was nobody trying to watch the roads, and Broyle's insistence on riding across at night seemed pointless. They were able to slip past several small villages easily enough, the inhabitants not even realising they were there. Now and then a dog would bark at them but they were able to fade into the night. And half the time, the people told the dogs to be quiet anyway. The lower part of Vales was hardscrabble poor, with thin people and animals, few crops and little that looked worth stealing. They still took sheep, chickens and even pigs and always ate well. But they were hungry for something different. Broyle led them north and east until he finally discovered a village big enough and prosperous enough to be worth their trouble. The king had smiled at him — he would not betray that by only tackling isolated farms or some stinking hamlet.

Every other night before a battle, there had been a real tension among the men, a fear of what the morrow would bring. But, as they sat around sharpening their weapons, waiting to attack this village, Broyle could detect none of that. There were plenty of jokes, lots of boasting and chatter, but nothing like he normally expected.

'Don't take these Velsh too lightly. They may not have our weapons or training but there're several hundred of them in that village and only a score of us. If we give them the chance, they could turn on us. So we take control! Kill a few to get the message across, take what we need and move on,' he told them.

They trusted him. He had brought them alive through battle after battle, had even saved them when their idiot officer had tried to get them killed, all because he did not want to bring a convoy in late. So they obeyed Broyle without question now.


Sendatsu found the next human settlement as the sun was sinking. He had walked all day and he was sore, hungry and tired. It had taken the edge off the excitement that had been bubbling within him all day but even the discovery this village had no elven buildings, only the low, rounded huts of the Velsh, was not enough to dampen his enthusiasm.

He walked among the houses, looking for whoever led the village and wondering what could be making that terrible smell.

'Who are you, stranger, and what do you want?' a tall, bearded Velshman asked, appearing out of a low doorway.

'I am Sendatsu, an elf from Dokuzen, and I need your help,' Sendatsu said eagerly.

The Velshman stared at him. 'Are you serious, boyo? An elf?'

'Look, I even have the ears,' Sendatsu offered with a smile. 'Now, what can you tell me about the old church in the woods ...?'

'Everyone! Come quick! There's an elf here!' the man bellowed.

'Well, I don't need to see everyone ...'

Sendatsu's words were lost as Velsh poured out of the surrounding huts.

'Is it true? Is he really an elf?' someone cried.

'Look at his clothes, look at his skin and eyes and ears — we have an elf here!'

Shouts of excitement and cries of surprise assaulted Sendatsu from all sides. Hands grabbed at him and dozens of faces pressed in on him.

'What are you doing?'

'Why are you back?'

'Can you help us?'

'Wait! Calm down! I'm searching for answers — who knows about the old church? Has anyone seen any magic?'

His words seemed to vanish into the hubbub, except for the last one, which had them all excited.

'Magic! Please, heal my son. He is sick and I don't know what from.' A woman grabbed his arm.

'My best cow has stopped giving milk. Use the magic on her and make her better,' a man begged.

'My wife is pregnant but the babe has turned and it will kill her. You have to save her!'

'How can we make crops grow all year round?'

'Can you show us how to build with stone?'

'Gold — tell us how to turn anything into gold!'

The hands reached out for him from all sides, people grabbed his cloak, his arm, his kimono, begged and shouted and demanded.

'I can't do those things, I don't know how ...'

'Help us!'

'That is not why I am here — I need your help ...' but he might as well have been speaking another language. The cries got fiercer, the Velsh now also turning on each other, as those closest to him tried to pull him their way, while those on the outside tried to push in.

'The elf is mine!'

'I saw him first!'

Sendatsu was overwhelmed by the noise, the anger and the desperation. He was also getting frightened by the way they were grabbing at him; he used his hands to fend them off but that only made them more desperate.

'Save us!'

'Give us your magic!'

Everywhere he looked, people were pleading or demanding or shouting. It was too much.

'I can't!' he bellowed.

He felt enclosed, squeezed. Frantically he fought his way through the grasping hands, pushing past them. But they kept pace with him, following, begging. The hands were even more insistent and he felt as though he might be dragged to the ground — and never get up. They might rip him to pieces. Genuinely frightened now, he shoved and pushed and clawed back, fighting his way clear and racing for open air and the outside of the village. Some kept pace with him for a while but he put on a spurt of speed and tore clear of the last hands.

He risked a glance over his shoulder only when he felt he was clear. They had given up but the wailing and shouted appeals for him to come back made him shudder. He had obviously made a huge mistake going in there. But how was he going to get answers unless he spoke to people?

He checked he still had everything; although his sleeve was ripped a little, the book he had found and the children's toys were safe, as was his bowstave. The top of his arrow bag was torn, and several of the feathers were crushed, but he could fix that.

He walked on, feeling his heart slowly calm down, but the sick feeling inside would not go away. Why would they not listen?

How would he get answers if they were all like that? Where would he spend the night?

Just as the sun was slipping below the horizon, he saw a thin trail of smoke ahead. Cautiously he investigated — and found a single farmhouse, surrounded by a cluster of beast sheds. One farm only — now that was a better prospect, he decided.

'Hello the house?' he called as he got closer.

'Who's there?' asked a suspicious voice and a heavily bearded Velshman walked out, holding a long spear.

'I am Sendatsu, an elf from Dokuzen,' Sendatsu replied, keeping an eye on the spear.

The Velshman roared with laughter. 'An elf! Very funny, boyo! Now, really, where are you from?'

'I'm an elf!' Sendatsu growled, pointing to his ears.

The Velshman's laugh dried up. 'Skies above! There's a shock for you!'

'I am looking for answers about Aroaril and magic ...'

'Well, come on in,' the Velshman offered.

Relieved, Sendatsu was happy to take up the invitation.

He quickly found himself the centre of attention for Bedwin, the Velshman, Blodwen, his wife, and their five children, two boys and three girls.

'Can you do some magic for us?' Blodwen asked excitedly.

'Hush, woman! Let the man — elf — talk first. There's honour for you now — an elf in my home!'

'I need to find someone who can read ...'

'Oh, can't help you there,' Bedwin warned. 'We don't read. No need for it, see?'

Sendatsu hid his frustration. 'Does anyone speak a different language?'

The Velsh looked at each other doubtfully. 'There's old Cei up the road, he talks to the sheep — and the birds if they listen to him ...' Bedwin offered.

'No!' Sendatsu decided to change his approach. 'Who knows why the elves left?'

'Oh, that's easy.' Bedwin grinned. 'They left to save themselves from us. We were too violent, so they went behind their magic barrier and we slipped back into darkness.'

Sendatsu sighed. This could have come straight from his father.

'Now, we need your help. The chances of an elf just walking into my home! What you can do for us! I barely know where to start ... you can tell us how to build stone houses, how to grow better crops, heal us with your magic ...'

'Wait, wait!' Sendatsu held up his hands. 'I am afraid I cannot do any of those things. I don't know how to build houses, nor grow crops. I am not here to be a leader or to change anything. And my magic is not strong enough to heal anyone ...'

'Surely you are jesting with us? You're an elf, you can do anything!'

'No, I can't,' Sendatsu promised wearily.

'Well, there's gratitude for you! An elf walks into my home and he's about as much use as a singing cow!' Bedwin said indignantly.

'Perhaps he doesn't think we are worthy of him, with his fancy clothes and his magic,' Blodwen added.

Sendatsu looked around at the unfriendly faces and could see another fight coming.

'Maybe he's not an elf at all. Maybe he's in league with the bandits on the other side of the hills ...'

'I killed them yesterday,' Sendatsu said immediately.

Instantly everything changed.

'Did you now? Well, that's good news!' Bedwin brightened.

'I seek only information — I would be willing to pay for it ...'

But while they were delighted to see a silver coin, nobody had a scrap of knowledge worth a piece of copper. They had not heard of Aroaril, let alone an old church, and as for being able to do magic ... Sendatsu made a flower bloom, which was about the limit of his powers, and while it delighted the children, none of them showed signs of magic. Sendatsu was disappointed but decided to give Bedwin and Blodwen the coin, to keep the humans friendly. They offered him their food, a hunk of half-raw, half-burned mutton that had him dry-retching, so Blodwen gave him a bowl of oatmeal, followed by some sort of leek stew. Neither tasted particularly nice but they were better than the mutton the rest of the family devoured. Sendatsu was appalled to see the children drop scraps onto the filthy floor, pick them up and stuff them back into their mouths. Seeing as goats were penned down one end of the hut, he dreaded to think what else was on the floor. Watching other people's children also reminded him painfully of his own, so far away from him. Time for more questions ...

'So, if you don't worship Aroaril, who do you worship?'

'We aren't good enough for Gods!' Bedwin chuckled.

'Aye — we're like the sheep in the thatch — keep quiet and the owners of the house won't hunt you out,' Blodwen agreed.

'Sheep in the thatch?' Bedwin nudged her. 'Don't you mean mice?'

Blodwen burst into laughter. 'Did I say sheep? Skies above, I wouldn't like sheep in the thatch — the roof would never hold!'

'To say nothing of what would be dropping from above!' Bedwin chuckled again.

'So who do you worship? How do you marry?' Sendatsu pressed, ignoring their byplay.

'We don't worship. We celebrate Midsummer, to say thanks for good weather, and Midwinter, to ask for better weather. We leave out food; dance and sing to the skies above. Those are the times of year we can marry as well. We Walk The Tree ...'

'Is this going to be like sheep in the thatch?' Sendatsu asked warily.

They both thought that was hilarious.

'No, we walk sunways around an oak tree, east to west, then we're married. If you don't want to be married any more, then you wait until the next festival and walk widdershins around the oak tree and you're not married.'

Sendatsu rubbed his eyes. This was not helping at all. He felt tired and frustrated. He needed to sleep, and think of a new approach.

'I am very tired. Do you have a bed for me?' he asked Bedwin.

'Of course — here you go.' Bedwin handed him a bundle of stinking fur.

'What's this?' Sendatsu held it at arm's length.

Bedwin roared with laughter. 'Your bed! Just wrap yourself up in it and you'll be snug as a bug!'

Sendatsu could only imagine how many bugs were indeed hiding in this badly cured hide.

'And what do I sleep on?' he ventured.

'The floor. Nice and soft, eh?'

Sendatsu forced a smile and, shuddering, laid the skin on the cleanest patch of floor he could find to sleep.

'He's a strange one,' he heard Blodwen mutter.

'Hush, woman — look at those ears — he can probably hear everything! Don't worry, he'll likely want to leave in the morning, find some autumn leaves to write a song about.'

'Autumn leaves?'

'Oh, elves are always doing that sort of thing,' Bedwin said knowingly.

Sendatsu closed his eyes and tried not to think too much of his children.

He woke up to see a wolf's head an inch from his nose and was on his knees and reaching for his sword before he realised it was just his bedclothes. He sank back down, wondering at the thin line between nightmare and reality.

Perhaps today he could find some Velsh who knew more — or at least knew what a bed was. He stood and his lower stomach gave a growl of protest. He had to find a privy. Now. He looked around desperately to see nothing but the family stirring awake, all wrapped in furs on the floor.

'The privy?' Sendatsu asked urgently.

'What? Can't you just piss in the goat pen, like me and the rest of the boys?' Bedwin asked.

Sendatsu stared at him wordlessly.

'We stick to the rules of good behaviour here. Men piss with the goats, women with the sheep, just like everywhere else. But I don't have sheep in my hall. We're not some hovel in Rheged, you know,' Bedwin said haughtily.

'There're beast sheds out the back,' Blodwen suggested.

Sendatsu obeyed instantly, running out and sinking up to his ankles in thick mud, but he could not let that stop him. The rain was fine but insistent, making his head and shoulders damp immediately, while all around him were the sounds of animals waking up. Behind the back of Bedwin's home was only a sea of muck, as well as several crude shelters where sheep and pigs huddled miserably. He looked desperately for something that offered some comfort and privacy but slipped over, falling in what he fervently hoped was mud. His bowels warned that time was running out so, heedless of the mess over his fine clothes, he climbed over the wooden rails keeping a trio of pigs penned. The animals backed away, grunting at him, and while he wanted to find somewhere clean to squat, there was nowhere like that. Almost beyond caring, desperately he hauled down his hakama — keeping them out of the mud was almost pointless, given what was already on them, but it was also impossible.

Just as he was beginning to relax a little, and become more aware of his surroundings, he realised two things. At home, a selection of dried sea sponges on sticks, moistened by running water, waited close at hand for him to clean up afterwards. There was nothing — *nothing* — like that anywhere near. And secondly, there was a very large pig staring angrily at him, from just a few paces away. And it might live in a pen but from its bristles, red eyes and massive shoulders, it was obviously not too far removed from the wild boar he had seen many a time in the woods — and learned to keep well away from.

'Get out of there! Nobody shits with the pigs!' Blodwen shouted. 'And certainly never twice!'

He realised his predicament and began to haul up his muddied hakama — but carefully, for obvious reasons. The pig saw its chance and timed its charge perfectly. Sendatsu took one look and decided not to hang around. With one hand holding his hakama around his knees, he raced for the dubious safety of the mud outside the pen as the pig snapped at his heels — and grabbed at his trailing hakama, ripping out a chunk as he leaped for safety, landing head-first in the mud.

He looked up to see Bedwin, Blodwen and the rest of the family doubled over, helpless with laughter. Slowly he got to his feet, looking down at the wreckage of what had been fine clothes.

'You — you need to go in with the sheep,' Blodwen tried to say, pointing towards the next pen and still laughing. 'There's a mess for you now!'

Sendatsu looked at his ruined clothes and the laughing family. No wonder his people had taken themselves behind the barrier. Surely anything was better than living like this. How could these humans survive? More to the point, how could he live like this?

'Grab some moss off the roof, wipe your arse and then get back in the warm and dry. My wife'll find something for you to wear,' Bedwin said kindly.

Sendatsu sloshed over to the low-hanging roof, its bottom level only waist-height, and its surface covered in thick moss. It was soft, damp and surprisingly effective, although he had a few shudders while using it — and had no idea what to do with it afterwards, so left it lying by the wall. He shuffled around to the hall's only doorway, feeling suddenly hungry.

As he avoided a puddle, it began to rain hard. Not quite as bad as the day before, but not far off it. He sighed. At least he could make some use of it. He stripped off his filthy clothes and stood there, wearing just his boots, arms outstretched in the rain.

'You should put some clothes on and come in for food — you'll catch your death, standing out there like that!' Bedwin shouted at him. He stared at the elf's rippling muscles, the huge arms, shoulders and chest.

Sendatsu was past caring. 'Have you oil and a wooden knife, so I can clean myself?' he asked instead.

'What?' They gazed at him in bewilderment.

'I need to be clean,' Sendatsu insisted.

Bedwin and Blodwen had a short discussion, then Blodwen disappeared, coming back with a lump of something strange and grey, smelling not of lavender, or mint, but rather the tang of an old fire.

'How about this soap? We use it to clean clothes,' she explained.

He tried to work it into a lather but while it worked well enough in cleaning the muck from him, the smell seemed to linger, became more pungent.

'What is this made of?' he demanded.

Bedwin shrugged. 'Just the usual. Ash, pig fat and piss.'

Sendatsu dropped it.

'Piss? You mean …?'

'Binds it together.' Bedwin nodded.

Sendatsu shuddered. 'And whose …?'

Bedwin beamed. 'Mine, of course. Nothing but the best for you! Try it on your hair as well — it'll turn it a lovely light shade!'

Sendatsu rubbed feverishly at his skin with his hands, trying to use the rain to cleanse himself of the soap.

'Get in, man — I mean, elf! Bathing too often isn't good for a man. Or an elf.'

Sendatsu thought about arguing but he was getting colder now. He stepped inside, his sopping, rank clothes held in one hand.

'What do they do in Dokuzen, to make you look like that?' Bedwin asked, pointing both to the rippling muscles and the scars that covered Sendatsu's torso.

'We train with the sword and the bow, every day of our lives,' Sendatsu said, examining his clothes sorrowfully.

'And the scars?' Blodwen wondered.

'I don't talk about those,' Sendatsu said shortly.

'Blod, find him some clothes — tunic and trews will do,' Bedwin suggested into the sudden silence.

He found Sendatsu a woollen blanket and gave him a bowl of porridge, as well as the honey pot, and Sendatsu ate hurriedly.

Blodwen returned then, bearing green shorts and undervest, a red tunic and brown trews.

'Here you are,' she sniffed.

'Thank you.' Sendatsu dressed swiftly. They fitted reasonably well, although it was tight across the shoulders and too long in the arms. And the underclothes felt rough and lumpen. Perhaps it was just him being accustomed to cotton, he thought hopefully.

'What are they made of?' he asked.

'Well, the tunic and trews are made of wool, the underclothes of nettles.'

'Nettles?' Sendatsu asked faintly. 'The stinging plant?'

'Aye, that's them. Delicious cooked and you can make clothes out of them as well. I thought you'd like the pretty green!'

Sendatsu fought the urge to rip the clothes off, contenting himself with a careful scratch.

'Thank you,' he managed to say.

'So what were your old clothes called?' she asked, sorting through the muddy pile.

Sendatsu sighed. 'These are called hakama. The top is a half-kimono and the belt is called an obi.'

The children took over then, pushing forwards and picking up his old clothes, chattering and asking questions, all at once.

'Amazing!'

'Where do they come from?'

'Why do we not wear them?'

'Where do the names come from?'

Sendatsu paused. 'We've always worn such things.' He shrugged. 'Our history records that we came from across the sea to this land. We must have brought them with us, as well as the names for them. It is from a language we do not speak any more but we keep the words as a reminder, I suppose ... that is part of my mission. I believe you had a different language as well. I need to find it.'

'Another language? Why, we have enough trouble with this one!' Bedwin chuckled.

'Have you perhaps heard of humans who can do magic ...'

The pair of them roared with laughter. 'You have more chance of finding a goat who can dance and sing,' Blodwen snorted.

'Well, there was word of that goat down in Rheged ...' Bedwin began.

'Oh, don't believe everything you hear,' Blodwen sniffed. 'Tell us of Dokuzen! Is it true you live in amazing houses, built out of the trees themselves, reached by staircases made from living wood?'

Now it was Sendatsu's turn to smile.

'No, we live in stone houses, which we call villas. They are all much the same. In the middle, each has a beautiful garden, with living areas around the outside, while servant quarters are at the end of the house, along with the kitchen. We bathe every day, in hot water, use oil and a wooden knife to scrape the dirt from our skin. We also have a toilet, where you sit on a stone seat with a hole in it and running water carries away your waste ...'

'You are making fun of me!' Blodwen accused.

'Not so. It is all true.'

'And do you make everything by magic? Do the birds and animals of the forest help you, sing for you?'

Again, Sendatsu could not restrain a smile.

'We live in harmony with the birds and animals but they do not play a part in our lives. We do everything for ourselves. To the north we have the mines and quarries, the fishing villages and the huge rice and cotton fields that keep us fed and clothed and housed. But Dokuzen itself ... the city is built around a huge park, with a lake in its centre. Everywhere there are beautiful gardens, statues, music playing. Only beautiful things are allowed there.'

'I can imagine,' Blodwen breathed. 'And is everyone always singing, or making up poetry?'

'No — we sing and dance at special occasions, but that is it. Most elves work during the day, everything from fishing to mining to making clothes and furniture ...'

'Why, that sounds just like humans. That doesn't sound amazing and beautiful at all,' Bedwin protested.

'That is what it is really like,' Sendatsu said firmly.

'Well, what about magic? How do you use that?'

So Sendatsu tried to explain, tried to remember the lessons from years ago, in Sumiko's villa.

'Life is like one great circle. Everything needs a spark of magic to be born, uses it to grow and thrive then, when we die, we release it back into the world. This energy, this power is all around us but only some people can feel it and use it for their own. But anything you use must be replaced by your own energy — the greater the task, the greater the strain on the Magic-weaver. I don't have much ability but there are those who can change the world around us ...'

'Well, is one of them going to visit?' Blodwen asked hopefully.

Sendatsu sighed. He had to move on — he was getting nothing from this couple, pleasant as they were. 'Sadly, no. Now, I thank you for your kindness but I must continue my search for answers.'

They gave him food and a bag to carry it, then waved him goodbye.

'He was strange,' Blodwen muttered, when she thought the elf was safely out of earshot.

'Aye. I don't think I'd like to live in that Dokuzen.'

'Me either,' Blodwen agreed. 'Now, we've wasted enough time on him. You need to re-plaster the back wall with pig dung, then fertilise our field.'

'I always get the shit jobs,' Bedwin grumbled, swinging a shovel over his shoulder.

# 7

*If they had not died, would everything be different now? That question is too hard for me to answer, and impossible anyway. For they did die. One moment they were there, strong and confident, unchallenged, the next they had crumbled into dust, as if wiped away from the pages of history.*

*For those of us who saw it, the world would never be the same. The foundation on which not just our people but our whole way of life was built was swept away.*

*Some of us, like myself, tried to hold on to it, tried to fulfil their last wishes.*

*But many others saw them fall, and saw their opportunity.*

*Rebellion, which had only been whispered about behind closed doors, now became their ambition. Never openly, of course, for I would have heard that. But the seeds of my own betrayal and death were planted that day, watered with the tears of a people for their lost fathers.*

It was just before dawn, with the first light streaking through the sky, when Earwen of Patcham rolled out of bed and stirred the fire into life. He had dreamed of his son, Huw, last night and woke feeling alone. Huw was down in the Forlish capital, living his dream of becoming a bard, and Earwen missed him terribly.

It was the culmination of Huw's life. For years he had been ridiculed by his whole village. His reputation had even spread to other nearby Velsh villages. The crazy boy who sang to sheep, who dreamed of being a bard. They had mocked him, jeered his dream and told him to his face he would fail and be forced to slink back home to be the subject of jokes for the rest of his life.

In the face of such opposition, Huw offered to give up and become a farmer, like everyone else, but Earwen had not let him. He had protected him, encouraged him and guided him. He had lost his wife in childbirth but taken no other, instead raising the boy as well as running the farm — something that by itself had excited much comment in the village. After that sacrifice, his son would be given the chance to follow his dream.

Although Huw had fretted about heading south and his Velshness being found out.

'The Forlish will never know you come from Vales.' Earwen had smiled. 'They see so few of us, they wouldn't know a Velshman if he bit them! They think we are all hairy monsters who live in muck and eat mud. Besides, after what we have been through these past few years, I would have thought that a few Forlish sneers would mean nothing.'

But when Huw still fretted, Earwen had taken a more serious tone. 'Look, once you start playing your lyre, singing your songs and telling your riddles, they won't care where you are from. I didn't raise you to live in fear. The Forlish have stone buildings, a king and his court and are growing an empire, but that does not make them better than us.'

Huw had smiled.

'There is no call for a bard in Vales,' Earwen told him. 'Well, that is not true, we need to hope and dream as much as any man and we love songs and stories and riddles more than most. But there is no money in it here. The Forlish have money aplenty to spend on such things. Money stolen from those weaker than themselves, but money nonetheless. To earn that honestly is no shame. Earn enough so that you can come back here and put food on your table. It is your dream and you deserve the chance to live it. I've done all I can to make it possible. The rest is up to you. But do me one favour.'

'Aye, Dad. Anything!'

'Well, two things. First, never forget who you are and where you come from. And second, never offer a promise so lightly! At least listen before agreeing to do anything!'

They had both laughed then.

When it had come time to say goodbye, nobody in the village had waved Huw off, although almost all had had something to say the previous day, along the lines of Huw was a fool and Earwen doubly so, to indulge him. Several of the elders had predicted Huw would be back within three moons, and would then have to do some real work, not swan around like a moonstruck calf.

The two of them stared at each other for a long moment. They had never been short of a word before but neither could find anything to say now. Earwen could not get anything past the huge lump in his throat, while he could see the tears in his son's eyes.

'Come back safe,' he managed to say.

'I'll come back rich. Don't work too hard on the field,' Huw said awkwardly.

Unable to say what he really felt, Earwen held out his hand and Huw shook it carefully.

'Better get moving. You've a long way to go.'

Huw looked as though he was about to say something, then simply nodded.

'I'll be seeing you,' he said hoarsely.

Earwen could not watch his son go. Firstly because his cursed eyes kept leaking but also because he had been struck with a terrible certainty he would never see his son again. That memory was thick within him as he downed a bowl of oatmeal and then walked out into the dawn, ready for another hard day in the fields.

Broyle led his men into the village at the gallop. The village was bounded by a low fence, suitable for keeping animals in — or out — but little more. It also had a wide opening, easily big enough for four men to ride abreast through, and completely unguarded.

Dogs barked at them and for a moment Broyle thought they had made a mistake, for these were big, powerful beasts, bred to drive off wolves — then owners called them back and he breathed again.

Men, women and children looked out of houses, curious but not yet fearful of the men on big horses, dressed in plain tunics and trousers.

'Who is the leader of this village?' Broyle bellowed, reining in his horse and letting his men spread out behind him, so they were not all bunched in together.

After a pause an older man, his dark beard shot through with grey, strode forwards.

'There are no leaders here. We have no need for them. We are a community and work together,' he began.

'Well, you can work together on this! My men and I have just moved into the area. We have had a long ride and are in need of food and drink ...'

'Which you may purchase from us, at a fair price,' the Velshman interrupted back, his voice big and booming. 'If you are good neighbours, you shall be welcome ...'

Broyle ignored him. 'We don't pay! Now, bring us food, and drink, and any gold or silver you might have!'

The Velshman stepped closer.

'Who are you? Forlish?' he demanded. 'Did the Crumliners hire you to threaten us?'

'Where?'

'The next village over. Did they hire you?'

Broyle was about to deny everything when he remembered his orders in time.

'We are Balian,' he boasted, certain this ignorant Velshman would not know the difference.

'You sound Forlish. And how could Balians make their way through all of Forland to reach us?' the Velshman declared. 'You are a liar. Now leave our village! You are not welcome here!'

Broyle's hand went down to his sword.

'Don't cross me, old man,' he warned softly. 'For I shall kill you and your people if you do not obey me. Now, tell your people to get out their food and drink and gold, and we shall ride out of here with smiles on our faces, and you get to keep your head. Be sensible, man. You know who we are, what we can do. The rest of your people are hiding, not standing behind you. Walk away, tell your people to do what we say and you'll get to sleep with your wife again tonight, hold your children.'

Earwen looked up at the big Forlishman without fear. He heard the truth in the man's words and knew his life hung by a thread. For a moment only he was tempted. He wanted to see Huw again, wanted to see the boy grow into a man. There was still so much he needed to tell him. But he could not stand before Huw if he did not live up to his own code. Death would be preferable to betraying everything he had lived by.

If only he could see Huw once more ...

'Wolves do not go away if you feed them,' Earwen shouted. 'Brothers! Sisters! We are many but they are few! Rally here!' He looked around, waved to the men he saw standing in their doorways. This village had more than a hundred men of fighting age. If they stood together, the Forlish would run. 'If we stand together, then they cannot ...'

He never got to finish the sentence. Broyle knew the truth of his words and spurred his horse forwards, sword leaping into his hand. With a battle cry, he hacked down viciously.

Earwen tried to dodge away but the Forlishman had been fighting for too long and was a step ahead. The last thing Earwen saw was the sharp sword whistling towards his head, the last thing he thought was an anguished hope for his son to be safe.

A cry of horror went up from watching villagers as the Velshman collapsed, his head all but severed, and Broyle signalled to his men, his blood-covered sword held high. They fanned out in all directions and that was enough for those watching.

Instinctively they backed into houses, trying to seek shelter and cover, rather than rushing out and fighting. Broyle was relieved to see it. He did not have the men to fight a whole village — there were enough men here to drive him away, did they but realise it. He had to use fear to make up for his lack of numbers.

'Get into those homes and get us some plunder!' Broyle roared at his men, gesturing with his bloodied sword.

Cheering, his men sprang into action, working as a team, as they had learned to do in a dozen Balian villages. One in four held their horses, while the other three raced off to the closest houses. One kicked the door in then the other two burst inside, weapons drawn. Shrieks and cries followed, as the house was ransacked and the occupants terrorised. Then the trio emerged, carrying sides of bacon, legs of lamb, bread and cheese, barrels of ale and, sometimes, small pouches of coins.

A couple even emerged with a screaming woman over one shoulder, often followed by one or two crying children, although those were silenced with a blow if they got too close or the noise got too much. As for the man of the house in that case, the only sight of him was blood on a Forlish sword, although one came out swinging a wood axe — only to be cut down in the open. Together the villagers might have stood a chance but one Velshman was no match for three veteran Forlish warriors.

Broyle watched with approval, only needing to help once, when a couple of men tried to attack one of his laden parties. But by the time he had galloped over there, the Velshmen were dead, their children and wives fleeing and his men had picked up their booty and carried it back to where the horses waited. After each group had been to two houses, and the pile of goods looked more than enough for the horses to carry away, he called halt. 'That's enough, lads. We have to leave these sheep with enough fleece so it's worth another visit!'

His men, all of them carrying valuables, and a handful with blood on their swords, cheered in response as they mounted up.

'How easy is this going to be?' Broyle grinned, helping himself to a loaf of fresh bread and tearing off a huge chunk. 'We'll find somewhere to store this, then see what other pickings are around.'

He looked back at the village, at the Velsh emerging from hiding and wailing over their dead.

'The king knows what he is doing. They'll run to him after a few more visits like that,' Broyle declared.

His men, laden and looking forward to enjoying the spoils they had taken, grinned in agreement.

Broyle had been on raiding missions before, many times, when his regiment needed supplies and they had outpaced the wagons. Living off the land was almost second nature. He pushed the men hard, making sure they put plenty of distance between themselves and the village. He was sure there would be no pursuit but refused to get complacent. He had kept his men alive by being careful.

It was late afternoon, the setting sun casting long shadows across the ground when they found a patch of woods on a hill, seemingly a long way from any villages, and the ideal place to base themselves.

'Take what we picked up this morning and make camp up there,' he instructed one of his corporals, Cenred. He had brought two with him and trusted Cenred far more than the other, Ricbert. Ricbert was a good fighter but a poor corporal. Cenred was the steadier man.

'What about the women?' Ricbert protested, as Broyle had expected him to.

'Will be waiting for us when we return. We shall sweep around the area, see who our new neighbours are.'

'But ...'

'There will be plenty for all,' Broyle said warningly. 'Another word and it could be your last.'

Ricbert subsided and Broyle watched Cenred lead ten men with laden horses, as well as the four captured women, up towards the woods.

'Come on. The king doesn't pay us to sit and watch,' Broyle said harshly, leading the rest of his men off to the south.

Sendatsu had made himself a rough camp in the woods. He had failed at another village, this time one with a handful of elven buildings at its centre. These were not villas, nor halls but what looked like barns or storage huts. Still, they stood out from the Velsh buildings and were being used as homes by what looked like a dozen Velsh.

But while these buildings were full of Velsh, the Velsh were empty of answers — and less friendly than Bedwin and Blodwen. They had endless demands for magic to save a prize cow or heal a sick child. Sendatsu tried to explain that magic was not that simple, and healing magic best left to a priest of Aroaril, for it took too much energy — but they would not listen, instead accusing him of keeping the magic to himself. At the very least they wanted him to tell them what to do, to 'lead them back towards the light', as one had said. They would not listen to his questions, nor believe him when he said his magic could not do all the things they wanted.

Like the other village, he found himself in the middle of a knot of angry humans, all trying to pull him in a dozen directions. He tried to reason with them but they would not listen. When one grabbed hold of his pouch it was the last straw and he broke clear and ran for it.

Now he was huddled next to a small fire, wondering miserably what his children were doing, back in Dokuzen, and how he might find answers when the humans would not even stop and listen to his questions. Then he heard the voices. They were close. The speech was different to that of the humans he had met in the villages, their voices lacking the lilt and singsong quality of the Velsh, being harsher and cruder. Mixed in with the harsh calls of the men were cries from women, and these seemed to be Velsh. He kicked dirt over his fire then grabbed his pack and his bow and faded back into the trees. Night was falling, and he had been staring into the fire for long enough that his eyes were struggling to help him tell where to go. Luckily his little stumbles and breaking of twigs underfoot were lost in the noise of the humans' approach.

He found himself a hiding place, between two fallen tree trunks, and settled there to allow his eyes to adjust to the gathering darkness.

Cenred ordered two of his men to gather firewood, the others to start building shelters. They were old soldiers, and moved to their tasks swiftly, their enthusiasm for what was going to happen afterwards making the routine move even faster.

Cenred stood and supervised, watching their four sobbing captives at the same time. Not that they were likely to run, given they were all tied together, but he was not about to take the chance. He had learned as much from his sergeant.

He was pleased with the day's work. He guessed they would probably have to kill more at the start, when the Velsh were more likely to fight back. Once the braver ones had been culled, like the older man that morning, the others would fall into place like the sheep they were.

Then he drew his sword and whistled sharply.

Instantly all work on the camp stopped and men raced for swords.

'I smell smoke. There's another camp nearby. Two to guard the horses — and women — the rest of you with me,' Cenred ordered.

Moving quickly and silently, with the ease of long practice, they slipped through the trees.

It was not long before they found the remains of a fire, a trickle of smoke easing out from where someone had tried to cover it with dirt.

'Single campfire. Probably a traveller.'

'Just one man,' Cenred agreed with his scout's prediction. 'We must find him and silence him. None can know we are here! Spread out!'

Sendatsu was close enough to hear them, and by now could glimpse them, shapes against the darkening sky. They looked and acted differently from the Velsh. The story that elves shut themselves away from the human world was probably false but now, seeing these men spread out, swords in hands, he had a sense of the sort of humans Dokuzen mothers used to describe to terrify their children.

For a moment he thought about fading away into the trees, sure they could not find him in the gathering gloom. After all, there were plenty of them and he had too much to lose to get involved in some scrappy fight in this nowhere woods.

'Find him! Those women we took from the village have been tormenting us all day and I'm not going to wait much longer!' someone shouted.

Sendatsu's face tightened in anger. So they were rapists as well as killers? He could not walk away, even though it was the smart thing to do. He could not leave women to the mercy of these men. That would haunt him for ever more.

'Come on! Find him! Kill him!'

That gave him a moment's fear. Then it was replaced with a surge of anger. They thought to hunt him? He would show them he was the superior being, they were just crude men. He had been trained in woodcraft for years, had worked with both the sword and the bow. They could not hope to match him. Swiftly he strung his bow and checked his arrow bag. He only had a dozen arrows and barely half were useable. The heads on the others were facing the same way as the bow, so they could slice through the ribs of an animal that walked on four legs, like a deer. He needed arrows with the sharp metal head at right angles to the bow, so they could pass between the ribs of a standing animal, like a man.

He moved with purpose, an arrow held lightly across his bow, at the ready. The longbow was not ideal for this sort of country, for there were too many bushes and hanging branches to offer a clear shot at any distance. It meant he had to get close. But he was willing to do that.

They were searching carefully, holding up torches to help them look. They obviously thought he had gone to ground, for the torches made a perfect aiming point, he thought with satisfaction.

Sighting on one man, he drew back the string, feeling the strain, and focused on what he could see in the flickering torchlight. This man was scarred and hard-looking, with big shoulders. The way he held the sword suggested he knew exactly how to handle it.

He raised his bow and released in one movement, not pulling it back to the full draw, the arrow whispering out. He heard the solid thunk as it struck but the man stood for a long moment and he began to doubt, wondered if he had missed — then the man toppled forwards silently, his torch falling with him.

The sight of the man falling gave Sendatsu a feeling of power and he felt his senses come fully alive again. All his fear for Mai and Cheijun, his anger at what was happening, hurt and frustration had been looking for an outlet — and now it had found one.

'What's going on over there?'

The shout brought a smile to Sendatsu's face and he circled out to his left, searching for a new target, picking his way carefully over the fallen leaves and twigs on the ground.

The men gathered around their fallen comrade, one of them inspecting the long arrow and in particular the arrowhead protruding out of his back.

'What in the name of all that's holy is that?' one man shouted.

'It's an arrow, idiot,' someone answered him.

'Arrowheads don't look like that — they don't stick two feet out of your bloody back!' the first voice cried.

The torches were giving Sendatsu a good look at them and he tried to spot the leader, although he was probably the one on his knees, inspecting the fallen man, making him an impossible target. No matter, there were far easier ones. Sendatsu drew and loosed, sending a shaft into the back of the closest. He lingered long enough to see the spray of blood blast into the faces of two men opposite as the sharpened head tore out the other side, then he ducked and ran, circling around still further.

'Drop those torches! Stay together! He's only one man!'

Sendatsu heard the shouts and almost laughed. He was more than just one man. He found another likely place for an ambush and stopped, standing behind a huge tree. The woods were darker now, but hardly quiet — the dying cries of the second man

Sendatsu had picked off still echoed but, in between, Sendatsu could hear a pair of men walking cautiously towards him. A pair was better than one, for they made a bigger target, walking one behind the other, the second a little to the left. Moving slowly, for fast motion was easier to see in low light, he drew back the bow and sighted on the lead man. He let them get close, barely ten paces away, before loosing.

The power of the full draw at that distance picked the man up and threw him to the ground, knocking the second one back at the same time. As the second one struggled to regain his balance, and his wits, Sendatsu snatched up another arrow, drew and loosed.

'He's over ...' the man began, but then all breath was punched out of him as the arrow slammed through his throat.

Before the screams and gurgles had barely started, Sendatsu cut to his right, running hard then ducking down.

'He's got Redwald and Uffa!' someone shouted, and Sendatsu could tell the confident calls of earlier were all gone. In their place was fear, even a little panic.

'Let's get out of here! He's picking us off, one by one!'

'It's only one man!' the one who was obviously the leader shouted. 'Remember your training. Work together!'

Sendatsu decided to silence that voice. He crawled carefully through the bushes towards where it was yelling instructions, and away from where the other men were gathering around two more of their fallen friends.

'This is no normal bow,' someone cried. 'This arrow went right through Uffa and buried the head into the tree behind — I've never seen a bow with enough power to do that before!'

Sendatsu silently acknowledged the man's comment, while wriggling closer to his target.

'Stop talking! We are giving away our positions. Sit tight and wait for him to make a mistake,' the leader called.

Sendatsu thanked him for giving away his own position like that and drew his sword as quietly as possible. Their leader was tucked in between two trees, making him a difficult target for an arrow at any time but near impossible in the little light available. Leaving his bow on the ground, Sendatsu eased himself close, then jumped to his feet and thrust his sword forwards.

The man reacted like a cat, spinning and blocking with his own blade.

'I have you now, you bastard!' he cried. 'He's over here!'

Sendatsu pressed in, knowing he had to finish this fast. All those years of training, of being beaten and hit by his father, took over and he parried one high blow, locking the two swords together. The man was a head taller than he was, and broad across the shoulders, but he had not been trained to the bow and Sendatsu's archer strength was more than enough to allow him to twist the swords aside. The man gasped as he felt the power opposing him, then Sendatsu's blade flashed like lightning away from the locked blade and through his lungs, using the reverse side stroke.

Sendatsu ripped out his sword and did not stay to clean it, for he could hear the other men running closer. It took him a moment or two of fumbling to find his bow once more on the ground, then he was off and running too, blood sticky on his hand.

'Cenred is dead! Let's get out of here!'

The shouts and cries as thoughts of revenge and duty were replaced by self-preservation were sweet music to Sendatsu's ears.

As they blundered back through the bushes, heading towards where they had left their horses and gear, he kept pace with them. There were only four left and they kept looking back over their shoulders, as if they expected him to appear out of the darkness behind them. So he sped up, outpacing them easily and letting their clumsy, crashing run through the bushes cover the noises he was making.

He waited for them, an arrow on his string and his last useable one plunged into the earth at his feet.

'See anything?' he heard one cry, listened to the harsh breathing of frightened running men and drew back the cord.

The leading man was running on rubbery legs, fear had lent him speed but had also robbed him of strength. They were like bullies, Sendatsu decided. They did not know what to do when somebody stood up to them. They had been so used to things going their way, they could not handle defeat.

He let the leading man get five paces away and then he loosed, the power of the strike picking the man up and throwing him backwards, where he brought down a second man and made a third stumble. The last of the quartet swerved around his friends instinctively — and realised he should have dived for cover. Too late, as another arrow slashed through his chest.

Sendatsu dropped his bow again and drew his sword. He was almost tempted to let the two humans recover, regain their feet and draw their swords. But his father spoke to him across the years.

'Never give an enemy a chance. No mercy!'

Sendatsu sprang out of the bushes like something from a nightmare. The fallen man looked up in time to have the dragon-tail stroke take his head, while the last man tried a feeble thrust before the figure-eight swept it aside and opened his chest to the night air.

The dying moans of the men with arrows in them floated across the woods as Sendatsu gathered his bow and worked his way back towards the men's camp. There would be a couple more guarding their prisoners and horses, he guessed.

The pair of them were standing close to a fire, swords out but talking to each other, rather than looking for trouble. Sendatsu nodded to himself. They obviously expected their friends to return, rather than be picked off one by one and killed. Behind them, four women were slumped together, but he did not spare them a second glance.

He checked his arrow bag. He had no arrows with man-killing heads left, only deer-killers. He was tempted to use them anyway, but then put down both his arrow bag and bow. Using the sword would be more honourable. 'Are you ready to die?' he asked as he stepped out of the shadows into the firelight.

The two humans reacted instantly, dropping into a crouch.

Sendatsu imagined he must make quite a sight, spattered with the blood of their comrades, his blade stained almost its entire length.

'Who are you?'

'Sendatsu of Dokuzen. And I have killed every last one of your friends. As I shall kill you, and rescue those women you hold.'

The two humans looked at each other, then back at the bloodied Sendatsu. He half expected them to keep talking but instead they split apart and raced at him.

He reacted immediately, moving to his left and driving the human there back and across to his right with a series of figure-eight strikes. None pierced the man's guard but it still forced the human to retreat to Sendatsu's right, where he blocked the approach of the second man. The humans tried to split apart again, to come at Sendatsu from opposite sides, but he moved back to his right, driving the humans back and keeping them entangled in each other's way, so they could not get to his flanks. It was an exercise he had practised scores of times before and, just when he could see the frustration on the humans' faces, he changed his tactics. Now he sprang to the attack as they tried to sweep back and around. Caught by surprise, he cornered one man and cut high and low, using the floating cloud style, too fast for the man to keep up. His third blow ripped open the man's throat and he pivoted smoothly to block the last man's approach.

The man backed away as Sendatsu advanced, raining blows from all directions, before sweeping low in the dragon-tail stroke to take the man's leg off above the knee. Screaming horribly, the man collapsed, clutching at his spurting stump, before Sendatsu finished him off with a swift cut to the throat.

As the man fell he could not restrain himself and had to roar his triumph to the skies. The women all shrieked and clutched each other as he strode around the clearing, shouting out his victory. As he came close to them they wailed in terror and he stopped. The four of them clung together, some turning tear-streaked faces away from him as he walked over to them. He also noticed how much food was piled up near the fire. His stomach growled and he hoped he would get a decent meal out of this, at least.

'Your ordeal is over. You are free. Your captors are all dead.' He smiled at them through the mask of blood. He kneeled down and used one of the human swords to cut the ropes — no sense in blunting his own blade.

'Wh-who are you?' asked the oldest of the quartet.

'I am Sendatsu of Dokuzen. I am an elf.'

'An elf?' The four relaxed a little at the news.

'You are safe now. I have freed you!' Sendatsu exclaimed proudly. He could not stay still; the reaction of the fight had him wanting to run back to Dokuzen and tell his father he was not useless after all.

The oldest of the quartet, the one who was first to speak, turned to him, wiping her eyes.

'How can we ever repay you? I am Delia and we shall never forget what you did.'

Sendatsu grinned. 'I am glad you said that. Because I need you four to do something for me.'

They drew away from him, drew together again.

'What is it you want?' Delia cried.

'Are you really an elf?' another asked.

'Of course I'm an elf!' Sendatsu roared at them.

'Maegen, if he is an elf, then he can bring the dead back to life, change the past and save all in our village of Patcham!' Delia clutched the second speaker

'What? I can't do that!' Sendatsu protested.

'Why not? I thought you were an elf?'

'I cannot do such a thing! Even our most powerful Magic-weaver cannot bring the dead back to life.'

'But all the legends speak of your powerful magic, how it can do anything!' the woman Delia had called Maegen cried.

'Well, I cannot do this. But speaking of legends, can any of you read another language, maybe an old language ...?'

'If you are truly an elf, then bless my elfbolt, give it the power to heal.' Delia reached into her dress and produced a small lump of stone on a thong, holding it out towards him.

'What?' Sendatsu had never seen such a thing, nor heard of them before.

'An elfbolt! All it needs is your blessing to become a powerful source of magic!'

Sendatsu just stared at them. Were they speaking another language? The emphasis on some scrap of stone totally confused him.

'He will not do even that! Don't trust him!' Maegen hissed.

Bewildered, Sendatsu looked from one to the next. What was the significance of the stone and why were they so obsessed with it? It infuriated him.

'Enough!' he bellowed. 'No more of this nonsense! Now you will stop this and listen to me or ...'

He stopped there, partly because he did not mean to threaten them but mainly because they had run away, racing towards the tethered horses.

'Wait! I am sorry — I mean you no harm!' he called, the anger gone from his voice. 'Where are you going?'

'Home!' Delia replied strongly. The four of them clambered into saddles and looked as though they would be galloping out of there.

Sendatsu could not believe it. He risked his life, saved them, and they were running away from him! Just what did these humans think of elves? To have such strange memories of elven magic ... what legends had been left behind?

'You could at least cook me some food!' he shouted as they clattered away.

He kicked a saddle in frustration and anger. Even allowing for what they had gone through, this was ridiculous. He could not talk with humans. And when he did, their obsession and misconception of magic spoiled things. This was going to be even harder than he thought. How was he to get through to these humans?

# 8

*It started with the Magic-weavers. They had been so firmly under the control of our forefathers that perhaps it was natural they would be the first to rebel. As the most gifted among us in magic, the most powerful, they saw themselves as something special. They were also the way to create the magical barrier and seal ourselves away from the rest of the humans.*

*To my face they smiled and bowed and promised to fulfil the wishes of the forefathers but, behind my back, they schemed and plotted.*

*They thought they should rule the elves.*

*That was bad enough but I didn't realise there were other elves who thought they should rule the world.*

'What was it like at court, sir?'

Hector turned in his saddle. He had been brooding on the bad luck that seemed to have cursed his life. Once again, with triumph almost in his grasp, it had slipped away. With many miles of road to travel and little in the way of company, naturally his thoughts turned inwards. Now the sergeant of the guards he had been given had interrupted his brooding.

He glowered at the sergeant for a heartbeat before his face was transformed by a broad smile. 'Like nothing you could ever imagine,' he said warmly. 'To stand in front of your king, to have the whole court on their feet and applauding you ... it is a feeling like no other. You are lifted upwards on that wave of adulation, it fills you to the brim and, at that moment, you can truly do anything.'

'So you performed as well, sir? I thought it was just your daughter ...'

'Of course I performed! You don't think she just woke up with that sort of talent, do you?' Hector snapped. 'I was the greatest singer the court ever heard! The women used to swoon all over me as soon as I opened my mouth.' He looked around at the guards, saw he had their full attention and basked in it. 'Sergeant, what is your name?'

'Edric, sir,' he reminded him yet again.

'Well, Edric, the king himself shed a tear the first time he listened to me sing.'

'The king cried, sir?'

Hector paused. 'So I was told,' he added hastily. 'But bards used to sing songs about how good a singer I was. All of Forland was going to learn of my greatness. Your parents would have sung you to sleep with tales of my prowess, used them to calm your crying.'

'My parents weren't into singing, sir. More into hitting me until I shut up. But how come I never heard of you?'

'I lost my voice,' Hector admitted, the fire that had filled him at those memories now dying down.

'Still, at least you have your daughter, sir. Everyone talks about her. You can be famous through her.'

'Famous through her? She owes me everything! She would be nothing without me. Nothing!'

They rode on in silence for a little while, as Hector brooded anew.

'So no chance you could give us a tune or two, help the miles along, sir?'

'No.'


Rhiannon threw back her head and laughed.

The first few days after leaving Cridianton had been like some sort of nightmare. Her father, the central part of her life, had gone. Every day she had been told what to do, what to wear, where to go and what to eat. To have that taken away was an enormous gulf in her life. The thought he had died to save her from Ward was even more devastating. Hector had prepared her for the court of King Ward, filled her head with stories about how wonderful it was and what a success she would be. To have that taken away from her at the same time as her father was almost too much for her. Without Huw, she would not have made it.

Back in Cridianton he had been her only friend. At the auditions for the king he had performed after her — and saved her when nerves left her tongue tied and her legs leaden, playing the lyre to break the spell she was under and release her ability. Then, during one of the king's war meetings, when they had been the entertainment, he had invited her to join him in seeing the city. Even now she marvelled she had been brave and daring enough to say yes.

Together they had run through the quiet servants' passageways and slipped out of the castle without being seen.

She delighted in every moment. She had never felt more alive. He showed her the magnificent Central Park, with its tree-lined paths and gorgeous statues, and then they watched a short play at an open-air theatre before enjoying pastries at one of Cridianton's many fine eating houses. They talked incessantly, about everything, from what they liked to eat, to music they liked and the people they had already performed for at Ward's court.

Rhiannon felt as though a dam had burst within her. She never got to talk much with her father, unless it was about dancing or singing — and then it was more a case of him telling and her listening. She had never had a friend to talk to, and the words poured out of her.

It became their little secret, to sneak out into the city. Her father had told her time and again that men only wanted one thing from her, that they were only interested in her face and body — but it was not like that with Huw. He told her they were only friends and she believed it.

When he revealed to her he was not from Forland but Vales she had been shocked — but also terrified for Huw. She knew as well as he did Ward's plans for that country. Hearing Huw say he had to leave Cridianton to warn his people had been frightening. The thought of losing him, of losing this precious freedom he gave her, was too much to bear.

She had always been truthful until that day. Lying to her father was beyond imagining. But she had seen him do it often enough, when he wanted something done for him, or to get his own way. She had sworn she would never do anything like that — but found herself asking Huw to stay on, trying to persuade him to delay his trip north to warn his father and the other Velsh. After all, the Velsh could not stop the Forlish, they had no army, no flag, no ruler and no organisation. Why should he go back there and get himself killed, especially when he was no warrior himself? What could one bard do?

When reasoned argument did not work, she held his hand and hinted they could become more than friends. It had felt wrong, it had brought a flush to her cheeks, but it had worked. Huw had instantly agreed to wait a little longer.

And not only had the lie worked, it had come back to save her. For Huw had witnessed King Ward killing her father and been able to get her out of Cridianton ahead of the king's men. As the only person she knew, and her only friend ever, she naturally leaned on him for that time. In those first days, still shocked by what had happened, she would have agreed to anything Huw had asked. The fact he had not asked anything, had done nothing more than take care of her, was now a relief. It would have made things too complicated. Since they had performed at Pontypridd, met that elf and fought the Velsh, it felt as though she had come alive. Huw was letting her decide which road to travel, where they should sleep and whether they should perform or not. After merely doing what she was told, the feeling of power was quite intoxicating.

Not that they were having any more luck in warning the Velsh people that the Forlish were coming. After the incident at

Pontypridd they had tried to talk to the people at another village, with a singular lack of success. They could not understand why the Forlish were coming, did not know what to do — and took little notice of a bard and a dancer. Some thought it was just an elaborate jest.

Now they had arrived at a mining village called Caerphilly, and had been drawn to its elven-built inn. This was another chance to persuade the people, Huw told her.

Rhiannon thought this was hilarious. 'The Velsh won't believe us — they think we are fools, like the pair we spoke to a day ago. What was that couple's name? Blodwen and Bedwin! They thought it was all part of an act, and wouldn't listen.'

'Yes, but they were both several sheep short of a flock, if you ask me. But leaving aside idiots, I think we need to try again.'

Rhiannon smiled fondly at him. 'Fine. One more time. But don't blame me if it goes horribly wrong!'


Sendatsu was tired and irritable when he came across the next human settlement. He had spent a wet and cold night in the woods and dearly wanted a hot bath, as well as some proper food. He had even resorted to eating animal flesh, rather than starve. He felt so dirty that even his teeth itched. And the business with the women of Patcham bothered him, more than fighting and killing their captors. He had no sympathy for murderers and rapists but having their victims run away from him had left him with a strange unease. Why were they so obsessed with magic? And the power they thought he had ... Sendatsu could do a few small things with magic but bringing people back to life ...! It was obvious they knew nothing about magic.

How was he going to find the evidence, the answers he needed to return home? What if he could never return ...?

That was eating at him as he wandered into the settlement of Caerphilly. This was a mining village carved into the side of a hill. A huge open pit showed where the humans dug out iron ore. Sendatsu knew of such mines, to the far north of Dokuzen, but he had never seen one before. One look was more than enough, he decided after a few moments, and walked into the small town.

What gave him a little hope was some of the houses here were obviously elven-built. They stood out from the low, rounded human huts like fires at night. Although, from the number of drunken men staggering in and out of them, it seemed the humans were using them as halls and drinking houses, rather than for their original purpose. He avoided a pair of humans sprawled in the mud and walked into the largest elven building he could see.

Inside was as bad as he had feared, just like the one at Pontypridd. The windows were all gone, while the tiled floors were ripped up in places, or covered in fetid rushes, while the plastered walls were smeared with grime, the delicate designs obscured by dirt or crumbling off the bricks. He looked around, horrified by the way the humans had treated it.

'Who are you?' someone asked, and he turned to see a table of miners staring at him.

'Sendatsu,' he said shortly, turning his back on them and walking over to another long wooden table, where a human stood, smearing dirt around on the top with a grubby rag.

'Are you the owner?' Sendatsu demanded.

'What?' The human glared at him. 'Who wants to know?'

'What do you know of this building's history?'

'I bought it off my uncle,' the barman replied, mystified.

'Where can I find him? Does he know much of elven history?'

'He's dead these past eight moons.' The barman shrugged.

Sendatsu cursed and looked around, wondering if anyone else in here might know something — it looked as though the drinking hall was full.

'Would anyone here know about the town's history?'

The barman sniffed. 'Who knows? But maybe you can ask the performers I've got. They're a dancer and a bard, all the way from the court of King Ward himself!'

Sendatsu stared at him. Was this the same pair from Pontypridd?

'Do you know them?' the barman asked.

Sendatsu shrugged and turned to leave, only to see a miner stand and stagger across to join him.

'Are you going to buy us drinks?' the miner asked.

'No,' Sendatsu said.

'Who is this? Do you know him?' the barman asked the miner.

The miner swayed to a halt beside Sendatsu, where he inspected him drunkenly.

'Well, shag me like a sheep if it's not an elf!' he exclaimed.

'Well, I certainly won't be doing that,' Sendatsu told him politely, hoping that was the right response to make the man walk away.

Instead he leaned in closer and Sendatsu was treated to the full blast of his foul breath, as well as a host of other smells. He had some food caught in his tangled black beard, and from the colour of his skin he had obviously only washed lightly after coming out of the mine — if at all — while his clothes had been changed perhaps last year.

'What are you doing here?' he demanded, grabbing Sendatsu's sleeve.

'I'm here to find some nice woods that I can make up a poem about,' Sendatsu said shortly, prising the man's fingers off his shirt. 'Now please leave me alone.'

The miner had arms and shoulders hardened by days in the mine but could not stop Sendatsu and gasped at a greater strength than his own.

'So it's true what they say about you elves — that you're magically strong!' He wrung his hand but did not seem too bothered by it.

'Absolutely. And we live forever.' Sendatsu could feel his patience slipping.

'Show us some magic! Go on!' the miner encouraged.

'Magic, we want to see magic!' the table behind him took up the cry.

'Come on! Do some magic. You're not getting out of here until you show us something,' the miner declared, grabbing hold of Sendatsu's pouch, where his children's toys stayed safe.

That was too much.

'You want to see some magic? How about watching a man fly?' Sendatsu growled.

'Aye!' the miner began, but Sendatsu pounced, grabbing him by the throat and crotch, lifting him up and hurling him onto the table full of his friends. Chairs, miners, drinks and food went in all directions and everyone else jumped to their feet as well.

Into the silence that followed, as Sendatsu glared around the room, a lyre struck a single perfect note and the dancer bounded into the room.

'Ladies and gentlemen, all the way from the court of King Ward of Forland himself, may I present Rhiannon of Hamtun!' the bard bellowed.

But nobody looked their way as they danced into the centre of the room; all were focused on Sendatsu and the groaning table of miners behind him.

'You!' Huw and Rhiannon exclaimed.

'Not again!' Sendatsu glanced around the room nervously.

'Is this some part of the act?' the barman asked.

Sendatsu did not hang around for what he was sure would come — instead he turned and raced for the door.

'Get back to your room — I'm going after him, I'll bring him back!' Huw hissed at Rhiannon and then tore after Sendatsu.

The inn full of Velsh miners watched the three of them race off, then looked at each other, dumbfounded. One began to clap doubtfully, then they all clapped, before turning back to their drinks with relief.

'If that was the best entertainment that King Ward's court can provide, I'm glad I'll never go there,' the miner Sendatsu had hurled through the air groaned as he emerged from the wreckage of his friends.

The barman watched him without sympathy.

'You just don't appreciate culture,' he told him, blowing his nose on his rag, before using it to clean out an empty tankard.

* * *

Huw raced out of the hall at Caerphilly not far behind the elf and tried to stay with him, ignoring the wobble in his legs and the burning in his lungs. He was not going to let the elf get away this time.

Nobody stopped them, although plenty stared — especially at Huw in his bright bard costume of red tunic and green trews. By the time they had reached the outskirts, Huw was panting like a dog and almost reeling from exhaustion. The elf, on the other hand, showed no signs of slowing down. Barely a hundred yards from the last house, a wood began. Huw was staggering by the time he reached it, the elf long gone.

'Wait! I just want to talk! Please!' he puffed as loud as he could, then leaned on a tree and sucked in great gulps of air.

When his legs stopped shaking and it felt like he could breathe again without coughing, he straightened and looked around. Nothing. He cursed. He spun around desperately and came face to face with the elf. His sword was in his hand and it was pointed at Huw's throat.

'You've got some explaining to do,' the elf said coldly. 'Talk fast.'


'What happened here?' Broyle demanded, stamping around the clearing, staring at the bodies of his men they had found littered through the woods. The ones killed by a sword were obvious enough but several had been killed by something else. At first he thought they were from a crossbow but they looked different, with a smaller entry wound.

'I knew we should have all stayed together. The women are gone!' Ricbert grumbled.

'Well, I think we can safely say they didn't do this!' Broyle snarled. 'Cenred was one of the best swordsmen in our regiment. There must have been dozens of them — enough to kill our boys and then enough to take their own dead away.'

'You think the Velsh did this?' Ricbert asked.

'Well, it wasn't a bunch of woodland elves!' Broyle growled.

'So what do we do, sarge?'

'Horse tracks lead towards that village we raided. We shall head back there. But slowly. Cautiously. I want them to think they got away with this,' Broyle said carefully.

'Why?'

'So when I do rip them apart, I can enjoy it more,' Broyle vowed.

Sendatsu had made the shelter of the trees easily and watched the bard stumble to a halt and then lean against one, gasping for air. He was the most unlikely opponent Sendatsu had ever seen but it never hurt to be cautious. He used the bard's heavy breathing to cover the slight noise of his own approach and to draw his sword. When the bard turned, he was ready.

'Talk fast,' he ordered the frightened Velshman. 'Why are you following me?'

The bard gulped. 'I need your help to save my people. We've come from the court of King Ward in Cridianton — he's the king of Forland, a country to the south of here that wants to rule the world. He's sending soldiers north to raid and attack my people and I have to warn them. You can use your magic to save them — what are you doing here ...' he gabbled.

Sendatsu sheathed his sword. There was no danger here. 'Do you want to slow down a little?' he suggested.

'Yes!' the Velshman breathed out. 'Only you said to talk fast, so I thought ...'

'Look, how about going back to the beginning?'

'Yes! Great idea!' the bard said excitedly. 'But maybe you should come with me first — I have a couple of rooms back at that inn and we can talk there in more comfort. Besides, Rhiannon wants to meet you, and needs to speak to you as well ...'

Sendatsu hesitated. 'Fine. Lead on,' he said shortly, to cut off the bard's flow of words.

'Sensei Sumiko, what can we do? The thought of Sendatsu out in the human world is eating me up inside. He could be dead already!' Asami declared.

'Hush!' The High Magic-weaver looked around dramatically, which set Asami's teeth on edge. She knew Sumiko's powers would have told her if someone had been within hearing distance, while her garden would have seized anyone who dared enter it without her permission. It was particularly vibrant today and Asami wondered what that meant for her.

This had been her first opportunity to come here. The Elven Council had forbidden mention of Sendatsu's name. Everyone was talking about it, of course — it was the topic of conversation in every part of Dokuzen. But only with trusted friends and family. Clans were quick to point the finger at each other for disloyalty to the Council and the Council Guards were always ready to pounce. Gaibun had also had many angry words about that kiss she and Sendatsu had exchanged in the garden.

'I know your feelings for him. But to do that in front of others! You shamed me!' he spat at her.

'And you taking lovers across half of Dokuzen does not shame me?' she fired back.

'At least I am discreet. At least I do not do anything in front of servants and mere soldiers!'

'No, just in front of enough people that all our friends gossip about it behind my back!'

'I would not expect a woman to understand honour!'

'If that is your version of honour, then I am glad it makes no sense!'

They had not spoken since, except for him to forbid her going near Sumiko. But he was out on patrol near the border and she was willing to take the risk — any risk.

'The Council has ears everywhere. We must be careful ...'

'Aroaril curse being careful! Sendatsu saved us and is now risking his life to help us again. We need to give him all the aid we can,' Asami argued. Behind her, a vine exploded into life, silently twisting and crushing the rose bush next to it.

'Agreed,' Sumiko said quietly. The vine slithered back into the earth, leaving the rose bush to collapse noiselessly to the ground. 'The best way is to do something here. We both saw the effect one scroll from the tombs of the forefathers had on Jaken and the cursed Council. One scroll! And yet there are dozens still in there. We must go through them, find what is inside.' Another bush burst into life, rich red berries on its stems tempting a pair of birds who sat on the wall overlooking the garden.

'But I thought that was what Sendatsu had to do, why he was sent into the human world?' Asami could feel the magic flowing around her, worried what it meant, but dared not look behind.

One of the birds could not resist the beckoning berries and flew down, looking for a place to land.

'Yes,' Sumiko agreed. 'But we would be foolish not to try this. If we can get the evidence first, overthrow the Council, then there is no need for Sendatsu to be out there and we can bring him home. We have already begun the process, the people are already being prepared ...'

Awareness came to Asami then. 'You were already planning this, even before Sendatsu,' she breathed.

Sumiko smiled thinly. The bird had now landed on the very top of the bush and was edging lower, looking at the plump, ripe berries with a hungry eye.

'Of course. We have seen the magic dying within the elves, the barrier protecting Dokuzen decaying. We had to find out why. The history of the Magic-weavers makes for interesting reading but that alone would not be believed. After all, the Council has seen to it that we are despised. Every child is taught we are not to be trusted, and should be watched always. But the words of our forefathers themselves carry even more weight.'

'But will it be in time? He will not know how to deal with humans ...'

'We have to move carefully. The Magic-weavers have been working towards this for too long to risk revealing ourselves too soon. You have to trust me,' she said persuasively.

Asami felt a chill. She could not turn back but neither would she walk blindly into Sumiko's plans.

'So you seek to use me to achieve your goals, with no guarantee that it will save Sendatsu?'

The vine suddenly surged behind Asami, rearing tall above the slim elf. 'Yes,' Sumiko admitted. 'But you asked me for help. And this is your only chance.'

'Then tell me what to do,' Asami said simply.

The vine disappeared back into the ground, leaving the plants to their ordered beauty, while beyond them the bird jumped down a branch and reached for the first berry. Before it could pick one, the vine exploded out of the ground and plucked the bird from the branch, taking it so fast that barely a leaf was disturbed, the both of them vanishing below the ground in the blink of an eye.

One solitary feather floated down, landing on the patch of disturbed soil.

'You are going to break into the tombs of the forefathers and steal every book there.' Sumiko smiled.


Rhiannon paced nervously up and down. The thought of meeting an elf was so thrilling she had forgotten for the moment what she was doing here and why she had fled Cridianton. Geography had not been one of the things Hector insisted she learn but even she knew Dokuzen, the fabled land of the elves, was to the north-east. If one elf was walking among the humans again, who knew how many might be out there? Perhaps they were even now thinking about rejoining the world!

The idea of dancing for the elves, with the elves, consumed her. She even tried out a few steps, to see how it felt. She was spinning around when a knock on the window almost made her fall. She rushed over, to see Huw and the elf standing there. It took her a moment to work out how to open the crude horn panel that served as a window, then stepped back as Huw waved the elf forwards. 'This is Rhiannon of Hamtun, the most talented dancer that Forland, perhaps any land, has seen. Rhiannon, this is ...' Huw paused as he realised he did not know the elf's name.

'Sendatsu,' said Sendatsu as he hauled himself through the window, dropping lightly to the floor and straightening up.

Rhiannon had a thousand things she wanted to say but her throat seemed too tight, while her feet seemed too big, so she did not think she was capable of speech or movement.

'Sendatsu?' Huw asked. 'I thought elven names were longer …'

Sendatsu looked from Huw to the blushing Rhiannon. Huw grunted and wriggled his way into the room, dropping in an ungainly heap on the floor.

'Well, it's Tadayoshi Moratsune Sendatsu,' he said pleasantly.

Rhiannon swallowed. It was as if something forgotten or long-hidden had come alive within her. She could feel everything around her, sense the mice in the walls, the insects under the floor. It seemed as if she had but to ask, and the world would do her bidding. It left her feeling faint. 'Tadayoshi Moratsune Sendatsu,' she whispered.

'Very good,' Sendatsu complimented her, feeling a little alarmed at the way she was looking at him — and the way she was looking in general. Was she sick? He had never seen skin flush red like that on an elf. Was it perhaps the unwashed smell he imagined was coming off him in waves? Self-consciously, he tried to step back a little.

'Anyway, you wanted to know the truth of what happened in the taproom,' Huw interrupted, not particularly liking the way Rhiannon was gazing adoringly at Sendatsu.

'You're warning people about the raiders roaming Vales.' Sendatsu waved him away. 'I understand that. Then you saw that I was an elf, realised I could not be working for King Ward and decided to try to make up for the damage you so nearly did.'

Huw paused. 'Yes,' he agreed.

'Good. Now we have that sorted …'

'But we need to talk to you!' Huw exclaimed. 'What are you doing in Vales?'

'Well, I think we both need to talk. I need answers from you as well …'

'Are there more elves roaming the human world? Does this

mean you are ending your exile?' Huw pressed. 'We need help, my people desperately need a hero like you ...'

Sendatsu shuddered at the thought. But he should go carefully with these two. He looked around and saw there was but one chair in the room, so gestured Rhiannon towards it.

'You might as well make yourself comfortable,' he suggested. 'It sounds like we have much to talk about.'

'Oh, the bed is more comfortable — and big enough for two to sit on.' Rhiannon smiled. 'Come, sit beside me.'

Sendatsu regarded her doubtfully as she patted it. It was just a straw mattress on some wood and not what Sendatsu thought of as a bed — but better than a rancid wolfskin on the floor. At least she was obviously not too concerned about his smell. He sat down gingerly, leaving a scowling Huw to take the chair.

'Well, there are no more elves in Vales. And my people are not planning to end their exile, as you call it, any time soon.' Sendatsu hesitated. They claimed to know about the elves. How much could they tell him, how much should he reveal of his mission, the fact his life was forfeit if he returned without some evidence and his role in possibly overthrowing the Elven Council? It was a delicate balancing act.

'I am here to try and find out the truth about why the elves left the human world, to see whether any humans have discovered Aroaril and if they have discovered magic. I am trying to find answers and I hope you can help me.'

'So what have you found out?' Huw asked instantly.

'And when are you going back?' Rhiannon said in the same breath. 'Would you be able to take us?'

Sendatsu sucked in a breath. 'As to when I return — I cannot say. I would like to go back tomorrow,' he admitted with feeling, 'but I cannot return until I have answers. As far as allowing humans into Dokuzen ...' He paused, knowing there was more chance of his father welcoming him back with open arms. 'I don't think that is a good idea.'

'But if we had a special talent, if we had a dream to one day dance with the elves ...' Rhiannon sighed, her eyes distant. 'If we could help you in your quest, would you take us back as a reward? And we can help, can't we, Huw?'

'Well, it depends what Sendatsu wants to know,' Huw said sourly.

'I promise you this — if you can help me finish my quest, I shall show you Dokuzen,' Sendatsu vowed. If you can decipher that book, or do magic, then I shall have to take you back — although it will put your lives in as much danger as mine, if not more, he added silently.

Rhiannon squealed with excitement and clapped her hands together at the thought, before regaining control of herself. I have to stop acting like a moonstruck maiden if I am to impress him, she decided. The strange sensation was fading now and she felt more in control of herself.

'We know so much about the elves. The dance you saw us doing back in Pontypridd was called the "Dance of the Elves", and is meant to represent the fateful day when they sealed themselves away from the human world. Huw and I learned our craft in different countries but we are both well versed in elven lore. Much of our songs are based on elves, or about elves. Did you recognise the song, or perhaps the dance?'

'A little,' Sendatsu admitted. 'There were notes there, as well as steps you made, that reminded me very much of dances back home. Song and dance have always been part of our culture. They have obviously survived our long absence from your world. But what about the elven lore?'

'Where to begin? There are many stories about you,' Rhiannon said excitedly.

'Believe me, I've heard many of them,' Sendatsu said wearily. 'I am after something more solid.'

'We have that!' Rhiannon squeaked. 'Huw, show him your elfbolt!'

Huw leaned forwards, pulling out the little stone elfbolt on the thong around his neck. 'Here it is. It is a lucky charm that worked for both Rhiannon and me when we auditioned for the king ...'

'What?' Sendatsu looked at it closely. This was the same thing the women in the woods had shown him — and then run away when he did not know what it meant. At least now he could study it properly. Back in the woods Delia had seemed to have a scrap of stone — Huw's at least looked like a crude arrowhead. But why did they call it an elfbolt? Why would elves use it?

'I have never seen that sort of thing before in Dokuzen. Whatever it is, this is not made by elves. We have never used stone arrowheads.'

Huw leaned back, his face crestfallen.

'What do you think they do?'

'Well, because they are from the elves, everyone thinks they have magic properties. They can bring you luck and, if you place them inside a bandage, can heal wounds,' Rhiannon said.

Sendatsu leaned back in disbelief. 'How can a stone do all that?'

'Because it is of the elves!'

Sendatsu shook his head. 'Well, it is not elven. Aroaril knows where they came from! Tell me, what else do the Velsh know about the elves, and Aroaril?'

'Aroaril we have never heard of — but we know plenty about the elves. They could all use magic, they showed us many things but could not cure us of our warlike natures. In despair they shut themselves away from the human world behind a magic barrier ...' Huw said.

Sendatsu gritted his teeth. That was not what he wanted to hear.

'Well, I am from Forland and we all know about the elves there!' Rhiannon said excitedly. 'You should visit ...'

'You would do well not to go to Forland,' Huw interrupted, wanting to change the subject and stop the devoted look on Rhiannon's face. 'We have just come from there, from the court of King Ward himself. His men are crushing the southern countries and now he plans to bring Vales under his control by sending his soldiers disguised as bandits here, to raid and kill. Skies above knows what he would make of an elf — but I doubt he would be welcoming. His men are vicious killers and his wealth is built on slavery and conquest. That was why we came home, to warn people what is coming for them. Please, you have to help us — we need a leader, a hero, something to unite us ...'

'That is not what I am here for.' Sendatsu shook his head. 'I have a more important task.'

'What could be more important than saving lives? We are running out of time, Ward's soldiers must be getting close ...'

'You are too late,' Sendatsu said, wanting to get back to what these two knew. 'I have met some of his men already. They are raiding even now.'

'No!' Huw cried. 'Where did you meet them? When? How?'

'It was near here. I was making camp when a group of them stumbled across me.' He tried to gloss over it.

'Finding an elf would have been their fatal mistake,' Rhiannon declared. 'What happened?'

'Well, I killed them and freed the women prisoners they had taken. Although the women just demanded I perform magic for them.' He shrugged.

'Wonderful! The women were so lucky they had a hero like you there!'

'Have you seen any more? Where was the attack?' Huw said urgently.

'Oh, some place called ... Patches? Patfull? No, Patcham!' Sendatsu dismissed it. 'Look, can either of you read another language, or speak another language?'

The mention of his home village was a thunderbolt to Huw. He never thought Patcham would be a target, for it was deep in Vales and he was positive none of Ward's men could be that far north yet. But it only took a few moments for the shock to wear off.

'Are you sure it was Patcham? Was it somewhere else?' he gasped, grabbing hold of Sendatsu's tunic.

Sendatsu shoved his hand away. 'Yes, I am sure it was Patcham. Why?'

Huw bounced up. 'We have to go. We have to leave now, we have to get there,' he gabbled, unsure whether to start helping Rhiannon pack or head to his own room.

'What?' Rhiannon and Sendatsu said together.

'Patcham — that is my village! Was anyone hurt in the attack?'

Sendatsu licked suddenly dry lips. This was an unexpected turn. 'I think there were a few deaths,' he said carefully.

'Do you know who was hurt or killed?'

'Well, I never saw the village but the women who I rescued were all young — probably about your age. They lost their husbands.'

Huw felt sick with worry, unable to take much comfort from that. 'I have to get back there. My father is there!'

'Oh no, Huw!' Rhiannon exclaimed, surging from the bed and rushing over to him.

'Well, you can't leave now. It'll be nightfall within the turn of an hourglass and there's no moon — it'll be black as pitch out there,' Sendatsu said sensibly. 'The raiders are all dead, the attack on Patcham was a couple of days ago, so rushing there through the night won't make any difference but could see your horse lamed or yourself injured.'

'You can guide us!' Rhiannon said. 'Everyone knows elves can find their way through the dark as if they were cats!'

'That's one story I hadn't heard before,' Sendatsu said incredulously, as they both stared at him eagerly.

'But everyone says you can see for miles and hear a fly's whisper!'

'No, I can't,' Sendatsu promised. He wondered why they had kept ridiculous stories, and forgotten the truth.

'Please, we need your help,' Rhiannon implored. 'The Velsh need a real hero. They need you!'

Sendatsu had no intention of getting caught up in this. Asami — to say nothing of Mai and Cheijun — were relying on him to find answers. Getting involved in human squabbles was not going to help that — and might even get him hurt or killed. Besides, apart from his children, he had successfully avoided responsibility in his life so far. Now was not the time to change his habits.

'Look, my father knows much about the elves and humans, about what really happened when they left,' Huw said desperately, seeing the elf's reluctance. 'If you accompany us, he will tell you all you need to know.'

'Such as?'

Huw cast around for a story he remembered. 'That we used to have our own language, different to what we speak now,' he declared.

Sendatsu leaped up from the bed, his heart pounding. A different language, like the one in the book he had found. Hope flared within him. There could be a way here …

'What are we waiting for?'

# 9

*You could say my fault was I was too trusting. But looking back on it, I had little choice. Even knowing where my choices led me, to this dark place and my impending death in the dawn, I could not say I would do anything differently. Hindsight makes wise men of us all but the reality was, I could only make choices based on what I knew at the time. You make your choices and live with the consequences. Or, in my case, die with the consequences.*

*I needed the Magic-weavers to create the barrier. To build it properly, tie it to the magic within us, so that it faded as our magic faded away, eventually allowing us to rejoin the rest of the world. They had to know my fears about some on the Council and the concerns of the forefathers that our people might rule the other human tribes. It was perhaps natural it put ideas in their heads. To perform magic — not the clumsy tricks that are the limit of most of our natural ability — but real magic, the stuff that changes the world around us, must be amazing. To stand there, feel the power of the whole world around you and know it is yours to mould and manipulate as you wish ... it must be a feeling like no other. Is it any wonder they wanted to wield that sort of power in the rest of their lives?*

'The tombs?' Asami could see this ending badly for her. 'But won't they be expecting that?'

'If I went near there, or indeed if any other Magic-weaver tried to enter the tombs, they would be killed instantly,' Sumiko admitted. 'But you have far more power than any Magic-weaver in fifty years. You were the first to break the barrier around Dokuzen! They will not be able to stop you, especially not on the Festival of Summer.'

Asami saw the logic. The second-biggest festival after the Test, only a handful of guards would be left, for all elves would join the celebrations.

'But the risk ...'

'It is worth it. If you can bring us back those books ... knowledge brought with us from the land of Nippon, where our forefathers first arrived when they left the service of the dragons, and from where they found wives and families to bring here. Knowledge also taken from the human lands before we left there. In there is the proof we need to bring down the Council.'

'But we cannot read them, they are in other languages ...'

'Follow me.'

Sumiko took her inside the villa, to the Magic-weaver's private office. Here she used the magic to open part of the stone wall and reveal a space inside. Then she reached in and produced a book, which she opened reverently.

'This has been handed down through the generations of High Magic-weavers. Inside this book are the details of the magic we worked, centuries ago, so that all humans — including us — spoke the same language. In here are many of the old languages — the Nipponese we once spoke and the human languages as well — Velsh, Forlish, Breconese ... this is the key to understanding them. With this, with magic and with hard work, we shall be able to decipher what those books say.'

'But will the people believe it? They have been told only what the Council wants them to believe for so long — and told we are not to be trusted.'

Sumiko smiled. 'The people are not happy. They see how the Council and the leaders of the clans live. They serve silently as the nobility dines on delicacies, then go home and eat rice and scraps, drown their misery in rice wine. They accept their lot — but they do not like it. We are already using this, already spreading the word among the people. We tell them the Magic-weavers are here to help, they want to make life better for everyone. We are preparing the way. Soon the word will begin spreading without us ...'

'And into the ears of the Council!' Asami gasped.

'Exactly. They will overreact, as always. Council Guards will rush out to arrest anyone under suspicion of passing on this message, or claiming the barrier will soon fail. That will play into our hands. It will confirm everything we are saying and drive the people away from the Council faster than we ever could.'

Asami bowed. It would be slow, at first, but then things would begin rolling, like a snowball, and become unstoppable. As long as she was able to get those books.

'Yes, much of it hinges on you,' Sumiko said softly.

'But I promised Sendatsu that I would get him back. What if something was to go wrong? Could I perhaps bring him back first and then try ...?'

Sumiko stood. 'Walk with me,' she instructed.

This time, tall hedges sprouted around Sumiko's garden. Asami felt as if she and the High Magic-weaver were walking through some sort of maze. Everywhere she turned, there was a wall of green blocking her view of the way ahead.

'You cannot trust anyone,' Sumiko warned.

Behind her the hedges waved, as if in a high wind, although their movement was silent.

'I know what you are thinking. Bring Sendatsu back, hide him somewhere until it is safe for him to come out. But that will not work, will not stay secret for long. I fear the Council has a spy among my ranks. I believe Jaken has subverted at least one of my Magic-weavers. You would return with Sendatsu only for you both to die in a shower of arrows from the Border Patrol. Do not underestimate the risks. The Council killed to gain power three centuries ago. They waded through blood! Any elf who stood up to them was destroyed. They will not hesitate to kill to preserve their power now. The stakes are too high for anything else.'

The hedges shook with fury and vines writhed out of the soil as she said it, although her voice was mild. 'You have to do it my way. And beware of Gaibun. Especially of Gaibun!'

'He would not betray Sendatsu. He and I may have our problems but once he has given his word, he would never break it. And he swore to help Sendatsu return.'

'You are so sure of him?'

'I would bet my life on it,' Asami stated. 'Gaibun has been raised from birth to always tell the truth and be honourable. It is a way of life for him ...'

'And the lovers he has taken?'

Asami flushed. 'That is different. They give him what I cannot.'

'And if Jaken can give him what we cannot?'

'No!' Asami cried. 'I cannot accept that. Gaibun's father has always lived by a code of honour and Gaibun has always followed that. For him to break his word would be the end of him.'

Sumiko looked away for a moment. 'As you said, it is your life at risk. Do what you wish but prepare for the tombs. I need you to do this. Sendatsu needs you to do this. We have come this far. We cannot stop now. You trusted me before, trust me now.'

'Even assuming I can get in there, I don't know what sort of book to take with me. When I was there last, there was a whole cabinet of them,' Asami protested.

Behind her, the hedges swelled and loomed.

'Do you want to help Sendatsu or not? The books with the blue leather covering are the ones we brought from Nippon. Get those books, return them to me and I can have the Council in my hand by the next moon.'

Asami bowed her head. Part of her said Sumiko was right, they had come too far to back out now. But the days she had spent away from Sumiko had given her time to think. She had always trusted her sensei, believed her tales of a better life for all in Dokuzen. But some of the things that happened the night Sendatsu had been sent away had jarred. Asami found herself questioning whether Sumiko had used magic on Hanto, to enrage him and force a confrontation with Sendatsu. And the mysterious message that so inflamed Sendatsu's father, Jaken. Who had written that? Sumiko had so wanted to send Sendatsu into the human world. Had she manipulated events to make that happen? And was she manipulating Asami now? Asami wanted to know why the Magic-weavers had not taken the books in the long years they had sat there, gathering dust. She sensed she was getting out of her depth, wondered if she was being used by the sensei she had once trusted. But, if that was true, then she was partly to blame for sending Sendatsu out into danger. She had to get him back. She had promised to return him, to reunite him with his children. His fate and the Magic-weavers' ambitions were now intertwined. She had promises to keep on both sides. This was the only way forwards.

'I shall do it,' she promised.

Behind her, the hedges stopped moving, leaving but one path forwards.

'It will be best if we don't speak again until you have the books,' Sumiko said blandly.

She watched Asami leave, her mind elsewhere. She had been thinking about her father, her sensei and the previous leader of the Magic-weavers. There had been no question but that she would succeed him as their leader.

Most elves did not even consider using magic until their lessons began. But she had been training since she could walk, working on her magic, her control and her strength. Some children would have rebelled, others found a different path. But her destiny was set in stone one sunny day, while walking with her father around the main Dokuzen markets. Her father, Oshi, was known by both name and reputation and, while many people gave them both a wide berth, the stallholders and common people gave him due deference.

Until a small party of noble elves, sons and daughters of a clan leader and their high-ranking friends, had pushed in front of them at a food stall.

'There is a line here,' Oshi said sharply. 'It begins behind me.'

The laughing young elves turned on him, one of them stepping in close.

'You dare to question us? Do you know who we are?' he snarled.

'A rude young man?' Oshi replied coldly.

Instantly the elf backhanded Oshi across the face, sending him tumbling to the cobbles.

'Dog! You dare to speak to me like that?'

Oshi sprang to his feet and the young Sumiko watched excitedly, sure her father was going to teach these arrogant young fools a lesson they would never forget. She had seen his power a dozen times and no youths could hope to face him.

'I am Oshi, sensei of the Magic-weavers and ...'

'I am Tadayoshi Moratsune Jaken,' the young noble interrupted, 'and Magic-weavers are subservient to us. Try anything and we shall see to it that every Magic-weaver is humbled, your entire family disgraced and sent to live as esemono.'

Oshi swelled up and Sumiko held her breath ... only to let it out again as Oshi offered a deep bow.

'My apologies, Jaken. I spoke out of turn,' he said through gritted teeth. 'Please forgive me.'

Jaken waved him away and a shocked Sumiko was dragged out of the markets by her father.

She turned to him once clear of the markets, when he slowed down enough for Sumiko to get her feet once more. She was about to demand why Oshi had not punished Jaken when she realised he was weeping, tears of frustration and anger. The sight of her beloved father, the man she admired above all others, with tears running silently down his face, made her angry words dry up in her throat.

'Remember this day,' he said softly, his voice furious. 'I could have destroyed those fools in a heartbeat, only there were too many witnesses and you would have paid for it. You are more important than my pride. But this should never happen. The Magic-weavers should be acclaimed above all others, not despised. It will fall to you to restore the order to its former glory. We should rule Dokuzen, not those petty fools on the Council.'

'I will make that happen, Father,' Sumiko had promised that day — and promised herself again.

Now her chance was coming. She would not fail her father.

A noise behind her made her spin, to see Oroku bowing low.

'Are we wise to put so much faith in a girl like that?' her deputy asked.

Sumiko smiled thinly. 'Oroku, you are gifted with the magic. But leave thoughts of strategy to me. She is the perfect tool for the job. She is stronger in magic than just about everyone else and she is also fitter than any of us, skilled with sword, bow and fist. And, best of all, she will do anything to restore her foolish lover to her side.' Sumiko leaned across and let her fingers brush across the petals of the nearest plants, which seemed to shiver with pleasure at her touch.

'And what if she discovers you were the one who sent the message to his father in his name, who inflamed Hanto so he acted rashly, who forced things along so Sendatsu was forced to flee?' Oroku pressed. 'What if she learns you needed to prove the barrier was fading but could not be sure and risked Sendatsu's life — and her own — to create the right atmosphere of fear to overthrow the Council?'

'By the time she finds out the truth it will be too late and our victory will be complete. She is a tool and, like all tools, may be disposed at the end of the task.'

Sumiko stretched abruptly and the flowers behind her instantly withered and died. It was all very well sharing your plans with those you needed to see them fulfilled but, equally, they did not have the wit to grasp the necessary subtleties. She sighed and unbent a little.

'They are of great help now but will only cause problems once we have taken power. They believe in concepts of honour, in love. They will try to hold me to my promises to make a better Dokuzen.'

'But, sensei, it will be a better Dokuzen!'

'Of course. For us.'

Asami left Sumiko's house, her frustration ready to boil over. She liked and admired her sensei, had thought her the wisest of the elves, been willing to follow her vision for a better Dokuzen without question. Now she doubted. Comments and actions she had dismissed in the past bobbed back to the surface and she wondered whether she had made a huge mistake in following Sumiko so closely. But now was not the time to back out. She had to return Sendatsu or she would not be able to live with herself. Get him back first and then she could worry about Sumiko.

The path from Sumiko's villa to the main part of Dokuzen was familiar to her after the years of study; she knew the sights, sounds and even the smells she would pass.

So she knew when something was wrong. Someone was following her and doing it so well that she could not tell who it was, or where they were. She just knew they were there.

Sumiko's words about the Council having a spy and being prepared to kill came back to her and, with a sick sensation, Asami realised she had no sword.

Sendatsu was thoroughly miserable. As he had predicted, darkness fell swiftly and, without a moon, it was soon too dark to see anything much. He had been forced to stumble along in front, using a torch to try to see the way ahead, leading Rhiannon's horse, while Huw followed behind. His boots were caked with mud, while cold water had slopped into the left one and was squelching around his toes with every pace. Back in Dokuzen he would have ordered a halt by now — although back home he would have been on the horse, expecting servants to lead him to light and a warm bed. The fact the humans were riding and he was walking did not seem right, somehow. He was praying for them to come across a village soon, where they could at least rest. But until then he had to keep slogging along. Telling himself this was for Mai and Cheijun did not make it much easier, or any more pleasant. But it did make him think about the role of servants in Dokuzen. They had to do whatever they were ordered, keep going no matter what. He had forced them to perform similar tasks for him before — and had not even thanked them for it afterwards. It was an uncomfortable thought.

He had little enough time to think on this, however, because Rhiannon asked him endless questions about what life was like in Dokuzen. What clothes did people wear? What did they eat? What songs did they sing? What dances did they perform? No sooner did he answer one than she had another. It was worse than Mai and Cheijun combined! He had to be careful, because he did not want to reveal too much about himself. He was out here to get information from the humans, not the other way around. When he stepped into a puddle for the third time, distracted when trying to answer one of her questions, he decided he had had enough.

'I'm sorry, I have to concentrate on the road ahead,' he declared and, to his relief, she accepted his excuse.

'Of course — I'm sorry, Sendatsu, I'm just so excited about the thought of travelling with an elf, with someone who has seen the glades of Dokuzen! There is just so much I want to know. But I shall keep my questions for another time.'

'I appreciate that,' Sendatsu said gravely.

He could not suppress another little sigh of relief when they slogged up a slight hill to see a small village laid out across the road, the light of fires a welcome sight in the middle of the night. Sendatsu stopped, looking longingly at the warm shelter waiting ahead, if he could just but get them into it. The sogginess of his left toes and the ache in his right heel were eloquent persuaders.

'We should push on — get as far as possible while we can,' Huw said immediately, and Sendatsu cursed silently.

Huw had been alone with his thoughts for the trip, and they had not been pretty ones. Guilt, which had been riding close behind him these past few days, was now firmly holding the reins. If only he had left Cridianton when Ward had announced his foul plan to bring Vales under his heel. He could have left after hearing the king's plans and been here almost a moon ago. Ahead, he could see Rhiannon by the fitful light of the torch that Sendatsu was using. She was the symbol of his guilt. If he had thought with his head rather than his breeches, then he would have been home long before the raid. His insides were knotting themselves into a ball and he just wanted to get home. Once he knew his father was safe, he would be able to relax again.

'I think we need to rest,' Sendatsu replied carefully. 'The horses need rest — and so do you. It might be dangerous to push on much further. You cannot help anyone if you are falling off your horse tomorrow. Besides, don't the people of this village deserve your warning as well?'

'I still think we should go on,' Huw said stubbornly.

'Rhiannon, what do you think?' Sendatsu asked, eager for support.

Rhiannon almost jumped in surprise. Hector had never asked her opinion and she was unused to offering it. 'If Sendatsu thinks we should rest, then I think we should believe him. He knows far more than we do,' she declared.

Huw gritted his teeth. He knew he would not sleep that night.

'Huw, I know how you must be feeling. But your horse needs to rest. We shall go even slower if you have to walk,' Sendatsu said gently, persuasively.

Huw cursed. 'Fine. But we shall leave at first light. I know elves need little sleep.'

Sendatsu managed to stifle a yawn. 'Where did you hear that one?'

'Oh, everyone knows that,' Rhiannon agreed.

'I must meet this Everyone. He obviously knows a great deal,' Sendatsu muttered.

The village headman was willing to let them eat and sleep in his home in exchange for a silver coin. He warmed up some sort of stew, which to Sendatsu looked like pieces of gristle floating in greasy water but Rhiannon and Huw wolfed it down.

'Haven't you got anything else?' Sendatsu grumbled.

So he found himself eating cold pease pudding and hard cheese. Sendatsu emptied out his wet boot and wondered if he had made the right choice by joining these humans.

'Do you have a bath?' he asked hopefully.

'What? Why would you want one of those?'

Sendatsu sighed. He was wet, cold and smelly. If he had more energy, he would have argued.

The goats were taken from their pen and out the back and fresh straw brought in for the guests, while Sendatsu shuddered as he was handed a bundled wolfskin as a blanket. He sniffed it warily. It smelled as bad as he did.

Huw and Rhiannon settled in happily enough but Sendatsu struggled to get comfortable and tried, with even less success, not to think about fleas and lice. He felt exhausted but forced himself to stay awake until he thought the others were asleep. Then he brought out his children's toys, held them close and tried to hold back the tears. Softly, under his breath, he sung Mai her special goodnight song. He felt if he still sang it every night, then he was not really away from her. He told Cheijun not to be afraid, he would be there. He had to get answers soon. If these strange two humans were the best way, then he would put up with anything — even smelling like he did. The discomfort of wet feet was nothing compared to the pain in his heart. He kissed the toys tenderly and tucked them back in his belt pouch.

'Stay safe until I return,' he murmured.

Huw lay silently, unable to see what Sendatsu was doing, or hear what he was saying — but knowing he was up to something.

Gaibun had seen inside the Moratsune villa many times — although usually just the garden and Sendatsu's room. He had never been inside Jaken's study and, after the stories Sendatsu used to tell him, he had never wanted to go in there. Yet here he was, looking around. At first glance it seemed ordinary enough — a huge wooden desk, a pair of chairs and a selection of swords and bows on the wall as decoration amid the shelves. But when he looked closer, he realised the shelves were actually made up of hundreds and hundreds of small compartments. Inside each one, Gaibun could see a scroll, and above each one was a name. Some of those names he recognised. He wondered what was in those scrolls — and if there was a compartment with his name on it somewhere.

'Apologies for keeping you waiting.' Jaken stepped into the study and Gaibun could not restrain a guilty start.

'No apology necessary, lord.'

Jaken settled himself in his chair, saw Gaibun seated and then poured tea for both of them.

This friendliness only unsettled Gaibun even more.

'How are your father and mother?'

'Both well, lord.'

'Really? I heard your father was quite sick. Too ill to receive visitors.'

Gaibun paused as he was about to sip his tea. 'No, I saw him just yesterday and I can assure you he was in perfect health ...'

'Too sick to receive visitors. That is what he needs to say. Especially when Daichi, or one of his representatives, comes calling. Understand?'

Gaibun coughed and tea nearly ran out of his nose. He used the time to get himself back under control.

'I understand, lord. I shall tell him,' he managed to gasp.

'Good. But be sure to tell me who it was that called around. If they send nobody, I shall be suspicious. It will at least be clan Kaneoki's leader, if not Daichi himself. Your father is the only other one with claim to be leader of clan Tadayoshi. They would be fools not to speak to him.'

'Lord.' Gaibun bowed his head. Everyone knew his father was an honourable man. It was how Jaken had outmanoeuvred him to take control of their clan.

'And your wife, how is she?'

Gaibun put down his cup. 'That is the reason I am here, lord. Asami is searching for a way to return your son.'

'And you — do you also wish for him to return?'

'No!' Gaibun said instantly. 'What they plan is to overthrow the Council, the clans, the order of everything!'

'Well, I am sure they are saying that. But what they are really planning is to overthrow the Council and replace it with themselves. I doubt life in Dokuzen will change much — the esemono will be ruled by Magic-weavers, not the Council, and the clans will bow to Sumiko, rather than Daichi. What I am planning is something different. I will change life in Dokuzen. Even the lowest of the esemono will have human slaves, and all shall live a life of luxury and wealth unsurpassed. Help me and you will become the next leader of clan Tadayoshi, when I become Elder Elf.'

Gaibun looked away.

'You do not trust me. You think I shall betray you as I betrayed your father.'

Gaibun nodded wordlessly.

'Then you may choose not to help me. It is your decision. But I warn you, do not underestimate me. You saw my shelves while you waited. You wondered what was inside. It is knowledge. Scraps of information, secrets and gossip about every elf that matters in Dokuzen. Some owe me favours, some fear exposure. All can be used — understand?'

'I do, lord,' Gaibun said hoarsely.

'I tried, for many years, to impress on my son the importance of duty. The more times I told him about his duty, the less he seemed able to grasp it. But I think you know more about duty.'

'Yes, lord.'

'I have been preparing for a very long time. All is nearly ready. I can do this with you, or without you. Which will it be?'

'I am ready to serve my clan and my people. And you, lord.'

'Good. You will be well rewarded. You shall not regret this. You are the perfect elf. The sort of son I wish I'd had.'


Sendatsu came awake with a start, to find Rhiannon and Huw dressed and waiting for him.

'What time is it?' he asked, trying to rub the sleep out of his eyes.

'Just after dawn. We need to be on the road now!' Huw implored.

Sendatsu agreed, only for different reasons.

'I need a horse if we are to make better time,' he grunted as he pulled on his boots, smiling a little to find they had dried out from the fire while he slept.

'I'll get the headman. I need to speak to him anyway about Ward's plan, so he can warn the rest of the village,' Huw declared.

As son of the clan leader, Sendatsu had been used to riding only the best horses. The scrawny nag that two silver pieces bought was apparently the finest riding beast in the village. As far as Sendatsu was concerned, it was good only for making glue.

'Are you sure you have nothing else?' he asked.

'There's a donkey somewhere — but it smells bad,' the headman warned.

As Sendatsu was trying to hold his breath anyway, standing next to a huge dung heap that did not seem to bother the headman, he had no interest in seeing something the man thought stank worse. He saddled the horse, reflecting gloomily that he would add old horse to the smell he felt sure was following him around. How could these Velsh not be affected by it?

Meanwhile, Huw had even less luck with his warning.

'Why would the Forlish come here? We have nothing for them!'

'They want you to obey their king, to become part of the Forlish empire. You have to protect your village!'

'How?'

That simple question left Huw speechless and he had no more time to waste anyway.

'Just keep an eye out,' he insisted as they rode away.

He caught Sendatsu looking at him and shrugged. 'I don't know what else to do. I'm hoping my father will have the answers.'

Sendatsu nodded. That was what he was hoping as well.

They plodded on through the day, taking only short breaks, whenever Sendatsu's horse seemed to be struggling. If he could give it a full moon of rest and good food, it might just about be ready for a small child, he judged. Rhiannon was more than happy to exchange horses with him but, even so, he reckoned it would be doing well to make it through the day without collapsing.

Rhiannon still had a hundred questions and he had no ready excuse for stopping them either. Her open adoration was beginning to get on his nerves as well. No matter how hard he tried to tell her that Dokuzen was not like her childhood dreams, she did not listen. To her, Dokuzen was a place of wonder — and nothing he said would change that.

Her earlier shyness and tongue-tied excitement only showed occasionally; if he looked at her, or his leg brushed against hers, it was too much. As it was she felt giddy, heady with her dreams coming to life.

She was painting a picture in her mind of Dokuzen, of the way it looked, the way the elves lived there, everything. In desperation, Sendatsu turned to Huw, who had been riding silently, lost in his worry and fear for his father. The bard looked as though he was about to vomit and Sendatsu thought talking about something else might help him — as well as give Sendatsu some hints of what the bard's father knew.

'So what did your father say was the reason for the elves leaving?' Sendatsu asked.

'My father never really spoke about that. But I heard it was because the elves could not compete against the brutality and the aggression of the humans. There were so many of us, always so hungry for land, for conquest — the elves shut themselves away to protect themselves.'

Sendatsu sighed. 'But even a huge human army could not defeat an army of elves, with their magic and their bows.'

'The cost in lives — on both sides — would have been huge. The elves made the choice to protect both sides,' Huw explained. 'What were you told?'

'Exactly the same thing,' Sendatsu admitted. 'But now I don't believe it. Are you sure you have not heard anything about humans doing magic? Or worshipping Aroaril?'

'Humans can't do magic. It is the preserve of the elves,' Rhiannon said with a smile.

'But how do you know that?'

'Everyone knows that.' Rhiannon shrugged.

Sendatsu bit his lip. The bard's father better have something more useful than this.

As for Huw, the anxiety eating him up from the inside was too great to ignore. 'Tell me, is there any way you can discover whether my father is all right?'

'And how can I do that?' Sendatsu asked sarcastically.

'Well, magic of course!' Huw said, surprised.

Sendatsu groaned. 'You really don't understand magic, do you?'

'Surely you just use it to see across huge distances ...'

Sendatsu shook his head irritably. 'The way to see across long distances is to use birds and animals. I can command a bird to go and look for something — but unless I know exactly what that is, the bird won't tell us what we want to know. And I don't know how far Patcham is. I could lose control of the bird, or it could fly over the village and not be able to see your father, if your father is inside ... I am not very good at magic and it would probably go wrong.'

'No!' Rhiannon gasped. 'But magic is part of your life!'

'A very small part. There are elves who could do that but I am not one of them. Then the energy it would cost me might be too much for me to keep riding. Magic is sometimes more trouble than it is worth, especially if you have little talent for it.'

He looked around and saw them both gaping at him. It was obvious they did not believe his words and thought he had some ulterior motive for not using magic. It took him back to those Patcham women in the woods.

'Why can't you humans accept that not every elf is magical?'

Huw shook his head. 'No doubt you have your reasons. I thought you might give me some peace of mind.'

Sendatsu bit his tongue, restraining himself from giving Huw a piece of his mind instead.

Huw spurred his horse on ahead, leaving Sendatsu and Rhiannon to ride behind at the speed of the wheezing horse.

'Is magic really that difficult?' Rhiannon asked wistfully. As a child she had often pretended she could do magic. She sometimes imagined things moved or changed at her bidding but, of course, that was impossible and it must have been her imagination.

'Perhaps one day you will find out,' Sendatsu grunted.

All three were delighted when they finally came within sight of Patcham, late that afternoon.

The village still stood, and Huw breathed a heavy sigh of relief when he saw the familiar wood and thatch homes. But something seemed wrong. Normally there was plenty of bustle and activity, men and children out tending herds, working on fences or on homes. But the village seemed quieter, as if in mourning, and solemn black smoke hung over the huts.

No one came to meet them either — and that was the strangest thing. The arrival of three people on horses would normally be enough to have half the village — and all the children — rushing over to see what was going on. Instead, doors were dragged shut and women with fearful faces hurried children inside. Barking dogs followed the newcomers, although quickly learned to stay away from Sendatsu's bowstave, which he used to clear a path.

'What is going on?' Huw shouted in frustration, as yet more people hid.

'They have been attacked, and fear us,' Sendatsu said harshly.

'It is me! Huw! Son of Earwen! I have returned from my trip with friends!' Huw stood in his stirrups and yelled at the top of his bard-trained voice. 'There is nothing to fear!'

A few cautious faces peered out, and Huw waved at them.

Finally a man strode out, a long spear held nervously.

'Glyn! It is me, Huw!' Huw called, scrambling down from the horse and hurrying to meet him.

Glyn stared at him for a long moment but did not smile in return.

'Huw. Welcome back,' he said dully. 'Who is with you?'

'My friends, Rhiannon of Hamtun and Sendatsu of Dokuzen. They have journeyed with me to bring a warning about raiders sent from King Ward of Forland.'

'Then you are too late,' Glyn said.

'We know that,' Huw admitted. 'But still, why does everyone hide?'

'Someone said they recognised the other one — Sendatsu — from the raid.' Glyn jerked his head at Sendatsu.

'You are mistaken. I have never been here — although I freed the women taken from your village by the raiders. Raiders who I killed,' Sendatsu said harshly. 'And if you thought we were raiders, why do you cower in your homes? There're only three of us — there are dozens of men here!'

'How dare you!' Glyn thundered, and Sendatsu smiled coldly.

'Better,' he said. 'More of that might have saved lives when the raiders came.'

'Peace!' Huw cried. 'Glyn — please forgive my friend. We shall go to my father's house now but ...'

Huw trailed off as Glyn's face went grey and a terrible fear gripped his heart. He could barely breathe.

'Glyn, tell me,' he managed to croak.

'Your father met the raiders. He told them to leave — and they cut him down ...'

Huw reached out and grabbed Glyn's tunic.

'Tell me it's not so!' he whispered.

'I am sorry ...'

But Huw did not hear any more. His world went black and his mind fled.

# 10

*After I told the Magic-weavers my plan for the people to seal themselves away behind a magical barrier, until we were safe to walk these lands again, they swung into action. Initially I thought they were helping me, for they went out to the people and warned them of the humans, said they were hungry for land. They painted a picture of humans too numerous to count, all armed to the teeth, all wanting what we had. I did not see the harm in it — at first. Most of my people had only seen the Velsh. But the Magic-weavers travelled much further south, spent time among the other countries. For the likes of the Landish, Balians and Breconians, they were the only Elfarans they ever met. As they spread stories among my people, they also spread stories among the humans. They claimed we were elves, invented this nonsense about how we could see in the dark, hear like cats, were unbelievably strong yet wise and kind.*

*They were supposed to be helping the humans, preparing them for when we would leave. Instead they were persuading the humans we were elves, not Elfarans. Worse, they were also hunting out humans with magical abilities, judging how much resistance the humans could put up.*

*I did not hear about these stories until it was too late. I tried to tell the truth but the lies had spread too fast, taken root and grown beyond the original telling. The humans would not believe*

*we were ordinary, and even my own people were convinced we
were special.*

*The Magic-weavers had worked quietly. And while I laboured
fruitlessly to undo their lies, they began their plan to seize power
and rule all.*

*I discovered that before it was too late — but it was still the
beginning of the end for me.*

Huw awoke to find himself lying in his old bed, in his old
bedroom. Everything was the same, from the carefully repaired
furniture to the carvings on the stone walls he had done as a
child, to the scribbled sagas he had written on lambskins. For
a long moment he luxuriated in the familiarity and the thought
his father would come in, give him that crooked smile, sit on the
side of his bed and ask him what had happened since he had left,
say it was all right and tell him what to do.

Then he remembered and had to stop himself leaning over
the side of the bed and throwing up. With difficulty, he forced
himself to his feet and opened the door. The main room was
also exactly as he had left it; the thick beams holding up the
thatch overhead, the heavy wooden furniture and the fire pit in
the centre. Earwen's house was one of the rare stone buildings,
built by his father, Derwin, Huw's grandfather. It was one of
the oldest buildings in the village, for wooden huts lasted only
one generation. It was small and simple, a main central chamber
and two side rooms, one at either end. Rhiannon was seated at
the table and Sendatsu was poking at the fire, trying to get heat
under a pot.

They both sprang up when they saw him.

'We brought you here — Glyn showed us the way,' Sendatsu
said awkwardly.

'Huw, I am so sorry.' Rhiannon crossed to his side. 'I know
how you feel — we have both lost parents to Ward now ...'

That was too much for Huw and he burst into tears, all the
fear and guilt of the past few days washing out of him in an
unstoppable tide.

Rhiannon held him and he clung to her, unable to do more than sob. It felt as though he was being punished for his sins.

'It's all my fault!' was all he could get out.

'Not at all. You did not swing the sword. It was nothing to do with you,' Rhiannon told him.

'But I stayed too long in Cridianton! I should have returned earlier, I could have warned them!' he howled.

Rhiannon felt her own tears start then.

'Huw, I am so sorry,' she sobbed, meaning every word of it.

Sendatsu felt like crying also — from frustration and disappointment. This had been a wasted trip. Then he looked again at the two humans.

'It is no comfort, I know, but I killed all the raiders,' he said uncomfortably. 'It probably means nothing to you now but at least your father's killer paid for his crime.'

Huw and Rhiannon did not react for a long time but slowly, slowly, Huw got himself back under control. Rhiannon, however, was inconsolable. 'Huw, this is my fault.' She tried to wipe her eyes. 'It was me who made you stay. I was selfish, I wanted your company and your friendship. I did not want to lose those and so now your father is dead. You saved me from Ward, after he killed my father, and this is how I have repaid you ...'

Her legs seemed to have lost all their strength and Huw helped her into a chair. He took a seat himself before her words stopped him in his tracks. The memory of his lies to her, and the guilt he carried, rose out of his grief like a hill out of the morning mist.

'No, it is not your fault. I could have left when I wanted. I made my own decisions, I have to live with the consequences,' he said hoarsely.

The impact of those words struck him to his core. He had made several choices, any of which could have saved his father — or at least brought him back here, where he was sure he would have been able to save him. He had done everything his father had told him not to. He had sacrificed his beliefs, his father's teachings, his sense of worth, even his own Velshness, in order to try to keep his dream alive. Then, after all that, he had thrown it away for Rhiannon, and lost his father into the bargain. It was a bitter price to pay and he could not see a way forwards. His father was not there to help him.

Sendatsu watched the pair of humans sob and found it hard to control himself. He tried to busy himself by stirring the fire into life and setting water on to boil. He was feeling raw inside. What was his next move? Where should he go? The village of Patcham had no elven buildings, no hint that here rested a secret store of knowledge. Perhaps it was time to travel south, see what the other countries knew.

With a last, vicious thrust at the fire, Sendatsu turned back to Huw and Rhiannon. Their grief at the death of their parents was hard to watch … he was not sure whether he would hurl himself on his father's mercy or draw his sword when next he saw Jaken. And seeing them hold each other made him think of Mai and Cheijun. Would they be weeping now, thinking him dead? What had Jaken told them, what was Jaken doing with them, what poison was he dripping in their ears?

'The oatmeal is nearly ready,' he said, just so he could do something. He supposed he would stay the night and then leave in the morning.

Rhiannon wiped her face on her sleeve.

'We need to decide what to do next,' she declared, sniffing slightly. 'We have to make up for what happened here.'

Huw wiped his own face clear. 'How can we do that?' he demanded. 'We cannot turn back time. My father will still be dead …' His face crumpled at the thought and he had to fight hard to control himself enough to finish the sentence. 'There are some things you cannot repay.'

Rhiannon shook her head.

'We cannot bring back your father. But we can make his sacrifice mean something. We have the knowledge of Ward's raiders coming. We can stop Ward's plan, we can protect the rest of the Velsh.'

'And how do we do that?' Huw rubbed his face listlessly. The enormity of his grief was preventing him seeing anything ahead of him. Just a short while ago that future had seemed golden, now it was bleak and hollow.

Rhiannon leaned forwards and cupped Huw's face in her hands.

'We have an elf with us. He can help us. He will be the hero your people need.'

Together, they both turned to look at Sendatsu, who had been lost in his own thoughts and was a little slow to catch up.

'What?' Sendatsu asked.

'You can help the Velsh people! You can save them from Ward!' Huw said excitedly. 'All you have to do is go back to Dokuzen and ...'

'No!' Sendatsu almost screamed. It was what he wanted to do more than anything else in the world — and the one thing he could not do yet.

'But surely, if you tell your leaders what is happening out here — I mean, the Velsh have lived at peace with the elves for centuries but if Ward takes us over, it cannot be long before his gaze turns to Dokuzen. He will have conquered everything else by then,' Huw argued.

Sendatsu shook his head. This trip was going from bad to worse. It was time to give these humans some truth. There was no point in being nice to them, for Huw's father was dead and any promise of information gone with him.

'The elves will not help. Not if their lives depended on it. The wars and the suffering of humans mean nothing to them. Asking them to come to your aid would be a waste of breath,' he said forcefully. 'The Velsh will have to help themselves if they are to fight Ward.'

'That's it!' Rhiannon said.

'What is?' Huw and Sendatsu said.

'You can teach the Velsh to protect themselves!'

Sendatsu groaned. He had to nip this in the bud. 'It took me years to learn the bow; nearly as long to handle a sword properly. I don't have that time and you certainly don't have that time ...'

'But there must be things you can do. You know so much — you must be able to help them! They need a hero like you.'

Sendatsu stared at her, at the expression of blind trust, and tried to find the words to convince her this was not possible. Even if he had not had a desperate need to find magic and knowledge enough to allow him to return to Dokuzen, this was the last thing he would have done. Without warning, an image of his father flashed into his head, and the memory of yet another humiliation.

'You must show your leadership ability. It is important not just for the Council to see but also for our clan. They must see you as a strong successor to me,' Jaken declared.

'But Father ...' the ten-year-old Sendatsu protested.

'Don't disagree with me, boy! You must take command at training tomorrow, when the Council arrives to watch. Show you know more than the others.'

Sendatsu had not slept that night for worrying and he had vomited his breakfast back up again. He dearly wanted to say he was too sick to train but Jaken's penalty for that would be too severe.

Sweating, he had stepped forwards first when his sensei called for a volunteer to lead the demonstration. But, under the gaze of the Council — and his father's glare — the familiar moves slipped from his mind. Gaibun, standing just behind, tried to help, whispering instructions, but the laughter of the other children had drowned that out and he had finally let his sword fall to the ground, his face red, tears rolling down his cheeks and his humiliation complete. Worse, the adults did not rage at him, the way he knew his father would do later. Instead, they merely shook their heads and sighed.

The adult Sendatsu remembered the feeling and shuddered. He could not risk that again. Much better to walk away.

'You said the village could have held off a score of men, back when we rode in here,' Huw said. 'How would they have done it?'

Sendatsu paused. He wanted to get off the subject but this was fairly safe ground. 'Well, the village needs lookouts, to give them warning. Then the animal fence around the village needs to be made bigger, a ditch dug so they can only come at you from one direction, then you concentrate the men there ...'

'See, you do know how to help them,' Rhiannon said excitedly.

'Well, that might help one village. But there are dozens of them out there ...'

'So we travel around to the other villages!' Rhiannon was exultant at the thought.

'She's right,' Huw agreed. 'There is much we can do. And once people know that you are an elf, they will be inspired by more than just fear to help us.'

Sendatsu gaped at them. 'This cannot happen. I have important work to do. I must find out why the elves sealed themselves away. I cannot do that if I am spending all my time building walls.'

'Well, you won't be spending much time on wall-building. The villagers will do that,' Huw said persuasively.

'But what can they do? Most of them will be old, or young, or women ...' Sendatsu trailed off, aware he was arguing the wrong point.

'They all know how to work. Trust me on this,' Huw assured him. 'They will surprise you with just what they can do.'

Sendatsu stared at them, horrified.

'Look, you must be thinking of going back to Dokuzen, that you did not come here to get involved in petty human disputes,' Huw said, correctly judging Sendatsu's silence but not the reason for it.

'Please, just talk to the people, tell them what you told us. What harm can that do?'

Sendatsu was tempted to agree, their expressions were so hopeful, so pleading. Aroaril knew these humans needed help. But his hand brushed against his belt pouch, he felt the outline of the toys within and he shook his head.

'No,' he said firmly. 'I did not come here for this. I do not have time to waste. Huw, I am sorry about your father but I came here for the knowledge he had. Without him, there is no reason to stay. I shall leave in the morning to find it, whether here in Vales or further south. I wish I could help you but I cannot.'

Rhiannon looked at Huw, seeing her own devastation at this news on his face. But while he looked like he would simply accept

Sendatsu's words, slump into a chair and dissolve into tears, she was determined not to give up. Her mind raced. She had persuaded Huw to stay in Cridianton when he wanted to return. Obviously that had been a mistake — but perhaps she could use something similar to make up for it.

'You will never find the knowledge you seek without us,' she declared.

Sendatsu stopped in shock, while Huw also stared at her.

'What do you mean?'

'Vales is the only place that really knows the elves. After all, this is the place where they lived among the humans. The elves only visited the other countries and what knowledge we have of them is more legend and story than anything. I know more about the elves than every other Forlish. It is my dream to dance with the elves and my father did everything he could to help make that come true. He purchased every book with elven stories in them he could find — including those our armies brought back from the other countries. And do you think I was much help to you?'

Sendatsu coughed. 'Well, some of the stories you heard were a little strange ...'

'You have spent the last few days telling me none of them are true! If you travel south, you will wander forever and find nothing,' she said forcefully, delighting in the way everyone was hanging on her words. Usually people just stared at her face, or legs. This was so much better! Having been robbed of her voice for so many years, finding it was almost as inspiring as the applause after a performance.

Sendatsu shivered at the thought of wandering, unable to find what he needed to get home. 'Fine. I shall stay within Vales then ...'

'But Vales will be gone soon. And the knowledge you seek will be gone with it. Already King Ward's men have come here and snuffed out a candle of knowledge. Imagine what they are doing across Vales. Men and women like Huw's father, who hold the answers you seek, are being hunted down and slaughtered. You will wander Vales hopelessly.'

'Then I shall just have to race the Forlish to find them first,' Sendatsu said defiantly, hiding his fear she was right.

'But you don't know where the information is, nor where the Forlish will strike next. And you are an elf — you will just be swamped by the people. They won't listen to your questions because they want your magic. They will surround you and drown you in requests to save their sick children, or bless their elfbolts, or tell you what you already know. You could be in the right village but you will never learn their secrets.'

Sendatsu said nothing. He had seen that happen too many times already. He did not understand these Velsh — and they certainly did not understand him.

'You need a pair of guides to take you around. We can bring you to the right villages, protect you from the people and help you find what you seek. In return, all you have to do is help the people protect themselves.'

'But we can't spend days and weeks at the one village ...' Sendatsu warned feebly. Rhiannon's argument was hard to fight against, although the thought of these people relying on him, of taking on a leadership role, was terrifying. Almost as bad as wandering helplessly across Vales, unable to return to Mai and Cheijun. If they could really help him ...

Rhiannon hid her smile. His objections had changed and she knew she all but had him.

'We told you before. The Velsh can work like nothing you have seen. The villages will be protected in a day or two and you can move on to the next.'

'But only until I have the information I seek. Only until I get my answers,' Sendatsu insisted. Talk of days made him feel sick inside. He wanted to go home now — but his troubles would not end with simply walking back into Dokuzen. The fight would begin there.

'As soon as you get what you need, you can return to Dokuzen — although I would ask that you at least tell your leaders of our plight, and what they might face from the Forlish,' Huw added his voice to Rhiannon's.

Sendatsu was torn. Half of him said this was a mistake, he should leave now, see what he could find on his own. Yet what if this was the best way? Rhiannon's words about the other villages not helping him were hauntingly real.

'We'll give it a try,' he said finally. 'But I will need a bath in exchange.'

'This is like finding a maggot in a cauldron of rice,' Hanto grumbled.

His two companions said nothing. They had learned silence was the best way to deal with the angry Council Guard. Silence — and instant obedience. They had faced the uncertainty of travelling through the magical barrier without flinching, had walked into a tree without knowing they would walk out the other side intact — but travelling with Hanto was far more dangerous.

'We can't reveal our presence here and yet the humans would be the only ones who might know where that accursed Sendatsu has gone. What are we to do?'

His companions exchanged nervous glances. This was a question they could not ignore. Their clan leader, Jaken, had ordered them to do whatever Hanto said and warned them they must succeed or suffer an eternity of pain at his hands. The bigger of the two, Jin, cleared his throat.

'Perhaps if we go in at night, keep our hoods on …'

'And that won't look at all suspicious — three hooded figures in kimono and hakama, asking about an elf, when one hasn't been seen in these lands in centuries!' Hanto spat.

Taigo, the other, adjusted his swordbelt.

'One of us could dress up in some human clothes, keep the hood — or use one of the cowls we have seen some wear. Then he could go in and ask some questions, perhaps get some information …'

Hanto struck Jin on the shoulder with his open hand. 'There you are — that's the sort of thinking we want!'

'And we should go into the human villages that have old elven

buildings — that's what Sendatsu would have been looking for,'
Taigo continued.

Hanto nodded. 'It is the best plan. We shall find and kill
a suitable human tomorrow. Be sure not to mark the clothing.
We shall perhaps get them to take their clothes off before death.
Then, Taigo, you shall wear the human clothing and go into
another human village.'

'Why me?'

'Because I can't trust Jin here not to say something stupid. And
because a good dose of human lice and fleas will teach you not to
be too clever.'

Asami had trained with both Sendatsu and Gaibun over the years
and had beaten many of the male elves at their Test. She was also
Sumiko's favourite student and the most gifted with magic for
her age so, even without a weapon, she was confident of besting
whoever was out there.

'Who's there? Show yourself!' she challenged, taking up a
fighting stance in the middle of the path.

A chuckle answered her and she clenched her fists, prepared to
reach into the magic to defend herself.

'You're getting better,' Gaibun commented, as he pushed out of
the undergrowth.

Relief flooded through her. 'What are you doing here? Why
were you hiding in the bushes?'

'I arrived home from patrol not to a wife's welcome but to an
empty house. I knew where you would be, so came to find you.
And to warn you.'

'Warn me?'

Gaibun walked to her side, smiling a little as she stayed in a
fighting stance.

'I am not your enemy,' he said gently. 'Please — we do not
know who is around ...'

Asami relaxed reluctantly and embraced him awkwardly,
stiffening again as he kissed her cheek — and whispered in her ear.

'I have been to see Jaken.'

Asami pushed away, looked around wildly, her heart thumping, expecting to see armed Council Guards appear out of the undergrowth.

'I have not denounced you. I would not have bothered coming all the way out here to do that, I would have simply waited for you to come home. No need to worry. Yet.'

'Then tell me what is going on,' Asami insisted.

Gaibun glanced down the path and then placed his arm around her shoulders, beginning to walk back towards Dokuzen, ignoring the tension radiating from her. 'We are being betrayed on all sides,' he said softly, their heads close together. 'Sendatsu is but part of a larger plot. We think we are helping him but in fact we will be bringing him back to his doom.'

'Can you stop being dramatic and just tell me?' Asami demanded.

'Jaken wants Sendatsu back here, he has even sent out Hanto and two warriors to bring him back. But they do not want him dead, they want him to return. They will even help save him out there, if necessary. But his return will be used by Jaken to overthrow Daichi and take control of the Council. He will use Sendatsu as evidence of Magic-weaver treachery and then crush both the Magic-weavers and Daichi,' Gaibun said urgently.

Asami forced herself to keep putting one foot in front of the other.

'What will you get out of it?'

'He has offered to make me clan leader, when he becomes Elder Elf.'

'And why are you telling me this?'

'Because you have to trust me. We are the only two who actually want to return Sendatsu. Sumiko wants him back so she can use his knowledge to topple the Council and rule in its stead. Jaken wants to use him to rule Dokuzen, then the world.'

'But do you want to return Sendatsu? You would make a fine clan leader, it would be good for you. You might be able to set me aside and marry whomever you wanted ...'

Gaibun stopped abruptly and turned her to face him. She was shocked to find his eyes brimming.

'Listen to me,' he said hoarsely. 'I have made so many mistakes. It is time to wipe the slate clean and start again.'

'What do you mean? You are frightening me ...'

'Please. Before we were married, we were friends. But I have always loved you. I hid my feelings, for I knew you only had eyes for Sendatsu. When he was forced to marry another, I was heartbroken for you both but I went to see Jaken and asked for your hand. I wanted you to be happy and thought this was the only way when you couldn't have the one you truly loved. After all, there are many such marriages in our circle. Two elves brought together for reasons of politics manage to find friendship, even love together. I thought you might have learned to love me. Perhaps not the way you love Sendatsu but something close enough ...'

'Gaibun, you don't have to ...'

'Yes, I do!' he cried. 'I pushed too hard, I did not give you the space and time you needed. I see that now but I was a fool then.'

'I am sorry too. If you had only told me even a little of this from the start ...'

'As I said. I have been a fool and blundered from mistake to mistake. The worst was the night when I tried to force you to my bed and you used magic on me ...'

'I don't want to talk about that,' Asami interrupted, turning away. That memory still sickened her.

'Then I shall not,' he said, catching her arm and turning her gently back. She hesitated before looking at him, seeing the tension in every line of his face. 'But please believe me when I say I burn with shame at my actions — and the way I behaved afterwards. In my hurt and anger I took mistresses to make you jealous, an attempt to make you change, when it was I who needed to. I betrayed you and I betrayed myself. I told myself such a thing is common in Dokuzen but it does not excuse it.'

'Why are you telling me all this now? Why not years ago?'

Gaibun took a deep, shuddering breath. 'Things have gone too far,' he groaned. 'Whatever happens, whether Sendatsu returns or not, things will change and perhaps not for the better. I have to change as well. I know these are only empty words but I want to prove to you that I mean them. Let me help you get Sendatsu back.'

'Gaibun ...'

He held up his hand, his gaze burning even more than usual. 'Please, let me help. We need to work together on this. Jaken thinks he can buy my loyalty with the promise of clan leader. The arrogant bastard! The position should have been mine to inherit. My father had the best claim to lead clan Tadayoshi, only Jaken tricked him, outmanoeuvred him and won it for himself. Now Jaken offers it to me as a consolation prize! He orders my father about as if he was esemono and seeks to play me like a lyre! I know he is sitting there in his study, like some evil spider, pulling on his strings and laughing as we struggle to escape his snares. Using me to trick others would be hilarious to him. He used my father's honesty against him, now he seeks to twist that in me for his own ends.'

'Your father was always honourable. Jaken was too devious,' Asami agreed.

'My father raised me to always speak the truth, to stand by your word and your friends. Even if it costs you what you really desire. That was the way he lived his life and the way he wants me to live mine. But look what it brought him. He wants me to follow in his footsteps but I shall find my own path. I will tell Jaken what he expects to hear, what he wants to hear. But we shall work together to bring Sendatsu back. We have to stand as one, for Sumiko seeks to use us, as does Jaken. If we lie to them both, then we might be able to play them off against each other.'

Asami looked up at him and saw the way he could not look at her as he worked to keep himself under control. She held him close, leaned in and kissed him.

'Gaibun, you are a true friend ...'

'Don't call me that! Please! Can't you see this is hard enough already?'

Asami laid her hand on his arm, feeling the muscles jump.

'Then let me say thank you. We shall work together, and together we shall bring Sendatsu home.'

'And us? What will happen with us?'

'One problem at a time perhaps?' Asami said carefully.

Gaibun nodded jerkily. 'Let me show you I mean what I say. What do you need me to do?'

Asami sighed. 'Sumiko wants me to break into the tombs of the forefathers and steal as many books as possible.'

Gaibun grunted. 'You do know Jaken expects that very thing, and has placed a strong guard there?'

'Yes. But he will not expect the both of us.'

'True. But don't tell me here — we shall talk once we are home.' Gaibun's arm tightened around her and he began to walk back towards Dokuzen. Asami went with him. This time she was willing to let his arm stay around her but, by his side, she missed movement in the bushes, as a vine slowly sank back into the ground.

# 11

*The plan to pull all Elfarans back to Dokuzen, behind the magical barrier, was a delicate and careful operation, requiring plenty of planning and even more diplomacy. There were many of us who did not want to hide behind a barrier. They had lived and worked with the Velsh for many years and were confident their friends and neighbours would not harm them. They did not want to go back to Dokuzen, especially those who knew its meaning. My forefathers had named it — apparently it meant 'self-righteous' in the old tongue of Nippon. It was an apt name for such a complacent and self-obsessed nation as we were.*

*Getting all the Elfarans out of human lands required plenty of work from the Magic-weavers. They had to transport Border Patrol, as well as guards loyal to me, out to far-flung reaches of Vales, then bring everyone back.*

*That was the idea anyway.*

*But when most of the forces loyal to me were spread thin and wide across Vales, the Magic-weavers unleashed their plot to destroy me and rule Dokuzen.*

Getting the village together was a challenge for Huw and Rhiannon, and it was only the respect the villagers had for Huw's father, Earwen, that brought almost all of them out the next morning.

But they were hardly receptive to Huw's suggestions. He had to bellow to make himself heard and there was plenty of muttering at the sides and back.

'The raiders that came here and killed my father and five others are just the first of many! King Ward of Forland wants to add Vales to his kingdom. He wants to terrorise us, to raid and rape, burn and kill, until we beg to be put under his protection — and live under his cruel laws and pay his taxes.'

That had the expected effect — they were listening but it was out of fear, not hope.

'But we can stop him!'

Huw ignored the ironic laughter and shaking of heads.

'I have here a friend — Sendatsu of Dokuzen. Yes, Dokuzen, the elven homeland. Sendatsu is an elf and he can show us how to protect ourselves. He is the hero we have all hoped for! Not only will we be safe from the raiders but you and your children won't have to bend the knee to an evil king!'

Rhiannon applauded loudly but there were just a few scattered hand-claps from the doubtful villagers. Huw gestured to Sendatsu and the elf nervously stepped forwards. He had washed and cleaned his clothes in the chilly stream next to the village — but now he was drenched in nervous sweat.

He surveyed the sea of villagers staring at him; most of them looked unfriendly, a handful were bored and quite a few were either talking to their partners or trying to chase unruly children.

'Er,' Sendatsu tried to begin, then had to clear his throat. Panic was gripping him.

'First thing you need to do is build a palisade around the village ...' he began.

'What's that?' someone called.

'A big fence, you clod!' another yelled back.

'And how will we build it? Who will pay for it? Who will work our fields if we work on it? We talked about it and nothing got done!' Glyn stepped out of the crowd to address the people.

'You have to work together,' Sendatsu tried.

'Why should we listen to an elf? What do they care about us?' Glyn shouted.

'Why doesn't he do it with magic?' a man up the back offered, to general enthusiasm.

'No, we must do this ourselves — not with magic!' Huw shouted.

'Well, why should we listen to someone who spends all their time making up poems about autumn leaves then?' Glyn warmed to the subject.

'Because I was the one who killed the raiders who struck here, and because I was the one who saved the women they took with them!' Sendatsu roared back, anger swamping his doubt and fear.

He glared out across the village and suddenly realised he had their full attention.

'Come forwards, the women I rescued!' he barked. 'Delia, Maegen and her friends!'

There was some shuffling among the crowd and then four women pushed forwards, or were urged forwards, all of them holding young children either in their arms or by the hand, until they were in a line. All four were wearing black hoods and three of their children were snivelling at the fuss being made. Sendatsu could see they were looking at him without any warmth and he hoped they were not going to start complaining again.

'Look at them! They are your friends and relatives and they are only here because I took them from the bastards who attacked you. I killed every last man that rode into your village. Just one warrior. Me!' Sendatsu found himself boasting.

'Only half,' Delia called.

Sendatsu saw her staring coldly at him.

'Half?' he asked.

'Half of them rode off somewhere. You only killed half.'

Sendatsu was thrown for a moment, while Huw felt a surge of anger. Half of them still lived? Was his father's killer among them?

'I killed half of them by myself.' Sendatsu recovered himself. 'While the rest of you did nothing.'

'And then after you killed them? What do you say about then?' Delia challenged.

Sendatsu had taken enough of this. Either they would listen to him, or not.

'I am sorry you don't understand the way magic works. But I swear to you now that I do not have the power to bring back the dead. No elf does! But these women are alive because of me. They are back with their children because of me. Now, if anyone here thinks they could have done that, let them step forwards.'

He looked wildly around, but could find not one. Even Glyn was silent, standing just behind the widows in black.

'Our time is wasting! Now, you need to work on the wall — unless you know something about magic, Aroaril or why the elves left ...'

Huw stepped in front of him. 'Maybe leave that until they are working. Best not to confuse people,' he suggested, then turned back to the village.

'Those raiders, or ones like it, will be back. We have to make our village safe. We cannot live in fear. We have an elf to help us, something no other village has. Are we going to listen to him, get his help and ensure the children can grow up without losing any more fathers?' he said passionately, looking around at the many familiar faces.

While many of them had mocked Huw behind his back — some even to his face — they had all respected Earwen and were all mourning the loss of friends and family in the last attack.

'Aye, we are,' Glyn spoke for the village's mood.

'Then we need to begin right away. There is no time to lose,' Huw called.

Slowly, but not reluctantly, the villagers began organising themselves.

'You were so inspiring,' Rhiannon whispered to Sendatsu. 'We all trust in you!'

Sendatsu had been looking around at the young faces of the village children, imagining he saw his own two among them; Huw's line about children growing up without their father had struck deep. Watching the Velsh playing with their children made him ache. He had to tell himself not to get too attached to these humans, nor forget why he was here. It was not to save the Velsh, it was to save himself.

'Where is the young bard, Hugh?' Hector demanded.

The village headman at Browns Brook looked baffled. 'I do not know who you mean,' he protested.

'Don't lie to me! If you are hiding him, I shall personally have the skin off your back — and take what remains to King Ward!' Hector snarled.

His journey south to Browns Brook had been swift, fuelled by his anger and need for vengeance. How could the stupid bitch have been so foolish? Hadn't he told her often enough men were not to be trusted, they only wanted one thing from her? She had nearly ruined everything and he knew he would have to work extra hard with her on the return journey, if he was to win back favour with the king.

He had destroyed his first chance at power and glory. After winning the king's coin, he had been sure fame and fortune were his. But it had gone to his head and he had used his position of favour to entertain the court ladies, in more ways than one. He had carved a swath through them, wooing, bedding and then moving on, leaving behind broken hearts. It had all gone to plan until he seduced the younger daughter of a minor noble, who happened to be one of Ward's former war captains. He had been about to leave when the little cow had got herself pregnant and ruined everything. Her father gave him a choice — marry his daughter and leave the king's service to live with her in a small village, where the family's shame could be hidden, or face him over blades. The noble might have been nearly forty but Hector knew he stood no chance of beating the ex-warrior. He had to take the first option, as well as a large bag of gold to ensure they could at least live comfortably. The only concession he won was the promise he could return the following year.

Only he had caught that infection, which ruined his voice and killed his new wife, although leaving the baby girl alive. So there he was, with plenty of gold to live on thanks to his dead wife's family, but no voice and no future. Until he had seen the possibilities in the little girl, and vowed to restore his fortune ...

Now, thanks to the idiot girl and the bard, it was all in jeopardy. He could not wait to be revenged upon the little bastard. He found himself dreaming up ever-more fanciful ways of making him scream on the long journey back to Cridianton. And it would be a long journey, for their horses were exhausted. But it would give the king's anger time to cool down, and Hector more time to work his revenge on Hugh. If he could just find the man!

'I am not lying,' the headman insisted. 'There has been nobody called Hugh in this village for two generations!'

'Then he must have used a false name. A young bard who went to Cridianton to perform for the king. You must know him.'

The headman looked into Hector's burning eyes and shuddered. 'Only one person from Browns Brook went to Cridianton — a juggler called Bertwald, who returned after being flogged for insulting the king with his lack of talent.'

'Well, where is he?' Hector demanded.

Bertwald was found, although he was less than keen to come and talk to armed guards wearing the king's livery.

'Tell me the truth, or the last flogging you had will seem like a hug from your sweetheart,' Hector threatened.

'What do you want to know?'

'There was a bard at the king's auditions, a man named Hugh, who claimed he was from Browns Brook. Did you know him?'

He could see the fear on Bertwald's face. 'There were no bards from the village — I was the only one who went there — it is the truth, sir, I beg you!'

Hector signalled to his guards.

'Give him twenty lashes, see if that helps his memory,' he ordered.

'Wait! I'm telling the truth!' Bertwald wailed.

'Then tell me more! A man does not just pluck a name out of the air — Browns Brook is not so well known that its fame would reach the capital! Did you speak with anyone, did you see any you recognised from other villages?'

Suddenly Bertwald was nodding. 'Hugh, you say?'

'Aye. What do you know?'

'I met a Velshman on the day before the auditions, who said his name was Hugh, although I think they say it differently — they can't speak their words properly and ...'

'A Velshman? What did he look like?' Hector snapped.

'Average height, dark hair, no beard like you'd normally see on the Velsh, lyre over the shoulder ...'

Hector sighed. 'How did you meet him?'

'He talked to me, tried to give me advice about performing to the crowd. It sounded good but then he said he was Velsh so I told him to rut off and not come near me again. Pity, maybe if I'd done what he said, then the king wouldn't have flogged me ...'

Hector waved the fool to silence. He needed to think. Could they be the same person? Could this foul Velshman have come south, met this idiot and pretended to be from an honest Forlish village to disguise his upbringing? That would be evidence of intelligence far beyond what he expected from those northern barbarians. Telling Ward the object of his desire was probably being defiled by a pack of hairy Velshmen was a sure way to disgrace — or worse. He had to get Rhiannon back and capture Hugh and have the king think the couple had been hiding out in some remote part of Forland. That was if this story was true ... Hector struggled to come to a decision. Chasing all the way into Vales would take time, and they might just run into some of the king's soldiers, sent to bring those lawless lands under Forlish control. Things could get confusing and nasty. Luckily he had the king's seal to help ease the way. But what if this was a wild goose chase?

'Give this fool twenty lashes and see if his story remains the same,' Hector said harshly, to give himself time to think. 'While you are at it, let the headman watch and tell him he is next unless his memory improves.'

Patcham was a swarm of activity. It had begun well enough. Sendatsu supplied the orders and Huw organised the people to make it happen. Six boys, all still a few years from manhood, were sent out on ponies to keep watch while each night, men with dogs patrolled the village. Half the men were felling and splitting trees; they had plenty of wood from the old animal fence but that needed to be pulled apart and fitted together as something far bigger. The rest of the men and all the women and children were digging around the village, making a deep ditch. Some were shown where to dig small holes outside of that, which could trap a horse's hoof.

'This is to stop them riding horses right up to the palisade,' Sendatsu had explained. 'They will have to approach on foot or, if they want to use the horses, attack the gate.'

A plan to protect the village was simple enough. He had made something similar when on patrol near the border. A strong wooden fence and a ditch would stop raiders. It would not turn back a real army but, from what Huw said and his own experience had taught him, these Forlish had only light weapons.

But the pace of the work chafed. He made Huw ask around the villagers, to see if they had talked with Earwen about elven legends or similar — with no luck. Earwen had spent his time with Huw — and almost all the village thought Huw was a lazy wastrel who would ruin his father's land. With nothing to help him here, he wanted to move on to the next village — except Huw and Rhiannon persuaded him he needed to make sure his ideas worked at one village before taking them around to all the others.

That the plan might not work was another fear. His father had ridiculed his ideas as a matter of course and although Jaken was Aroaril-knew-how-far away, his presence still lingered. If the villagers found they had put their faith in someone as useless as his father had claimed he was ... fear made him quick to anger, while frustration left his temper short.

It was not helped by the villagers. The women had not been pleased to be told that all but a few must leave their children, the cooking and their homes to dig a ditch. And the men had been angry they could not tend to their livestock and fields while they either split logs or dug instead.

'It is only for a few days,' Huw tried to explain. 'Each man can take a couple of turns of the hourglass each day to feed animals or water crops. But we need everyone to work on this. The faster it is done, the safer the village will be and the sooner we can get back to normal life.'

'I thought the elf was going to protect us,' Glyn summed up the protest. 'Why do we have to dig holes and fell trees? Why can't he just do it by magic?'

'Because it doesn't work like that! You have to do things for yourself. There is a reason humans can't do magic ...' Huw tried to explain.

'But he can just wave his hands and have it done ...'

'How do we learn how to protect ourselves then? It will all depend on the elf — and what if something happens to him, or the magic?' Huw said reasonably. 'Besides, magic does not work like that. Sendatsu explained it to us. It would take one Magic-weaver far longer to build a stockade around the village by magic than it would take the whole village to do it by hand ...'

'But it would be so much easier for us!'

'How stupid are you?' Sendatsu snarled, before Huw could say anything. 'I thought you were smarter than the sheep you herd, but perhaps I was wrong.'

'Listen here, you pointy-eared bastard ...' Glyn stormed forwards. He was nearly a head taller than Sendatsu and his arms and shoulders were corded with muscle after a life of working on the land.

But the elf was both stronger and quicker. His right hand was held out, fingers stiffened and pointing like a spear, and he drove that into Glyn's stomach. As the man folded over he chopped down once with his left and Glyn toppled over, moaning.

'Now, anyone else who is too stupid to understand why we

can't use magic, step forwards and we can discuss it now. Or should I try to explain what I'm doing to the sheep and have them tell you?'

Everyone looked at him, looked at the groaning Glyn, rolling on the ground holding his stomach, and got back to work.

Huw and Rhiannon exchanged looks and gently eased Sendatsu away from where a group of women and children were digging feverishly under his angry gaze.

'Sendatsu, we really appreciate what you are doing, but perhaps there is no need to be quite so harsh on the people,' Huw suggested gently.

'What do you mean?' Sendatsu felt much better after hitting Glyn.

'They are afraid. The attack has scared them. They are willing to listen, but they need to be led, not pushed,' Rhiannon agreed.

'But this is not like our agreement. We said it would only be a day or two — this is going to take a quarter-moon at least — and we agreed there was to be no more ridiculous talk of magic,' Sendatsu snapped.

'We are making great progress. It's just they are frightened. They will follow you happily if they believe in where they are going but they will dig their heels in if they are unsure,' Huw tried to explain.

Sendatsu grunted. 'Well, they had better hurry up. We need to move on to the next village. Who knows when the Forlish will strike.'

He stamped away to yell at the men splitting logs. That was a much easier target for his frustration.

'We need to stay close to him,' Rhiannon stated. 'I always thought the elves never got angry, never displayed emotion?'

'This one does,' Huw said. 'I don't think he is like those elves we sang about. He's not the hero I expected.'

'No, he is better!' Rhiannon sighed, looking devotedly over at Sendatsu.

Huw held back angry words and instead shyly reached out and touched her arm. 'Thank you for this. Sendatsu may be making it happen but it is your idea. You were the one to suggest this and the one to persuade him to help.'

Rhiannon smiled back. 'We are both making it happen. I am just pleased you still want to talk to me, after ...' She slowed to a halt and bit her lip, thinking again about how she had stopped Huw from leaving Cridianton.

Huw squeezed her hand. 'Of course I still want to speak to you!' His own guilt prevented him from saying more. 'Besides, you are the one with the good ideas ...'

Rhiannon squeezed back. 'Thank you. And here is one more, although I don't know how good it is. Perhaps we should get Sendatsu to help with the work, rather than just supervising? That way they can see him working with them — it will bring him closer to the people ...'

'Brilliant!' Huw exclaimed. 'We'd better hurry — before he fights someone else. One more thing, though — just be careful around him.'

'What do you mean?' she bristled.

'He has a secret — something he carries around in his pouch. I think it might be magical or something ...'

'That is silly. We can trust him,' Rhiannon insisted. 'Come on!'

Huw said no more, except to add his voice to hers when she told Sendatsu her idea. Sendatsu was a little reluctant but gave in under gentle persuasion from Rhiannon.

'It will make everything go faster,' she said enticingly.

He could not argue against that. 'But you can work too,' he told Huw.

'I don't have the skills!'

'Anyone can dig,' Rhiannon pointed out.

So Huw found himself sucking in his stomach and stripped to the waist, digging the ditch. He had traditionally avoided much of the heavy work around the farm, shielded by his father — and of course the past few moons had seen him relax and indulge himself in the castle of King Ward. The wooden spade he was using was hardly the best tool for the job, but the soil was rich and soft, and it was easy enough to heave out of the ditch and up onto the growing bank, which would become the first line of defence. As the bank grew, men came along and made a channel in the middle, readying it for the logs. It soon grew more difficult with every spadeful but he found the menial work strangely comforting. His grief at the loss of his father was still red-raw but the feeling of working to protect the village, as part of a community, seemed to help. Secretly, it also felt like a penance for his failure to return home quick enough. Either way, he almost rejoiced in what he was putting himself through.

Of course, his hands were soon blistering, while his back, legs and shoulders were burning from the unaccustomed effort. But the women and children around him were not complaining, nor were they slacking off. Huw could not stop, so he just wiped the sweat away from his face, gripped the rough handle of the spade and kept going.

He knew all the women by sight and name, and most of the children as well, and it was easy to talk to them about what they were doing, about how this would protect them.

'So, did you really perform at the court of King Ward?' a woman called.

'That I did,' Huw admitted, wiping away the sweat and glad of the chance for a momentary break. 'I can show you the gold coin he gave me, stamped with his head, when he asked me to stay for a year.'

They absorbed that for a little while.

'Will you give us a song then, to keep us going?' another asked.

Huw shovelled out another spadeful.

'Join in if you remember this one,' he suggested, then began a traditional Velsh song about a farmer waiting for the spring rains.

His rich voice rolled down the trench, men, women and children pausing in their work to listen and turn and watch. After a few moments, several women began to join in, followed by the men. Huw increased his volume slightly, leading the tune, and finding himself smiling, just a little, as he did so.

Sendatsu watched the men working on the trees with grudging approval. They had sped up appreciably. He had already decided the palisade did not need to be enormous. Ten feet, including the earth foundation they were digging out now, would be plenty. These raiders had no more equipment than their swords and horses, and their best weapon was the fear they spread. They did not have the time or the weapons to try to smash through a wall, even one as low as the palisade Sendatsu was planning. That meant trees could be split into quarters, then sawn down further, so they were only cutting down as many as they needed. He took his turn with the axe, shearing off the smaller branches, which were being collected for firewood by young boys — as well as Rhiannon — and also worked on the saw. He stripped his tunic off to keep it clean and caught sight of her staring at him. He hurriedly turned back to the saw, pretending he hadn't noticed her, and tried to lose himself in the physical exertion. He had not used a saw before but refused to let any discomfort show. It was a habit he had learned — the hard way — from his father's lessons.

Although he did not want to be distracted by feeling anything for these humans, it was hard not to have some kinship with the man on the other end of the saw as they sweated together. Sendatsu even found himself offering a nod of approval to the man, before moving back to the axe. He heard Huw singing and turned to watch for a moment, seeing the way the people seemed to move to the rhythm of the song, spades and picks rising and falling together. Rhiannon began singing as well, then the men joined in. Sendatsu looked at them, noticing how they took strength from the act of singing and working together. It was interesting to watch. He had seen the esemono at work before — and it had been nothing like this. The humans were working better than elves. When he had first read the other Sendatsu's words he had thought nothing could be worse than elves becoming like humans. Now he was not so sure.

# 12



*One of the most shameful things that went on was the way the worship of Aroaril was taken away from the other tribes of humans, the Velsh, Forlish and so forth. For many years they had worshipped the same God as we had — many of us had even shared a church. But, to those of my people who looked down on the humans, seeing them perform magic was, as I was later to learn, an 'abomination'. It also ruined their stories of so-called elven superiority. How could you argue one group was better when they were both equal before the same God? They fought this two ways. Human priests and priestesses of Aroaril were killed, sometimes horribly — and elves always rushed in to explain to the rest of the village that this terrible tragedy was because humans were not meant to worship Aroaril. In fact, they claimed, Aroaril was offended by humans worshipping Him and, if they continued, even worse things would happen. Instead, humans could only pray to the sun — ceremonies at Midsummer and Midwinter were the best.*

*It was monstrous — but the tactics worked.*

'You have worked fairly quickly,' Sendatsu said grudgingly, as they sat around the dining table that night. There was a mutton stew that had been cooked for the whole village and he was hungry enough to force it down. 'I'd like things to be moving faster, of course.'

'The music helped,' Rhiannon added. It had really helped her. She had been caught up in her idea to help the people but, once she was out there, she had been beset with worries. She was Forlish, the attackers were Forlish — would the Velsh hate her? She had also been a little afraid of them. Her father had said they were all hairy barbarians with no culture. But while none had spoken to her at first, the singing had changed everything. They had heard her voice, sung along with her and the ice was broken. By the end of the day she was chatting with everyone, and some of the women had even offered to braid her hair. 'It really inspired people. I loved hearing it as well,' she told Huw.

Huw grinned as he cradled his spoon between blistered hands. 'I'm glad. Luckily my voice was stronger than my back and arms — by the end of the day I was out on my feet. Even a spoonful of stew is almost too much for me to lift!'

Sendatsu chewed a mouthful down and pondered the way the two humans seemed to have recovered their spirits. Yesterday they had been in tears, barely able to function, but now they had a purpose and it had given them energy. Watching the whole village work together and take strength from each other had also been something of a revelation. He was sure the Elven Council would have been shocked to its core to witness it. He had walked around the village and been amazed by what he had found.

His little tour began at the far end of the village. There, downwind from everyone else — unless a rare southerly blew — the tanner was working away, scraping hair and fat and flesh off a hide stretched tight. Between the smell of his waste and the chicken dung he rubbed into the leather to make it tanned and smooth, he needed to be far away from everyone else.

Sendatsu had hurried away from there but stopped at the fields to watch the men work, which was a fascinating sight in itself. Sendatsu had never seen the rice paddies but had imagined they must be huge fields, as far as the eye could see. The humans did not farm like this. Instead, the village shared one huge area, dividing it up into strips for each family, each strip bounded by a slim grass section to allow access to all sides. Different crops sat side by side and dozens of boys covered the long strips — weeding, watering, hoeing, planting — while the men worked on the palisade.

The women, when not digging or looking after the children or cooking, gathered nuts and berries, or made clothes. There were many vats of berries and plants bubbling away, making a smell nearly as bad as the tanner but also staining the woollen clothes they all wore. And all the females, right down to the little girls, spun wool wherever they went.

Everyone seemed to be working all the time, from dawn to dusk, and he found himself comparing that to life back in Dokuzen.

There the lower classes slaved just as hard, but the middle classes had a much easier life and the upper classes worked not at all. And things were only done on the orders of the Council. Here, people did what was needed, when it was needed, without thought of political advantage or whether it would demean their family or clan to do so. He had thought life in Dokuzen was perfect and, while it had many advantages over here, he had to admit there were still things the humans did better ...

'What are you thinking?' Rhiannon asked.

'Nothing.' He shrugged. 'Are you sure there is nothing I can use as a bath?'

'There is only the stream,' Huw pointed out.

Sendatsu grunted. Of all the material things of Dokuzen, clean clothes and a hot bath were the ones he longed for. Perhaps he could get the wall-builders to make something up for him ...

'Once the palisade goes up — what then?' Huw asked, breaking Sendatsu's train of thought.

'How do you mean?' Sendatsu swallowed the mutton and scooped up another spoonful. His hunger had overcome his distaste for animal flesh. It was livened with salt and mint and quite tasty, although he longed for some greenery and especially some rice.

'Well, it will make them stop and think. But if they attack anyway, how do we stop them?'

Sendatsu sighed. 'You need weapons. And we do not have the time to teach these people ...'

'Not to use a sword or a bow. But there must be other weapons, easy to use and able to drive back these raiders,' Rhiannon suggested.

Sendatsu was about to tell them there was nothing, but the expectant expression on Rhiannon's face stopped him. He thought hard, and was pleasantly surprised to come up with an idea.

'There is one thing — have you heard of a crossbow?'

'Of course. But they are too expensive — there is no way we could get enough, even if the Forlish would sell them to us,' Huw grunted. 'And they take so long to reload that even a dozen of them would not be enough ...'

'Yes, but there is a different type of crossbow. The problem is, I only saw it a few times, in the tombs of my forefathers, where rest many things that we brought with us when we left the dragons and sailed to this continent ...'

'Do dragons still live at Dokuzen?' Rhiannon interrupted excitedly.

'My people once served the dragons. Centuries ago. But none have been seen in Dokuzen.' Sendatsu shrugged.

'How I would love to see one,' Rhiannon sighed. 'I used to dream of dragons when I was a girl. They would take me for a flight and tell me I could do magic ...'

'The new crossbow?' Huw interrupted.

'It is a repeating crossbow. Instead of needing to be wound up after every shot, it can loose a dozen bolts rapidly, one after another. The drawback is range — it has little power and would be useless beyond about twenty yards. But if you were able to make enough of them, they would give you a chance to turn back the raiders.' Sendatsu smiled at Rhiannon. 'Sadly, I doubt you have the ability to build such a thing.'

'Nonsense!' Huw said. 'We have many men who are brilliant with their hands. Give us the design and we shall build it.'

Sendatsu paused. This was the flaw. He had only seen the thing a few times and, while he had been fascinated with it as a boy, he had no idea how it would work. But he had no intention of admitting that. Instead he would draw it from memory and then blame it on the incompetence of the craftsmen if it did not work. After all, how could they possibly replicate something of the elves? That way it could not be his fault.

'Get me some paper and ink, and I shall sketch it out,' he declared.

Although Rhiannon watched, entranced, he was horribly aware a memory was a difficult thing to get down on paper — or scraped, chalked lambskin. He remembered it looked roughly like a normal crossbow, but built in two parts. The top half could be moved backwards and forwards by a wooden lever, with the backward motion cocking the weapon, as well as dropping a new bolt into the firing slit from a box at the top. Then the forward motion propelled the bolt out. He drew confidently enough, although how anyone was going to make his drawings a reality he had no idea. But he showed no sign as he handed them over to Rhiannon and Huw.

'Give that to your best men and see what they can do. But don't let them waste too much time on it. After all, the design is elven, so it is far beyond what they are used to,' he suggested, which he thought would help disguise any flaws in his drawings and things he might have forgotten.

'We might surprise you yet,' Huw said stoutly. He needed the elf if he was going to avenge his father's death and stop the Forlish — but he did not have to like him. The fact Rhiannon was both entranced by the thought of seeing Dokuzen and by Sendatsu himself had hardly anything to do with it.

Asami welcomed her parents into her main reception room with a fixed smile, ensured they had both tea and food, then sat carefully, wondering what their purpose was. Of course she could not come out and say such a thing. She had to make polite conversation and wait for them to come to the point. Given her father was known as Jaken's right hand, she had no doubt he was here on the orders of their clan leader.

'I was at the marketplace yesterday and I have never heard the like,' her mother said. 'Rumours and gossip fly around like birds at sunset. Sendatsu's actions have created more of a stir than anything I have ever seen or heard before.'

'Well, you can hardly blame them. Nobody has used swords and magic on Council Guards before. Why, it must be fifty years since someone even dared to fight them,' her father added.

'I look at that and thank Aroaril you never married him,' her mother sniffed. 'I mean, first there was the business with his wife and children — and now this!'

'Not to mention the way he has lived his life for the past few years. He has a position almost every other elf in Dokuzen would give their right arm for — and he did nothing with it! Everyone expected Jaken's son to be a leader in our society. Instead he sat at home and played with the children,' her father sniffed.

Asami bit her tongue, for she had heard it all before — many times. In the past, when they thought she might marry the clan leader's son, they could not praise him enough. As soon as Jaken had blocked their union, their opinion changed overnight.

Her mind flashed back to those days and when she had first met Sendatsu, at his fifth birthday party. Her parents had ordered her to be nice to Jaken's son, for he would be clan leader one day, and she had been determined not to have anything to do with him. Rather than talk with him, she would sit in the corner and say nothing. Young elves were running around wildly, wrestling with each other and shouting. She had found a peaceful corner of the garden, only for a boy to come and sit next to her. They had watched the others for a while, then begun to talk. He showed her some of the nearby flowers and where to get a plate of food.

'I am so glad you were here,' Asami had confessed as they ate their treats together. 'I thought this was going to be a nightmare. I thought all of Sendatsu's friends would be like that,' and she gestured to where a handful of boys were running into each other with bloodcurdling shouts. 'He's probably the one with the loudest voice!'

'I thought the same thing,' her new friend confessed.

They chuckled at the way the others were behaving and then shared the last honey cake together.

Asami had sat there in warm silence for a few moments more, then a tall, beautiful woman strode into the garden.

'Sendatsu! The Elder Elf is here! You must come and greet him now!' she ordered, her voice cutting through the boisterous noise.

Asami looked around, waiting to see which of the buffoons answered the call. Then her new friend sighed and stood.

'I have to do what Mother wants, or Father will be furious,' he said. 'Do you want to come and meet the Elder Elf too?'

He held out his hand. Shock and embarrassment made Asami hesitate for just a moment, then she took it. She had never wanted to let go since. But, of course, life was never that easy. Her father was still talking and she forced herself to listen. 'I do hope you plan to have nothing more to do with him. After all, what was it all about? Some ridiculous claim that the elves may not be born with magic and the barrier is fading!'

'But the barrier is dying, otherwise I would not have been able to send Sendatsu through it.'

'Well, you can repair it then,' her mother said fondly. 'Just look at you — you are proof of the power of the magic within the elven people ...'

That was too much for Asami. 'How many people do you know who use magic in their everyday lives?' she snapped.

'Well, you can hardly blame them. It is hard work and tiring. Doing something yourself, or having a servant do it for you, is far easier,' her mother pointed out.

'But if magic is our gift, if it is as natural to an elf as breathing, why do you not use it?' she demanded.

'Do not use that tone of voice on me,' her father warned.

'We know what you are saying, dear,' her mother said defensively. 'And you are right. Too many people pass their Test and then set it aside. But you have to understand, when you work for a living, when you have children to feed and look after, you do not have the time to devote to study. And when you are already tired, you do not have the energy to use on magic ...'

'Excuses. The truth is, fewer and fewer of us have true magic power, other than the ability to perform a few tricks,' Asami interrupted.

'This conversation is ridiculous. And we shall talk of it no more,' her father snapped.

Asami bowed her head. Her frustration was a hard thing to control. She loved her parents but she wanted a different path for herself. Blindly obeying what her clan leader and the Council told her to do just felt wrong. And once she'd seen what her clan leader and sensei were really like, and realised they did not deserve her full respect, it was hard to keep her tongue still.

'How is Gaibun?' her mother asked. 'Are there grandchildren on the way?'

'Not just yet. I need to concentrate on my studies with sensei Sumiko,' Asami said carefully, preparing for another conversation on another familiar topic. The Festival of Summer was less than a moon away. More importantly, in a couple of days' time she could reopen the gateway and see if Sendatsu was there. Until then, she just had to bite her tongue.

Work went on in the village, with the pace hardly slowing. Huw and Rhiannon led the people in song while Sendatsu directed their efforts. The cut trees were lashed together in panels, dragged across by horses and raised with poles and ropes, then the soft earth packed around them, rammed down hard until they were fixed solid. Bracers were propped against them inside the village perimeter, while children and women dug more holes outside — horse pits, simple holes only a foot deep and no wider than the span of two hands. Once one section of the palisade was complete, they went to work until the ground outside was so full of holes that it resembled a cheesecloth. But, as Sendatsu said, any horse that put its hoof into a hole would end up with a broken leg, both breaking up a charge and slowing it down.

For the gate, two trunks were left whole, then had spikes of wood hammered into one face, so that side resembled a hedgehog, then thick rounds attached to the whole, acting as wheels, so it could be dragged across the gate opening.

Although he was chafing at every day they spent there, Sendatsu was impressed at the way the villagers worked, each day still cheerful and willing to sing. The palisade grew swiftly and he had to admit no elf could have worked harder, nor faster — although they would have worked with stone, not wood.

Of course, they had plenty of motivation. It was a rare morning when smoke did not stain the sky in one direction or another, the signal that another village had been raided. The villagers worked harder than ever on those days.

Sendatsu had washed again in the stream — but it was not the same. However, several women from the village saw him trying to clean mud off his tunic and, when he returned to work looking much the same, offered him fresh clothes. He mumbled his thanks as he took them, relieved he could at least wear something clean, even if he did not feel clean.

Then came the day — which he was half dreading — when the village's best carpenters came to see him, Huw and Rhiannon.

'It has taken us longer than we thought,' their leader, Kelyn, admitted.

Sendatsu was about to launch into his prepared speech about the difficulties of humans replicating something an elf had invented when Kelyn produced a crossbow with a grin.

'But we have one that works — watch!'

Kelyn dropped a handful of simple wooden bolts, with no proper head or crossvanes on them, into the little box hopper, then pointed it at the palisade, about ten yards away. Holding it with his left hand, he worked the handle with his right hand, back and forth, each cycle sending another bolt whistling out, where they bounced off the wood, although one or two stuck into the rough-sawn trunks.

Sendatsu took the crossbow from Kelyn and inspected it, struggling to hide his awe as the humans applauded each other. How had that man managed to come up with this from his rough drawings?

It looked different from the one back at the tombs of his forefathers, the wood was darker, but it worked fine. Not that he had seen the other one work but he could not imagine it doing much better than this. The bow itself was a series of pieces of wood, laminated and secured together, while the string was the rolled sinew of some beast. A lever pulled the string back until it dropped into a narrow trigger slot, which then allowed one of the bolts to drop into the firing groove. Pushing the lever forwards triggered the action, loosing the bolt, then pulling the lever back repeated it. It was just as the elves had built.

'What do you think?' Kelyn asked.

Sendatsu glanced over and saw they were all desperate for his verdict. He hid his genuine admiration.

'Well done. It has taken you a while but the wait was worth it,' he said pompously. 'Make a dozen, and then I'll be happy.'

'They'll be done in two days,' Kelyn promised.

'That is brilliant,' Huw said fervently. 'Wonderful work, all of you!'

'You have done something worthy of the best of the elves!' Rhiannon agreed and, grinning, the carpenters hurried away.

That comment set Sendatsu's teeth on edge. Comparisons between elf and human were the biggest barrier to his quest. He waited until the carpenters were a safe distance away before turning to Rhiannon. 'They have done better than I could have hoped, but you need to be careful comparing things to the elves,' he said quietly. 'Unless you have seen Dokuzen, you should not say such things ...'

'Well, take me there and then I can judge it all for myself.' She pouted.

Sendatsu was reminded of Mai, when she wanted to have another plum, or some other treat.

'Just be careful with what you say. I am having enough problems with the huge difference between what humans expect from elves, and the reality of our differences,' Sendatsu said hurriedly. 'Now I must go and supervise the last section of palisade.'

'He'll take me there,' Rhiannon predicted confidently, once he had moved away.

'It may not be all you hope,' Huw warned.

'How can you say that? It's Dokuzen, the home of the elves! We've both dreamed of seeing it!'

'There is something he is not telling us.'

'What are you going on about?'

'This quest of his, to find the truth about what happened three centuries ago, and to find evidence of human magic or worship of Aroaril. Some of it does not make sense. Surely they know all about it back in Dokuzen. And why the rush? Why does he have to find it out so quickly and then hurry to return home? I feel there is something else, something he is not telling us ...'

'I think you are seeing problems where none exist,' Rhiannon said firmly. 'We are just lucky he is here with us, showing us how to protect the Velsh. We have to do all we can to keep him here as long as possible — and that means making him happy, and not saying anything to upset him!'

Huw sighed. 'Look, have you noticed — each night he takes something out from his pouch and sings at it. He has something secret and magic in there, I tell you!'

'Well, I have never seen him late at night,' Rhiannon said defiantly.

Huw silently thanked his lucky stars for that. Rhiannon had his father's room, while Sendatsu had Huw's old room and Huw slept in the main chamber. He had wanted his old room but Rhiannon had insisted that was impossible, the elf deserved it. It had become their custom to talk together each night, after the day's work, though not for long — Huw was exhausted by day's end, as was Rhiannon, for neither was used to heavy manual work. Huw's hands had been agony for the first two days and he had been genuinely afraid it might affect his lyre playing at one point. Only thoughts of his father, anger and guilt gave him the strength to keep going.

They talked of many things — the day's progress, the mood of the people, singing and dancing. But, after failing to find anything written down in his father's room that might provide some answers, they had not really spoken of legends of the elves. And while Rhiannon often dropped hints about being taken to see Dokuzen, Sendatsu swiftly changed the subject. Huw had spotted the pattern but he doubted Rhiannon had. She was too busy giggling and hanging on Sendatsu's every word, he reflected bitterly.

Several times he wanted to sit Rhiannon down and talk about her father, what had really happened at Cridianton. But he was afraid that would drive her away, or into Sendatsu's arms, which was worse. He could see the looks Rhiannon gave Sendatsu, the way she brushed her hair when she spoke to him, the way she took every opportunity to touch his leg or arm. The elf was not giving her much encouragement but it drove Huw crazy. He might be an elf but Huw doubted Sendatsu could stop himself if a sobbing Rhiannon flung herself into his arms, begging for comfort. Huw certainly would not be able to resist that — he could barely resist her now.

It was a stupid, selfish reason not to tell her the truth but he could not risk losing her completely. After all, they were still good friends, and she had been a great help in the first few days, when his grief had been a raging animal inside him. Just sitting with her, holding her hand as he talked about his father, helped ease the crushing pressure inside his chest. He had high hopes their friendship would become something more. Telling her the truth would end that hope. Perhaps if he waited a little longer, things would happen naturally between them, and she could be told the truth afterwards, when she might be able to put it into perspective.

'I just don't want to see you hurt. I know you would dearly love to see Dokuzen — but maybe such a thing is impossible. Or it may be as Sendatsu said, and not this wonderful place we have built up in our minds. Maybe we would be disappointed if we ever went there.'

'I doubt that!' Rhiannon smiled. She knew Huw was in love with her. It was impossible to miss. She had grown used to seeing adoring looks thrown her way. She had also been used to lustful gazes, which only confirmed everything her father had told her about men.

As for Huw, sometimes she felt going to him might expunge her guilt, absolve her from the way she kept him in Cridianton and, unwittingly, led to his father's death. But she instinctively felt a relationship begun like that would be doomed to fail. Besides, there was so much to see, so much to explore. Dokuzen, for one! She dreamed every night of going there and hoped with all her heart Sendatsu would take her there. Away from the dirt, the work, the fear of raiders and the brutality of this world. To somewhere peaceful, beautiful, where art, music and dance were given their due honour. Sendatsu was the key. She would use whatever it took to reach him. The fact he was an elf was attractive enough but to see him with his tunic off ... There was also something about him, a hint of sadness, of darkness even, that he tried to hide, which she sensed and found immensely appealing.

'Come on, Huw — let's see the last piece of the fence go in.'

She linked arms with Huw and instantly his scowl disappeared, as she knew it would, and he accompanied her willingly to join the rest of the village, smiling at the people and the children they knew, as a sweating gang of men, stripped to their waists, moved the last section of palisade into place. As they hammered it home, rammed the earth around its base, the whole village cheered and applauded.

'We have done a great thing!' Huw roared, his voice echoing over the cheers. 'It has been hard but you, your children and your children's children will be safe because of the work we have done here!'

This time they clapped each other, patted each other on the back and Huw waved for Sendatsu to step forwards.

'And here is the elf who has helped us!'

Sendatsu could not help but feel a surge of pride as they cheered him. True, they were only humans and would be the subject of contempt back in Dokuzen. But the palisade was tangible evidence he had done something useful. Perhaps his father was wrong, he was not hopeless.

'You did well,' he managed to say. 'I was pleased to work with you.'

His few words had them all cheering each other again. He looked around and could not keep the smile off his face.

A feast was planned to mark the occasion and, although the people were tired from the days of hard work, they were happy to prepare a celebration.

Fire pits were dug, men drank, women rebraided their hair and children played. Even Sendatsu found himself laughing. It had all gone well here and tomorrow they would ride on to a new village, the neighbouring Crumlin, which had elven buildings. The four widows from the woods had spoken to him, Delia and Maegen telling him they were grateful for being saved, very happy to be back with their families and how it had all been a misunderstanding due to the shock and stress of what had happened on that fateful day.

Then, when he found himself actually tantalised by the smell of roasting meat, it all changed.

'Raiders!'

The shout, delivered at the top of a breaking teenage voice, silenced the laughter instantly.

In the same move, all looked towards Sendatsu and he realised, with horror, they expected him to save them. He managed to calm his hammering heart and control his voice.

'Where? How many?'

'A dozen, riding towards us! They're about a mile off!'

Sendatsu could see the fear rippling through the crowd and he felt it himself. He did not think he could face them if it all went wrong and the raiders got in here. He wanted to rage at Huw and Rhiannon for getting him into this. But he took a deep breath and got himself back under control, a little. He waved at the villagers.

'Get a weapon and get to the gate,' he snapped.

Now they moved with a purpose, and he led the rush back to Huw's house, where his bow and arrows waited.

'What should we do? Do you think they will ride in and attack?' Huw asked. He was torn between fear and hatred of these raiders. 'Can you kill them all?'

'We'll see,' Sendatsu said grimly. He was confident of his bow but unsure of how the villagers would act, after the way they had not fought back when the first raiding party struck.

He took his sword, while Huw selected a long knife that his father had used for butchering sheep.

'What can I use?' Rhiannon demanded.

'You need to stay here, in safety,' Huw said instantly.

'What's safe about it? I would do more good being out there,' Rhiannon insisted. 'I don't want to sit here and worry — I am not some housewife, to be ordered to stay behind!'

But the pair of them had already run out. Rhiannon swore — she had learned some good ones from the woodcutters — and hunted around for another knife.

Sendatsu forced himself to run to the gate, knowing the people were expecting to see a warrior elf, would take confidence from him, although his bowels were churning and his palms sweaty. Huw was at his shoulder, sure being with an elf was the greatest guarantee of safety.

Glyn and some of the other villagers who lived closer to the gate had already dragged the hedgehog across to block the way in. The trunks bristling with wooden spikes made an impressive barrier and Sendatsu took heart from it, knowing that few, if any, horses would be prepared to jump that.

Villagers clutching axes, saws, hoes, shovels and sticks were bunching up behind the gate now, nervously, but taking comfort from their numbers.

By now the raiders were in sight, a small group of men on tall horses, dressed not in armour but in tunics. All carried bright swords or axes. They rode along steadily until about one hundred and fifty yards away.

'That's close enough,' Sendatsu decided, hoping a warning would scare them off. He nocked an arrow and loosed, sending it arching down to land in the road just in front of them.

Instantly the raiders stopped, the leader dismounting to pick up the arrow and inspect it, before climbing back on his horse. They sat there, just watching, for what seemed like an age, then turned and rode back the way they came.

They could not have failed to hear the roar of mingled triumph and relief from the villagers as they disappeared.

Men embraced each other, patted Sendatsu on the back and cheered themselves, as if they had won a famous victory.

'That showed them!' someone crowed.

'They won't be back,' Glyn vowed.

'What do you think?' Huw asked Sendatsu quietly.

The elf shrugged, unwilling to commit himself.

'They'll be back,' Rhiannon warned. 'They are Forlish. We don't give up that easily. They just didn't have enough men to get in through the gate. They'll get more men and they'll be back in a few days.'

'So what do we do?' Huw asked Sendatsu.

Sendatsu could see not just Huw, not just Rhiannon, but all the villagers were waiting for his answer. The temptation to leave now was strong. Then he looked around at the crowd. Women and children had joined the men and they were all staring at him mutely, desperate hope in their eyes. They were all depending on him. He could not stand to think of these children, of these people, being slaughtered by Forlish raiders. He cursed himself. He had told himself not to become involved with the humans, reminded himself not to fall into the trap of caring for them. But it was too late. He could not leave them. He longed to have Mai and Cheijun run into his arms, ached to hold them close. But to sacrifice these families to get that was too high a price to pay. 'We need to get ready for them,' he said grimly.

# 13

*The Magic-weavers' attack on myself and the other clan leaders was well planned and carefully thought out. It would have succeeded — and I would not be writing this now — had it not been for my wife, who was also a Magic-weaver. Unsurprisingly she knew almost nothing of the Magic-weavers' plans — especially as she was spending almost all her time by my side. It was sheer chance she chose that morning to visit her sensei and discovered their plan of co-ordinated attack. On such things do kingdoms rise and fall.*

*There was not enough time to return to our villa but she was able to send word to me through the birds. I received the warning, but it cost her life, for her companions turned on her. Outnumbered ten to one, she was no match for them, talented as she was.*

*I did not know what had happened and barely had time to warn half the other Council members before Magic-weavers attacked us, teams of them striking at our villas. Forewarned, we were able to muster enough clan members to frustrate them. Luckily the magic was still strong in all of my people then. Even the lowliest Elfaran could do much. While the Magic-weavers were truly gifted with magic, they were also few in number — and while it cost many lives, we exhausted them, drained their powers and then killed them.*

*Their attempt to overthrow me and rule Dokuzen was finished and I made sure all of the people knew about their treachery. I broke their power, made the survivors swear magical oaths of loyalty to me, to ensure they would never rise again.*

*That was a success but I had no heart to tackle all the problems still ahead of me. My wife had died to save me and I was more interested in grieving than anything else. Instead, I handed many of the tasks over to my best friend, closer to me than a brother.*

*It proved to be a fatal mistake.*

Broyle of Readingum was an angry man. He wanted to be back down south, smashing the Balians and bringing glory to his king, fighting a war he knew and understood. Losing Cenred and nearly half his men had been a bitter blow. The fact he had not been able to find those responsible was nearly as bad. Rain the day after had washed away the tracks, and he had wasted days searching the surrounding country for some sign of a large band of Velsh, carrying wounded with them. He could not imagine Cenred and his men being killed without exacting a high price in return.

But he could find nothing.

Of course he was still there to strike fear into any Velsh he found, and his anger made him vicious. He slaughtered a family in an isolated farmhouse in their sleep, leaving the bodies for their neighbours to find. Fear was a powerful weapon and Broyle planned to use it as often as possible.

On he rode, striking at a farm here, a traveller there. Each time they were killed swiftly and their bodies left for friends and neighbours to find. Finally he found himself approaching Patcham again. He expected to ride in, find the women he had taken the first time and get answers from them, one way or another. But, unlike last time, he was surprised to see young scouts spot his approach from far away and race off to deliver a warning.

Normally he would have ducked away, changed his route, but he had unfinished business with this village.

He was doubly surprised to see a palisade around the village, as well as the evidence that it had just been built — but this was replaced by fury when an arrow was sent arching down at him.

He thought it a crossbow at first but the missile had not looked anything like a crossbow bolt. His first impression was it could be instant death for any of his men it struck, for he had not brought armour and shields, as that would have given away their cover as simple bandits. He also thought armour pointless, as the Velsh were basically unarmed peasants. Obviously this had been proved wrong. But, more importantly, it looked like a weapon that would inflict wounds just like the ones he had found on Cenred's squad.

Broyle wanted to know what was inside that palisade. He wanted revenge but he needed more men — so he went looking for them.

It took him two days to find another band, a bigger one this time, more than thirty men, under the command of a man he did not know, a lean, tall man who introduced himself as Oswald of Eoferwic. He and his men had heard of Broyle — or rather of his reputation among the veterans of the Balian fighting. But while they had heard of Broyle, the greater numbers meant that Oswald appointed himself as the overall leader.

'A Velsh village has been fortified? And you think they are using it as a base to attack our men — and might even have elven archers inside it?' Oswald had been unable to keep the disbelief out of his voice.

'At least one person, elf or man, using an elven-style bow,' Broyle said softly. 'Maybe more. Maybe a dozen. We need to find the truth of this. I have seen no other Velsh village so protected. They had scouts out, and they definitely loosed an arrow near two hundred paces at us. We shall need to be careful. This Patcham is no ordinary village.'

'I think you are seeing dangers where there are none,' Oswald snorted. 'We have been here for a quarter-moon and have not seen any evidence the Velsh will even fight.'

'Look at this then.' Broyle handed Oswald the arrow he had picked up from the road.

'This means nothing,' Oswald dismissed. 'One arrow does not mean a pack of elves — it does not even mean one! Skies above, we haven't seen hide nor ear of an elf in hundreds of years!'

Broyle ground his teeth at the disbelieving expression on Oswald's face.

'They're Velsh peasants, man! They might have a bit of a fence around them but we'll just ride in and smash the place up,' Oswald insisted.

'It's not going to be that easy ...' Broyle tried one last time but Oswald cut him off.

'You might think this is Balia all over again but the most danger we've been in is catching some skin disease off the women! Now, if you want to join my men in attacking this village, you will follow me — or we shall ride away and you can tackle it by yourself.'

Broyle hesitated. All his instincts told him this was a bad idea, but the longer he left that village, the more prepared they were going to become. Besides, there were nearly fifty Forlish veterans here. No one archer could stop them.

And Oswald knew his business, at least. He, Broyle and a pair of scouts eased forwards to check out the village before attacking.

'There're no farmers out in the fields, and it looks like their flocks must have been driven to safer pastures. They have a fence around them, true enough, but it's not very high — and it's just tree trunks, all cut to different sizes,' Oswald mused. 'That spiked thing across the gate area looks formidable and no doubt they are massed behind there, ready to slaughter any of our men who try and get past it.'

Broyle nodded agreement. Oswald might not take advice well but you did not reach sergeant in the Forlish army without demonstrating cunning and intelligence.

'So we do the unexpected. Your men, and a squad of mine, go up the front to draw their attention, then I'll lead the rest around the side. We'll loop ropes across the top of the fence posts and use the horses to pull several sections of it down. Then the two of us will meet in the middle.'

'And if the place is full of elven archers?' Broyle asked sourly. He did not really think that, but could see his men were more likely to suffer and die by the gate than Oswald's flank attack.

Oswald laughed. 'With an imagination like that, you should go and tell tales for the king's amusement! Elven archers!'

Broyle took control of a small group of sullen men, bringing his numbers up to twenty, while the rest of Oswald's men massed behind them.

'Charge at the gate — we'll swing out to the right. You'll know we're inside when the gate defenders start running. Don't kill everyone. Keep the women alive, at least. But once we have the village we shall burn it, as a lesson to any others who might be thinking of protecting themselves,' Oswald ordered.

Broyle agreed with that — it was exactly what he would have done. But he would have liked to take a few men in tonight, have a really good look at the fence. From this distance it looked as though it could be ripped down with a little work — there were no bracers on the outside, so a team of horses, pulling together, should be able to haul down a section. But it just felt too easy, although Oswald would not listen to him.

'Attack!' Broyle called. He signalled and led them forwards at the trot. He rarely felt fear these days, he liked to inspire fear in his enemies instead. But he could feel it stirring in his stomach now as they emerged from among the trees and rode up the rough dirt road at Patcham.

'Charge!' He pumped his arm and then spurred his horse, making sure to let Oswald's men among his group get to the front. No sense in risking his men unnecessarily.

There was no reaction from the village. Oswald waved his arm and led the bulk of his men out in a wide sweep to the right. They were close enough now that Broyle could see the massed men behind the spiked gate and he actually began to relax a little, to wonder if this might just be as easy as Oswald had predicted.

Then it all went horribly wrong.

Huw called the villagers to an assembly again.

'Should we not just leave? Take the children and get to safety?' someone asked the obvious question.

'Run where? Where is safe? The raiders are arriving here now, more and more of them. Soon every village will face the terror they bring — they have to, if all are to agree to become part of Forland,' Huw declared. 'And if we leave, we shall only be able to carry a few things. Remember, they all have horses, so they shall be able to follow our trail and catch us if we try to take too much. And that means they will burn the village. Your homes, your possessions, the fence we all worked so hard on. Gone. Your animals. Gone. Your lives, everything you worked for and your parents and grandparents left to you. Gone. Or we can stay here, and teach them to leave Patcham alone.'

'Can we hold them off? Running and being alive with nothing is better than staying and being dead among all your possessions,' Glyn pointed out.

Huw turned to Sendatsu.

The elf felt a moment's fear again. This was not like taking on a couple of bandits out in the woods, or even tackling an unsuspecting group in a dark forest, where he could split them up. This was beyond his skills alone. He would have to do something special. *Why are you all looking to me for help? Don't you know how useless I am?* He wanted to run and hide from their belief that he was their saviour, the elf from magical Dokuzen, come to rescue them. He took a deep breath. They had all the advantages here. The fence was strong and they had plenty of men inside it. From his lessons he knew a properly defended stronghold could hold off an attack from a force at least three times its size — and there would not be hundreds of Forlish coming here — more like fifty, at the most.

'We can hold them off. Kelyn has managed to make elven crossbows, which can loose a dozen bolts in the time it takes to say that. And we have the time for the rest of us to prepare. Huw is right. If you run, you only put off the day when you must face the raiders. But if you fight them off, they will go looking for easier targets. They will leave Patcham alone.'

The villagers looked at each other, waiting for someone to take the lead.

'I shall stay and fight. Who's with me?' Huw stepped forwards.

'I shall!' Rhiannon joined him instantly.

'We all shall,' Glyn judged.

There was no cheering.

The village was a hive of activity over the next two days.

Kelyn and the other carpenters were kept busy churning out every crossbow they could make, as well as stacks of the simple bolts. Once the design had been perfected, it was relatively easy for a man with tool skills to recreate Kelyn's work, while the bolts were just stout straight sticks with sharpened ends. Even the older children were making them. Looking at them compared to one of his arrows, Sendatsu knew just one could not kill a man — and would not be able to penetrate armour — but the way they could be pumped out in a cloud of missiles was fearsome enough and any man or horse with a couple of those stuck in them would quickly lose interest in trying to sack the village. They were also almost impossible to aim, requiring the arbalester to press the butt of the stock into their hip for support but, again, the sheer volume would make up for that.

Other men built crude fighting platforms at different sections around the inside of the palisade, so that could be easily defended, while all had to spend several turns of the hourglass each day practising with weapons. Sendatsu was under no illusions that one of these Velsh farmers was going to be a match for a hardened Forlish warrior, so he did not even attempt to show them swordplay, even if the village blacksmith could have somehow forged enough swords in the limited time. Instead they took long hoes and other farming implements and put crude spearheads on them. At the very least, they might be able to keep the Forlish at a distance. He also organised the men into groups, each with a different task. Some were to man the gate, others be prepared to use the fighting platforms around the wall to push back any Forlish trying to climb over, while a dozen of the crossbowmen were kept back as a floating force, ready to rush to wherever needed.

'How do you think they'll attack?' Huw wondered.

Sendatsu took a small party outside the village palisade to consider the problem.

'They'll probably come straight at the gate then, when we throw them back, try around the sides,' he suggested.

'You don't think they'll try something smarter than that?' Rhiannon asked dubiously. 'I was there for the king's war meetings and his captains always had plans to take towns and cities protected by high walls.'

Sendatsu once again swallowed his self-doubt.

'They don't have armour, or siege equipment. They'll have to try something direct. Besides, they think us just Velsh peasants, unworthy of a proper invasion,' Huw said bitterly.

'He's right,' Sendatsu agreed thankfully. 'And they won't expect the crossbows. Once we surprise them, they'll probably turn and run.'

Despite the hard work, it was a nervous wait to see if the raiders would return. Sendatsu suffered in particular, having to put on a brave face at all times. The people were confident because of him. The crossbows helped, of course, but they saw him with his bow, saw him practising with the sword and declared no Forlish warrior could stand against the elf. He had to pretend to be the invincible elf, the hero of their songs and dreams, offer reassurance when he was the one who really needed it.

The scouts did their job again, galloping back to the village to announce a large party of raiders was coming their way. The men wanted the women and children to lock themselves into houses, to stay safe that way, but Rhiannon suggested at least some of them could carry spare bolts to the crossbowmen — and Sendatsu had agreed, saying every man might be needed to fight off the raiders.

So while the children and most of the women hurried to safety, Rhiannon and a dozen other women stacked bundles of crossbow bolts and hoped they would not be needed.

The men tried to cover their fear with jokes and loud laughter but Rhiannon noticed there was a steady stream of them heading over to a dung heap behind a nearby house, then hurrying back, pulling up their trousers. This got worse as the wait grew longer.

'Where are they? Surely they should be here by now?' Huw had managed to get one of the crossbows and he was both afraid, and eager, to use it. Every time he worried about what might happen, he forced himself to remember his father — and then hatred swamped the fear, for a little while.

'They are probably watching us,' Sendatsu predicted, trying to cover his own fears.

'There!'

The shout went up from a dozen throats and all craned to see the tight bunch of raiders riding swiftly up the road towards them.

'Get ready!' Sendatsu licked his dry lips.

They had built platforms to either side of the gate — although Sendatsu worried about crossbowmen using them as they had to expose the top half of themselves in order to point the crossbow in the right direction. But they had not seen the raiders bring any crossbowmen of their own, so it was a risk that had to be taken.

Men scrambled into position and Sendatsu strung his bow, succeeding at the second attempt. They had nearly twenty of the crossbows at the gate, with another ten held back, to rush to wherever they might be needed. He hoped that would be enough.

For now the raiders were doing exactly what he expected, sending their entire force at the main gate. He only had a score of arrows, so he wanted to keep them until they could do the most good. He was just bending the bow, and wondering whether he should aim at horse or man, when more than half of the raiders peeled off from the group and rode to his left, heading for the side of the village.

'Follow them! And get up on the platforms!' Sendatsu bellowed, and the men held back from the gate obeyed, scampering off to the left, towards where the bulk of the raiders were going.

He grabbed Glyn. 'Take five crossbowmen and follow the others — we can handle these at the gate,' he snapped.

The Velshman nodded then tapped several of his fellows on the shoulder and raced away.

Sendatsu turned back to the charging raiders and drew his bow once more. By now they were barely seventy yards away, and coming fast. He aimed at the lead horse, a chestnut, let out the air in his lungs and, in the pause between breaths, loosed. He watched the arrow bite home deeply and gazed with some satisfaction as the horse bucked and reared, tossing its rider and forcing those behind to slow and swerve around. He took another arrow and loosed at a rider this time, taking the man in the chest, the force of the strike sending him tumbling backwards out of his saddle. A third arrow missed, then the fourth struck another horse, bringing it down, and as he reached for his fifth arrow, the raiders were barely thirty yards away, big men on big horses, shouting their challenges and war cries, waving long swords and axes as if they intended to leap across the spiked barricade at the gate.

To either side of Sendatsu, he could see villagers edging backwards, terror on their faces. He knew he should say something to encourage them, but had no words.

'Kill them all!' Huw roared, stepping forwards, his crossbow held tight into his hip. He walked closer to the barricade, past the men edging backwards; he held the bottom part of the bow with his left hand and his right hand was on the cocking handle. He did not know if these were the raiders who had attacked Patcham the first time but imagined the lead rider was the one who had killed his father so aimed the crossbow in his direction, as best he could. He slammed the handle forwards, sending the small wooden bolt flicking out the front and towards the Forlish and making the top half of the weapon slide forwards. He pulled the handle back, grimacing a little at the effort, and the top half slid back, allowing another bolt to drop into the firing groove, and locking the bowstring behind the firing pin. He jerked the handle forwards and another bolt zoomed out, only a few heartbeats after the first.

He could not see where they were going but his shout, and his action in walking forwards, was enough to stir the rest of the villagers. The other crossbowmen around him, as well as the four on each platform on either side of the gate, began loosing their weapons also, a hail of stout bolts with tips that had been sharpened to a wicked point.

The Forlish raiders screamed to a stop as they were enveloped by the cloud of bolts. They were going in all directions, peppering the ground as they missed, but the cluster of Forlish warriors on large horses was too big a target. Men and horses cried out as stout wooden bolts, each the thickness of a man's middle finger and near a foot long, sunk into arms, legs, chests and faces.

Men and horses went down in a pile and all the time the bolts kept flying. As soon as a crossbowman finished what was in the crude box-magazine on the top of his weapon, a woman fed handfuls more in and the men worked the mechanism, overwhelming the Forlish by the sheer rate of fire. One crossbow broke, another jammed, but enough remained to make an assault on the gate impossible.

'Keep it up! Huw, hold them here — I need to see what the others are doing!' Sendatsu yelled, then raced off to his left.

Broyle ordered his men back — there was no way inside that gate. He had never seen anything like the bolts that were flying out of those strange bows at an impossible rate. He had seen many crossbows, had used them a few times himself, and they were massive things, needing ages to rewind for a second shot. This was something out of his experience and he had no intention of sacrificing his remaining men to help Oswald. As it was, all of Oswald's men who had ridden with him were dead or down, as well as a pair of his own men, while another three had one or more of the strange bolts in them. Luckily they did not seem to have the range to bother him once he was fifty yards away — some still loosed but they were falling short or bounced away.

He glanced over to his right, where Oswald was leading the main charge, and hoped the man suffered for his stupidity — but still opened a way into this cursed village. He wanted to get inside more than ever.

He got half his wish.

Oswald's charge stopped as horses began falling over — and not just falling but tumbling over, sending the men flying, to crunch into the ground with bone-shattering force. The sound of screaming horses echoed across, drowning out the howls of the wounded Forlish by the gate. Broyle stared at the ground. It was as if the horses were all falling into holes … they were! He could make them out now, dotting the ground in a thick border around the village, small holes that were hard to see but deadly to any horse that stepped into them.

Oswald was standing in his stirrups now, shouting something at his men, who tried to dismount and rush forwards at the crude palisade, ropes in hand. But Broyle knew what was going to happen before it did — a cloud of bolts reached down and covered the men on foot, knocking some over and sending the rest running for their lives.

Oswald shouted at them, rode forwards — and was struck by several of the bolts, both he and his horse falling as one.

Broyle glanced back towards the gate and the Velsh packed thickly there and made an instant decision.

'Follow me!' he shouted, riding hard for where Oswald's Forlish still struggled and died under the lash of the strange crossbows.

Sendatsu reached the platform nearest the fighting — a pile of old barrels with planks stacked on top — and hauled himself up, joining Glyn and a dozen crossbowmen working their machines as if their lives depended on it — which they did. A few others, who could not fit up on the platform, pointed their machines in the air and loosed bolts randomly over the wall in hope.

'We're beating the bastards!' Glyn grinned.

Sendatsu could only agree with him. Injured horses lay thickly on the ground, brought down by the holes the villagers had dug, while men screamed in agony or lay silently where they had fallen. There were still plenty of Forlish there and he ordered a crossbowman down to give himself room to draw his bow, for some of the Forlish were trying to organise the others and stopping them called for more accuracy than that provided by the crossbows. He drew back on the string, sighting on a Forlish warrior shoving men towards the wall. The man thought he was safe, a good fifty yards from the wall — but that was no distance at all to a longbow. Sendatsu loosed and the arrow jerked the man off his feet. He looked around for another target and saw a Forlishman trying to ease his horse past the many holes dug so carefully in the ground, a file of others behind. By now Sendatsu was not even thinking. These were not men any more, they were targets. Years of practice had taken over and he aimed, drew and loosed in a smooth movement, knocking the man off his horse.

'They don't like that!' Glyn roared.

The other Velsh were jeering now at the Forlish, not loosing so many bolts but instead trying to pick their targets, for few Forlish were willing to come close enough.

Sendatsu ignored them, instead watching a new group come galloping close. This group did not join the rest of them in their futile attack but rather the leader waved for the surviving riders to follow him further around.

'Glyn, stay here with three men! The rest of you follow me!' Sendatsu shouted, jumping down from the platform and stumbling slightly, before running further around the wall.

Looking carefully, Broyle could see the ground was uneven all the way around the palisade — obviously those damned holes were everywhere. But perhaps there was a way through, as long as they were there before those cursed crossbows.

'Dismount!' He flung up his hand and looked over his shoulder. More than twenty men had followed him — more than enough for the job, if he could just get them inside the wall.

'Lead your horses to the wall and then use them to get over it!'

The ropes were almost all back with the remnants of Oswald's disastrous attack, tied to the saddles of a dozen horses who were even now screaming with broken legs, a hideous sound that was even more distressing than the cries of wounded men. But Broyle blocked both noises out.

The holes were scattered thickly but, by walking slowly and deliberately, it was possible to get the horses past them and close to the wall. Of course, walking so slow made them easy targets for the crossbows — but they were not here yet.

'Hold the horses here — and use them to get over the wall and onto the battlement on the other side!' Broyle shouted.

He waited until one of his men held his horse steady, then stood in the saddle, holding onto the rough timber wall for balance, and looked over — to see a ten-foot drop on the other side. Looking right, he saw a rough fighting platform ten yards down, to his left there was another twenty yards away, but a group of Velsh crossbowmen, led by the archer, was already racing towards that one.

'To the right! Ten yards!' Broyle pointed, and the men following him led their horses further down.

While one man held a horse's head, others stood in the saddle then clumsily swung over the wall to the fighting platform — in reality just some straw bales and planks. Three, four, five men were over and jumping down to the ground, swords in their hands and running at the group of Velsh. Broyle grinned. Now his men would get some revenge. He held back from joining the race to get inside so he could watch what happened first.


'Get on that platform and stop them! Leave these to me!'

Sendatsu was hardly aware of the words as he shouted them. Gone were the doubts, the fears, the uncertainty. Instead he knew what had to be done. If these Forlish were not killed, the village was doomed. They would not show any mercy.

He dropped his bow and drew his sword, running hard at the first Forlishman, a huge man with a rough beard and a long sword. As the Forlishman brought his sword around in a massive swipe, Sendatsu tucked his head down and went smoothly underneath in a forward roll, feeling the draught of the sword as he slipped past the first man. He came to one knee and braced his elbow, thrusting forwards in the same motion to drive his sword deep into the guts of the second

Forlishman, who was not expecting to be attacked. Quick as a flash, Sendatsu ripped his blade clear and whirled to where the first warrior was trying to recover from the massive blow that had only just missed. He never got the chance. Sendatsu rose and slashed in the one movement, ripping through kidneys and spine with the thunder-strike, blood exploding from the wound.

He turned smoothly, hearing the battle cry of the third man, who raised his blade and swung it down with all his strength. Sendatsu did not try to block it, instead spinning to his left. The sword sunk deep into the ground and, before the Forlishman could rip it free, Sendatsu swung his sword around in the dragon-tail stroke, the sharpened steel slicing through the leg just below the knee.

Screaming, spraying blood in all directions, the warrior clutched his stump but Sendatsu was already up and moving, to where the last pair had slowed to a stop, horrified at the way their comrades had been taken apart. Before they could think of what to do, Sendatsu was upon them. He leaped high, his sword coming down over a despairing block to slice deep into the shoulder of the one to the left, sinking down into the man's chest and heart beyond in a windmill stroke.

The blade caught on the man's collarbone and he used his foot to kick the dying man away to free his sword. The last Forlishman saw his chance and swung furiously. Sendatsu could only partly deflect the blow, the tip of the sword opening a line along his ribs. But he had many lessons with his father when he had taken wounds and been forced to keep going. He ignored the stinging pain and went on the attack. The Forlishman parried a pair of blows desperately, before Sendatsu used the reverse side technique, cutting low and, when the Forlishman moved to block, slicing up to rip the sword through his neck. Blood flew and the man spun away to hit the ground in a puddle of gore.

Up on the fighting platform, another three Forlishmen who had sprung from the saddle over the wall hesitated, hardly able to believe what they had seen and not sure what they should do —

hold the wall or try to attack this strange warrior, who moved and fought like nothing they had ever seen.

But then the Velsh were there, working their crossbows, and the three were peppered with bolts, ducking and covering up and finally falling to a hail of the sharp wooden points.

'Get up there and kill the rest!' Sendatsu roared, blood caking his arms, chest and face.

Broyle watched the archer throw away his bow and draw a strange sword, gently curved and with a slimmer blade than the broadswords they were using now and the short swords they favoured when fighting in the battle line. To Broyle, there was only going to be one outcome. Five veteran Forlishmen against one man — it was no contest. He was right in one way, he realised, as he stared in horror at the way the warrior cut apart the men. To be sure they were Oswald's men, not his own, but still ...

'Kill the rest!'

The warrior's shout snapped Broyle out of his shock. The platform was clear, bar for three more Forlishmen, who twitched as they slowly died from the impact of a dozen of those nasty little bolts, and there were enough Velsh crossbowmen taking their place to slaughter the rest of his men.

'Back! Pull back! Retreat! Leave the horses!'

Broyle had never had to say that before, and the words tasted sour in his mouth as they raced to safety. Getting the horses out would have taken too long but, he was furious to see, several of Oswald's men still tried. The ones who led their horses out were cut down in a swarm of crossbow bolts, while those who tried to ride out hit a hole and were sent flying, their horses left screeching with the pain of their broken legs.

He glanced back, to see the crossbowmen stop as the last of his men dragged themselves out of range. He stared hard, wanting to see the strange warrior one more time, but the man did not appear. Broyle turned away, began to lead what was left of his men to safety.

'What now, sarge?' someone asked.

'We walk away. But we'll be back,' Broyle promised. He glowered at the palisade. He was not finished with this village, nor with the strange warrior inside. He would get his revenge, no matter how long it took.

Sendatsu watched the Forlish slink away, dragging some of their wounded with them, and leaving others, as well as plenty of horses, screaming in agony below the palisade.

'We did it!' Glyn bellowed, and all around the village people were cheering, embracing, laughing and crying. Women and children rushed from the houses where they had been sheltering, to join in the celebrations. Others saw the dead and dying men left by Sendatsu and hung back, or ran the other way, to where the gate was a mass of cheering Velsh.

Leaving the pile of crying men and horses beyond the palisade, Sendatsu jumped down from the fighting platform, to where Glyn and the other Velsh crossbowmen had gathered. The only Forlish alive in the village was the man whose leg he had cut off, and he was dying, his lifeblood seeping into the earth. Sendatsu paused for a moment and sliced down once, ending his suffering.

'Here he is — our hero!' Glyn roared at the cautious crowd that had gathered nearby.

Sendatsu suddenly could barely take another step without men and women and children wanting to embrace him. The only thing that kept him from being swamped was the blood that drenched him.

'Are you hurt?' someone called.

Sendatsu found a dry patch of tunic and wiped his face reasonably clean.

'This is Forlish blood!' he shouted, glossing over the wound down his ribs, and they bellowed in approval.

He retrieved his bow and made his way back to the gate, shaking hands and being patted on the back and shoulders all the way. It was as if every Velsh villager wanted to touch him, so the luck would rub off on them.

At the gate it was a similar scene. The Velsh were cheering themselves, while outside, a pile of Forlish men and horses heaved and sobbed and bled.

'We did it!' Huw emerged from the crush to see a blood-covered Sendatsu. 'Didn't we?'

'Just like I said we would!' Sendatsu boasted, conveniently ignoring his doubts from earlier. 'Your father is avenged, Huw!'

But Huw shook his head. 'My debt is nowhere near being paid. This is only the beginning.'

'They won't be back,' Sendatsu announced, not listening to the bard's words.

'Of course they won't be back! These crossbows saved us. With these, we can drive away the raiders every time — they don't stand a chance.' Rhiannon arrived to hear the last words, then she caught sight of Sendatsu, who was surreptitiously looking at his cut ribs. 'You're hurt!'

Sendatsu smiled through the smears still left on his face. 'It's just a scratch.' He shrugged.

'He killed five of them with the sword — it was unbelievable, I tell you!' Glyn announced. 'There's skill for you!'

'Here, let me help you.' Rhiannon rushed to where buckets of water had been left, along with a pile of torn tunics, for crude bandages.

'Three cheers for the elf!' Glyn cried and the village erupted.

Sendatsu looked around at the grinning faces, the smiles and the applause and stood a little straighter. He was no closer to the answers he sought but this was a good thing he had done today.

'Come with me, you need to do something with that wound, or it'll fester and make you sick,' Rhiannon insisted, trying to dab at it with a grubby tunic, soaked in dirty water.

'What were you thinking of doing?' Sendatsu stepped back rather than have that scruffy rag near his cut ribs.

'Well, bind it up with an old tunic and put an elfbolt in there to keep away the evil that turns it bad,' Glyn suggested.

'Oh no you won't!' Sendatsu found he was more afraid of the Velsh treatment than he had been of the Forlish who injured him.

'The bandage needs to be cleaned and boiled, and then a herbal poultice used,' Sendatsu insisted. 'The edges of the wound should be bound together with stitches ...'

'Stitches? Like clothes? I have never heard anything so revolting!' Glyn choked.

'What sort of herbs?' Rhiannon asked.

'Well ...' Sendatsu thought hard. 'There are many. Do you have the long-leafed, spiky plant we call aloe vera?'

He looked around the confused faces and realised that was too much to ask.

'What about goldenseal? Or comfrey? Sage is good as well ...'

'Delia knows about herbs.' Glyn pointed to her.

Delia was ushered forwards.

'I have those herbs but we only use them for rashes, fevers and the like — they do nothing for cuts ...'

'And the dirty old tunics and elfbolts do any better?' Sendatsu asked sceptically. 'Give me the herbs and they will work.'

'Everyone knows that an elfbolt is best for those, to keep out evil spirits that make it go bad ...'

'I'll take my chances,' Sendatsu said hurriedly.

'Come with me, I'll boil up the bandages and help you,' Rhiannon offered.

Sendatsu was not sure if she had the experience — but did not trust the other villagers not to do something strange. At least Rhiannon would do what he asked.

'Let's go then,' he agreed, the pair of them following a dubious Delia to choose herbs from her home.

'The elf and the dancer, eh? Sounds like a good tale for you to sing!' Glyn nudged Huw as Delia led Sendatsu and Rhiannon away.

Huw watched them leave, feeling as though someone had sunk a blade into his stomach. After the battle, he had been filled with exultation, a soaring certainty he and Rhiannon would be together. But the elf was the real hero of the day — Huw was just a man who knew how to talk and could use the elven crossbows. And what could he ever say to stop them?

'Get some men together — we need to collect the wounded Forlish raiders, put the horses out of their misery and find as many bolts as we can out there,' he said gruffly.

'Of course!' Glyn clapped him on the shoulder and then began shouting.

# 14

*One of the side effects of all the plans going on was that I heard little of what was happening with the humans. Once, Velsh had been welcome to walk through the streets of Dokuzen. A few Forlish and a handful of Breconians had even made their way north to see us. But now, those that tried were killed before they got to me. Afterwards, of course, I could see the pattern, I could understand why reports of what was happening in Vales, in Forland and elsewhere were not getting back to me. Of course, hindsight is always the clearest vision.*

Huw walked slowly back to his house. The villagers had spent the rest of the day cleaning up after the battle. Wounded horses had been killed, then dragged away to be butchered; that much fresh meat was not to be wasted. As for the Forlish, most were dead or dying — the ones still able to move had crawled away and then been rescued by their fellows. Their weapons were stacked up inside the village, their bodies were burned in a huge pyre. Everywhere there were small bolts, and women and children had gone over the ground carefully, retrieving every one that could still be used. They were too valuable to be left.

At the end, there were still six Forlish living, and these were all in a bad way. Struck by several of the bolts, they had all lost plenty of blood and the village argued what to do with them while these men still bled.

'They would have shown us no mercy,' Glyn pointed out.

'But we cannot just kill them, like they were animals!' Kelyn said doubtfully.

'They are animals. And we would not let a good sheepdog suffer, were it dying. We should at least show them that mercy. We don't know how to draw out our bolts without killing them anyway,' Glyn snorted.

'Perhaps we should send them back to their king,' Kelyn suggested. 'We have a few living horses they left behind. Put them on there and send them south. Then their fate is their own and out of our hands.'

'No,' Huw spoke up. 'We must not send them back to Ward. He must not know what is going on here. If he thinks we are resisting him, he will send his armies. We have to protect ourselves first.'

'So what do we do?' Glyn asked.

Huw waved him down. He was still thinking this through himself. He had worked hard to clean up the battlefield but had been unable to get his mind off Rhiannon and Sendatsu, neither of whom had reappeared. Now he had a different thought to follow. They could not send the wounded back to King Ward. Patcham had defences sufficient enough to hold off a pack of Ward's raiders but the Forlish armies could smash through stone walls and towers, bring down entire cities. They could wipe Patcham off the map in less than a day, if Ward thought it was a threat to his plan to bring the Velsh under his control. For now they were safe, for the survivors would not go running back to Cridianton with the tale of how a Velsh village defeated them. Not yet. But there would come a day when Ward would hear the Velsh were defying him. His reaction would be swift and brutal.

So they had to protect not just Patcham but all the Velsh villages. One village the Forlish could destroy in a day — but if every village was protected, ready and waiting for Ward's men ... Huw's imagination raced ahead. The Forlish were fighting wars in two southern countries, had troops patrolling the two they had previously conquered. If the raiders failed, then Ward would face a choice — begin a third war or leave the Velsh in peace. He sighed to himself. Ward would never choose peace. So they needed some way to defeat the Forlish army. There was only one possibility — the elves. Nobody else could hope to defeat Ward's Forlish.

So the key to all this was Sendatsu. Not only did he need to use the elf to go and show every other Velsh village how to protect themselves, he needed him to persuade the elves to break their self-imposed exile. As well as being archers and peerless warriors, they had the magic no human could wield. Not even the Forlish could stand against that.

But this was going to take some work with Sendatsu. It was clear the elf had his own agenda. He was helping them now but for how long? He said, time and again, once he found what he sought, he was off to Dokuzen. Huw's head said he wanted Sendatsu around as long as possible to help the Velsh but his heart said he wanted the elf gone now. Not that he had shown much interest in Rhiannon but, with him around, Huw stood no chance. Huw knew he was no warrior, he had no idea about magic and he possessed little of the elf's knowledge and almost none of his physical prowess. He was not a hero, a saviour of the village. Nor did he offer the excitement of being a fairy tale come to life — or the hope of taking her to see Dokuzen, where she had dreamed of dancing and singing with the elves since she was a little girl. Put like that, it made sense for her to choose Sendatsu over him. But it hurt. Skies above, it hurt! Worse, he had to hide his feelings and pander to the elf, to get him on side. His people needed a hero — and there was only one choice available. No matter how unpleasant, he had to do this.

'Kill them. None must live to tell the Forlish that the rabbit has grown fangs,' Huw said harshly, gesturing to the Forlish wounded.

'But ...' Kelyn began.

'If they live, we shall die. It is as simple as that!' Huw snarled.

'He's right,' Glyn said after a moment. 'We cannot let Forland know we have an elf and can defeat the raiders they send.'

The big Velshman took up a Forlish sword and finished off the badly wounded men swiftly, mercifully, as he would an animal marked for slaughter.

'What are you planning?' Kelyn asked.

'Once we are sure Patcham is safe, I need to take Sendatsu and journey to the other villages — we all need to be protected,' Huw said simply. That was enough for them to know now. In fact, it would be better if he kept his plans to himself, at least for now. Sendatsu always acted strangely when they asked him about Dokuzen and returning to the elves. One step at a time, that was the best way. Huw could almost hear his father telling him this, sitting in his chair by the fire, talking about farming but also about life. Huw had not always listened, instead begging his father to tell him stories about heroes, about elves and magic. But now he was surprised how much seemed to have stayed in his memory.

Reflective, he walked back to his house, not sure what he would find there but knowing he had to swallow his pain and concentrate on getting Sendatsu to help him. In this Rhiannon would no doubt prove to be the greatest help, which made it doubly difficult. Huw could almost see them now — the elf had his shirt off and Rhiannon had her hands on him, the way he often dreamed she would touch him ...

He waited outside the door for a moment, forced himself to hide his feelings, so nothing would show on his face when he walked inside. But when he pushed the door open, it was to find nobody in the main room.

Huw knew where they were, because he could hear them.

The door to his father's bedroom, where Rhiannon had been sleeping, was shut but it was thin wood and Huw could hear the sounds coming from behind it, including the rhythmic creaking of his father's old wooden bed.

That was almost too much for him. He did not know whether to rage, or cry, or both. Tears of hurt, of frustration, of despair and anger streamed down his face and he cuffed them away furiously. That Sendatsu could be in his father's bed, with the woman he loved … for a moment he wanted to storm in there, hit the elf until the hurt stopped. Of course, he knew that would be pointless — Sendatsu would have no more trouble beating him than he'd had in winning Rhiannon.

His next thought was to disappear. The village was safe, his father avenged, he could go away, far away, forget all about the pair of them, about Ward and his plans for the Velsh.

But the sight of his father's chair by the fire stopped him.

He could never say whether a whim or something deeper made him cross the room and sit down. He had not sat in his father's chair since his return, had not even gone near it. It had too many memories. But now he sat back and thought. Just being in the chair seemed to clear his mind.

He had ignored, deliberately walked away from many of his father's teachings down in Cridianton. His father would never have tolerated the slavery, the cruelty, the evil that festered at the heart of Forlish civilisation. Huw had managed to convince himself he was doing the right thing by staying, when all he was doing was indulging his own selfishness. He had rationalised staying there, taking on a new name, pretending to be Forlish, refusing to speak out against the brutality he saw every day, just so he could go on pretending he was doing the right thing. Not only that, so he could entertain the foolish hope he and Rhiannon could be together one day. And look how that turned out!

No, it was time to stand up, to take responsibility. It was time to be the man his father wanted him to be. He reached up to the elfbolt that hung around his neck and, with some difficulty, tore loose the thong. He looked at the charm for a moment and then hurled it into the fire. It was time to stop putting his hope in a small rock; it was time to put the trust in himself. He sat there in the chair, the tears rolling down his face for the mistakes he had made, the things he desperately wanted to tell his father and the things he would have to do now. The noises from the bedroom were like salt in those wounds. If he had not been in his father's chair, he would never have been able to stay in the house. But he used it, as well as the realisation of his own mistakes, to turn inside himself. His father was no longer there, there was nobody to protect him, to shield him from the harsh world and the truth. He had to stand up for himself. He had to face it all. He forced himself to stay there until the noises stopped, until his tears stopped also.

Then he busied himself with getting the fire going, hung a pot and set water to boil, so he could cook some oats. He was not quiet about it, trying to use the everyday tasks to blank out everything else. It hurt, it stung like nothing he had ever known, but he gritted his teeth and kept going, because there were more important things at stake.

He put the oats in the water, added salt and stirred it vigorously, slapped three plates on the table, hunted along shelves until he found some honey in a comb, in a small wooden bowl covered with cloth. By the time he had judged the oats were almost ready, the creak of the door opening made him turn.

'Huw! How long have you been here?' Sendatsu asked as he walked out, wearing just a pair of trews. The muscles of his upper body were in sharp relief, rippling in the firelight. Huw hated him.

'Long enough,' he said shortly, staring directly at the elf.

Sendatsu flushed under his gaze and Huw took that as a small victory, although a feather to weigh against the lead weight in his gut.

'Sit down. Have something to eat. We need to talk.' Huw took the pot from the heat and began spooning porridge onto plates.

Sendatsu stared at Huw with a mix of shock, horror and guilt. He had not meant this to happen. He knew Rhiannon had built up this picture of him as a fairy tale come to life and was obsessed with meeting an elf. He also knew Huw yearned for her. He was not out here to get involved with anyone, let alone a human woman. His love was Asami, although she was untouchable.

The wound along his ribs was painful but, when he took off his tunic, proved to be relatively shallow. He had instructed Rhiannon on how to boil a cloth clean, as well as a needle and thread, then boil the herbs they had selected from the bunches hanging inside Delia's roof and put them into a compress. She had been obviously nervous but determined enough to sew the long wound together, add the poultice and cover with a clean bandage.

'You've done a good job.' He smiled as she washed her hands clean.

'It was a pleasure to help a hero,' she replied. 'I'd better check there's nothing else. Are you sore anywhere?'

Sendatsu admitted his shoulder ached where he had dived forwards under a sword stroke.

Instantly Rhiannon was running her hands across his arms and shoulders, down his back and stomach.

'It all feels good to me,' she said, a little huskily.

Until then he had looked at her as merely helping fix up his wound. But the feeling of her fingers over his skin made the goosebumps stand up. The battle had left him on top of the world. Having the whole village hail him as their saviour had him feeling ready to burst through a stone wall. She was so close to him, her lips slightly parted. It had been over three years since he had been with a woman; since Kayiko's death he had been with no other. The closest he had come was Asami's kiss in the garden, just before he fled Dokuzen. Rhiannon's hand went down his side, brushed the top of his trews and he felt his control crack. She might be a human but, this close, she looked no different to an elf. The feeling of her hands set him on fire. He had to have her, simple as that.

Getting her into bed had been a blur. He was not sure what he had said or promised to get her into bed with him.

She had wanted to talk about Dokuzen almost as soon as they had finished, while he lay there, horrified at what he had done. Surely this was a mistake that would come back to haunt him. Part of him should have been disgusted he had slept with a human. Back in Dokuzen that would be considered little better than a sheep. But that was not bothering Sendatsu. He was struggling to see the difference between elves and humans now. He knew the truth of what happened three hundred years ago was hidden but he was wondering how much else might be hidden. Certainly there had been little difference in the firelight. It had been a long time but it hadn't been *that* long. No, he was more concerned about Rhiannon's reaction. He needed to get out, needed time and space to think, to come up with a way to fix what he had just done. They could never have a future — but that was exactly what she was talking about. He needed to let her down gently, find a way to leave her that did not break her heart. She would not understand.

He mumbled some excuse and walked out into the main part of the house but was shocked to see Huw cooking porridge. Had Huw heard what was going on in the bedroom? How was he to cover this up, how would Huw react ...

'Huw! How long have you been here?' he asked, to give himself time to think.

'Long enough,' came the reply, while the knowing gaze was enough to make Sendatsu flush. He knew how Huw felt about the dancer — even a blind man could see the attraction the bard had for her. And Huw had shown him nothing but kindness, had even shown him how to lead this village to victory, then had waited out here, listened in, known Sendatsu and Rhiannon were in his dead father's bed ... Sendatsu burned with shame. This was all a terrible mistake. He should leave them now before he did any more harm.

'Sit down. Have something to eat. We need to talk,' Huw said, serving up the porridge, thumping it onto the plates as though it had offended him.

'I'm not really hungry,' Sendatsu lied.

'Sit!' Huw thundered, his trained voice almost rattling the rafters.

Sendatsu sighed. He supposed he owed the bard this much. He would have to explain himself, apologise and then leave.

'What do you want to talk about?' Sendatsu sat down tiredly. He felt a little sick but, strangely, also hungry. He hauled a plate of porridge towards himself.

'Today was a victory. But we need to repeat that at every village across Vales,' Huw stated, taking a seat opposite Sendatsu and reaching out for a heaped plate, then for the bowl of honey.

'What do you mean, every village?' Sendatsu took the honey himself. This was not what he expected Huw to say.

'We need to travel to every village and show them what we achieved here. We need to protect every Velsh village, not just this one. We have to show them how to build the crossbows, how to protect themselves with palisades, ditches and walls, so that Ward's Forlish raiders will be thrown out, wherever they try to attack.'

'And how long will that take?'

'As long as it has to. We won't need to stay for days at each village after a while, for they will get the idea, and we can leave them to finish the work themselves. Of course, for the bigger villages, there will be a need to think of different ways to protect them. So you'll need to talk to all of them.'

Sendatsu was wrong-footed by Huw's approach. They both knew what had been going on in the bedroom. Why was Huw not talking about that? He forced himself to think. He might feel guilty but he was not going to commit to what sounded like moons of travel and effort — and little promise of the answers he so sorely needed to get back to his children.

'No. I can't do that. Surely you can do it now — it's simple enough: build a wall, craft a few dozen crossbows and surprise the raiders, teach them to fear you Velsh.' Sendatsu scooped up a huge spoonful of porridge and swallowed.

'It has to be you,' Huw told him coldly. 'Only you can make it happen. If I walk into a village, I am just some strange Velshman with crazy ideas. But you — you are an elf. They will think you a hero. They will listen to you. My people are crying out for a saviour. It has to be you.'

'I am here to find the answers I seek, nothing more. You want an elf from your legends. I am not that person,' Sendatsu warned.

Huw leaned forwards. 'You have to be. There is nobody else! You can't tell me that today did not change you. I saw your face as the village cheered you, as people hailed you as their hero. Imagine that happening every day, at villages right across Vales. And then there're all the men, women and children's lives you will save. I know they do not mean as much to you elves but I think these people's lives and dreams, even if they are short, are worth fighting for. Think of them — all alive if you help them, dead if you do not. Will the revels in Dokuzen be as sweet with those deaths on your conscience?'

'Aroaril curse you!' Sendatsu dropped his spoon. 'Of course I care about their lives — that is why I fought for your bloody village today! But I have other responsibilities. I have to get back to Dokuzen as soon as possible. They are counting on me! And I don't want to be a hero — I never did. I have never cared what people think of me, never wanted to be a leader. You have the wrong elf.'

Huw stared into his eyes. The spirit of his father was with him now and the words were easy to find. Fear, which had so often stilled his tongue in the past, was not a concern now.

'There is no other. I am sorry but you will be who I need you to be. This is the price you must pay for the knowledge you seek. Rhiannon was right: you will never discover what you need by yourself. Either the Forlish will kill my people or they will run from you. Aid me and I shall see to it that you return to Dokuzen with everything you need. But if you refuse to help, then I shall spread word that none are to speak to you. Every door in the land will be shut to you. You will wander alone, friendless, shouting your questions helplessly.'

Sendatsu nearly hurled himself across the table at the bard but managed to control himself — just. Huw was right, Aroaril damn him. He did need the bard's help. But there was still a chance to make him see sense ...

'Be reasonable, Huw! What will it achieve? If we protect every village, surely the Forlish will just return with their army and lay waste to Vales anyway. And a few crossbows and a wooden wall won't stand up to a proper attack.'

Huw smiled. 'You are right. Which is why, after we have

protected the villages, you are going to take me back to Dokuzen and we will persuade the elves to come and help my people.'

'What!' Sendatsu surged to his feet.

'It makes perfect sense. This is the perfect solution.'

'That is not going to happen,' Sendatsu warned.

'Why not? You can tell your elders, your king or whoever rules in Dokuzen that they need to become part of the world again. They have to stand up now, or they will have their worst fear — a warlike nation at their door. Bring me back to Dokuzen and I will show them Ward will not stop until he has sacked not just our homes but theirs as well.'

Sendatsu almost choked on his porridge. His return to Dokuzen was going to be fraught with danger as it was. Bringing humans back as well would be impossible.

'Huw, they will kill you if you come back with me. No human has been beyond the barrier for three centuries. They have patrols that do nothing but look for humans. If they ever found any, they would kill them on sight. You would never get to speak to the Council ...'

'You would protect us. Because Rhiannon and I would have the information you and the Council seek. We would give it to them at the same time they hear our plea for help,' Huw said simply.

Sendatsu gazed at Huw with a mixture of awe and hatred. The bard's plan to blackmail both himself and the Elven Council into getting his own way was bravery far beyond anything Sendatsu could imagine. Yet it was also immensely foolish, for the Council did not want to hear what Huw knew — they wanted him silenced. Killing him would be their instant solution. He considered telling Huw everything: explaining about the scroll, his father, about Mai and Cheijun. Yesterday he might have but this new Huw, determined to get his own way, was a different story. If Huw knew the truth, would he turn the Velsh against Sendatsu? It was a risk he could not take. He would have to agree to Huw's accursed demands — at least until he had the information.

'And don't think you can pretend to go along with this and then run once we have the knowledge. You won't be allowed to speak to the villagers — only me. Only when we are done will I tell you ...'

That was too much for Sendatsu ... before he knew it, he had leaped across the table and grabbed Huw by his tunic.

'You can't do this to me!' he howled.

Huw did not move, his hands kept by his sides.

'I am sorry but I have to,' he said. 'Hit me all you like. It won't gain you anything.'

Sendatsu wanted to punch him until the bard agreed to help but hesitated. Angry as he was, he struggled to bring himself to strike the young bard. There was a new determination in Huw's eyes and he knew the bard would not give in.

'Sendatsu! What are you doing?'

The pair of them turned, frozen in place, to see Rhiannon hurrying out of the bedroom, pulling her tunic straight, her hair dishevelled.

Neither answered her.


Rhiannon stretched out on the bed, feeling as though everything was right with the world, for the first time since Huw had given her the shocking news Ward had killed her father and was now after her. Everything had seemed so crazy since then but now it made sense. She was going to live in Dokuzen, she was going to dance for the elves — she was going to marry an elf — all her dreams were coming true!

The battle in the village had shaken her — she had been determined not to be one of those helpless maidens from the songs; the ones who waited nervously while the hero saved the day. But the reality of the battle had been dramatically different from the ones she sang about. The noise, the blood, the smells, the sights of men and horses dying ... being so close to death, seeing it all around her had made her feel more alive than ever before. Every breath, knowing it could be your last, was impossibly sweet; every little detail was fixed in her brain.

Victory had been the best moment in her life. The feeling as she realised she was going to live, that they were all going to live, had been indescribable. Exultation had swept through her, her blood felt like it was bubbling with joy — a kind of delight that she had never experienced before.

Seeing Sendatsu save them all, hearing how he had defeated no less than five of the vicious Forlish raiders, seeing him return to the cheers covered in blood, it had been natural to want to help him. She wanted to show that she was just as valuable. Then he had taken his tunic off and she wanted to see him up close. From afar he had looked just like a man and she was sure he had to be different somehow. At first it had been easy, he had sat there like a statue, but then something changed and he reached up and kissed her ... She shivered a little, remembering it. How had it happened so fast? She had never intended to do that. But she had been swept up in the moment and, before she knew it, Sendatsu had brought her in here. All the way he was telling her how beautiful she was, how she was the most stunning human he had ever met, the only one to compare with the elven maidens at home. And all the time he was kissing her, touching her.

It had been so easy to just go along, caught up in the mood of ecstasy from the battle, from having everyone's hero tell her she was special, the one human he had actually been attracted to.

Even so, she had baulked when he had tried to take off her tunic.

'I'm not ready ... I don't think we should,' she had said breathlessly, placing her hand on his rippling chest.

'Of course we should! You can't stop what we are both feeling,' Sendatsu said hoarsely, head dipping to kiss her neck.

She thrilled to the feeling for a moment, then gently pushed him away.

'No,' she said firmly. 'I can't lie with a man until we have Walked The Tree together, sealed our marriage before the people ...' Thinking of the people made her imagine Huw, with his burning brown eyes and his gentle smile, watching her Walk The Tree with Sendatsu and she drew back.

'But elves don't Walk The Tree,' Sendatsu pointed out, drawing her back in again, his hands slipping down her body. 'We exchange vows before Aroaril.'

All thoughts of Huw vanished from her mind.

'What do you mean? You will take me to Dokuzen with you — will we exchange vows there?' she breathed. 'We shall marry?'

'Yes, oh, yes.' Sendatsu's hands were roaming lower, while his lips were on her neck. But she listened to his words, not the meaning behind them.

Thoughts of seeing the elves, of achieving all she had ever dreamed, filled her and the exultation sweeping through her was even greater than after the battle. She kissed him deeply, barely even aware as his hands went to her tunic once more, began to lift it upwards.

Every time she thought about stopping, she imagined Dokuzen and the wonders they would see together and that promise filled her with a great warm feeling, more pleasure, even, than what they had done in the bed, amazing as that had been.

Now she lay here, torn between regret and excitement at what the future held. Perhaps this was all meant to happen, she mused. She had lost her father but that tragedy had brought her here, had enabled her to meet Sendatsu and have the chance to go to Dokuzen. Obviously this was her destiny, just as Sendatsu said. An elf and a human ... the songs and the lore said such a thing could never work but Sendatsu was not so different from a man — just better. But she would rewrite the songs, would go to Dokuzen and create new ones. In her mind's eye she saw herself wandering the fabled streets with Sendatsu, hand in hand, as he pointed out the marvellous sights. She could see herself being introduced to his parents, being embraced by his friends and family. Best of all, she could see herself dancing for them, singing for them, performing in some great arena that put even the stone theatres of Cridianton to shame. And she could hear the cheers as they acknowledged her talents, rose as one to applaud her performance. It warmed her, even more than Sendatsu had been able to do.

But slowly, noise from outside intruded on her comfortable daydream. Sendatsu was arguing with ... Huw! A tiny sliver of fear, of uncertainty, shot through her. She thought about staying in bed, hiding away for as long as possible, but the voices grew louder and she could not bear to imagine Huw seeing this. He was her friend, her first friend, and she had no intention of hurting him. If Sendatsu had not been here ... She pushed that thought aside with the fear Huw might see her like this. She hunted for her clothes, carelessly strewn on the floor. She had better get out there and try to pretend nothing had happened.

She hurried out, to see them locked together, Sendatsu about to strike Huw with his fist.

'Sendatsu! What are you doing?'

Neither answered her.

'What is going on? You are friends, you worked together to save this village — why are you fighting?' she demanded.

Huw was the first to recover, with Sendatsu struggling to think of something that would get him out of this situation.

'Sendatsu and I are discussing why he should take me back to Dokuzen with him, so I can persuade the elves to come and save my people from Ward and the Forlish armies,' he said coolly.

Rhiannon smiled. 'But that will be fine! He is taking me back with him, of course he can bring you as well! We are going to marry!'

'He is taking you back? You will marry?' Huw gasped.

'I am?' Sendatsu was almost as horrified and frantically had to compose his face. Had he really said that? Could he truly have been so stupid? He couldn't remember promising anything so rash but Rhiannon's expression warned that he had.

Sendatsu looked from one human to the other as they stared at him, and realised how deep a hole he had dug for himself. With a snarl, he shoved Huw away and the bard tumbled across the floor, landing almost by the chair next to the fire. How was he going to get out of this?

'Sendatsu! What are you doing?' Rhiannon cried, rushing over to Huw's side.

Sendatsu could not talk, he was so furious, with himself and these two humans.

'He doesn't want to help us humans any more. He wants to go back to his own kind.' Huw shrugged off Rhiannon's helping hand and pushed himself back to his feet. He had been a little afraid Sendatsu would hit him but, after the pain of what he had listened to before, he almost welcomed a real blow. Being thrown across the room was nothing, although his hip and back were telling him he would feel it tomorrow.

'That's not true! He's going to help us and he's going to take us back to Dokuzen,' Rhiannon said stubbornly, staring at Sendatsu, who kept his back to them.

'Sendatsu! Tell him! Show Huw he's wrong!'

Sendatsu thought fast, and desperately. 'It's Huw's fault,' he said quickly. 'I can't go back to Dokuzen until I have some answers for the Elven Council. But Huw wants me to stay out here until the Forlish are defeated. He seeks to keep us from going to Dokuzen!'

He watched with satisfaction as Rhiannon swung her attention to Huw.

'Huw, is this true?' she demanded.

'We need his help and this is the only way to ensure he does not slip off to Dokuzen in the night, without either of us,' Huw stated.

'He would never do that! He is not some man, he is an elf — they only speak the truth!'

Unseen behind her, Sendatsu winced.

'Well, we shall be as quick as possible. But we cannot leave the people here to be killed by Ward's Forlish, as he killed your father,' Huw said craftily.

Rhiannon clenched her fists. 'No, you are right.'

'And I want to go to Dokuzen as much as you. It is just a question of waiting a moon or two.'

'True,' Rhiannon agreed.

'Then it is all settled?' Huw smiled, his eyes firmly fixed on Sendatsu's face.

'It sounds like a plan!' Rhiannon enthused. 'And I have a wonderful idea for when we travel around the villages. We shall

240

arrive and sing a song about Sendatsu, tell them he is here to help!'

'What?' Huw and Sendatsu asked together.

'A song to announce him and praise him, tell everyone how he's a hero, here to help them,' she exclaimed. 'We can start work on it tonight. Oh, I can just hear it in my head! We'll sing it as we enter each village, let them know how lucky they are to have an elf to help them.'

Huw ground his teeth. He knew he would not be able to sing Sendatsu's praises. The words would choke him.

Sendatsu instinctively shied away from this. But he had no choice, he just had to go along and pray he found a way out.

'So what do we say?' Rhiannon asked.

'Fine,' Huw grated, feeling Rhiannon's eyes on him.

'Perfect,' Sendatsu lied.

'That's settled then!' Rhiannon smiled.

# 15

*The Magic-weavers were defeated, their power broken and their leaders either killed or forced to swear their lives to me. The shattered survivors were willing to do whatever asked of them. But, in Dokuzen, appearance is everything and my standing had been humbled by their revolt. The loss of several clan leaders, the death of my wife and the fact that they had dared to attack me had the people whispering: 'The forefathers must have made a mistake'; I was 'not strong enough to lead the people forwards'. The whispers were being led by my old friend Naibun. I trusted him to finish what I had begun. Instead he smiled to my face and worked behind my back. Everything I did fell into his trap.*

*When I mourned my wife he said I was weak. When I tried to lead the discussion he said I was distracted. And all the time he was murmuring that the forefathers were wrong. I had let the Magic-weavers nearly seize power. I was leaving the humans with the power to destroy us.*

*I did not hear — but others listened.*

Huw had been worried the village would react badly to the news they were leaving. But while there was some concern, the spirit of the victory from yesterday allowed him to convince them this was the best thing to do.

'The raiders are not going to come back here quickly — not after what we did to them!' Huw told them, to roars of approval.

'They have learned to fear us and instead will seek easier targets. That is why we must go, to help protect the other villages.'

'Can't we let them burn Crumlin to the ground first?' Glyn called, which brought a gale of laughter.

'That is what I fear they will do. And we cannot let that happen. So Sendatsu, Rhiannon and I will journey around Vales, trying to get to the villages before Ward's raiders.'

'But what about us? What if they come again?' someone called. 'Without the elf …'

'You do not need the elf to defeat them any more! We shall have more than enough crossbows in a day or two so that we can post men — and women — around the entire wall,' Huw fired back.

'But what if they get inside the wall?'

Sendatsu had been watching, sourly, as Huw spoke but now, with some prodding from Rhiannon, he stepped forwards. He could not see a way out of this and the knowledge was heavy on him.

'We shall leave tomorrow so today I shall show you how to fight,' he announced and felt a little sick as they cheered enthusiastically.

It was not going to be enough. They needed months and years of training to take on the Forlish and what little he could teach in a day would merely allow them to survive a few heartbeats against a proper warrior. But he wanted to move on and, in that, Huw was in agreement with him — every day more of the Forlish raiders had to be arriving in Vales.

Training started almost immediately, with normal village life suspended while the men worked. Crude wooden swords were quickly fashioned by Kelyn and his carpenters, basically just branches cut to the right size and rough shape. The real swords, the ones seized from the dead Forlish raiders, were kept hidden away, for fear of the villagers doing more damage to themselves.

The men were all excited. The tale of how Sendatsu had taken on five raiders had been told and retold and even grown in its retelling, to the point where there were now almost a dozen of them falling to the elven blade. The older boys were all running around, pretending to be elves and slaughtering Forlish warriors by the hundred. Something of that was within their fathers, who lined up, crude wooden swords in hands, ready to listen to Sendatsu.

But instead of making them duel each other, he formed them into three lines and spent the whole day drilling them, teaching the three basic blocks and six sword strokes, from the double-strike to the figure-eight, and making them practise these over and over, until even their work-toughened hands were blistered and muscles aching and they were cursing both their own enthusiasm and, quietly, the elf himself.

'You must do that every day, until you can do them in your sleep. In battle, your mind will be swamped by fear, by the thoughts of what you have to do. You must know those strokes so you can make them without thinking,' Sendatsu finally explained. 'That is the only way you will survive.'

Huw watched Sendatsu for a while. He thought about learning himself, but he worried it would affect his lyre playing — his hands had only just recovered from all the digging. More importantly, he knew he would look clumsy and foolish compared to Sendatsu if he tried to use a sword. It was stupid, particularly as Rhiannon had already made her choice.

Instead, he worked with Kelyn for the day, preparing a series of models to show how the elven crossbow could be built, so that — in Kelyn's words — any half-sober carpenter with more than one hand could make them. With them went a huge bag of the bolts, as well as three working crossbows — one each for Huw and Rhiannon and one to use as an example as they travelled around. He started to understand how the crossbow worked, watched Kelyn make one from scratch and felt much happier about going out to a strange village and telling them how these would save them.

He also practised with the crossbows. Holding them at the hip made it almost impossible to aim but he persevered, loosing an endless stream of bolts, and began to feel he could direct them with some confidence. Of course, the fact they were only useful within twenty yards meant the target had to be close anyway, so it made accuracy possible.

Finally, he also found a couple of teenagers, sons of older farmers, and used some of the gold he had brought back from Ward's court to make sure his father's farming strip and various animals would be looked after and run well, in his absence. Truth be told, he had never been good with crops, much less animals. A pair of young farmers' sons, both of them a year past their manhood of sixteen, would do a far better job than he ever could.

It was warm in Kelyn's workshop and, even better, Rhiannon was nowhere in sight. He could not bear the thought of seeing her with Sendatsu but, equally, he could not think of leaving her behind.

Rhiannon could not stop thinking about going to Dokuzen, about showing the elves how she could dance and hearing their applause. None of her dances seemed to be good enough, so she spent the time working on new ones, trying to outdo what she had already achieved at the court of King Ward. She also worked on a song for Sendatsu and, when she took a break, more practically made sure they had plenty of twice-baked bread, salted meat, dried oats and dried fruit to take with them. The villages would feed them, she was sure, but there would also be nights when they would have to make camp.

She also decided to repair her relationship with Huw.

After extracting the promise from Sendatsu, the rest of the night had been somewhat uncomfortable, with nobody speaking much. Huw had finished a bowl of porridge, then disappeared into his room. Rhiannon had wanted to speak to him but he had been quick to make his excuses. Strangely, Sendatsu was much the same with his behaviour, curling himself into a blanket by the fire. She glanced over at Sendatsu — and saw him tucking something away in his belt pouch, the pouch he had been careful to hide from her when she had been treating his wound. She thought about asking him but his eyes were now closed and he seemed to be asleep.

The next morning, when she walked out, it was to find the pair of them had already vanished, leaving her alone with the dirty plates and the bowls.

'Do they think I am some sort of servant?' she muttered.

She found herself some bread and cheese before working on her dancing, but thoughts of Huw nagged at her and she finally went to find him. She had to ask around before finally discovering him in Kelyn's workshop.

'Hello Huw,' she had greeted cheerfully. 'Greetings Kelyn!'

'And a good afternoon to you,' Kelyn had responded warmly. He had been smiling since Huw told the village Kelyn was just as much the hero of the battle as Sendatsu, for designing and building so many crossbows in so quick a time.

Huw just grunted.

Kelyn chattered about the weather and the villages they would need to visit but gradually the awkward atmosphere reached even him and he found an excuse to be elsewhere.

'I thought we should talk,' Rhiannon said immediately.

'About what?' Huw replied surlily. Seeing her was tearing him in two.

'Last night should change nothing between us. We are still friends.'

Huw held back what was on the tip of his tongue.

'We have been through too much for this to come between us,' Rhiannon continued. 'I shall always be grateful to you for how you saved me from Ward, after he killed my father.'

As usual, mention of her gratitude for his lies silenced him, even more effectively than fear of driving her away.

'What is happening between Sendatsu and me ... it might bring our two races closer together! We could be the start of a new relationship with the elves. And he has promised to take me to Dokuzen! I shall meet his friends and family, dance and sing for the elves — and you can visit us whenever you want ...'

'Oh yes? And was this before or after he rutted with you?' Huw asked nastily, unable to help himself.

Rhiannon flushed and this time he was afraid he had gone too

246

far. 'Now that is not something a friend would say,' she told him stiffly.

'I'm sorry — it is just because I care for you, am worried about you,' he said quickly. 'After saving you from Ward, I do not want to see you hurt by Sendatsu. He might intend to take you back to Dokuzen but what if the other elves disagree? What if he really has an elven girl promised to him back there, waiting for his return? I'm sure he did not come to our world thinking to fall in love.'

Rhiannon paused and he kept his face still, just a hint of honest concern there. Referring to Ward was a risk but he had thought hard last night — sleep being difficult — and come to the conclusion Rhiannon was going to end up in tears, her heart broken. And who better to pick up the pieces and provide the shoulder to cry upon than her only friend?

'I know you only want the best for me, that you're trying to do what my father would, if only he was here ...' Rhiannon said slowly.

More likely he would be offering to sell you to the elf for a sack of gold and a pledge the elves would recommend his performing academy to the boys and girls of Forland, Huw thought cynically.

'But I ask you, as a friend, to be happy for me and to trust me — I know what I am doing.'

Huw bit his tongue once more and merely nodded his head.

'Of course I trust you!' he lied.

'Then we are friends still?' she asked, a little nervously.

'We are friends still,' Huw confirmed.

So they worked a little on Sendatsu's song but mainly on a new dance for her, Huw coming up with music for her new moves. It had been hard for him to watch her — since last night, she seemed to have acquired a new grace, a new fluidity to her movements. What had occasionally seemed awkward or uncomfortable now flowed together and had him struggling to keep his mind on the music and off her lithe body.

All he could do was curse himself for not acting sooner — and curse the elf. If only the Velsh did not need a hero so much — and if only there was a better one than Sendatsu.

'You know, I saw him putting something back into his pouch last night,' she said.

'Did you see what?'

'No, but I shall ask him.' She smiled.

Broyle watched three riders leave Patcham, heading west towards the twin village that waited just a few miles away. The pair riding with the elf looked strangely familiar. He stared at them and then remembered — it was the dancer and the bard from Cridianton! They had been there when King Ward explained his plan for Vales. That made them traitors and Broyle burned for revenge.

'Do we take them, sarge?' Ricbert asked hoarsely.

'Not yet,' Broyle said scornfully.

He only had a dozen men — several of the wounded had died, for he had no way to treat them, while most of Oswald's surviving men had all left, heading back south to their homes or their units — Broyle did not care which. The men he had left were all battle-hardened but he was not going to rush in again. Not after the disaster last time. He could still hear the screams as men died — and could remember only too clearly how the elven warrior had sliced apart his warriors. There was something going on here — something the king needed to know about. But not yet. Broyle knew better than to return with just bad news. He had to return with this elf and those two traitors in ropes — and those crossbows as well. If word of these weapons reached down south, it would be a disaster. The Balians and Landish had learned not to face the Forlish armies in battle. They had been defeated too many times by the implacable shield wall that turned their best warriors into so much carrion for the birds. Now they skulked behind walls and tried to hold their cities. And they even failed there, for the Forlish armies were used to breaking down tall stone walls and taking their swords to the terrified people inside. But if the walls were packed with men and women using those crossbows ... Broyle could see the enormous cloud of shafts that would cover any Forlish attack, dooming it to failure. This could change the course of the wars, could even see the king's armies

forced to retreat. Bringing both the elf and the crossbow back to
the king would get Broyle his own company of men.

But, above all else, Broyle wanted revenge. He hated losing his
men — and he hated being beaten even more. Seizing those three
was more important than the king's praise.

'We follow them. We have to attack where they can't escape —
and where we won't be followed. They've got horses, remember,
and we have none. We'll strike when they least expect it,' he
vowed.


Huw had never been to Crumlin. For one they were rivals for
grazing land and, in times of drought, for water. They were like
brothers, always squabbling. Patcham was definitely the younger
brother in the relationship. While Patcham had been founded
barely a century ago, Crumlin dated back before the time of the
elves and elves had actually lived there once. Several former elf-
built buildings still stood at the centre of the village. A hall, a
villa and three outbuildings had, over the years, been turned into
the heart of Crumlin. All had brick walls, tiled roofs and light,
spacious rooms. All were home to several families, the richest and
the oldest in the area.

As ever when he found examples of previous elven life in this
part of the world, Sendatsu was fascinated. How had these elves
and humans lived together? Had the Velsh been the servants,
even the slaves of the elves? Or had they been neighbours,
working together? Had a Velsh rebellion seen the elves draw
back into the forest, hide behind their magic barrier and their
bows? The Velsh had tried to preserve the buildings as best they
could but, as always, it was obvious they lacked the knowledge
to do so properly. He stretched. His side was healing well,
although the stitches Rhiannon had put in were pulling when
he rode.

He wanted to ride across, talk to the oldest Velsh and find out
more about them. Could he find the answers here that would
lead him home and let him escape his foolish promises? Then he
glanced across at Huw, saw the bard watching him closely.

'Don't try and speak to them. I shall do it for you. Remember our deal,' Huw told him and Sendatsu had to grit his teeth and nod reluctantly.

Rhiannon began singing, telling the villagers how wonderful Sendatsu was, how a hero had arrived to save them. It was enjoyable to listen to, although Huw's playing seemed less than enthusiastic. But she did not get the chance to reach the best bit, about him being an elf, before they found themselves surrounded by villagers.

'Who are you and what are you doing here?' someone accused, and Rhiannon stopped singing as she looked around at a small crowd of partly angry, partly nervous Crumliners.

'I am Huw the bard, son of Earwen of Patcham,' Huw called out. 'These are my friends, here to help you!'

There was a short discussion, while several of the men peered uncertainly at Huw and then whispered to each other.

'We do know of Earwen, and that he had a crazy son, who sang to the sheep!' an older man declared.

'That is me,' Huw admitted.

'So what are you doing here? You know Patchamers are not welcome here,' the man cried. 'Are you spies for the raiders?'

'If we were Forlish raiders, we'd have ridden in here with swords in hands, not sat and introduced ourselves. And we'd have cut you down while you talked,' Huw told him. 'Gather up the people so we can tell them why we have come ...'

'Why should we listen to a Patchamer?'

Huw pointed at Sendatsu. 'Because we have brought an elf to help you!' he shouted.

'An elf? Where?'

'We have an elf here!'

Almost immediately the crowd began pushing forwards and Sendatsu felt like turning his horse and galloping out of there. This was exactly like the other villages ...

'Stand back! Calm down!' Huw used his horse to push people back. 'Do you want to listen to what he says or drive him away?'

For a long moment, nobody moved, then Sendatsu relaxed as the people eased back.

'I am Dafyd, and my family has lived in this village for ten generations. We shall listen to the elf's words.' The older Velshman stepped forwards.

Huw forced a smile. He nodded at Rhiannon, who began singing again, all about the wonder of Sendatsu.

Sendatsu breathed again as the people kept their distance, although all watched him. The bard had proved his worth there.


Sendatsu had half expected everyone to crowd into the old elven hall to listen to his words and he thought it would be the perfect venue. But, apparently, it was home to Dafyd and his extended family, so the village merely stood outside in a rough semicircle to hear Huw — and especially Sendatsu — speak.

The story of the attack on Patcham had reached them and left them fearful, so they actually cheered the news the Forlish had been defeated and sent running for their lives.

'We have been seeing smoke on the horizon for the last few days — in all directions,' Dafyd explained. 'Everyone is wondering what is going on.'

They accepted news of the Forlish raiders, and how they were trying to force the Velsh to submit to King Ward's rule — but it was Sendatsu they wanted to see, they wanted to talk about.

Huw seethed at the way they fawned over Sendatsu, falling in love with him even faster than Rhiannon had. But he hid it and helped Sendatsu explain why magic was not the best way to keep the village safe.

'You must do the work yourself, in order to be truly protected,' Huw said and they nodded solemnly.

Within a turn of the hourglass of the three of them riding in, a pair of carpenters and six other helpers were poring over the elven crossbows, while the rest of the village was harnessing horses and dragging both rocks and trees to begin a palisade for the village. Unlike Patcham, Crumlin fields were full of stones and rocks, which made them harder to plough and prepare for planting. It was just one of the little differences that had provided much of the rivalry between the two villages. More importantly, it provided plenty of material that could be used as a crude wall to protect the village. Meanwhile, Dafyd and his son Edwin had climbed onto the roof of the hall that was their home and the heart of the village and were building a crude lookout platform, to give the people warning of approaching raiders.

'If they see Patcham protected, they will come here next — and we don't want that,' Huw told Dafyd.

'Really? A Patchamer caring about us?' Dafyd sniffed.

'We like to see you look foolish — we don't want you dead. Besides, if the Forlish burned you out, who would we have for rivals then?' Huw smiled.

Dafyd's laugh boomed out and the Crumliner invited the three of them to eat with him that night.

'Who is the girl?' he asked. 'Yours?'

'No, she is with the elf. She's Forlish but no friend of Ward — he killed her father and she only escaped with my help,' he explained, the effort of keeping his thoughts hidden making his eyes water.

'There are many like that in Vales now. Forlish who are afraid of their own king; who fled his guards and his taxes for a taste of freedom in Vales. A man should not have to bend the knee or hand over his goods to make rich men even richer,' Dafyd declared.

'But if the alternative is having your home burned out and your children killed ...' Huw pointed out.

'I would have agreed, if it meant the village was safe,' Dafyd admitted. 'We wouldn't have liked it but we would have still done it.'

'This way is better,' Huw agreed, hoping Dafyd would not take it a step further and ask what the plan was when Forlish raiders were beaten back and Ward turned to his regular army.

Luckily there was plenty to be done and, once again, Huw and Rhiannon led the village in songs to help the work. The huge piles of rocks that had been unearthed over decades by farmers, cursed as they were rolled and hauled into cairns at the edge of fields, were loaded into wagons and dragged into place around the village. They served a double purpose — not only did they provide a barrier, and a way to stop raiders from riding into the village, but they were also an effective defensive position. Crossbowmen could hide high up and stand almost in safety as they poured a devastating cloud of bolts down at any attackers. And, finally, the smaller rocks could also be hurled, used as missiles themselves.

In between these crude piles of rock, trees were dragged around to fill in the gaps. It was different from Patcham's palisade but would prove just as effective, Sendatsu judged. The Crumliners had a reverent attitude to him, bowing whenever he walked past. It was strange but far better than the way some Velsh villages had swamped him in his first days out here. Living in elven buildings, seeing these examples of elven civilisation every day, had left the Crumliners feeling they were close to the elves. He was sure they had the secrets he wanted — but Huw seemed to follow him like a shadow, while Rhiannon was never far away either.

'If only we knew how to make the tiles to repair the roofs — or the glass to replace the windows. Storms have taken their toll over the years. We take care of the buildings as best we can but we lack the knowledge to keep them up to your standard,' Dafyd explained, before showing a collection of broken tiles, kept stored away safely. 'Do you know the secret?'

Sendatsu held the fragments of tile, examined them gently and carefully handed them back.

'I am sorry. That was not my job,' he admitted. 'I know they are made from clay, fired in a hot oven somehow, baked into shape and strength — but whether they add sand or rock or something, I do not know ...'

'That must be it! Well, the ingredients will be in here — we shall grind up a few and then bind the mixture with water, mix it with clay, try to make them ourselves!' Dafyd said excitedly. 'If we fail the first time, we shall try again — and again, until we get it right!'

Sendatsu smiled — and was about to ask him about Aroaril, when Huw grabbed him.

'Sorry, Dafyd, but the palisade needs elven expertise,' he interrupted.

'Of course! Still, we can talk more over dinner tonight ...?'

'I would like that very much,' Sendatsu said hastily.

'There are strange tales of an elf, travelling with a bard and a dancer,' Jin reported, pulling off his human clothes and scratching himself.

'Can't you stand still?' Hanto asked irritably.

'Sorry, sir. I think I have lice or something from these human clothes,' Jin grumbled.

Hanto sighed. 'Where has Sendatsu gone?'

'North and east.'

'Interesting. We shall follow him but we'll need to be careful. There are bands of armed humans roaming around. While you were in the village we spotted the trail of one large band going in that direction. We should move fast to catch him. The last thing we want is for Sendatsu to be killed by a human.'

'Jaken will have the skin off our backs,' Taigo muttered.

'Aroaril curse Jaken! I want to kill Sendatsu myself.'

Dafyd's family made the three of them more than welcome. Sendatsu was relieved to be inside a proper structure again, with real floors, real walls and stairs. However, it had been made to look more like a human house, with rough wattle walls put up to divide the large space into something that could house Dafyd's extended family, including several sons-in-law, daughters-in-law and grandchildren, as well as his and his wife's parents. Dafyd's mother proved to be very knowledgeable about herbs and helped replace Sendatsu's bandage and poultice, clucking with approval at the way it had been treated and was healing without infection.

They were given the best seats, as well as first choice of the roast pig. Sendatsu was able to eat this flesh now, although he made sure he chose well-cooked pieces, but he longed for some fish, some vegetables and above all rice. He needed something fresh to go with all these oats, meat and rough, grit-filled bread.

Progress had been excellent during the day and the Velsh were talking excitedly about what they had done, while Huw and Rhiannon played and sang for them. Sendatsu watched the small children laugh and play, chase each other in and out of the sitting adults — and felt a sharp pain in his heart. Each child's laugh made his heart leap for a moment, then sink deeper down.

'Now, who would like to see the secrets left behind to us by the elves?' Dafyd asked with a smile.

Sendatsu sat up immediately, ignoring the stares he was getting from Huw. Dafyd opened a small cupboard to bring out his treasures.

'Nothing like these over in Patcham, eh?' he said with a wink at Huw, before bringing them out to show.

The adults held back the children, who wanted to get close enough to look, and, from the way Dafyd handled them, it was obvious they were the most precious things in the village.

'I dread to think what would happen if the Forlish raiders got their hands on these,' Dafyd sighed. 'They are priceless.'

Heart in his mouth, Sendatsu leaned forwards to see as Dafyd placed them on a long wooden tray. Would they be evidence of worshipping Aroaril? Then his heart sank. It was a strange collection of household items. There were a few clay plates and pots, fragile with time; ordinary things with little value, and a handful of better items — all with flaws. A chipped pot with engraving around the base, a broken plate with a pretty design painted on the edge, a glass bottle with a crack in it. Strangely, all seemed to be marked with soot, or charred.

'These were not found in the houses, but in the fields, left behind by the elves when they left our world,' Dafyd explained.

Sendatsu was initially disappointed — then thought again. Why had they not been in the houses, why in the fields? And why did some look they had been rescued from the fire? Was this evidence of violence, or even a rush as the elves fled for Dokuzen? He would ask questions, and damn Huw!

'What do you know of the time when the elves left you?'

'I don't think Dafyd needs to bore everyone with that ...' Huw began.

'Little enough. My family has lived here for centuries and yet I do not know the truth of it. The memories passed down to me speak of great fear. Humans had attacked elves and they warned us any attempts to follow would meet with death. We cherish these objects, for they remind us of how we have fallen,' Dafyd said solemnly. 'Once we could have made objects like this — now we cannot. When the elves left, they took their knowledge and we have gone backwards, instead of advancing. Our craftsmen can only offer crude copies, with neither the patterns nor the quality. But one day, we dream, they will return and once again we shall reach for the stars!'

The other humans muttered agreement, and Sendatsu leaned forwards.

'How do you know humans attacked elves? Did it happen around here?'

'Oh, of course not!' Dafyd chuckled. 'You have nothing to fear! No, we would never attack the elves. It happened elsewhere.'

'You don't know where?' Sendatsu pressed.

'Far over the hills,' Dafyd said vaguely.

Sendatsu buried his face in his hands. It was a tantalising hint of what had happened but not enough. Nowhere near enough.

'What do you seek?' Dafyd asked.

'Humans worshipping Aroaril, humans who can speak a different language, who can read, maybe even humans with magic ...' Sendatsu said tiredly.

'What on earth do you want to find that for?' Dafyd's son, Edwin, blurted.

'There is no need,' Huw interrupted.

'Well, there's no magic around here. Skies above, I wish there was!' Dafyd smiled. 'If only the elves would return to us, live among us once more.'

Then Rhiannon stood.

'Well, they shall return! Sendatsu here has promised to take both Huw and myself to Dokuzen, where we shall meet the elven elders, tell them of events in the outside world and persuade them to come to our aid!'

Suddenly the roast pork was rising back up Sendatsu's throat. He swallowed and tasted bile.

'Skies above but that is the best news I have ever heard! With the elves on our side, the Velsh shall be safe, and enter a new golden age!' Dafyd exclaimed. 'Thank you, Sendatsu — and thank you, Huw and Rhiannon! If you can do that, we shall sing your praises forever! We shall tell everyone tomorrow — they will be delighted to hear ...'

Sendatsu groaned. Seeing Huw stare at him, a smile on his face, just rubbed salt in this wound.

'The elves are coming! The elves are coming!' several of the children began singing and dancing, making up their own steps, while the adults clapped along. The children's voices were the last straw. In them he could hear echoes of Mai and Cheijun, the last time he had heard them, as they had been coming down the passageway of his father's villa. He had heard them but not seen them for that one, last time ...

'Enough!' Sendatsu roared. 'The elves are not coming back — they care nothing for the struggles of humans. And if you hope elves can solve all your problems and make everything golden and happy, then you are fools — the stories of the glory of the elves have been handed down from village idiot to village idiot!'

He glared around the room and a couple of the smaller children began to cry. Stunned silence greeted him from the adults.

'Well, time we were all abed, don't you think?' Dafyd's wife, Vivien, said brightly and loudly into the gap.

Instantly the family was up and about, collecting plates, treasures and children and moving as one, as though all knew what the others were doing.

In no time at all, the three of them were left alone in the room.

'There are blankets there, and fresh straw for beds. We'll leave you to it — you must be tired,' Dafyd said hurriedly as he was tugged away by his wife.

'Wait, I am sorry ...' Sendatsu called, too late, as the last of them disappeared.

'What aren't you telling us?' Huw asked softly.

'What?' Sendatsu replied defensively.

'Your reaction just then. It is as if there are things about the elves we do not know and you don't wish to tell us ...'

'Well, you don't wish me to speak to the Velsh by myself, so I count us even on that score. If I had spoken to Dafyd alone, this would never have happened. So it's your fault as much as mine,' Sendatsu told him sharply.

'What about Rhiannon then?' Huw fired back. 'Perhaps you could tell her — I am sure she has proved worthy. After all, you are going to take her back to Dokuzen ...'

Sendatsu glanced at Rhiannon and felt a new surge of guilt. But she was his best weapon — his only weapon — against Huw.

'I want to return to Dokuzen. And I know Rhiannon wants to go also. I'm just trying to complete my mission and get back home swiftly. If you and Rhiannon do not want to go there ...'

'I want to go to Dokuzen!' Rhiannon interrupted.

'There you are then,' Sendatsu pointed out, restraining the urge to wince at what he was doing. 'It is Huw holding us back ...'

'I am trying to save lives,' Huw spat, outraged that Sendatsu was using Rhiannon against him. Well, two could play at that game. 'The Forlish are raiding my people every day and they killed my father. I would have thought you, Rhiannon, would want some revenge on the men who killed your father and wanted to rape you ...'

Rhiannon gasped and Huw had to fight to keep his thoughts off his face. The lies were eating him up inside but he had to do whatever it took to get the elf to help his people.

'We can do both,' Rhiannon insisted. 'We just have to work together, and not argue among ourselves.'

Huw and Sendatsu glared at each other.

'We need to move faster,' Sendatsu said. 'We can't spend days on one village.'

'We should leave tomorrow,' Huw agreed.

'There. All settled. And we can be friends again.' Rhiannon smiled.

Sendatsu managed something closer to a smile than grimace. 'I am going to bed. We have another early start.' He stood abruptly and hurried over to where the straw and blankets waited. He thumped some straw into shape and rolled himself into the rough blanket. He wanted the pair of them to go to sleep quickly, so he could say goodnight to his children. They seemed very far away at the moment. He waited as long as he dared before taking out the toys …

'What are you doing?' Huw demanded.

'Nothing.' Sendatsu tucked them away again and rolled over.

# 16

*The Velsh knew far more about mining than we did. So while we were happy to pretend that we were wiser, more knowledgeable than any other humans, we were also happy to steal their knowledge. We set up our own mines with their help, we created our rice paddies with help from Breconia, we set up a fishing fleet thanks to the Skillian Islanders. We were happy to work with humans when we could take something. Giving was another matter, of course.*

The village was a hive of activity when they left the next morning, as Crumliners worked on their protective wall and a couple of them practised with their finished crossbows.

Sendatsu had wanted to speak with Dafyd and the other older humans who lived in the elven homes — but Huw had insisted on doing the talking with them while Sendatsu gave the villagers a last chance to use his knowledge on the protective wall they were building.

'They did not know anything valuable. They know nothing about Aroaril or magic,' Huw told him as they rode away.

'How do I know you will tell me the truth?' Sendatsu accused. 'What if they did know everything I seek but you plan to wait until we have visited another fifty villages before telling me?'

'Oh, Huw wouldn't do anything like that. He doesn't lie,' Rhiannon said immediately. 'You can trust him — I do.'

Huw pasted a smile over his guilty conscience. 'See?' he said.

'I think I need to talk to them anyway. There could be things you don't understand in their replies, things that lead to new questions,' Sendatsu said sourly. He had been unable to sing the goodnight song to the toys. This whole situation was getting worse by the day. He was now riding further away from home and getting no closer to answers. Last night Asami would have opened the gateway home for him … but he had not been there.

Now they were heading into a thick wood, which divided Crumlin from the next village.

'Well, you can hardly blame Huw for wanting to keep Dafyd and his family away from you after the way you yelled at them last night,' Rhiannon pointed out. 'You have a duty to these people. All the centuries the elves have been away, we have kept alive their memories. They think you something special — and when you act like that, yelling and abusing them, it does two things. First, they begin to wonder if the old stories are true and second, they are less likely to help us. You have to remember you are a hero to them. You need to act like one all the time …'

'I don't care what they think about me and I don't want to be a hero,' Sendatsu interrupted.

'But you should! They need you to be a hero — and you are the first elf anyone living has seen! Children will remember you and speak of you for years to come. You must think of the children next time …'

That was too much for Sendatsu, who began to laugh — because if he did not laugh, he would cry.

'Why are you laughing? What is even funny here?' she shouted.

Sendatsu shook his head and wiped his face. 'There is nothing funny,' he assured her.

'Then what was that?'

'You wouldn't understand.' He shrugged. Explaining this would reveal things he had to keep hidden.

'Why not? Because I'm a woman, or because I'm a human?' she accused.

Huw was thoroughly enjoying this little exchange and wondering how he might be able to provide a comforting shoulder for Rhiannon, when he heard something off in the bushes to his right.

'Quiet!' he snapped.

'What? Don't tell me you are on his side as well!' Rhiannon stormed.

'No — I think there's someone out there.' Huw gestured.

Instantly all three fell silent, watching the low bushes where Huw had pointed.

Sendatsu drew his sword slowly, keeping the sound of steel slithering out of the scabbard to a minimum, while both Huw and Rhiannon reached for the elven crossbows strapped to their saddles.

Nothing moved.

They looked around in all directions, listening as hard as they could.

Sendatsu could feel his heart pounding. The woods were silent — not a bird or an animal noise could be heard. That was not good. He glanced over his shoulder, back to Crumlin and safety. But the trail took them past huge rocks, covered in plants, as well as fallen trees and thick bushes. If anyone was waiting for them back there, they would be easy prey. But the woods ahead stretched out in front of them, miles and miles of uncertainty. It was decision time and Sendatsu knew it was pointless talking it over with Huw and Rhiannon. The humans were aiming their crossbows nervously off into the bushes — crossbows that were almost useless from horseback and in this terrain. Going back seemed the sensible option — but what if that was what the watchers wanted? Anyone who could remain unseen in the undergrowth for so long was not going to make a basic mistake like rustling bushes long enough for even someone as inexperienced as Huw to notice. Surely the intention was to make them turn back — right into the trap.

So Sendatsu did the opposite.

Before they had a chance to question him or argue, he shouted at the top of his voice and kicked his horse into a gallop. The big

Forlish horse reacted instantly, racing forwards down the trail. As he went past both Huw and Rhiannon, he slapped the rumps of their beasts with the flat of his blade, stirring them into a gallop as well.

The trail was relatively open here, being used by Crumliners for hunting and for grazing pigs among the trees, and he rode as fast as he dared, knowing the other two were close behind from the sound of the hooves beating on the earth. The back of his neck was itching and he slowed down, sure the other half of the trap was about to be sprung.

Just as he feared, four men jumped out of the undergrowth ahead, swords in hands. They were obviously Forlish raiders but whether stragglers or part of a larger group, he had no time to wonder. They spread out a little, to attack him from either side. He glanced from one to another, judging if he could crash through them — and hope to emerge safely on the other side. But all looked solid, tough men, all were handling their swords confidently so he hauled on his reins instead.

'Off the horses!' he shouted at Huw and Rhiannon, intending to unstrap his bow and use that to clear the way — and hope he could do that before the rest of the Forlish arrived.

But while Rhiannon managed to drag her horse to a stop with one hand — she had the packhorse tied to hers and it slowed her down — Huw's hands were full of elven crossbow. In fact, he was barely staying in the saddle as it was. While he tried to pull on the reins, the horse did not stop and instead kept going towards the four Forlishmen, although it was slowing down so would not even have speed and momentum to crash through. However, it was doing a fine job of hiding the Forlish from Sendatsu, so he dared not loose an arrow.

Sendatsu swore and kicked his horse back into a gallop. Even as he did so he knew he could not reach Huw in time. The sensible thing would be to jump down, string his bow and wait for Huw's fall to allow him to loose at the Forlish. He would be able to clear the way ahead and, at the very least, avenge Huw. Risking his life for a man who was stopping him from getting back home was stupid — but Sendatsu did not think of that. He only knew he could never live with himself if he left the bard to die without trying to help him.

He shouted at the top of his lungs, brandished his sword in the vain hope the Forlish would be distracted. But they knew what they were doing. They were concentrating on killing Huw — and there was nothing Sendatsu could do. Instead of stopping he pushed his horse even harder, overtaking Huw but not fast enough ...

Huw managed to get his crossbow around and worked the lever twice, as best he could from the saddle, although where the bolts went, nobody could say.

The Forlish were about to strike when arrows flickered out of the bushes to the right, throwing three of the Forlish backwards like rag dolls.

Sendatsu stared in shock at the familiar look and sound of longbow arrows striking home — but that was nothing compared to the effect it had on the last Forlishman. He forgot about Huw and instead stared in horror at what had happened to his comrades. Too late he remembered about Huw, whose horse smashed him backwards and then blundered onwards. Huw still held his crossbow and the impact knocked him from the saddle. The bard fell heavily to the ground, losing his crossbow, while his horse kept going at a trot.

Sendatsu arrived a moment later and jumped down, landing lightly beside the bard.

'Are you all right?' he shouted.

A dazed Huw got his arms beneath him but he was obviously winded and struggled to stand. Sendatsu hoped that was the only thing wrong with him.

'Bastard!'

The surviving Forlishman rolled to his feet and raced across, sword held over his right shoulder, ready to be brought down in a massive blow.

Sendatsu sprang to meet him and thrust forwards even as the Forlishman began his extravagant stroke. The Forlishman ran onto Sendatsu's blade and died there. Sendatsu flung the body away and stared back down the trail. More Forlish had appeared from the rocks and bushes closer to the village, just as he had feared they would do. While they were running now, they were too far away to be a threat. Of more concern was how they had been saved by mysterious archers. A quick glance told him these were expert bowmen — three arrows and three Forlish had been downed instantly, impaled on the classic long arrow. One was already dead, the other two not far behind. And perhaps these archers had saved him twice, for who had given them the warning by rustling bushes in the first place?

'Rhiannon! Quick!' he roared, for she was still fifty yards down the trail. He turned back to Huw, who was on his knees now, and got his arm under the bard's shoulders, supported him as he hustled him down to where both their horses waited, ten yards away.

'Wait! The crossbow!' Huw protested, wheezing.

Sendatsu told him what he thought of the crossbow.

'No, we need it!' Huw tried to turn back, fought Sendatsu's effort to keep him moving until Sendatsu swore again, shoved the bard towards the horses and turned back to grab the crossbow. He picked it up as Rhiannon raced past him.

'Keep going!' he ordered. Despite his reluctance to go for the crossbow, in truth there was little risk. Those Forlish were on foot and too far away. He turned around, intending to race for his horse, when a whisper of noise made him turn again.

A sword whistled for his head in the unmistakeable dragon-tail stroke and it was only his years of practice that allowed him to block it.

'You're coming back with us, Sendatsu — dead or alive!' the familiar face of Hanto snarled at him.

Sendatsu was so shocked to see Hanto he nearly dropped his guard, and deflected a tiger-claw cut only with difficulty. Sendatsu was about to launch his own attack when, behind Hanto, he saw a pair of elves racing through the bushes. Without thinking, he stepped back and levelled the crossbow at Hanto.

He knew it could not be used with one hand — and had no idea if it would work ever again after Huw dropped it — but pointed it anyway, guessing Hanto would not know it was an empty threat.

The elf instinctively dived for cover and Sendatsu used the opportunity to turn and sprint for the horses.

'Stand and fight!' The Forlish shouts did not scare him — in fact they reassured him. If the Forlish were that close, then Hanto and his companions could not chase him without fighting them first.

Ahead, Huw had managed to get on his horse, while Rhiannon was leading Sendatsu's horse back towards him. He sheathed his bloody sword and leaped into the saddle.

'Let's get out of here!' he roared at them.

Only as they were galloping down the trail did he wonder if they had seen him fighting another elf.

Broyle slowed to a stop, watched them ride away and cursed loudly and fluently. It had been a clever trap — but had proved too clever. He had expected the elf would be able to spot an ambush, so held his men far back from the trail. But when he had seen the trio arguing he had been unable to close in fast enough for an attack. Then the elf had been able to break out past his men. He could have sworn there was no way the elf could have got past four of his best men without a scratch but it had happened.

'Willibald's dying, sarge,' his corporal, Ricbert, reported from the side of the trail.

The other three men were already dead but it was the arrows that interested Broyle.

'It's the same thing we saw back in the woods, with Cenred,' Ricbert grunted.

Broyle nodded, not trusting himself to say anything. There was a bigger mystery here. The elf and his companions had help. But Broyle had seen him also exchange sword blows with one — and threaten them with one of those strange crossbows. So were they his allies or not? Broyle only knew they had killed his men, so that made them his enemies.

'We need to get out of here and get after them,' Broyle snapped.

'What are we doing, sarge? There're only seven of us now.'

'I can count,' Broyle said coldly. This was the third time he had been defeated. It would be the last, he swore.

'How could he have got away?' Hanto spat.

Taigo said nothing, because that was safest.

'Do we finish off those humans back there?' Jin asked.

Hanto hit him across the head. 'No, idiot. We don't have time to waste on them. We follow Sendatsu. Next time, we shall put arrows into his legs — see if he can run then.'

He signalled and the three elves began to lope after the horses, the fact they were running through woodland, not on the trail, making no difference to their speed.

Sendatsu finally slowed them down when they emerged from the woods, a good five miles away. Out in the open he felt safe enough to halt the horses before they became too tired — or one of the humans fell off.

'What happened back there?' Huw gasped. He had managed to stay on the horse but it had been a near thing once or twice.

Sendatsu had no idea where to start. He was struggling to come to terms with it himself. Hanto was out here, and obviously hunting him. It was a terrifying thought. The Council — and his father — were so desperate to silence him they had sent elves into the human world to kill him. More than that, they would have needed a Magic-weaver to help get them through the barrier. Had Sumiko turned against him, or was there a traitor in their midst? Knowing his father, that was the more likely of the two but it was still very discomforting.

'They were waiting for us. Down the trail was the only way out of the trap,' Sendatsu said shakily.

'Huw, you need to thank Sendatsu. He rode after you and picked off those three Forlishmen with arrows from the saddle before killing the last with his sword. I can barely believe I saw it!' Rhiannon exclaimed.

Sendatsu closed his mouth. She must have been facing the wrong way, or imagined seeing him draw his bow ... thank Aroaril he did not have to explain what had happened with the three elven archers in the undergrowth — for he had no idea what he would have said.

Huw turned to the elf. 'I know. You did not need to risk your life for me. After our arguments, I do not know I could have done the same, were our positions reversed.'

'Thank Aroaril for that — I don't think I'd like to see you fight four Forlish warriors.' Sendatsu tried to smile.

'Seriously — why? You are always going on about this mission of yours, how you have to get back to Dokuzen ...'

Sendatsu shrugged. 'I could not live with myself if I let you ride to your death.'

'Then I thank you. Those Forlish would have killed us without a second thought or worse, taken us back to Ward,' Huw said fervently.

'That is worse than death?' Sendatsu really smiled at that.

'Ward would make us beg for death — and he would make sure he wrung every drop of information out of us, so he could smash my people and destroy Vales,' Huw said soberly.

'What he has planned for me is little better,' Rhiannon said with a shudder. 'You saved us, Sendatsu! They were all around — I saw you fighting them off when you went to get Huw's crossbow.'

Sendatsu reached for the crossbow, using it to hide his relief. He had been unbelievably lucky. Hanto must have warned them about the trap, then turned his bows on the Forlish when it seemed as if Sendatsu was to be killed ... that meant his father wanted him back alive. He wondered if he should lie in wait for them. He could kill Hanto easily enough and then get information out of his companions ...

'What is it?' Rhiannon asked.

Sendatsu handed the crossbow back to Huw. 'Nothing.' He smiled. 'Just reliving that ambush.' He could kill Hanto but the other two would have their orders to stop him. If one of them put an arrow into him — it was too risky, he decided.

They rode on together, much more warmly this time. Once a good three miles from the woods, with no sight of any pursuit, Sendatsu found them a spot on a small hill, which gave them a good view of the way they had come, and stopped for a break.

Huw made a point of shaking Sendatsu's hand.

'I have sung enough sagas about heroes to know one when I see him in action,' he said.

'I am no hero — I don't want to be.' Sendatsu shrugged. 'I'm just doing what I have to.'

'Well, it was enough to save me!'

The bard wandered off to grab some firewood, leaving Sendatsu to hope he might get the bard's help in speaking to the Velsh at the next village, and beyond. When he had not really done anything to earn the bard's gratitude, this was fortunate indeed.

Sendatsu joined Rhiannon, who was brushing down the sweating horses. As soon as they were hidden by the horses, she embraced him.

'Thank you for saving us, and risking your life. I shall not forget it.' She reached up and kissed him.

Sendatsu stood there awkwardly. He did not want to do more harm, or leave her with even more of a broken heart, but she was warm and lithe against him and other parts of him were saying something different ...

'I think Huw's returning,' he forced himself to say, then returned her kiss before they broke apart.

No sense in telling her the truth too early, he decided. He might need to use her against Huw, if the bard still insisted on keeping him away from the Velsh. The way her trews sat tight around her legs had nothing at all to do with it ...

The narrowness of their escape left him both a little shaky and feeling elated — it had affected them all the same way. He found himself needing to laugh as they ate and drank.

'What's the next village?' Sendatsu asked.

'Catsfield,' Huw replied, breaking apart an oatcake.

'Sounds like a good name,' Sendatsu commented. 'Do they farm them, or eat them?'

The two humans looked at him.

'Are you serious?' Rhiannon gasped.

'Sure.' Sendatsu winked at Huw, unseen by her. 'Cat is a great elven delicacy. You can expect to be served fresh cat in Dokuzen every day. Isn't that right, Huw?'

'Well, it is mentioned in the sagas, many times,' Huw agreed, fighting to keep a straight face.

Rhiannon stared at them with such a look of horror that they could not keep up the pretence any longer and Sendatsu rolled around in hilarity, while Huw burst out in laughter as well.

Rhiannon glared at them for a few moments, then dissolved into giggles herself.

The reaction to their escape bubbled out and they all found themselves helpless with laughter. It was a long time before they could get themselves under control again.

'I didn't think you elves liked jokes,' Rhiannon accused.

'No, only cats!' Huw gasped and that set them all off again.

Sendatsu lay on the grass, his chest heaving, and wiped his eyes. He laughed a great deal with his children but there had been few smiles with other adults since he was forbidden to marry Asami.

'We like to laugh as much as you,' he said finally. 'But perhaps nobody made a song out of that.'

'Then we shall have to be the first,' Rhiannon decided.

'A song about eating cats and laughing. That should earn us coin aplenty.' Huw grinned, rolling over and sitting up.

'No more about the cats! Please?' Rhiannon pleaded.

'Well, we had better get to Catsfield before we are unable to say the name without laughing,' Huw agreed, 'especially as the Forlish may not be far away.'

Hector looked across the valley to where the edge of the civilised world stopped, and Vales began.

'Are you sure of this, sir?' his guard sergeant asked nervously. 'The king was sending men up here to fix these damned Velsh and I wouldn't like to run into a group of them. Then there's our accents. If our boys have been going through here like they've been ordered, it's likely the Velsh won't want to talk to a bunch of Forlish ...'

'Sergeant ...' Hector paused and the soldiers willed him to finally remember the name. 'Edric!' Hector announced and the soldiers silently sighed with relief. 'We have been ordered by the king to bring back my daughter. I hold the king's seal! Would you like to return to Cridianton and tell him his orders were too difficult for you? Do you think he will be happy to hear that?'

Edric gulped. He had been in the king's service for nearly a decade and knew mercy was not one of the king's many qualities.

'Besides,' and here Hector softened his voice a little. 'I have a plan.'

After all, he needed these men to go along with him. If he was to return to Cridianton empty-handed, then all his dreams would go up in smoke. How could the girl have been so stupid? He had been sure she was his puppet, willing to do whatever he told her to. And not just willing but happy to! That had been the real triumph. Any fool could get a child to do what they were told — it took real artistry to get the child thinking it was actually the best thing for them. When his wife had died in childbirth, after he had lost his voice from the same fever that had left her weakened and unable to make it through the rigours of birth, he had thought his golden run was at an end. First he had lost his place at court, then his talents, then his wife; now he was being left with a child to care for — a girl child as well, one that would only be a burden.

But it had been his genius to see the opportunity in despair. The girl was tall and well formed — between his gifts and his wife's beauty, surely she would have ability he could mould, talents he could use to restore his fortune.

And so he had begun his careful scheme, refining it over the years. Sadly the girl had not proved quite as fair of face as her mother, not the beauty to instantly grab the king's attention. But she was tall, and graceful, with long limbs and a natural ability to move well — and really, he reflected, that was more important than a pretty face in the bedchamber, once the lights were out.

His dreams, his golden future, had been in his grasp. A few days' work and everything would have been sealed. Only for it to be dashed away by his daughter's stupidity and a foul Velshman. They were an odious people and fully deserving of what was coming their way, he decided.

The trip north had been both quick and relatively comfortable. Wherever they went, whatever they wanted, the king's seal had been able to supply. One look at that, backed up by the hulking presence of the king's guards, and shopkeepers and innkeepers alike swiftly offered up horses and food for free. Hector had thoroughly enjoyed the feeling, although he would have much preferred to be back in Cridianton, enjoying the fruits of his long years of hard work. Did she not understand how much it had taken to look after her, to work with her? All those ridiculous tears, those petty fears ... he had virtually turned himself into her slave for the past twenty years. Did he not deserve something from that? Who else would have been willing to spend that much time working with a young girl? And afterwards, when Ward had finished with her, he would have found her a husband somewhere, ensured she had sufficient money to live on.

'Your plan, sir?' Edric prompted him.

Hector cleared his thoughts. 'We shall leave your armour and uniforms at the last Forlish village. Without them, we shall be able to move much easier, remain unseen by the crude Velsh. All we have to do is find my daughter and her captor, free her and return to Cridianton with him in chains. And that will be easy enough. This Hugh, or Huw, or however he says his name doesn't know we are after him — he thinks us still searching in southern Forland. And one or two of us can slip into a Velsh village, ask a few questions and then get out again without any suspicions being raised.'

Edric rubbed his surcoat between finger and thumb. 'And what do we wear then, sir?'

Hector flashed the king's seal. 'This will get us whatever we want,' he promised. 'Within a few days we shall be returning to Cridianton in triumph, I promise you!'

* * *

Catsfield was another small village, surrounded by rich fields — and by a number of isolated farms.

'How are we going to protect this?' Rhiannon wondered as they looked across at the scatter of small farms around the village. 'We can't possibly build a wall around this lot!'

Sendatsu scratched his chin. 'There are no elven buildings either. This looks like a great deal of work for nothing. I think we should ride on to the next village.'

'No!' Huw snapped. 'We can't just leave them here, unprotected! We have to save them, we have to save all of them!'

Huw's vehemence, after the earlier friendliness, was all the more unexpected.

'We can't save everyone,' Sendatsu said.

'That was not the deal. We need to save as many as we can. And just because they don't have elven buildings here does not mean they have no answers for you.'

Sendatsu sighed. 'Perhaps we could get them to build up each one,' he suggested, 'make each of them into a stronghold?'

'They're made of wood and thatch. Two torches and they'll go up in smoke,' Huw pointed out. 'The only way is to make them move into the main village.'

'And you think they'll do that?' Sendatsu asked.

'No. But we have to try anyway,' Huw said grimly.

'And the Velsh? Can I speak to them this time?'

Huw hesitated. From his conversation with Dafyd, he doubted Sendatsu would ever find the answers he sought. Huw's father, Earwen, always said his knowledge of the ancient times was barely half that of the Crumliners. Yet Dafyd only had the same stories Earwen had told. And Huw did not think the Crumliner was holding anything back — he genuinely did not know any more. So this quest was going to become a delicate balancing act. He needed to give the elf a little hope, to keep him working on protecting the villages. If Sendatsu discovered the answers he sought were not in Vales, what would happen then? Already he was complaining about helping villages without evidence of elven history.

'I tell you what — any village without elven buildings, you can speak directly to the people,' he offered, hoping this compromise would buy him enough time to protect most of Vales.

'Then we should stop wasting time out here.' Sendatsu spurred his horse forwards.

The people of Catsfield flooded out of their homes and in from the fields, regarding the trio suspiciously, even with a fair amount of hostility, which turned to fear and then wonderment as Rhiannon and Huw sang their Sendatsu song.

Once they knew they were with an elf, they clustered around him and Huw and Rhiannon were forced to push and order them back. But, with that achieved, the villagers listened with complete attention to Huw's tale of what had happened at Patcham and what Catsfield needed to do. As he had predicted, the idea of leaving their homes and moving into the village proper did not meet with their approval. Even Sendatsu was not enough to get all of them to agree, although perhaps half reluctantly decided to pack up and move into the village until it was safe again. They had the usual debate about magic, before a mixture of persuasion and Sendatsu's orders saw the villagers begin work on a ditch and a wall, carpenters on crossbows.

The biggest issue, Sendatsu felt, was their lack of knowledge. The best thing, really the only new thing he got from them, was a comment from a blind old man.

'We don't worship Aroaril — trying to do that will see you struck down,' he said.

'How do you know?' Sendatsu pressed.

'He's the elven God. Any human who tries to call on Him will be destroyed.'

'And you've seen that?' Sendatsu asked eagerly, then winced at his own words.

The old man chuckled. 'Of course not! But who would take the chance?'

'So nobody has tried to find out?'

'I know I'm going to die if I stick a knife in my heart, why would I want to prove it?'

Sendatsu felt his frustration rise anew. 'But where does this come from? Surely someone must have told you ...'

The old man shrugged. 'It was something from my grandfather. Kind of a saying he used to have when he was asked to do something he didn't want to: I might as well pray to Aroaril. I was but a lad and asked him what that meant, so he told me.'

'Thank you for your help,' Sendatsu said absently. He could not see Aroaril destroying humans for daring to pray to him — but perhaps it tied in somehow with the church he had found destroyed. Had the elves spread this story, backed it up with magic? Should he try to get some Velsh to pray and see what happened? If only he had more knowledge of Aroaril or even a prayer book ...

He thanked the man and left — only to run into Rhiannon.

'Any luck?' she asked.

'None at all,' Sendatsu grumbled. 'We should move on and try another village.'

'But this one has hardly begun ...'

His desperation to get back to his children outweighed any regard for sense.

'If you want to go to Dokuzen, then you need to help me against Huw. We need to move faster around the villages,' he said.

Rhiannon nodded immediately. 'I can't wait to go there, to meet your friends and family, walk through the beauty and the wonder ... oh, I can see it now!'

Sendatsu forced a smile onto his face. This is for Mai and Cheijun. I can explain everything to her later, say sorry then, he told himself.


It worked. Smoke on the horizon the next morning, far across to the east, helped inspire the village to greater efforts. Thanks to Rhiannon's persistent arguments, Huw agreed the village's progress was so good they could also ride on.

'We shall keep a good lookout. The beauty of Catsfield is none can sneak up on us — they must ride across miles of pasture to reach our village,' the leading farmer in Catsfield, a grim-faced, grey-bearded man called Llewellyn, promised as they left.

'Keep a good watch. That is your best defence,' Sendatsu agreed. 'Use the dogs too. I know you Velsh like to have them sleep beside you but a dog's nose is the best warning you have. Then use a horn — anything you can find to warn your people as soon as something is spotted. Then get everyone behind the walls and drown any Forlish who attack in a sea of bolts.'

'Oh, that we can do,' Llewellyn vowed. Whatever the doubts they had about moving, and about spending the next few days building a wall, they had all been impressed by the elven crossbows.

'Maybe we should have stayed a little longer,' Huw fretted as they rode away, the wall not even half finished yet.

'We could stay for a month and they would not all be safe. Some of those farmers won't leave their homes until they are in flames. And by then it will be too late,' Sendatsu said grimly. 'We cannot save everyone. We just have to give as many as we can a chance.'

'We have to save as many as possible,' Huw insisted.

'How? There're only the three of us,' Sendatsu pointed out. 'How can we be everywhere at once?'

'He's right, Huw,' Rhiannon agreed.

Huw opened his mouth to argue but could not find the words to convince them both. But there were so many people who still needed to be helped. Sendatsu might have won Rhiannon over but he still had a secret weapon — neither of them knew Vales like he did. He decided to take them south, into the poorer province known as Rheged. There would be less knowledge but plenty of people to help.

# 17



*I had known Naibun since boyhood — and he had always hated humans. His father was one of those who thought of himself as an Elf, not an Elfaran, and raised his son the same way. It was the main reason the forefathers chose me and not Naibun to lead. But, while I mourned my wife, Naibun decided to make sure the humans learned their proper place. Humans who knew how to use magic were tracked down, while any churches of Aroaril were also marked. Naibun also created what he called a Border Patrol, ostensibly to protect Dokuzen but, in reality, to drive humans away from elven areas.*

*Humans who knew the truth about us were rounded up and books and scrolls that contained the real history were taken; in their place was left stories about a human rebellion and how the humans had betrayed elves with their lust for violence. He intended for the humans of these lands to never dare challenge elven supremacy. He did it slowly and carefully — and very effectively.*

Much of the smoke seemed to be coming from the south each morning and Huw was bursting to get down there and help the people. He steered them that way, although it did not take long for Sendatsu to realise which direction they were travelling.

'It's too late for the people down south,' Sendatsu growled. 'We should cut our losses and worry about saving those who still have a chance. If we hurry, we can protect many of the villages in this central part of Vales before the Forlish can get in there.'

'And we condemn the people living in Rheged to a nightmare of rape and fire and blood!' Huw spat.

'Better a few than many. Who knows how many more bands of Forlish raiders are heading north every day? Would you have us waste our time saving ones who are already lost? Remember, it takes days to build a wall around a village. Do you think the Forlish will sit and watch us do that — or will they come rushing in one night, through a half-finished palisade? We could doom more people that way ...'

'We still have to try!' Huw cried, stopping Sendatsu's flow of reasonableness. 'We have to try,' he repeated. 'I cannot walk away when I know people are suffering. Think of the children!'

Sendatsu was silenced instantly. It was all he thought about. Huw, not knowing, pressed his advantage.

'Can you bear to see them dead, can you stand to ride away knowing all those tiny faces will cry out in fear, will haunt your dreams for ever more?'

Sendatsu shuddered at the thought. *Curse the bard — he has found my weakness.*

'That's enough, Huw — can't you see how it hurts him?' Rhiannon cried.

Sendatsu managed to give Rhiannon a smile and congratulated himself for getting her on his side — even if he had been forced to lie to do so. But he could not hold his tongue when Huw declared they would also stop at villages on the way to Rheged.

'If we are going to do this, we need to get south as fast as possible, give ourselves time,' he argued.

'But we can't just ride past villages and not tell them, not help them protect themselves,' Huw said.

'You can't have it both ways! You have to make a decision about who you want to save!'

Huw could hear the sense in Sendatsu's argument — he just could not bring himself to accept it. He knew, deep inside, that if he rode past a village, then the Forlish would strike it, people would die and it would be his fault. It was stupid, perhaps, but it was how he felt.

'Perhaps he is right, Huw …' Rhiannon ventured.

'But we can't let people die! Not if we can save them!' Huw said in anguish.

'Huw, I know how you feel,' she tried to begin.

'No, you don't!'

That was too much. 'You are not the only one to have lost your father!' she snapped.

Huw, as ever, was silenced by the memory of his lies to her.

'Look, we can stop at these villages but if we get to Rheged and there're too many raiders, we agree to come back.' Sendatsu seized his chance.

Reluctantly, Huw agreed.


King Ward had given up on his two sons some years before. Their mother, Queen Mildrith, had poisoned their minds, until all they cared about was slaughter and glory for themselves. She also hated him for his philandering but he could not blame her for that. But the way she had filled his sons' heads with foolishness and frippery was too much. Still, of late, he had felt time slipping away from him, so called them in once more.

'What are we doing here, Father?' Wilfrid was the older, a powerful young man with a flat face and vicious eyes.

'Captain Edmund here will brief you on our campaign in Vales and how we shall bring them under our control. When they are begging to become part of Forland, I shall send one of you north to make it happen.'

'Why don't we just kill them? They're a pack of sheep-shaggers and there's nothing worth taking up there,' Uffa grunted. He was shorter than Wilfrid but had the same eyes as well as wide lips, which made his mouth always look vacant.

'Listen to Captain Edmund and find out,' Ward said, controlling his temper.

'Why do we need to know?'

'Because you are princes of Forland and must learn to use your minds as well as your muscles! I did not devote my life to this kingdom to have you throw it away after I am gone!' he roared at them.

Instantly their faces closed down and he cursed.

'Edmund, see what you can do with them,' he snarled, stalking out of the room before he said something worse. He did not have the time or patience for them.

They left the villages of Glottenham and Abergavenny protected but, by the time they left Pigstrood, both Huw and Sendatsu were about to blow — for completely different reasons.

Huw was furious with the way Sendatsu was using Rhiannon against him. If only he could discover the elf's secret, tucked in that belt pouch, he was sure he could stop that. But Sendatsu kept it hidden. Then there was Rhiannon herself. She was obviously happy, laughing at the funny names of villages such as Pigstrood. He found himself resenting her. She was glowing, as well as growing, obviously revelling in her new-found freedom — and in Sendatsu. He hated that she was so happy to be with the elf and he could not make her feel that way.

Weighed against that was the work Sendatsu was doing in those villages. Thanks to him, they were all protected. He was keeping up his end of the bargain — but he was growing more frustrated with the lack of answers these villages were yielding. Huw longed to see the elf go, yet was afraid Sendatsu might find something that would take him back to Dokuzen — and take Rhiannon and hope for the Velsh away with him. He was torn.

When the third village had yielded nothing, Sendatsu was about to put his fist through a wall. The fear was growing inside him that there were no answers. He had even showed the book to a few Velsh in Glottenham and Pigstrood but they had no idea what the strange writing meant. Huw had claimed the people of Abergavenny knew nothing either. What if Sumiko was wrong? She had been so sure all the evidence the Magic-weavers needed was out here but all that remained were fragments. Every day took him further from his children and just saying goodnight to their toys was not enough any more. Especially when he suspected Huw was trying to catch sight of what he was doing. Several times he had nearly been caught by the bard. He dreaded to think what would happen with Rhiannon if she found out he had children. He found himself contemplating just returning to Dokuzen. He lay awake at night dreaming about seizing back Mai and Cheijun, persuading Asami to leave with him and all of them coming to live here, far from his father and the reach of the elves.

Then he recalled Hanto's angry face in the bushes and knew it was hopeless — he would never be able to relax.

But he was left tired and irritable, more so by his inability to find something familiar to eat or have anything resembling a bath. Being forced to endlessly repeat the same things to Velsh villages hardly helped his mood. If only he could get something, some hope to keep him going ...

'Where do you Velsh get your names from?' Sendatsu asked, as they rode away from Pigstrood, Rhiannon still snorting with laughter but able to add her thoughts.

'Aye. Why are there names you can barely pronounce and then others that are just obvious?'

Huw's vow to keep what he knew to himself could not survive this provocation. 'It is not a joke. Some of the names are our own, while others are in the tongue we all use now, after the elves took away everyone's languages,' he blurted.

Sendatsu stopped laughing. 'What do you mean?'

'It is nothing.' Huw tried to cover it up.

'Nothing? This is what I have been seeking and you have had it all the time!' Sendatsu roared.

'Come on, Huw, you have to tell us — this could be our ticket to Dokuzen,' Rhiannon said excitedly. 'Please, Huw, tell us what you know.'

Huw cursed himself but there was no going back now.

'Well, you have probably seen there is a connection between the names of the villages and when they were founded. My father told me those with strange names, like Abergavenny, are much older and date back to a time before the elves came here, when we had our own language. Those names have meanings in old Velsh, meaning that has been lost through the centuries, with only the strange words remaining to us. Newer villages, built since the elves left, have more ordinary names, that we can all understand.'

'So this is all to do with your father's belief that the Velsh had their own language?' Sendatsu accused.

Huw hesitated but Rhiannon's glare made him open up. 'My father said once we all had our own languages — the Velsh, the Forlish, the Balians — everyone. Maybe even the elves. That's why the names we call ourselves are so different, why older towns and villages sound like they're from another place. He thought the elves did something, used magic to give us all the one language ...'

'Why, it's a brilliant idea! That way everyone could talk and understand each other — what a wondrous thing for the elves to do!' Rhiannon exclaimed.

'Was it? My father used to say that a country without a language of its own is a country without a heart. Said the elves might have given us new words but also took something from us. That's why villages and towns that have been built since they went away have such ordinary names, no matter whether they are here or in Forland, Balia, or elsewhere. Like Catsfield and Browns Brook, rather than Pontypridd or Hamtun.'

'The cost in magic must have been enormous,' Sendatsu breathed. 'What else is hidden away in plain sight, I wonder?'

'Probably many things,' Huw admitted. 'My father told me there are ruined buildings, relics of old settlements, hidden away in the woods — woods that the elves made grow overnight, to hide what was there. One day we humans knew how to build, how to make things — the next, all the knowledge was gone.'

'But how could that be? The elves would never do anything bad,' Rhiannon insisted.

Sendatsu dug into his saddlebag and produced an oilskin-wrapped bundle with shaking hands. It was time to share.

'I found this in a burned-out Velsh church to Aroaril,' he said solemnly. 'It is written in a language I cannot read.'

'A Velsh church to Aroaril?' Huw gasped.

'Something you cannot read?' Rhiannon gasped.

Sendatsu explained about his find in the woods near Pontypridd, while Huw inspected the book with great care.

'I saw something similar once before — in the tombs of the elven forefathers. There were books there written in all different languages, none of which I could read,' Sendatsu said.

'I would dearly like to see that church, and see those books,' Huw said thoughtfully. 'If only we had time now!'

'Well, you'll be able to see the books when we go to Dokuzen. Sendatsu will take you there himself,' Rhiannon said brightly.

'Why don't we travel to that church now? Maybe we could ask around there?' Sendatsu tried to drag the conversation back to where he wanted to go.

'We shall return there — but we have work to do here first,' Huw said defiantly.

'You seek to turn back the tide with a wall of sand. There is no way we can protect every village, nor stop every raider. Do you really think just the three of us can save Vales?'

'Maybe not — but we have to try, not go running back to our safe little home, protected by our nice magic barrier!' Huw yelled. 'Sometimes you have to make a stand. Sometimes you have to take a risk to do what is right. You elves just hid rather than do something. I won't do that. Perhaps I can't save everyone but at least I shall try.'

Sendatsu had heard similar things from his father all his life, and from Asami of late, and was not prepared to take it from this human bard who was keeping him from his children with his stupid plans. He swelled up, ready to explode.

'But none of this explains a name like Pigstrood,' Rhiannon said hastily.

They swivelled to face her.

'Obviously they love their pigs in this area,' Rhiannon continued. 'But what is a Glotten-ham? Is it a pig that's eaten too much?'

Huw and Sendatsu stared at her.

'We shouldn't fight among ourselves. There are too many other people who want to kill us,' she said defiantly. 'Come on, there will be answers for us aplenty in Dokuzen!'

She eased closer to Sendatsu, who forced a smile to his face to avoid another conversation and another lie about taking her there. He thrust the book back into his bag.

'Come on. We are wasting riding time,' he said shortly.


Sendatsu lay in bed, Rhiannon asleep beside him, and thought about Asami.

They had arrived at Five Ashes, the last village before they were officially in Rheged, although there were no borders, just a line of hills to mark where one district ended and one began. As usual, the people had been willing to do whatever an elf wanted. But they could not give him answers. He even resorted to trying to see if any of them had magic. He had to keep that one quiet, because he did not want Huw to know. He gathered a handful of young Velsh and made a flower bloom for them, tried to see if any of them could feel the magic as he worked it.

None had — and then Rhiannon had come looking for him, so he had to hand the flower to a young woman and hurry away.

'Everything all right with the wall?' he asked.

'Of course. I just had a … feeling … I should find you,' she said. It was foolish but she could have sworn the world had shifted somehow, the plants, animals and insects ready to speak to her. For a moment she had been sure they would do her bidding, all she had to do was ask … then it faded away. 'Why did you give that girl a flower?'

Sendatsu glanced back and saw the young woman smile at him, holding the magicked flower as if it was the most precious thing in the world, surrounded by a throng of excited friends.

'They asked to see a little magic,' he tried to dismiss.

She took his hand and pulled him along, to a hut further away.

'The headman of Five Ashes has given this hut to us. But Huw is away talking to him,' she said.

'It's … lovely,' Sendatsu said lamely as he saw the pile of skins on the floor that would be a bed.

Next moment Rhiannon was pressed up against him.

'We have not been together since Patcham. And you have said little more about our plans to go back to Dokuzen together, and marry before your God. Are — are you having second thoughts? Do you think it a mistake?'

I never had first thoughts, Sendatsu wanted to say. I've made many mistakes and this one is right up there with the best.

'There hasn't been the time, nor the opportunity …'

'You haven't found another, thought others more beautiful?'

Sendatsu would have laughed if this was not so deadly serious. 'I have not found another, nor do I think any other human is more beautiful than you,' he said. She was very close to him, her lips just a few inches from his, while the rest of her was pressed against him. He could feel his body respond to her. One of her hands was running down his back, the other was slipping up his side …

'So we shall return to Dokuzen together?'

Sendatsu dearly wanted to tell her the truth — but she would be devastated and both she and Huw would never help him. Besides, her hands were slipping lower …

'Yes,' he managed to say without the word choking him.

She leaned in and kissed him, hard, pulling him close to her.

He knew he should be strong, should not give in. But he was weak, oh, so weak.

Now he felt guilty and dirty in spirit as well as body. He hated that he was building a false dream for her, lying to her with every breath. He was doing to her what his forefathers had done to humans all those centuries ago — used them for their own pleasure, without thinking of the consequences. But how could he get himself out of this mess?

On top of it all, he felt like he had betrayed Asami — even though she was married to another. What was she doing? Were she and Gaibun living up to their promise to help him home? Should he just try to travel back, talk to them and find out what was happening?

He rubbed his face with his hands. He had achieved little except create more disasters out here. Mai and Cheijun seemed so far away. Leaving Rhiannon to sleep, he dressed and went out to see what he could do to speed things up on the wall. He had never felt so pained after an afternoon of pleasure. He decided to try one more village in Rheged. If they could not give him some hope that answers waited out here, then he would leave Huw and Rhiannon, journey back east and implore Asami to bring him home.

The next day, they rode into Rheged.

The change was dramatic. The wide valleys and rich farmland of Gwent ended in a line of hills. Over the other side, nothing was flat. The villages were gone — instead there was isolated, scattered farms, or perhaps two or three families close together, working a small valley and trying to eke out a living from the thin land.

They rode most of one day without seeing anyone, which was unusual in itself. Then they came over a rise to see the first farm of the day. But it was not a pretty sight.

Someone had taken time to build it. By Velsh standards it was a large holding. There was the usual round hall, as well as a series of beast sheds and shelters, neat, fenced fields and paddocks for the animals. It had a wonderful view down across the nearby valleys and a small stream trickling down the hill. It was the sort of place to make a life.

Until Forlish raiders had come through and robbed everyone there of life.

Animals lay dead in the fields, while every building was a burned-out shell.

'We should go and see if anyone's alive,' Rhiannon said immediately, starting her horse forwards.

'No!' Huw was even faster than Sendatsu in grabbing her horse's bridle. 'We don't want to see what is in there.'

'Should we not at least give them a proper burial?' Sendatsu asked.

'They would be ash and bones. And we don't have proper burials like you elves,' Huw said bitterly. 'There is no Aroaril for us, no dream of a paradise waiting for us. We are born, we struggle and we die. Nothing else. Remember?'

'I didn't do this! I'm the one helping, remember?' Sendatsu flared back. Yesterday with Rhiannon had put him in a dark mood and nothing they had seen today had lightened his spirit. 'And I didn't even want to come down here. I was the one who said this was a bad idea. How are we going to save families like this? How can they hope to defend themselves?'

'So we just leave them to be killed in their sleep, the smoke of their passing left to terrify others?' Huw snarled.

'I don't have the answers. You are the one with all the big ideas!'

'Enough! This is not helping anyone.' Rhiannon shouldered her horse between the two of them. 'There are people we can help here. We should find them.'

'Good idea,' Sendatsu said coldly.

Huw held his tongue, but only with an effort.

They rode in on silence, as it began to rain gently, a fine mist that dampened everything.

Finally they came across a smallholding with living people — although these ran into the trees and took some persuading to come and speak with them.

'We saw the smoke and thought they were coming for us next,' the father, a short man made old before his years, told them.

'There are Forlish raiders everywhere. You are not safe. You need to leave here and find shelter in a village somewhere,' Huw told them.

'But if we go to a village, where will we live, what will we farm — will they give us land?'

Huw admitted he could not answer that. 'But if you stay here, the Forlish will come for you.'

'I'd rather take my chances,' the man snapped. 'Why would the Forlish bother with us? We've got nothing and there's little enough around here.'

'Once we have thrown out the Forlish, you can return ...' Huw began.

'And when will that be? When the elves come marching out to help us? Yes, I can see that happening!' the man snorted.

'What do you know of elves?' Sendatsu demanded, before Huw had a chance to keep arguing.

'I know they are not what people think,' the man sniffed. 'Folks in these parts go on about how wonderful the elves are but I know the truth about them.'

'Come on, he's not going to listen to us.' Rhiannon half turned.

'Wait — what truth?' Sendatsu pressed.

The man looked at him. 'The elves didn't want humans bothering them — so they killed hundreds of us, to teach us a lesson.'

'That can't be!' Rhiannon exclaimed.

'Why would it be a lesson, if nobody else knew about it?' Huw pointed out.

The man shrugged. 'Nobody believes that elves can be anything other than good. But I wouldn't trust them. I know they killed us, lots of us. For no reason.'

'Let's get out of here. The man's obviously mad.' Rhiannon grabbed Sendatsu's arm but the elf did not move.

'Do you have proof? Do you know where it happened?' he asked urgently.

'Somewhere north. They invited all the humans who had befriended them, shared their knowledge, told them they were going to give them a gift — and then killed them!'

'That has to be wrong. Elves would never do anything like that,' Rhiannon insisted.

'And how did you hear about it, when nobody else did?' Huw asked reasonably.

'I'm alive, and living down here, because my ancestors saw it happen and ran, rather than join them. We kept quiet because it kept us safe. And even when we did speak, folks had their heads stuffed with nonsense about the elves, about how kind and good and wise they were. But I know different.'

'Well, for your information, this is an elf with us now — and he can tell you the truth, about how wonderful the elves are and how you have been believing lies all these years,' Rhiannon said hotly.

The man laughed shortly. 'He can tell me the sky is green and the grass is blue for all I care. I have more important things to do. So ride on and find someone who wants your help.'

'Wait — do you know anything about the worship of Aroaril?' Sendatsu asked.

'I have said all I am going to,' the man sniffed, and turned back to his crops.

'We are wasting time here. We need to go, find others — find a village,' Huw said frustratedly.

'He was mad. Saying that elves weren't good!' Rhiannon agreed quietly.

Sendatsu ignored them and hurried after the man.

'Listen — I believe you ...'

'Of course you do. You're an elf. You know the truth of my words.'

'That's exactly it — the elves have been lied to, the way the humans were. They think it was humans who attacked them. I'm trying to find out what really happened so I can change things. Can you at least take a look at this book I found ...'

The man brushed off Sendatsu's hand. 'You're an elf, so I can't trust you. My family's survived for so long by keeping away from your kind and I want to carry on their tradition.'

'I'm not here to hurt you, but to help ...'

The man spat in disgust. 'Go away. Leave me alone. I've told you all I can.'

'Listen ...' Sendatsu growled, trying to keep his temper.

But the man hurried away, back towards the trees.

'Sendatsu! Come on!' Huw called.

He hesitated for a moment longer but he could not force answers out of the man. And perhaps he did not know much more anyway. But at least it was a valuable clue.

'He was never going to leave his farm and go into a village for safety,' Huw sighed as he rejoined the other two. 'But I thank you for caring about a man like that.'

Sendatsu opened his mouth to correct Huw, then shut it again. They were not ready to hear the man was right and elves were not all good.

'Come on, we need to find a village and help them.'

One more village, Sendatsu silently swore. I have to get something there or I shall leave.

Twice more they saw homesteads, but both times they had been abandoned. One had been left untouched, while someone had tried to set fire to the other, only to be defeated by the Velsh weather. Part of the roof was gone but the rest was unharmed.

They found a hamlet, a collection of some six roundhouses and assorted beast sheds and fields.

'It is too small to protect itself ...' Sendatsu warned, but Huw had already spurred his horse across to them. Cursing, Sendatsu followed.

'Wait!' Rhiannon cried. 'We need to do the song!'

Huw ignored them both, pulling up his horse amid the buildings. 'Hello! Anyone here?' Huw called. 'We are Velsh, from Gwent. We are here to help!'

But there was no answer.

'You do know this could be a trap. Forlish could be using this as a base.' Sendatsu caught up with him.

'This far from all the big villages? I don't think so.' Huw jumped down from his horse, wincing a little at his sore thighs. They had been riding for nearly a half-moon but he was still not used to the horse.

Sendatsu drew his sword. 'I'll go first,' he announced.

'If there is anyone here, you'll terrify them,' Huw pointed out. 'And what if they attack you?'

Sendatsu was prepared to argue but Huw just ducked into the nearest house. He waited a few moments for his eyes to adjust to the gloom — and was nearly knocked over as Sendatsu sprang inside after him.

'There's nobody here,' Huw told him.

'But what if there had been?' Sendatsu countered. 'Could you fight them off? What good would it do if you get killed?'

Huw was about to retort when Rhiannon called.

'Quick! Come quick!'

Huw and Sendatsu both ran for the door, almost collided, only for Sendatsu to use his size to be first through. Furious, Huw followed to see Rhiannon holding her hand over her nose and mouth.

'There's a terrible smell coming out of that far house.' She pointed, choking a little.

'What were you doing, wandering off to have a look?' Sendatsu snapped. The lack of people and now this deserted village had him even more on edge. 'If there were Forlish here, they would have killed you before we even knew about it. How can I protect you like that?'

Huw mentally rubbed his hands together, expecting Rhiannon to take the elf to task. He had sounded just like Hector then!

But Rhiannon merely hung her head. 'You are right. I am sorry, I was not thinking,' she apologised.

Disgusted, and disappointed, Huw pushed past and led the way down to the last house. As he got closer he saw what she meant. The village had the usual smells of mud, dung and mould, the things he expected and strong enough to mask what was coming out of the last house. Almost. Until you got closer to it, when its stink of corruption hit you like a wall.

Huw found his steps getting slower — and then he stopped altogether when a fat, sleek crow hopped out of the doorway, saw him and strutted away. He did not want to go in there, could well imagine what he might find but took a deep breath, held it and strode forwards. One look inside was all he needed to turn and hurry away, fighting to hold his noonday meal down.

Sendatsu grabbed his shoulder.

'Are they all in there?' he asked, choking a little at the smell.

'Probably. Maybe some escaped, maybe they let a few go to spread the tale around the surrounding hills and vales,' Huw gasped. 'But there's a pile of bodies in there. Men, women and children.'

'Children?' Sendatsu spat. 'They have killed children?'

Huw pointed to where a small hand lay outstretched in the side of the doorway. Huw staggered away, as did Rhiannon. Sendatsu stood there, frozen — and then he heard it. A soft cry for help. He raced over and ducked inside, heedless of the stink of death. Dead, staring eyes gazed back at him wherever he looked — then he saw a small hand reach up. He pushed aside the dead body of a man to reveal a young boy. He was probably Mai's age, just old enough to begin exploring the world around him. Then someone had slammed a sword into his back. Dried blood was thick on his tunic but he was still alive — barely. Sendatsu gently turned him over, to see more blood on his chest, while a wound on the top of his head had also bled heavily, covering his eyes.

'It's all right, you're safe now,' Sendatsu said gently. He did not know much magic but he had learned how to take away a little pain — perfect when Mai or Cheijun tripped and grazed themselves. He reached into the magic and tried to give as much as he could to the young boy.

His laboured breathing seemed to ease a little and Sendatsu hoped he had helped. He began to gently open the boy's tunic, discover how deep the wound was and if he might save the boy.

'Dad, is that you?' the boy whispered.

Sendatsu thought about telling the truth but a glance inside the tunic told him the boy did not have long to live.

'Yes, it's me,' he said hoarsely, holding the boy's hand. 'I'm here. You're safe now.'

'I'm so cold. And I can't feel my legs ...'

Sendatsu held him close. 'Your legs are fine. You'll be running before you know it,' he whispered.

'It hurt so much. But now I want to sleep.'

Sendatsu had to clench his jaw to hold himself together. 'You go to sleep now. As long as you like. No chores in the morning.'

'Can you sing to me?'

For a long, long time Sendatsu could not. But, somehow, he managed it. He had promised Mai that her goodnight song was for her only but he knew she would want to help this dying boy.

Slowly, haltingly, he managed to sing her song, listening as the boy's breathing slowed, eased, then slipped away.

He finished the song and then held the boy close, unable to let him go until the tears had stopped.

'Sendatsu? Are you all right?'

Rhiannon's voice made him look up.

'No,' he said softly.

He laid the boy back down, filled by an anger greater than anything he had ever felt before. If there had been Forlish there, he would have shown them no mercy. He had to find some, let out this colossal fury inside him.

He stood up. 'We should light a pyre.'

'I thought we didn't have time ...'

'We will make time. The bastards who did this will pay,' Sendatsu swore.

'But won't the smoke scare others, or maybe even warn the Forlish ...' Rhiannon asked tentatively.

'I'm doing this. Either help me or not.'

The blood on his tunic and face did not invite argument.

There was plenty of firewood stacked around, so Huw and Sendatsu hurled logs into the house, disturbing a pair of ravens that flew off, cursing at them, while Rhiannon stacked more around the sides. They worked until they were tired and sweating.

The thatch of the roof was damp, and fire would not take easily, but Sendatsu reached into the magic, used it to heat the straw underneath until the roof seemingly went up in flames all at once.

Sendatsu closed his eyes, prayed with all his heart and soul that Aroaril would take this boy and his family, give them peace. He wiped his face clear and looked once more at the fire. 'We are done here. We must find some Forlish to pay for this,' he said flatly, turning away.

'Don't you mean, find a village to help?' Rhiannon asked.

'No.'

Rhiannon and Huw looked at each other doubtfully, before following him back to the horses.

On they rode, but they found no villages that day. They saw more farmsteads, some of them with people working the fields. At the first the people ran for the trees as soon as they saw the three riders but while they listened as Rhiannon sang Sendatsu's song, it still took all of Huw's persuasion for them to come out and talk.

'Every time we see riders, we run. That's why we are alive,' they said.

But they would not listen to Huw's suggestions to find a village for safety.

'Do you want to ask them questions?' Huw offered to Sendatsu.

'No. I want to find some Forlish,' Sendatsu said harshly.

This was what Huw had wanted but now he found it worrying, while Rhiannon did not feel able to say anything, so they rode on.

Sendatsu slowly steamed in the gentle rain as they rode past a series of hills and across a small valley. There were Forlish around here. Let them take on someone their own size, see how long they lasted.

'Smoke!' Rhiannon cried.

They followed her pointing finger to where the first fingers of smoke rose above the lip of a hill.

'Come on!' Huw raced his horse forwards, followed by Rhiannon and Sendatsu, who swiftly overtook him.

He knew he should never show himself on the crest of a hill — but he was beyond caring. He boiled over the top to see a small village, barely a score of houses, nestled in the valley below — where it was under attack from a dozen Forlish raiders.

Two houses had already been set on fire, while the Forlish rode through the rest of the village, daring the Velsh to fight back — and killing any that tried. A handful of bodies already lay sprawled on the ground, while the screaming and crying carried right up the hill. Sendatsu ignored the noise, for he had eyes only for the small girl running, screaming, away from a laughing Forlishman who was stalking her on foot.

He grabbed his bow and leaped down from the saddle, staggering slightly in the wet grass, as Huw and Rhiannon reined to a halt behind him.

'What are you doing?' Huw cried as Sendatsu strung his bow in a heartbeat, drew and sighted on the Forlishman, who had trapped the girl beside a water trough and now raised his sword.

It was a difficult target, aiming downhill nearly a hundred yards away, but there was an ice-cold anger bubbling inside Sendatsu and he knew he could not miss. He loosed and watched the Forlishman get thrown back by the power of the strike.

The terrified girl looked around and Sendatsu waved for her to hide.

'Are you mad?' Huw jumped off his horse and ran to Sendatsu's side. 'We can't take on that many Forlish!'

'They are dead,' Sendatsu said simply. He laid another arrow on his string, spotted a Forlishman dragging a woman out of a house and loosed in the next instant. This time the Forlishman spun around and fell.

When a third man went down screaming with an arrow through his guts, the Forlish noticed the three figures up on the hill. Only four of the Forlish were mounted — and they galloped up the hill, determined to avenge their comrades.

'Better get back,' Sendatsu advised Huw. He drew and loosed, watched with grim satisfaction as it snatched a Forlishman out of his saddle.

A second man was sent reeling away with an arrow in the arm, then Sendatsu put down a horse with a third arrow — dropped his bow and drew his sword as the last Forlishman leaned out of the saddle to chop him down.

Except Sendatsu was not there. He darted to his right, away from the Forlish sword, and slammed his own blade into the horse's mouth. As it screamed and bucked, the Forlishman tried to keep his seat, only for Sendatsu to rush behind him and slash through his back with a brutal thunder-strike.

By the time Sendatsu turned back, the remaining Forlish had found their horses and were riding away, having seen enough.

'What were you doing?' Huw demanded.

'What you wanted — stopping the Forlish,' Sendatsu snarled, with such force that Huw recoiled. 'Now we need to go and help those people.'

He strode down the hill, stopping only to finish off the Forlishman thrown by his horse, both of them lying, screaming, with broken legs.

'I have never seen him like this,' Rhiannon said shakily. 'We have to get him out of here before he gets himself killed.'

Huw had wanted to see the elf punish the Forlish invaders — but this was too much even for him. 'I think you're right,' he agreed.

'Do you think it has something to do with what's in his pouch?'

'No, it was seeing the dead children. But I didn't realise he cared so much for humans,' Huw mused. He was shaken by the elf's intensity. He thought Sendatsu cared little for the people they met and only for the knowledge they might hold.

'We'd better catch up to him,' Rhiannon said. 'We might need to do some fast talking to get him to agree with us, rather than go hunting Forlish.'

Huw nodded agreement. Of all the things he had imagined happening in Rheged, this was not one of them.

# 18

*The reports did not alarm me at first for they were little incidents, things that I had expected might happen. I stupidly did not think they were all the work of Naibun. Elven homes were set alight, human mobs dispersed outside elven settlements in the far north, where the rich mines yielded tin and iron. Worse, I did not see the effect they would have on the people. Already nervous of being told to leave their homes and return to Dokuzen, they spread tales of angry human mobs.*

*Naibun skilfully wove these tales up, until the people were convinced the barrier was the only thing between us and destruction at human hands.*

Sendatsu only agreed to leave Rheged to protect the remaining villagers he had saved, when Huw insisted they could find new homes in Gwent. The terrified villagers were in no mood to argue — and certainly not with Sendatsu, whose burning eyes were making them even more nervous. They escorted the villagers to a plump Gwent village called Lewes, just across the border. The people there were on edge, having woken up to see smoke to the south almost every morning. They were willing to let the Rhegeders stay — Sendatsu would brook no argument — and raced to build a wall and the elven crossbows.

'See, we were right to come north. We will help far more people this way.' Rhiannon smiled.

Sendatsu was not convinced. What he had seen in Rheged left him feeling raw. 'We should follow the smoke,' he suggested, something even Huw was not willing to try.

Both Huw and Rhiannon were worried at this turn of events. How would other villages react to this new, angrier Sendatsu? He was not even looking in his pouch any more.

Luckily the next village was Harlech.

This was a large, prosperous village, one of the biggest in the central Vales district. Harlech dwarfed the likes of Catsfield and made even Crumlin look like a hamlet.

It was also burying its dead when they arrived.

Half a dozen homes on the outskirts had been hit overnight, families killed, then the huts fired. When their neighbours rushed out to help, they saw figures running off into the night, carrying both goods and women. Consequently the village was in a volatile mood when they arrived — a strange mix of anger and fear.

'Who are you? What do you want?'

The trio found themselves surrounded by a mob of worried and angry people who were not inclined to listen to a song.

It took some quick talking from Huw, as well as a quick demonstration from Sendatsu, before the village accepted the three travellers. A delegation of farmers, led by a massive man called Gareth, sat down with them.

'It is a shame you did not get here a few days ago — even yesterday,' Gareth said bitterly. 'We slept like lambs, not knowing wolves were stalking us.'

'Did you not see the smoke on the horizon, wonder what it was?' Rhiannon blurted out.

Gareth was a head taller than Huw, and twice as wide. Even Sendatsu looked small against the size of his arms and chest. He also had easily the most impressive beard the three of them had seen, a true Velsh beard. He regarded her slowly.

'Listen, girl. We see and hear many strange things here. But they have never affected us before. We live our lives in peace, attacking nobody. Why should we expect anyone would strike at us?'

Rhiannon flushed at being addressed as though she was a fool but Huw touched her arm and gave her a quick warning look.

'We wish we could have been here sooner. But we do not know where and when these raiders will strike. Now we are here, we can provide you with the way to protect yourselves.'

'We need more help than that. They took some of our people — you can help us get them back,' Gareth rumbled. 'I am going to lead a party of men into the woods. I cannot abide the thought of people I know suffering while I do nothing.'

'These are not mere bandits — they are veteran Forlish warriors. If you go after them, you will be lucky to return alive,' Huw warned.

'And you need to listen to me, lad. I shall not leave my people to suffer,' Gareth vowed. 'You say you want to help. This is your chance.'

'I know how important it is to protect your people,' Huw said with feeling. 'But I also know when the Forlish are setting a trap. At least give us time to build some of our crossbows, let Sendatsu train some of your men. They can't hope to take hunting spears against swordsmen ...'

'We go, with or without you,' Gareth said implacably. 'If you are really here to help us, as you say, then you join. Otherwise you are welcome to leave at any time.'

'I'm ready.' Sendatsu half rose but Huw grabbed his sleeve.

'Of course we shall join you,' Huw said firmly. 'But Sendatsu is only one man — elf. You have to be prepared for this to end badly. The Forlish are not foolish. If they let you see them take prisoners away with them, you can be sure they had a reason.'

Gareth levered himself to his feet, followed by the other men of Harlech.

'We shall leave within the turn of an hourglass. Be ready or be gone.'

'We shall be there,' Sendatsu promised.

'This is a bad idea,' Huw said, as soon as Gareth and the other Velsh had left. 'The Forlish will be waiting for us. They want the bravest and strongest men to come out to meet them, so they can slaughter them and have the rest of the village at their mercy.'

'Then we shall have to stop that happening,' Sendatsu said calmly.

Huw stared at him. 'What is it you're not telling us? Why did Rheged affect you so deeply?'

'It didn't. I've been fighting the Forlish since I got here,' Sendatsu dismissed.

'No, not like this. It makes no sense. You know as well as I that the Forlish are planning a trap and Gareth is foolish to walk into it. Why do you want to join him? I thought your quest was more important?'

'I don't want to talk about it.' Sendatsu turned away. He had been able to walk away from things back in Dokuzen but life out here with the humans was different. Seeing children slaughtered before his eyes was too much to take. He saw the face of the boy who had died in his arms every time he closed his eyes. How could he embrace Mai and Cheijun when he had done nothing to stop the blood on his hands?

'It's our lives you're risking as well — talk to us!' Huw demanded, grabbing hold of Sendatsu.

The elf was about to hurl the bard across the room when Rhiannon stepped in between them.

'That's enough! Both of you!'

The two of them glared at each other past her, until she grabbed Huw and forced him to turn away. She chose Huw ... she was not sure why but she instinctively felt he would respond to her, while Sendatsu would not.

'Calm down! For me, if not for anything else,' she told Huw.

Instantly he smiled, a little sheepishly. 'I shall.'

'And an apology for Sendatsu?'

'What? I just asked a question!' Huw protested.

She leaned close to him and he thrilled to her lips being only a few inches from his, looking deep into her eyes.

'We are about to go out to find and fight the Forlish. Don't you think it would be better to do so as friends? Trust me, I know

Sendatsu has our best interests at heart. If he is hiding something, there is a very good reason.'

At that point, Huw would have agreed with almost anything she said.

'Sendatsu, I am sorry,' he said over Rhiannon's shoulder.

Sendatsu still glowered, so Rhiannon turned to him.

'And Sendatsu — you too.'

'I'm sorry — that I thought you wanted to fight the Forlish as well as I,' he growled.

Rhiannon was about to demand a better apology when Huw tapped her arm.

'I don't need one. Look, I have an idea how we might be able to help out there,' Huw offered, eager to show Rhiannon he was the bigger man. Well, he was the only one but that was not the point ...

'What?' Sendatsu said shortly.

'Sendatsu, you go with the lead group, because you can move through the woods better than anyone here and might be able to spot a trap before they spring it. Rhiannon and I shall be towards the rear, where we can either cover a retreat or come to your aid. We'll take every bolt we have with us — the elven crossbows might still prove the difference.'

'Don't you think Rhiannon should stay here if it is going to be dangerous ...'

'I am not staying behind, like some milkmaid!' Rhiannon snorted and Huw smiled.

The pair of them had been using the crossbows every day, demonstrating them at each village. Rhiannon was fitter than most women but most Velsh farmwives, their arms toughened by a lifetime of work, were stronger and had no problem using the crossbow.

'I'll take care of Rhiannon.'

'I don't need taking care of — any more than you do!' Rhiannon said hotly.

'Great, you can save me and carry me back here in your arms.' Huw turned it into a joke but Sendatsu did not smile. He felt he might never smile again. The emptiness inside him could only be filled with blood and death.

Huw did try once more to persuade the village not to leave the safety of the houses and go into the woods.

'Skies above, I know how hard it is to sit back and not help your friends. But the Forlish will be waiting for you. You can have your revenge on them if you stay here, if you build a wall and prepare the elven crossbows, they will get frustrated and attack — and you can pay them back ten-fold for what they have done, rescue your friends then ...'

'We cannot wait that long. A true Velshman does not sit back while his friends are being abused.' Gareth shut that down swiftly.

'A true Velshman does not get his friends killed to prove he is a true Velshman,' Huw retorted.

'Enough talk! We go!' Gareth roared.

The mob he had assembled rumbled their approval, although Huw reckoned barely half of them were genuinely enthusiastic. The rest were coming along because it was expected of them. They had no stomach for this and would probably run the first chance they got.

They were all men in their prime, none bowed by years of back-breaking work, all at least three years over manhood. But the weapons they carried were less impressive. There were hunting spears, as well as hoes and scythes, although there were plenty of axes and quite a few knives as well. But no armour, no shields and nothing that was good for fighting swordsmen in woods. There were enough of them — more than fifty assembled together. But that would be just perfect for the Forlish. The biggest and bravest men all brought together and, with their deaths, the village would be helpless.

They could not work together either. They straggled in small groups after Gareth, who held a long-handled wood axe over one shoulder, staying close to friends and family for safety and comfort, while few seemed to want to be near the front. Those who found themselves there often slowed down, or stopped to adjust a shoe or the grip on their crude weapon, allowing others to get ahead of them.

Sendatsu observed all this grimly. He had his bow strung and a handful of arrows pushed into his belt — but expected to use his sword. He hoped the Velsh would be able to help him.

'Have you any plan for when we find the Forlish?' he asked Gareth as they walked, almost alone, at the front of the mob.

Of all the Velsh, Gareth did not seem worried by what they were doing. He strode out, setting a fast pace, neither slowing nor deviating from the path he had chosen to the woods.

'We shall follow the trail they left until we see their camp, then we shall rush in and slaughter them,' the farmer replied gruffly.

'And will you have groups ready to take them in the flank, if necessary?'

'No.'

'And I suppose there is no proper formation with the longer weapons at the front?'

'No.'

Sendatsu sighed. These Velsh would only get in his way. They didn't know the first thing about fighting. The Forlish had left a broad trail even a child could follow. But this did not bother Gareth. He just plodded on, aiming at a gap in the trees, where the trail the Forlish had left seemed to vanish into the bushes. Sendatsu glanced over his shoulder to see the Velsh were spread out over another fifty yards, from the ones who were close behind Gareth to the stragglers, who were getting slower all the time.

He tried to see Huw and Rhiannon — but they were staying with the rear of the column, which was quite a distance away now.

'Drink?' A stout-looking Velshman just behind him offered him a skin. Sendatsu was about to accept when he smelled the man's breath. It was mead. From the glassy eyes and unsteady walk of several of the Velsh behind him, there was plenty of it as well.

'I'm not thirsty,' Sendatsu said dryly.

* * *

The advance across the fields was a new experience for Huw, and not a pleasant one either. It was one thing to talk about helping everyone but deliberately putting their heads in a noose to do so was something else again. He found his mouth was dry and his bladder full, while his hands were sweating badly and he had to keep wiping them on his tunic.

'It's just like the time before a show,' Rhiannon said softly. 'We'll feel much better once it starts.'

Huw smiled. 'This is one case where I don't think that is true!'

'I know,' she admitted. 'But I thought we might both feel better if I said so.'

They walked along in silence for a little longer. The fields were different from those he was used to. Patcham, indeed most of the villages he had visited, had one giant field divided into strips for each family. At Harlech they had strip fields, of course, but also large paddocks fenced with stone. He would have liked to ask someone about it but thought they had their minds on something else. Quite a few of the Velsh were doing their best to walk in any direction but towards the woods. All around the column, men were drinking from skins. Huw thought they must be suffering from the same dry mouth he had — until he got a whiff of what was inside. Mead. A potent liquor at the best of times but the way some of them were drinking, it was perhaps no surprise they were not walking straight. Others too, mainly the ones right at the back and sides, were stopping to drop their trousers and void their bowels.

Rhiannon averted her eyes, while they did not look up, out of embarrassment as much as modesty.

'I hope Sendatsu will be all right,' she worried.

'He'll be fine — the Forlish have never fought anyone like him before. I'm more worried about us.'

'We shall work together. You begin first — loose a few bolts quickly, then I shall begin as well. That way we shall not run out together. We'll tell each other when we are reloading, so we can cover each other,' Rhiannon suggested.

Huw thought about it and liked the idea. They both had makeshift quivers, cloth bags really, tied around their waists, each filled with the short, wicked bolts. Each elven crossbow could take about a dozen of them, and they had filled the hoppers and had at least another hundred bolts apiece in the bags. He hoped it was enough.

# 19

*Naibun took it to the next level when he began systematically killing humans — those with magic, priests of Aroaril and human leaders who had worked with us in the past. He had captured the lists from the Magic-weavers and now used them as they had planned.*

*Unsurprisingly some humans fought back — and Naibun was able to bring reports of dead elves before a Council meeting I missed. Coming from my most loyal supporter, he was able to win support to punish any humans who came close to the barrier — and he stretched that definition as far as it could go, pushing the Border Patrol far out beyond Dokuzen.*

Gareth finally raised an arm to call a halt a good ten yards from the start of the woods. For a moment Sendatsu thought the man had lost his courage, for the woods were silent, ominously so, and while he had not seen anything, he could feel eyes on him. But then he realised Gareth just wanted everyone to catch up.

'Hurry! They will get away!' Gareth boomed.

Sendatsu doubted the Forlish wanted to go anywhere, although it was a different story with the Velsh.

'Are they going to be able to fight?' he asked Gareth.

'Oh, they will fight,' Gareth promised.

By the time there was a solid group of Velsh standing there, all peering nervously at the woods, Sendatsu seriously doubted it, although Gareth was confident enough.

'When I give the order, we shall all rush in together. Stay close and kill any Forlishman you see!' Gareth told them. 'They will learn the strength of Vales today!'

That raised a ragged cheer, so Gareth turned and waved his axe. 'Follow me!'

It was less a determined charge and more of a cautious trot, but the Velsh broke into a run and, led by Gareth, plunged into the woods.

Sendatsu made sure he was just behind the lead group of Gareth and his cronies, ones who had been passing around the skins of mead on the walk from the village. He put away his arrow and slipped his bow into a holder across his back. In here, the sword was going to be the better weapon.

The trail led across flattened bushes, to a small clearing where a fire burned, around which three lifeless, naked women were tied to stakes.

It all reeked of a trap but, before Sendatsu could shout a useless warning, Gareth bellowed with rage and raced into the clearing, heading right for the stakes, his men close behind him.

Sendatsu immediately scanned the undergrowth, searching for the Forlish he knew must be hidden, allowing more Velsh to slip past him, men carrying hoes and scythes that bumped on low-hanging tree branches and got in each other's way.

By now Gareth had reached the first of the women, lifted the head and roared with fury as he looked into dead eyes. Even from where he stood, Sendatsu could see their throats had been cut. The Velsh were now milling around the stakes, with Gareth trying to cut the bodies free of their bonds with his axe.

'Watch the trees!' Sendatsu ordered but, even as the first of the Velsh reacted sluggishly to his call, the Forlish struck.

Sendatsu reluctantly had to admire it. The timing was perfect. The Velsh rush had lost all momentum, the ones eager to fight were standing around uselessly, while the rest were tangled with each other and the trees as well.

Forlish warriors raced in from all directions, picking their targets, crashing home with devastating force. Velshmen swung axes or poked spears or hoes and had their crude weapons swept aside by veteran soldiers, who got close and cut and thrust viciously with their wicked swords.

Gareth swung his axe in huge arcs, forcing back a pair of Forlish, while a few of the others were clever enough to stand together, holding out their spears to keep the Forlish at a distance. But a dozen others fell in a matter of moments, alcohol-inspired bravery and farm-bred strength no match for training and discipline.

Sendatsu raced forwards, to where the Forlish trap was about to close and cut off Gareth's group, eager to pay these Forlish back for what they had done.

To his left a warrior lunged at him but Sendatsu just slipped past the point and delivered a short slash to the neck, sending the man backwards. On his right another cut at his head but he blocked that easily and used the momentum from his first blow to send his blade deep into the man's chest. His sword caught on ribs and he cursed, brought up his foot and tried to kick the gasping man off his blade.

'Come on! Fight!' he roared at the Velsh, ripping his sword free and shoving the dying Forlishman towards his advancing comrades.

But the mass of Velsh was collapsing in on itself as the Forlish pressed in from all sides. Everywhere he looked, men were dying. He raced to help a young Velshman who was prodding desperately with his pitchfork, trying to keep a swordsman at bay. As the Forlishman pushed the rusty tines away and drew back his sword for the killing thrust, Sendatsu jumped in and cut off his head with a huge dragon-tail stroke.

That got the attention of other Forlish and a pair changed direction and pressed in on him.

Sendatsu shoved the Velshman he had saved towards a fallen sword.

'Pick it up! Fight!' he ordered.

Instead, the Velshman raced away. Sendatsu could not do more, for the Forlish sliced and cut at him from opposite directions. But this was no more than an exercise to Sendatsu, a drill he had practised scores of times, and a chance to use the floating cloud style. He jumped towards one man, forcing him back, then turned swiftly to block a blow from the other, rolling his wrists and chopping over the top. Before that Forlishman had collapsed, he had spun again, to parry another lunge. He cut off the Forlishman's hand, then sliced his throat as he screamed in pain, silencing him in mid-cry.

'Stay together, use your spears!' he shouted again, wiping blood off his face and trying to see what Gareth and the other Velsh were doing.

Behind him, the nervous fighters, led by the man he had saved, were flooding back down the trail, running for their lives. In front of him, Gareth and a dozen men stood, surrounded by the bodies of a score of others, while Forlish pressed in from three sides, tightening the noose around them. Sendatsu could see they had no idea how to fight.

'To me!' Sendatsu bellowed.

At last they heeded his words, hearing them over the screams of the wounded and dying and the war cries of the Forlish. Sendatsu counted swiftly — there were more than forty Forlishmen and each was the equal of three or four Velsh.

The Velsh were running towards Sendatsu. Only Gareth remained, his feet planted solidly, swinging his axe wildly from side to side, as though he was chopping at a tree. It only took moments — one Forlishman waited until the axe had swung past, then stepped in and thrust his sword into Gareth's belly. The big Velshman dropped his axe and grabbed his killer around the throat but, before he could crush the life out of him, other Forlish stepped in and their swords sank deeply into Gareth, who toppled over.

'Stay with me!' Sendatsu tried to slow them down but, once they began running, it was hard to stop. They raced for the village and the Forlish flooded after them in pursuit. Sendatsu had to back away himself, wondering where Huw and Rhiannon had gone.

Then the Forlish raced in, and he had no more time to worry about them.

'Come on! Stick together! Get those spears out!' He tried to hold the last of the frightened Velsh together as the Forlish pressed in, eager to finish this slaughter.

Huw and Rhiannon had been caught at the back, slowed down by the stragglers, who had been caught up in the trees and with each other. When the fighting began, the first they heard of it was the screaming of men dying on steel blades. Almost immediately, men began pushing backwards, heading for the sunlight and the village. One man dropped his scythe and ran, next moment a dozen of them were pushing and shoving to get clear, everyone getting tangled up with each other.

'Come on — let's get around them!' Rhiannon shouted. She was frightened, but not just for herself. Sendatsu was up there somewhere, near where all the screaming was happening. She knew he could handle himself but he was relying on them to help.

Huw did not want to go near the fighting. Every instinct told him to turn around, let the tide of frightened men carry him out in the sun once more. But he could not leave Rhiannon. He jumped over a low bush and hurried after her.

More and more men were now running backwards down the trail, while the screams and the shouts were louder up ahead. They could hear Sendatsu bellowing for men to stay with him and looked at each other.

'Come on then.' Huw waved and they pushed through the bushes, until they could see Sendatsu fighting furiously. Few Velsh were helping him and plenty of Forlish were trying to kill him.

'Do it! Quick!' Rhiannon cried and Huw levelled his crossbow in response.

He worked the crossbow's lever, sending a steady stream of bolts at the Forlish to Sendatsu's left side. Men stopped, ducked and covered up as wicked bolts sunk into flesh. Rhiannon added hers and that whole side backed away, collapsing in on itself. Sendatsu used the respite to turn on those in front of him. He deflected a wild swing and cut viciously, sending the Forlishman screaming back into his fellows, then he danced clear of the pursuit, encouraging a few of the slightly more sober Velsh to stand with him, to use their hunting spears to hold back the Forlish. Now the narrowness of the path worked to the favour of the Velsh, for it was the Forlish advance that was being held back, compressed by the path and the crossbow bolts slicing in from the flank. These bolts rarely took a man down with just one. But they rarely hit with just one. The narrowness of the Forlish advance allowed Huw and Rhiannon to concentrate their bolts on a small space. One was a painful annoyance, two slowed a man down, three or more and that Forlishman was out of the battle.

'Keep going! Stay together!' Sendatsu urged the Velsh, trying to get them to hold together and walk backwards at the same time.

It was almost impossible.

One by one, the Velsh disappeared down the trail.

'Take your friends!' Sendatsu darted from left to right, his sword cutting down Forlish who pressed too close, trying to give the wounded a chance to be dragged to safety.

The Forlish used short swords, ideal for close work and the shield wall — and more than enough to deal with the untrained Velsh. But Sendatsu's blade was considerably longer, giving him more reach — and he had far more skill as well. The Forlish held their swords in their right hands, used their whole arms to stab or swing fiercely, yet wildly. Sendatsu had two hands on his hilt and used wrists and forearms to move the sword too swiftly for them to follow. He dazzled them with a variety of styles — using the cross, the dragon-tail, the wagonwheel, the eight-side, tiger-claw and thunder-strike. They raised their swords to block a blow heading for their necks, only for Sendatsu to subtly change direction and slice off an arm, or cut open chests or stomachs. They were brave men and pressed in — but seeing their comrades fall to this blade naturally slowed them down a little, and they were content to push the elf back, rather than try to bring him down.

He beckoned them forwards, lost in the moment, his whole body alight. The fury that had filled him in Rheged had found an outlet. He was painted from head to foot in blood and the sight of him, wild eyes glaring from a red mask, was enough to give the Forlish reason to hesitate.

Huw and Rhiannon backed away as well, although few Forlish were going near them — they preferred to try to hide behind trees, duck away from the swarm of vicious little bolts hurtling in. The pair of them worked together as if they had practised this for months, instead of talked about it once.

'I'm out! Loading!' Huw called.

As he burrowed in his pouch and fed the bolts into the hopper on the top of the crossbow, Rhiannon slowed her rate of fire slightly, watching her targets and making sure nobody tried to rush in.

'I'm here again!' Huw cycled the crossbow through, sending his first bolt into a man's thigh.

'Sendatsu's falling back!' Rhiannon cried, unable to keep stealing glances over to where the elf dared the Forlish to come near.

'Pull back ten yards! You go and I'll cover you! Call me when you're ready!'

Rhiannon did not argue, turning and racing back, jumping over small bushes and dodging trees.

'Huw! Now!' she called, aiming her crossbow up a little to get more range as she loosed bolts.

Huw spun and ran, his back itching as he went. It was an effort to stop, to turn and use the crossbow again, but having Rhiannon beside him made it easier.

'I'm out! Cover me!' Rhiannon called.

As she reloaded, a Forlishman crashed through bushes at them. Perhaps he had seen Huw turn and run, perhaps the lack of bolts made him bold. Whatever, he raced at them, sword raised high, lips pulled back from his teeth in a snarl.

Time seemed to slow for Huw and he could see every detail. The fresh blood on the Forlish blade, the dried blood on his tunic and trews, the hatred in his eyes and the anger on his face. He could see the small bushes, beginning to flower, leaves broken and torn by the heavy feet of running men. Run! Every instinct told him to turn but he knew Rhiannon stood beside him, so he braced himself and levelled the elven crossbow. Until now he had been aiming at groups of men, not one individually. He had been able to loose bolts without looking into the eyes of the men he was trying to hurt and kill. But there was no such luxury here. He had to stop the man, or the Forlish warrior would cut him down and then get his hands on Rhiannon …

Huw loosed his first bolt, teeth gritted to stop himself from crying out, watched it flicker past the Forlishman's right shoulder. He adjusted left and loosed again, saw it sink into the man's chest, high up, watched his foe grimace in pain but keep going. Again he loosed, struck in the middle of the chest this time, but the Forlishman kept coming, eating up the distance between them a yard at a time with each stride. Again and again Huw loosed, watching the man check slightly with each strike, the shafts of the bolts bristling from his chest. Blood was now spilling out of the man's mouth but he still ran on, sword held high.

Huw was shouting now, a wordless cry of mixed fear and anger as he loosed one final bolt, which hit again in the chest. He cycled the crossbow again but nothing came out and, with a sick sense of horror, realised he was empty. For an instant he thought about dropping the weapon and running but then he stepped forwards, holding it like a club, trying to turn his cry of fear into a battle shout and bracing himself for the agony of the Forlish sword cutting into him.

The Forlishman's eyes widened in triumph and he drew back his arm for the killing blow, his mouth and beard covered in a bloody foam.

Then another bolt appeared in his left eye, or rather disappeared into his left eye, and the fury vanished in an instant, replaced by the blankness of wood in one eye and the darkness of death in the other as the Forlishman flew backwards and lay still.

'I'm here again,' Rhiannon said, voice shaking. 'Time to pull back. I'll cover you.'

Huw turned numbly, on legs that were wobbling and seemed barely capable of holding his weight. He wanted to be sick, he wanted to keep running — the edge of the trees was just paces away — but somehow he forced himself to stop by a thick oak tree and, with trembling hands, fed bolts into the hopper again.

'Ready!' he shouted, his voice sounding shrill, even to his own ears.

Rhiannon raced back and joined him.

'Thank you,' he tried to say to her.

'It's nothing — you stood there to protect me, so I had to do the same,' Rhiannon gasped.

The stories she had read, the songs she had sung — none of that had prepared her for the reality of this. It missed out the screaming, the blood, the stench of entrails, the foul, graveyard smell of bodies torn open to the air, men shitting themselves in fear and crying in terror. She clung to two things. She had to help Sendatsu, who was still fighting furiously — but most of all she drew strength from Huw. Sendatsu looked at home here, looked like he was enjoying himself as he used his skills to send another man to his death.

But Huw looked as scared as she felt, although he stood by her side, his jaw locked tight as his hands worked the elven crossbow. As he had held off that charging Forlishman, she had been terrified — for him. Her fingers had slipped on the bolts and a task that she had completed so many times it was second nature suddenly seemed almost impossible. But she had finished just in time, loosed the killing bolt. She wanted to run, she wanted no more part of this — but she was the one who had insisted she would not be left behind in the village like every other woman. She had forced herself into this situation, now she could not get out of it. It was ironic — she had pushed so hard and now she was in the thick of it, she wanted to be anywhere but here.

'We're almost out,' Huw cried.

She felt a surge of relief then, the thought it would soon be over. The sunlight seemed to promise safety and it was just paces away.

She risked a glance over at Sendatsu and saw him block a blow, kick a Forlishman between the legs, slice off a man's hand and then elbow a third in the face, before turning and running, a pack of Forlish on his heels.

'Come on!' she shouted.

She and Huw loosed bolts at the chasing Forlish, slowing the pursuit as the Forlish instinctively ducked and covered. Sendatsu outpaced the chasers easily, disappearing out of the gloom into the light. The two of them glanced at each other and, in unspoken agreement, raced out for the sunlight and the open fields around Harlech. They tore out into the sunlight and ran on for another fifty yards, racing over to where Sendatsu was slowing to a stop, breathing hard, his hands on his knees, blood covering his face and arms and chest and caking his sword.

'Are you all right?' Rhiannon cried.

'A couple of little cuts. But most of this isn't mine,' he gasped.

'We did it! We're all alive!' Huw rejoiced.

They stared at each other, glanced across the field to where the Velsh were alternately running and staggering towards the village — and then heard the roar as a horde of Forlish erupted from the woods, swords in hands and vengeance in hearts.

'We're not free yet! Come on!' Sendatsu pushed Huw and Rhiannon back towards the village. 'Get on — I'll hold them off ...'

'Don't be a fool! Out here they'll swamp you! The crossbows are the only hope!' Rhiannon snapped.

'That wall over there!' Huw pointed.

They raced back to a low stone wall that divided a pair of Harlech's fields and tumbled over the top of it. The two humans used it to brace their crossbows, while Sendatsu sheathed his sword and pulled his bowstave away from the holder on his back and swiftly strung it.

'I only have six arrows,' he warned.

'Make them count. Because we only have about thirty bolts left,' Huw replied grimly.

The Forlish obviously intended to finish what they had started, because they did not pause in their charge forwards, although Sendatsu could see a couple limping at the back, no doubt carrying one or more bolts in them.

Sendatsu stood and drew back, sighting on the leader and loosing.

Compared to the little crossbow bolts, the impact of a yard-long arrow was hugely impressive. It struck the Forlishman in the chest, picked him up and threw him backwards into two more, knocking them all over and slowing the charge instantly. Sendatsu swivelled and drew back a second time, loosing smoothly and sending a second man over. They were still too far away for the crossbows to be of any use, so Huw and Rhiannon just watched Sendatsu at work.

The strain of drawing the huge bow, coming so soon after the exertions of running and fighting desperately in the woods, hurt badly. He tried not to let it show but he could feel his face redden beneath all the blood. It took all his discipline to draw and hold the big bow, wait until he had a proper target. The Forlish were running to either side now, spreading out, darting around in all directions, anything to give him a harder target. He missed with his fourth arrow, sent the fifth through a man's leg, then drew back his last, changing his aim several times before loosing it, sending a Forlishman flying.

'Come on! We can't stay here — they'll get around us!' he snapped, breathing hard as he unstrung his bow.

Huw and Rhiannon did not hesitate. Instead of a nice, tight group that would have been an easy target for the crossbows, the Forlish had spread out into a wide line — and were sweeping around to the sides.

The three of them raced back across the field, not stopping until they reached the next wall. Huw glanced over and saw the Forlish still coming, slower now but just as implacable. There were probably fewer than thirty left — but there was little between them and the village of Harlech — and even less to stop them there.

'This isn't going to work! We'll just lead them right into the middle of the village,' Huw spat.

'Well, do you have any better suggestions, oh great-general?' Sendatsu growled.

'Get back to the village and round up as many men as you can. The Forlish have us on the run but, out here, we can swamp them with numbers,' Huw replied.

'Are you mad? The bravest of them are dead back in the forest — the rest are half drunk and shitting themselves with fear — the Forlish will tear them apart!'

'We don't have a choice,' Huw told him coldly. 'They don't have a choice. They fight or they watch their families die.'

'But I don't have the words — you're the one with the silver tongue. You go back there. I'll take your crossbow.'

Huw opened his mouth to argue his case, then saw the sense in what Sendatsu was saying.

'There're not many bolts left,' he warned, handing Sendatsu the crossbow and unstrapping the pouch with the remaining reloads inside and passing it to the elf too.

'We'll give you as much time as we can. But they're going to try and sweep around us, give us too many targets to aim at. We can't sit around for too long and these crossbows don't have much range on them,' Sendatsu said, tying the pouch around his waist.

Huw nodded. 'I'll be back soon,' he promised, then sprinted for the village.

'We'll let them get within forty yards, then loose half a dozen bolts before running for it again,' Sendatsu told Rhiannon. 'Can you do that?'

'I've been doing it all along — helping save your life,' she replied defiantly. 'I stood when the men ran.'

Sendatsu grinned wolfishly. 'You're right. I'm sorry. Just stay with me and I'll make sure we get back safe.'

'Really? Or perhaps I'll protect you.' Rhiannon levelled the crossbow, using the wall to give her support, then worked the lever twice, seeing the bolts soar high in the air, then fall close to a pair of Forlish, who dived for safety in response.

Huw found the village in an uproar. Women and children searched for missing husbands and sons, wounded screamed for help, men looked for their families, others shook and wept as they remembered what they had seen, how they had escaped. Huw was almost completely ignored. Twice he tried to talk, twice he went unheard.

'Listen to me!' he roared, his bard-trained voice finally cutting through the noise. He waited for a moment, as more and more turned to face him

'The Forlish are coming!'

That had the opposite effect he had intended. Women screamed, children wailed and people turned to run.

'Stop!' Huw thundered. 'To run is to die!'

A handful were already disappearing into the distance but most stopped to look at him again.

'Out there is an elf and a young woman. They are all that stands between you and death. For we have hurt those Forlish and they will show you no mercy. Women, children — all will fall to their swords, if you let them. Or you can stand together, join me and fight ...'

'They slaughtered us back in the woods!' someone cried, and the crowd began to edge backwards again.

'Because you were led into a trap! Gareth was a brave man but he killed your menfolk as surely as if he had cut them down himself! But this is different. Now they are coming here. There is nowhere for them to hide — and nowhere for you to hide either. It all comes down to this. Stand with me and we shall defeat them. I look around now and I see easily a hundred men. There's only a score of the Forlish left. If we all go out there, they will run, because they know to stand and fight is to die. But if we cower and hide, they will think us sheep and, like wolves, they will rip us apart.'

He paused for a moment, trying to see if they were with him. He was not sure they believed him but he was conscious the

Forlish were getting closer every moment — and Sendatsu and Rhiannon were out there.

'I know you are scared,' he tried one more time. 'I am scared. But I also know you are Velsh. The Forlish look down on us, think us barbarians, but being Velsh means something. It means you will stand up for your friends, you will not hide when a woman is fighting for you! You all lost something when you ran, when you left Gareth and the others to die. Come with me now and claim it back! Come with me and prove that you're not just men, but Velshmen!'

A pile of makeshift weapons, mostly farming implements, lay scattered around where men had dropped them. At least most appeared to have brought them all the way back — probably because they were worth too much to just throw away, even in terror-filled flight.

Huw bent down and grabbed a hoe. He had used axes to cut wood before — every Velshman had — but he could not imagine using it on another human. At least with the hoe, there was a comfortingly long handle to it, even if the head was blunt and scarred from years of being scraped on rocks in the fields around Harlech.

'If you want to save your families, if you want to avenge Gareth and your friends and family the Forlish slaughtered, then follow me!' Huw hefted the hoe defiantly but there was not exactly a huge rush to the pile of weapons.

'Come on! If you are truly Velsh, you will help me now,' Huw called, then thought of Rhiannon and was struck by a sudden inspiration. 'If the men are too afraid, then any woman who wants to save her children needs to go instead! If we stand together, they cannot defeat us!'

For a moment he thought he was going to have to lead a rag-tag dozen or so out to face the hardened Forlish warriors — then there was a rush for weapons, led by the women. Seeing them grab axes, knives, scythes and the like, the men could not stand back and joined in.

'Men and women of Harlech! Stay with each other and they cannot hurt us!' Huw shouted the words confidently, although he dreaded to think what would happen if the Forlish charged home. The Forlish would die, eventually, but would take a fearful toll.

With a huge mass of men and women, even a few children, Huw led the way back into the fields. He was tempted to run, for he sensed Sendatsu and Rhiannon would need help as soon as possible — but he remembered the straggling advance led by Gareth last time and wanted to keep everyone together, so made this more of a deliberate march. All could keep up with the pace he set — he just hoped it would be in time.

Sendatsu loosed three bolts in quick succession and cursed. This stupid weapon might be wonderful from behind a wall, with a dozen others all loosing at the same time, but, in an open field, he might as well be spitting at the Forlish. He didn't think his bolts had struck one warrior yet. Rhiannon had brought one down with a bolt in the lower leg but that was the best either of them had done. The Forlish advanced in short rushes, a few at a time, from all different points. It was hard to keep track of them and twice they had nearly been caught, forced to race away as a group pressed in on one flank or the other.

'Loading! Cover me!' Rhiannon called.

Sendatsu stood and loosed bolts at a running group of Forlish but they were too fast, and too far away, and the bolts all fell short. Then he realised that was his last one.

'I'm out too!' he spat, fumbling in Huw's pouch for the last few bolts.

With neither of them loosing anything, the Forlish charged in.

'Run!' Sendatsu grabbed Rhiannon and pushed her back towards the village, ignoring her cry of surprise and anger as she dropped a handful of bolts into the grass, rather than into the crossbow hopper.

They raced back to another wall, where they both feverishly pressed bolts into their crossbows.

'You have to listen to me! When I say I am loading, you need to watch for me — loose only when you have a target,' Rhiannon protested, levelling her weapon across the wall once more.

'These things are useless. We would do better hurling them at the Forlish,' Sendatsu grumbled.

For answer, Rhiannon loosed twice, bowling over a running Forlishman.

'Let them get closer. I'll deal with them then,' Sendatsu added, loosening the sword in his scabbard.

'Keep to the plan! Huw will bring the village to help us!' Rhiannon insisted.

Sendatsu snorted with disgust, then swore.

'To the right!' he called, working the lever on the crossbow furiously. Three, four bolts shot out, then the mechanism jammed.

Cursing furiously, Sendatsu tried to dig out the stuck bolt, while more Forlish raced in on his right.

'Back! Come on!' Rhiannon cried and they raced across another field.

This time the Forlish followed closer, intent only on revenge.

'Keep going!' Rhiannon shouted, glancing back over her shoulder. Running like this, being pursued, was far different from her rigorous training as a dancer, and her lungs were burning, her legs leaden with the combination of fear, adrenalin and exertion.

'Keep going where? The Velsh have fled, Huw with them. I'll deal with these Forlish myself.' Sendatsu dropped the blocked crossbow and drew his sword.

Rhiannon grabbed his arm. 'Don't be a fool! They'll kill you! Stay with me,' she pleaded.

He saw the numbers facing him and had a sudden vision of Mai and Cheijun. Then it changed to the dead boy in Rheged. Maybe these were the ones who left him to die, alone, surrounded by his dead family.

'Go. I'll be right behind you,' he said grimly.

But Rhiannon did not move. He could barely believe it. Did the woman really want to argue with him now? He glanced over his shoulder, to see her staring, a broad grin on her face, as the village of Harlech advanced grimly, climbing over the stone wall into the field.

Huw was at their head and there was a huge mass — men, women and older children. The ones at the back surely had no weapons, for there were not enough implements even in a village the size of Harlech to arm all of them. But there were too many to count and the ones at the front and sides all held something — from axes, knives and clubs to hoes and scythes.

'Death to the Forlish!' Huw roared, and the huge mob howled its anger.

The Forlish, spread out in a rough half-circle and closing in on Sendatsu and Rhiannon, stopped in their tracks. It was as if the wolf pack had been confronted by a mass of angry sheep — and they did not know what to do. But they could count, and their confidence was shaken by the sheer size of the mass of villagers. In ones and twos, then as a group, they began backing away, then turned and ran.

'After them!' Huw bellowed and the crowd shouted its agreement.

Sendatsu and Rhiannon ran with them, catching up to Huw as they went over a wall together, the Forlish in front streaking away for the safety of the woods.

'It has gone beyond sense now — we have to chase them away or this village will never be the same,' Huw explained.

'Are you sure?' Rhiannon called.

'No — I know what they are thinking and feeling! Trust me!' Huw cried, his face alight.

The feeling of bringing these people together, of driving away the Forlish almost from the gates of the village, was roaring through him. His fear from earlier was forgotten. He knew the Velsh had to regain their pride. Driving the Forlish away was no longer enough.

A pair of wounded Forlish, bolts in their legs, had fallen behind the rest — and were caught by the mob. They turned, swords held ready, and the village checked instinctively. But Huw kept going, knowing the Velsh mood was a fragile thing. If it stopped, it could be turned. The thought of taking on a pair of Forlish was terrifying but he forced himself on, hoe held out like a crude spear. The Forlish looked like they would sell their lives dearly, then Sendatsu charged in. He unleashed a series of blows, his sword flashing from side to side in the eight-side pattern. One man blocked desperately then went down, the other backed away and was swamped by the mob. It rolled over him and kept going.

The Forlish were disappearing into the woods but Huw refused to hesitate outside, instead racing on, Sendatsu and Rhiannon just behind him. The path through the woods was littered with broken and bleeding men, while the clearing was horrid with them, a heaving, sobbing mass of dying and dead, stinking of blood and shit. The Forlish had stopped here, but when they saw the mass of Velsh still after them, they turned and ran again. They led the Velsh further into the forest, to another clearing, where they began climbing hurriedly onto horses and trying to make a proper getaway.

'Don't let them escape!' Huw tried to yell, but his breathing was ragged after so much running.

Sendatsu led the way here and took on a Forlishman who was struggling to get onto his horse. The warrior hacked out with his sword but Sendatsu blocked it almost casually and chopped down once.

Huw threw his hoe, the long pole entangling a horse's legs and bringing down another Forlishman, who was pounced on and beaten to death by a dozen enraged Velsh, while Rhiannon sent her last bolts flying into the backs of the Forlish as they raced away through the trees, leaving behind their camp.

The Velsh looked around, looked at each other, realised with surprise what they had done, then someone began to cheer and they all joined in.

'No time for that!' Huw shouted, trying to get his voice back. 'We need to carry this back to the village, we need to get every helmet, sword, axe and weapon dropped — and we need to find our wounded, help them — and bury our dead.'

He half expected someone from the village to take control, to disagree even — but all seemed willing to listen to him. Groups began to work at his direction, splitting up naturally. Women went to look for wounded and dead men, while men picked up food and weapons, as well as the possessions the Forlish had already looted from their village. But first an older woman, a long knife in her hands, stepped forwards.

'Three cheers for our saviour!' she cried, thrusting the knife in the air.

Sendatsu reluctantly stepped forwards.

'To Huw! A true Velsh hero!' the woman shouted and the people roared their approval.

Sendatsu whipped around, shocked, to see an equally surprised Huw step forwards.

'Please — I did not do this alone. My friends Sendatsu and Rhiannon saved me, as well as you ...' Huw tried to tell them but, the cheering done, the people of Harlech went back to their tasks.

Huw shrugged sheepishly at Sendatsu and Rhiannon.

'Most of them do not know what happened out here — all they saw was you coming into their village, inspiring them and then leading them out here to chase the Forlish away,' Rhiannon said.

'I shall tell them. Even though we have driven away the Forlish, the village still needs to be protected, still needs our help,' Huw said defensively.

Sendatsu sniffed. 'I am not here to be the hero,' he said.

'You may not want to be the hero but you are one,' Rhiannon told him.

'Without Gareth, I think these people are lost. They are used to someone telling them what to do — and any that might challenge me are lying dead back in the clearing.' Huw shrugged, then smiled at Rhiannon. 'Thank you for saving my life.'

'It wasn't so hard.' Rhiannon grinned. 'Although my legs can't seem to stop shaking, everything feels wonderful — the air is sweet, every sense is alive!'

'It's the aftermath of battle — just as we used to sing about.' Huw nodded.

Sendatsu cleaned his sword on a discarded tunic. He felt flat, rather than wonderful. He had taken some revenge but it did not seem enough. More people had died, and still Forlish had escaped.

# 20

*The stories grew, got out of control. Attempting to spread the truth soon became impossible. Humans and even the Elfarans did not want to hear it any longer.*

*They wanted to believe they had been given magic by the dragons, wanted to think they were special.*

*Who wants to hear something mundane, when there is a wonderful alternative?*

*Our forefathers left the service of the dragons because they were frightened of what the magic was doing to them. Their faces were changing, stretching, becoming more like dragons, their cheekbones getting higher, their ears longer. Then they arrived in Nippon, where the people naturally had almond-shaped eyes, high cheekbones and golden-coloured skin. Thanks to the magic, the forefathers outlived many wives, creating huge families or clans — until the Nipponese drove them out.*

*Hardly wondrous.*

*And as for wisdom — well, I am the perfect example of the mistakes we made. But perhaps the worst of them was the so-called brilliant idea to have one language, so we could speak with the Velsh and Forlish, and they in turn with the Landish, Balians and Breconians. How much easier would life be if we could all understand each other! Why the forefathers agreed to let the Magic-weavers try this, I do not know. The simple answer is they could make mistakes like the rest of us. It was a massive*

'Have you seen a bard and a dancer pass through these parts?'
Hector asked, for what seemed like the hundredth time.

It was a frustrating search through Vales. News did not seem to
travel well through the little valleys and into the grubby villages.
As well, he had to be careful. The king's seal held no value up
here and, as the Velsh were known to be mad barbarians, it
would not do to anger them. Hector rode into the village himself,
taking no more than two guards with him — although making
sure it was always the largest ones. If he was questioned, he told a
version of the truth — she was his daughter and had eloped with
a bard.

It earned him rough sympathy, even if it did not always bring
news with it. Gradually a pattern began to emerge. The villages
that sprawled across the fields had not heard of them but the ones
that had walls around them had all seen the bard and dancer —
and an elf, travelling with them. Some even seemed to think the
dancer was with the elf, rather than the bard!

This was all somewhat confusing for Hector, although he tried
to make some sense of it. If there really was an elf — which he
found hard to believe — it was no surprise to hear Rhiannon
was with him, rather than with a lowly Velsh bard. She had
always been fascinated with the elves, judged herself against their
mythical ability. The chance to visit Dokuzen — she would have
jumped at that. Of course, that presented a new problem — if
there was an elf and he did take her back to Dokuzen, how was
he going to follow them there?

326

'If they pass through here again, should we tell them you are looking for your daughter?' the Velsh usually asked.

'No,' Hector said, time and again. 'They will only run if they know I am looking for them.'

The Velsh had laughed knowingly and Hector had forced himself to join in.

All Hector could do was keep following, as best he could, and hope they made a mistake — or he got lucky.

The mood of the village was mixed. Many families had lost husbands, sons, brothers — all had lost friends and Harlech had lost the only leader it had known for the last ten years.

Into that gap came Huw.

He had given the people their courage back, and now he cajoled, enthused and encouraged them to feel they could protect themselves once more. The elven crossbows had proved their worth — and the knowledge they could be used by a woman impressed all. The wall went up, as did lookout towers, while the carpenters worked day and night to make enough crossbows.

'We are going to have to leave soon — or they won't want you to go,' Rhiannon joked.

Sendatsu was not in the mood for jests.

'We are wasting time here,' he snarled at them. 'We've saved these people, now we have to move on. Every morning we can see smoke, every morning there are children being killed out there by those bastards.'

'I thought you'd want to find those precious answers you seek, that will let us go to Dokuzen?' Rhiannon added.

'That too!'

But Huw found he was enjoying being a leader. People asked questions and he had the answers. For years he had been despised for his dreams, for wanting something more than just to follow in his father's footsteps. Now the people needed someone with ideas. He had so much to make up for — and at last he felt like he was achieving something. It was heady stuff.

But the pressure from Sendatsu, with help from Rhiannon, became too great to ignore, so they rode out of the village to cheers and waves, as well as pleas not to go. But it was a very different village from the one they had found.

'There's a village that will never be surprised again,' Huw predicted as they rode out.

'We did a fine job there. Saved them and then gave them the knowledge to save themselves, the next time,' Rhiannon agreed.

Sendatsu just grunted.

'He'll cheer up if we can get him an answer or two,' Huw predicted.

But now they found village after village that had already been raided. Rather than convincing them they needed to protect themselves, the task was persuading them to stand up for themselves.

Whether it was the band of Forlish that had struck Harlech — and been almost destroyed now — or whether it was another group, the surrounding villages had all been hit hard. Crops had been torched, homes burned, livestock killed, women taken in the night, men left dead. The people were more terrified than angry.

Many of the people thought they should simply flee, while almost all were too afraid to go hunting alone or cut wood. As Huw had learned at Harlech, they had to regain their courage before they would stand up for themselves. Having an elf in their village was reassuring for them but, strangely enough, Rhiannon now proved to be the key. The Velsh were a traditional farming people. While their womenfolk were valued and respected, their place was in the home and it was the men who were seen as the defenders and protectors and leaders. To have a young woman walk among them, showing them she was not afraid of the Forlish — and was prepared to fight them with her elven crossbow — tipped the balance. The Velshmen could not be seen to sit back when a woman was challenging them to fight.

She was also crucial when it came to solving another problem. Few of the villagers here were runaway Forlish, unlike Rheged, which was always short of people to work hard fields. But there were some and the news the hated raiders were Forlish led to these settlers being regarded with, at best, suspicion. In a couple of villages, they wanted to hang them, crying they must be spies for the bandits.

'They have suffered, just like you. In fact, they have more to lose. If King Ward finds them here, if he becomes the ruler of Vales, they will be flogged to death. To leave Forland carries with it a terrible penalty,' Rhiannon told angry, frightened villagers.

And if that did not work, she challenged them directly.

'I was born in Forland. My life is forfeit, just like theirs, should I return. Just because we live in Forland does not mean we love King Ward, nor support his cruel rule. But there is no choice for us, like there is for you. I have stood and fought, I have killed Forlish warriors who were seeking to slaughter Velsh. If you doubt your neighbours, you also doubt me. Any who think they should hang the Forlish needs to start with me. Just try it!'

She stared them down, crossbow in hand — and none were prepared to try anything. Partly because she looked so fierce, so determined — but mainly because Sendatsu was standing behind her, glowering, hand on sword.

He found it easy to glower. At each village he was finding, not the answers he sought, but pain. Sobbing parents begged him to heal their wounded children, or even to bring them back to life. His protestations that his magic could not save them sounded lame, even to his own ears. These people did not want truth, they wanted hope. He felt he could not give them either. They could see the smoke that marked the passage of Forlish raiders through Vales. But although he longed to lure them into some rash attack on Velsh walls, they could not spot a war band.

Huw, and particularly Rhiannon, noticed the change in Sendatsu. He was driven to move onwards but not in search of answers, instead to hunt Forlish. Huw sent him off to find wood and seized the chance to speak to Rhiannon.

'He scares me,' Huw whispered.

'What do you mean?'

'Twice now he has risked all our lives. He does not seem to care about finding those of us with magic, or people with memories of Aroaril — he just wants to search out and kill Forlish.'

'But I thought that was what you wanted — to have a hero like that?'

'Not like this! And if he doesn't kill us, he is going to get himself killed — and then what use will he be? He's changing — he doesn't even ask for a bath any more. And he just takes and eats what's put in front of him, doesn't even ask for rice. It is unnerving me.'

'Well, what should we do about it?'

Huw gritted his teeth. 'Maybe you should talk to him,' he forced himself to say. 'Maybe the secret is inside that pouch of his.'

'Should we just try to find out what he wants to know — would that help?'

Huw shook his head. 'We don't want him to leave, we just want him to do what we need ...'

'I think you are trying to be too clever,' Rhiannon warned. 'We should be grateful he is helping us this much.'

Huw knew he was asking a great deal. But his people needed a great deal. He had to do whatever it took, use whatever was on hand. His father's memory demanded no less.

'What are you talking about?' Sendatsu returned with an armful of dead wood.

'We are worried about you,' Rhiannon said immediately. 'All you are worried about is killing Forlish.'

Sendatsu dropped the wood with a clatter. 'I thought that was what you wanted,' he said coldly.

'Well, yes, but it should be about protecting people, not hunting down Forlish.'

'They're one and the same,' he grunted.

Rhiannon glanced at Huw, who urged her on.

'We noticed you keep looking at something inside your pouch. Is it something to do with that ...'

'No!' Sendatsu roared, causing them both to rock backwards. 'What is in there is not for you. And I shall not talk about it. Goodnight.'

He turned his back on them and wrapped himself into a blanket. Thinking about his children's toys made him think about his children — and that was too painful. It was easier just to hit things.

Huw and Rhiannon exchanged a long look.

'We're going to have to do something,' Rhiannon whispered. 'He's changing. He would never have done that a quarter-moon ago.'

'Just a few more villages,' Huw begged.

'One more. We have to stop then, ask around, help him somehow. What if he was just to walk away from us?' Rhiannon shuddered at the thought. No Dokuzen, no dream, no dancing for the elves.

'One more then,' Huw agreed, wondering what he could offer the elf.

And then they arrived at Dale Hill.

This small village was sandwiched between a pair of small hills, and had a good view of the land around. But what they found there left Sendatsu infuriated and Huw horrified.

'We leave food outside the village, in case they come back. Then they will leave us alone,' said the gloomy village headman, even his moustache seeming to droop.

'You don't get rid of wolves by feeding them lambs — any shepherd will tell you that!' Huw protested. But the villagers were afraid, like their headman, Iddig.

'You cowards! I have heard some foul things since I arrived in these lands but this is surely the worst,' Sendatsu raged at Iddig.

'We are not elves. We can't protect ourselves with magic ...'

'No, you need to use courage! Don't you know it is better to die on your feet than live on your knees?'

'Easy for you to say. You don't have children to worry about!' Iddig retorted.

That was too much for Sendatsu and Huw and Rhiannon had to jump in front of him to stop him.

'We need these people to work with us — hitting them will not help!' Huw gasped as he strained to hold back Sendatsu.

'You will fight these Forlish if I have to throw you at them myself.' Sendatsu shoved Huw and Rhiannon back and turned instead to the shocked villagers surrounding them. 'I don't care how long I have to stay here, you will not give up to the Forlish. Is there just one of you with the courage to stand with me against the Forlish, to stop the baby-killers?'

He glared around the villagers and Huw was sure nobody would have the courage to step forwards. He had no idea how to restore the situation either and was thinking how he might get Sendatsu out of there when a young man, no older than Huw, took a big pace forwards.

'I am Powell. Forlish raiders killed my parents and burned out my farm, a day's walk to the south of here. I will gladly fight the Forlish,' he said fiercely.

Sendatsu glared around the rest of the village. 'Good. Powell is now your leader — does anybody object?' he snarled.

Iddig opened his mouth, then thought better of it.

'Good. Now we shall start working.'

The villagers reluctantly began making a wall — with little in the way of trees around, they had decided on an earthen bank, with stakes at the top to keep back horses — but progress was incredibly slow. A couple of families even walked away — loaded up a small wagon or cart and rounded up animals and left.

'We want no part of fighting. We just want to live in peace,' they declared, when challenged by Huw.

'There is no peace. Wherever you go, there will be Forlish raiders. You must stand firm, protect what is yours,' Huw had tried to tell them — but it was no use.

By the end of the first day, Huw was ready to walk away.

'We could stay here for a moon and still achieve nothing. The people have no spirit,' he said sadly.

'I won't let them give in,' Sendatsu swore. 'They will come around. Besides, the Forlish know to come here for supplies. We have to stop that.'

Sendatsu sat up most of the night, hoping a party of raiders would come to the fire he set outside the village — but nothing happened.

In fact, little happened for days. The people were reluctant to work and nothing Sendatsu did could change that. Huw came to his rescue, however, working with Powell to make him a true leader. The combination of Huw and Powell eventually meant even the most reluctant left their fields and animals and helped finish the wall or work on crossbows.

By the sixth day, progress was so good even Sendatsu felt able to ride away, leaving Dale Hill ready to hold off a Forlish attack and, with their thick earthen rampart atop the slope that led to the village itself, probably one of the best-protected of all they had visited.

But Huw was not prepared to go through another village like that and, even before Rhiannon had a chance to say anything, knew he had to speak to Sendatsu.

'We can't do that again. If this village is like Dale Hill, we have to walk away. We took far too long there — who knows how many others were attacked while we wasted time on them? How many lives were lost because we spent so much time on them? How many children, eh? What are you going to say to the parents when we walk into the next village that has been raided?'

'Don't you dare tell me that!' Sendatsu stormed.

'We need to calm down,' Rhiannon said soothingly. 'We've all spent too much time arguing with people lately and it has left us short-tempered. We need to eat something and relax for a turn or two of the hourglass.'

Sendatsu reluctantly agreed but he still felt on edge. While Rhiannon was getting a fire going and Huw was seeing to the horses he walked away and opened up his belt pouch, took out his children's toys for the first time in days. The reminder from Huw was the last straw. He had tried to stay away from the toys, thinking that only weakened him, but he needed them. He kissed them and held them close. Once they had even smelled of Mai and Cheijun ... now even that was gone. He felt lost. Why, oh why had he taken that scroll? Why couldn't life have just gone on as before? Anger and despair warred within him.

'What are you doing?' Huw asked.

Hurriedly, Sendatsu stuffed the toys back into his pouch and wiped his eyes on his dirty sleeve.

'Nothing,' he said roughly.

'What is in that pouch? What is it you are hiding?' Huw demanded.

Sendatsu pushed past him. 'It is nothing for you. Now leave me alone.'

Huw staggered back under Sendatsu's shove. Once he would have taken that, would have walked away. But that was a different Huw. He flung himself at Sendatsu, aiming for the belt pouch. Sendatsu reacted instinctively, spinning away. But Huw had a firm grasp of the pouch and the thin leather fastening tore from Sendatsu's belt, leaving the pouch in Huw's hands.

'Now we shall see what your secret is,' Huw declared.

'Give that back!' Sendatsu roared, raw anger swamping through him.

Huw was alarmed by the red fury suffusing Sendatsu's face and raced over to the fire.

'Stay back — or this goes in the flames,' he warned.

Sendatsu drew his sword. 'Give that back to me or I swear I shall take it from your still-warm corpse.'

'Sendatsu! Calm down! And Huw, for sky's sake give him back the pouch!' Rhiannon jumped to her feet, alarmed.

But Huw was not ready to give in.

'I want to know what is in here, why he cannot show us — why he threatens to kill me for it.' He ripped open the pouch and hauled out the children's toys.

For a long moment the three of them stared at the two objects in Huw's hand.

'What are these?' Huw began.

Sendatsu lost all control. A red mist descended across his eyes and he sprang forwards, intent on getting Mai and Cheijun back by any means.

Huw was distracted by the toys, the last things he had expected to see in there, and was slow to react. But Rhiannon was faster and saw the menace in Sendatsu. She leaped in front of him.

'Stop! Wait ...' she called but Sendatsu was in no mood for reason. He hurled her aside.

She shrieked as she flew through the air, then her voice was cut off as she thumped into the ground and lay there.

'Rhiannon!' Huw cried, dropping the pouch and the toys and racing to her side.

Sendatsu's only thought was for the toys, the symbols of Mai and Cheijun, and he gathered them up, leaving his sword in their place. His next thought was Huw and he turned to pursue the bard — to see Huw on his knees beside the unmoving Rhiannon.

For a moment more, Sendatsu's anger burned hotter than the sun, but such intensity could not be sustained and it flickered out as he stared in shock at Rhiannon. He ran over and joined Huw on his knees, as they tried to see what was wrong with her.

'Rhiannon, speak to me!' Huw patted her hand, stroked her face — but she continued to lay unmoving.

Sendatsu was seized with a terrible fear he had truly hurt her, perhaps even killed her, and he leaned over and slapped her cheeks, not hard but strong enough to gain a reaction.

'Wh-what ...?' Rhiannon's eyes flickered open and she stared about wildly for a moment before focusing on Sendatsu.

For a long moment they locked eyes, then he felt the prickle of horror as he saw the fear in her gaze.

'Get away from me!' She scrabbled backwards.

'No, please — I am so sorry.' Sendatsu held out his hands.

But Rhiannon kept backing away, her jaw set, her eyes cold.

'I think you should explain,' Huw said softly. 'What are those toys and why you are willing to kill us for them?'

Sendatsu looked at the toys in his hands, then back at Rhiannon, who was gazing at him with something close to hate — and he dissolved.

The fear and anger that had been inside him for so long burst out, like poison from a wound.

Huw and Rhiannon gaped at the weeping elf, then looked at each other, then back to the elf.

Sendatsu was incapable of words now, hands holding the toys, arms wrapped around his chest, rocking back and forth.

Huw wanted a reaction from the elf — but he had not expected anything like this. He had always known there was something strange about that pouch but this was more than he had imagined. Huw had to know the truth. And there was only one way to get it. Besides, the sounds Sendatsu were making were uncomfortable to listen to. It was too personal. He had to do something for the man — elf. He locked eyes with Rhiannon and then gestured towards Sendatsu with his head.

Rhiannon's eyes widened with surprise. Was Huw really suggesting they go and comfort Sendatsu, after what the elf had just done? She shook her head furiously. Her glittering future with Sendatsu, the glorious life together in Dokuzen, lay in ruins around her. She had not even begun to work out what that meant — but she knew she wanted nothing more to do with Sendatsu. But Huw was gesturing insistently, while Sendatsu's wailing had not stopped.

She looked at Sendatsu, now in the foetal position on the ground, sobbing in a way she had not heard before. It was as if his heart was being torn out with every breath and, despite the anger and hurt she was feeling, she had to know why.

Slowly, reluctantly, she joined Huw as they edged towards the stricken elf. Huw was the first one to reach out, patting Sendatsu on the back. Rhiannon reached out hesitantly, then stroked his hair.

Sendatsu reacted instantly to their touch, curling himself into a ball, and his sobs redoubled.

'Talk,' Huw said gently, patting the elf. 'Talk to us. Get it out. Whatever it is, it is poisoning you inside.'

But Sendatsu was unable to do anything more than wail.

Huw gestured at Rhiannon and she gritted her teeth, then reached out and held Sendatsu, unable to stop remembering how she had held him before, when they were in bed together.

'Tell us,' she managed to say, almost choked by those memories.

Huw stretched out as well, enfolding both Sendatsu and Rhiannon, until all three were locked together. For a long moment Sendatsu resisted them, then he clutched them back, like a drowning man reaching for a helping hand. The two humans looked at each other, a little dumbfounded, as he clung to them but his sobs seemed to slow, to drop off in intensity until, at last, he was silent.

'Tell us,' Huw said into the silence. 'What is it?'

'My children,' Sendatsu managed to say, in a thick, almost strangled voice. 'I had to leave them behind in Dokuzen.'

Huw and Rhiannon stared at each other and he saw the shock in her eyes, the flare of anger, but he held up a hand, begging her not to say anything yet.

'Well, of course you want to go and see them. But surely they are safe with their mother ...' Huw suggested gently, pleading to a fuming Rhiannon with his eyes.

There was so much she wanted to say, and Huw's warning was not enough to stop her — then Sendatsu raised his head and she saw his face.

He was red and blotchy from crying, his eyes and nose were running — but he had such an expression of utter desolation that her angry words died in her throat — for now.

'My wife died years ago. My children are with my parents. But I cannot visit. My life is forfeit unless I can return with evidence of what really happened when the elves left. Unless I find the answers I seek, I can never see my children again.'

Huw and Rhiannon stared at him with a mixture of shock and horror.

'So the elven leaders haven't sent you on this mission?' Huw found his voice first.

'No,' Sendatsu admitted. 'They've sent elves out here to kill me, or at least bring me back. If I do find my answers and go home, I must overthrow my father and the Elven Council.'

Huw and Rhiannon sprang to their feet, equally horrified, but for different reasons.

'So our plan to get the elves on side can never happen — we are teaching my people to defend themselves, just so we can invite Ward's armies here to finish the job and crush us properly?' Huw exclaimed bitterly.

But Rhiannon's voice was louder.

'So you lied to me? You were never going to take me back to Dokuzen? You just said all that to get me into your bed?'

Sendatsu thought about lying but, really, what was the point now?

'I am sorry. I know it was a mistake and I have regretted it ...'

'Not as much as me!' Rhiannon stormed. 'You were just using me for your own pleasure!'

Sendatsu nodded sadly. 'I was weak. I am sorry.'

'Don't tell me that now! So why did you not say anything? Why did you promise me a life back in Dokuzen?'

'I had not been with another woman since my wife died. I stopped thinking and lost control. You are beautiful and I could not help myself. Then I had to keep up the pretence because thinking you were going back to Dokuzen made you the perfect tool to use against Huw ...'

Rhiannon turned away, fighting tears of humiliation, hurt and fury. She had thought herself special but, all the time, he had been lying. Like a fool, she had fallen for it all. She did not know what was worse — how he had manipulated and lied to her or how she could have been so stupid to believe it. Her father had always warned her about men like this — she just never thought an elf could be like a man. And Huw had tried to tell her, tried to warn her — and she had laughed at his concern, even accused him of trying to trick her because of his own feelings towards her.

'Rhiannon, please believe me — I am so very sorry,' Sendatsu said, but she just held up her hand.

'I don't want to listen to you any more. I have heard too many lies in the last moon, been given so many false promises that I cannot hear you now.'

She realised she could not bear to look at him. If she did, she might act on her feelings, which told her to grab one of the elven crossbows and pump a full dozen bolts into his lying face. How he must have lain awake, laughing at her stupidity, after using her! Her face burned with shame and anger at what she had done — at how she had behaved.

She needed time to come to terms with this. Abruptly she started walking away.

'I need some space,' she declared. 'I am going for a walk.'

Huw heard her say the words he had longed to hear — and it gave him no pleasure at all. The devastation on her face at Sendatsu's lies was wrenching to see. Without thinking, he hurried after her.

'Rhiannon ...' He reached out for her arm but she ripped it away.

'Don't touch me! I do not want to be touched by a man now!' she snapped at him.

'Sorry — I was just worried about you ...' Huw stepped backwards.

Her face softened a little. 'I am sorry too. Sorry I did not listen to you. You have been such a good friend to me, Huw, saved me from King Ward at Cridianton, tried to warn me about Sendatsu. At least I know you would never lie to me.'

'Of course,' Huw agreed, the knowledge of his lies to her sitting heavily in his gut.

'But I really need to be alone, need some time to think.'

'I don't want you going off by yourself. You never know who or what is out there.'

'The mood I'm in, any Forlish need to stay away from me,' she said grimly, but with the ghost of a smile.

'At least take a crossbow with you.'

She shook her head. 'It would be too tempting to use on that lying bastard. I can't believe I lapped up his stupid lies! You were the one to see through it, and I wouldn't listen to you either.'

'Don't blame yourself,' Huw urged. 'I believed him as well. As did thousands of Velsh! Look at all those villages we told would be safe when the elves returned to protect us ... what are they going to think now?'

But Rhiannon was not thinking about Velsh villages.

'I hurt you, Huw,' she said softly. 'You have never acted on your feelings for me but I know they are there. And I flaunted my desire for Sendatsu — my desire for glory with the elves — in your face. That must have hurt but you never said so. You never let it show.'

Huw turned away then — the memory of that time in his house, sitting in his father's chair and listening to Sendatsu and Rhiannon making love, was still red-raw.

Rhiannon reached out and gripped his shoulder briefly. That was all the contact she was prepared to have.

'I am sorry, Huw. I am not fit company right now. There are things I need to think about. Give me a little time.'

With that she walked away.

Huw was torn between a fear of what might happen if she ever found out about his lies, and a little thrill at the thought of what she had just hinted at. But that was swept away by his worries about the Forlish and how he could protect the Velsh, now elven help was impossible.

He turned to Sendatsu, wondering what his next move should be.

The elf was sitting listlessly, holding onto his children's toys, eyes streaming.

Huw stormed across to him. 'Listen to me!' he snarled. 'You feel bad? That's good — you should feel terrible. Your lies have hurt Rhiannon but, more importantly, they have put at risk every Velsh man, woman and child in every village we have been to! The defences we have built are there to stop a few raiders — they will not hold a Forlish army. Ward will bring his men north, those people will die — and it will be because of you!'

Sendatsu looked up. 'Because of me? You were the one who forced me to do this! I just wanted to get some answers and go home but you had this idea that I could save your people. I told you I wasn't a hero, I told you I didn't want responsibility. But you thought you were being so clever by tricking me into helping you!'

Huw paused for a moment — but only for a moment. 'You are an elf! Of course I was going to think you were a hero! Don't try and blame me for your lies. If you had been honest with us from the start, none of this would have happened.'

'Well, if you hadn't forced me to try and save everyone …'

'You wanted to help them too — remember? You came away from Rheged wanting to slaughter every Forlishman we found!'

Sendatsu heard the truth in Huw's voice but did not want to accept it.

'It's still not my fault …'

'What about Rhiannon? Are you going to say you are innocent there?' Huw spat, his memories of that time still burning inside.

Sendatsu stopped there. 'I can never make up for what I did to Rhiannon. That was a huge mistake and I wish with all my heart I had not done that to her,' he said shakily.

Huw quashed the angry words that rose in him. 'No, you can never make up for that,' he agreed, his voice cold as ice.

Sendatsu sighed. 'I am sorry, Huw. I cannot do this any more. I have to go home. I don't know how but I am doing nothing of use out here.' It was time to face facts. He was no closer to finding answers and every day he spent out here was harming more than just his children.

Huw swallowed angry words. 'You can't leave. Not only are you the best warrior in Vales, but you know so many things that could help make people's lives better.'

'I just want to go home,' Sendatsu sighed. 'That is all.'

Huw thought quickly. Sendatsu was still the best, indeed the only hope for his people.

'Just give me one more moon and then I will see you will return to Dokuzen with all the answers you need. I know you want to go back, I know today has shaken you up but you said it yourself — you can't return without evidence of humans doing magic or they will kill you.'

Sendatsu shrugged. The way he felt now, he was willing to risk it.

'What good will it do your children if you are dragged away to be executed before you can even hold them? What will happen to them then?'

Sendatsu forced himself to think about that.

'They will be raised by my father, the one thing I swore would never happen,' he admitted.

'Well then — help me for one more moon and then we shall travel east, search for the ruins my father spoke about, find the answers you seek.'

'And what good can one more moon do? Why can't we travel east now?'

'Because people will die — because scenes like that hamlet in Rheged will be repeated all across Vales. Do you want that on your mind?'

'No,' Sendatsu reluctantly agreed.

Huw sighed. 'What is the secret they will kill you for?'

Sendatsu did not have the energy to lie. 'The barrier around Dokuzen is fading. Soon it will be gone and we shall be part of this world again, whether we like it or not. The magic is also dying within the elves. When we have no more magic than humans, the barrier will be gone.'

'The elves you serve, the ones who will overthrow your rulers — will they help us against the Forlish?'

Sendatsu looked into Huw's eyes. 'Don't think you can make bargains with them. I have to trust them, because they are my only hope. But they will not hold to a deal with you.'

'They might — if you make it a condition of you helping them.'

'And why would I do that? I am in no position to make deals. And why would I demand such a thing? All you have done is try and trick me into helping you.'

'Well, I would say we have been tricking each other. But, leaving that aside, you make that deal because that will save the lives of women and children across Vales.'

'This is a dangerous game you are playing. You gamble not just with your life but with many lives,' Sendatsu warned. 'And I have not even agreed to help you again.'

'But you will — for you have no choice. Listen, my father taught me not to live my life as a lie. I was not able to do that and, as a result, my father died. I learned a bitter lesson. You too are facing a hard test now but you refuse to learn from it. You ran away from Dokuzen and you are running away still.'

'What?'

'You see yourself at the mercy of me, of your doubtful allies back in Dokuzen — everyone. You are letting others dictate your life to you. You need to step forwards, run your own life, seize control of your own destiny.'

Sendatsu heard the words — they were but a variation on things he had been told many times before — but they washed over him.

'You don't believe me, do you?' Huw accused. 'You think everything can go back to the way it was, that you can overturn the rulers of Dokuzen and just go home and hug your children like nothing happened?'

Sendatsu opened his mouth to protest, then shut it again. Nothing would be the same.

'Look, I will help you — but you have to help me as well. You think that crazy old man back in Rheged was right, that the elves massacred humans and there was a terrible injustice when the elves left this land? Then make up for it. Do something for the humans, unite elves and humans once more!'

Sendatsu shuddered at the thought. That was too much for anyone, let alone him, to achieve.

Huw could see the vision but, sighing inside, realised this was not the elf to do it. Or at least not yet ... he needed to play this carefully. Already, another idea was forming in the back of his mind, a way to use Sendatsu's knowledge to save his people. But it required more thought before he said it aloud — and much more thought as to how to persuade the elf.

'You want to get back to your children, yes?'

'Of course!'

'Then help us for one more moon and I promise you on my father's grave that I shall not stop until you can go home and hold your children.'

'Nothing more?'

'That will be the whole of our deal.'

Sendatsu looked at Huw doubtfully. He knew the bard well enough that there was something else hidden. But, for the life of him, he could not see what it was. 'What about Rhiannon? Will she still let me travel with you?'

Huw opened his mouth but then shut it again, slowly. He had been so concerned with getting through to the elf he had not thought about what came next. Rhiannon would want nothing more to do with Sendatsu, while Huw wanted everything to do with Rhiannon.

He was furiously thinking how to get around this when a faint cry made him look up.

'Where is Rhiannon?' he asked in sudden fear.

# 21

*It was a time of death. My loyal supporters were slowly whittled away, although I did not see it that way. I still thought I had almost all the people behind me — including Naibun. But while his supporters were unharmed, those who were loyal to me only were dying in all sorts of ways. Accidents, rogue Magic-weavers, human attacks — all of them at the hand of Naibun.*

*Meanwhile, the people were afraid of the humans and the humans were being taught a false history about us.*

*And I sat in my villa and grieved for my dead wife.*

*Looking back on it now, I could have brought a stop to it. If only I had led more, pushed more, taken more control, then none of this would have happened. Probably. But I sat back and drifted, went along with the flow, trusting that my friend was steering me right. Only the ship of my life was being directed towards rapids.*

Rhiannon stalked away, not caring where she went, as long as it was far away from Sendatsu. The land around here was hilly, full of cuttings and folds in the ground. She crossed one of them, finding a quiet spot, a large stone to sit on while she tried to come to terms with everything.

As much as she wanted to blame Sendatsu — as much as he was to blame — her conversation with Huw had revealed a nasty truth. Sendatsu had lied to her, had tricked her into bed — but she had still gone there of her own volition. She could have walked away but she was so blinded by her own desire for a better life, one with the elves, she fell prey to Sendatsu's desires.

She looked back at how she had been behaving around Sendatsu, how she had been infatuated with the idea of the elf, rather than with who Sendatsu was. She had doted on his every word, flattered and admired everything he did. Now it seemed so obvious, and she cursed herself. She thought about her father, and how he had warned her about men like Sendatsu. Well, of course they had been men, not elves, but it had been for the same reasons. If he had been here, would things have been different? She grimaced at that. Things would be very different if her father was alive. Apart from everything else, she would not have been allowed to do anything. Fighting Forlish, riding horses — he would have rather swallowed broken glass than let those things happen.

It was strange. At first she had missed him bitterly but had barely thought of him recently. What would she have been doing if her father was still alive? Then she shook herself. It was a pointless thought, for Ward would still have wanted to drag her to his bed.

Not unlike Sendatsu, she told herself darkly. Only his methods were more subtle and even more reprehensible. He was an elf! He should know better! How could he lie to her? Yes, she had helped him with her own foolishness and naïvety but he had still looked her in the eye and lied. Elves were not supposed to do that! How could she possibly look at him again without wanting to put a crossbow bolt through his lying tongue? She could not bear to see him again. They did not need him. Huw could do just as good a job.

That made her think of Huw. She had not ignored him, exactly, but — compared with the excitement of an elf and the lure of Dokuzen — his careful courtship had been rebuffed. She buried her face in her hands. She had made so many mistakes. She had to learn from them. It was the one thing she was sure of. For most of her life she had been kept away from everything, sheltered from not just men but life itself by her father. Like a bird caged for too long, she had ached to spread her wings and fly but had learned there were reasons for a cage, even though hers had been too small and the key kept from her for too long. But she was a fast learner and she swore no man would ever take advantage of her or lie to her like that again.

In a perverse way, she was almost grateful to Sendatsu. It was not a lesson she wanted to learn but she felt stronger for it. It had changed her. She had been walking along with her head in the clouds, dreaming of Dokuzen and the glory that waited for her. The romance had blinded her to the truth. Having that taken away allowed her to see things far more clearly. She could not thank Sendatsu for it but knowledge was power and although it had come at a bitter cost, she was wiser now.

That led to the question of what to do about Sendatsu? Apart from taking a sharp knife to his groin, that was. Without him, what would happen to their mission to protect the Velsh? The elf gave them respect and attention. Suspicious villages warmed instantly as soon as they saw Sendatsu and heard his stories of Dokuzen. Then there was his skill as a warrior. There were still dozens of bands of Forlish roaming around and neither she or Huw had the ability to fight them off. But, even if she swallowed her anger — after he had grovelled out endless apologies — where would that leave them? They could hardly lie to the people and tell them the elves were coming. The idea of parading Sendatsu in front of people, singing that song about him, making them look up to him made her want to vomit. Things had to change — but she could not think how. They could not leave the Velsh to their fate but, equally, how could they save them?

'What are you doing out here?'

The strange voice made her look up, to see five men walking towards her, grinning. Her heart stopped for a moment, then began pounding rapidly. All five were wearing old clothes — but had swords at their hips and the voice of their leader was unmistakeably Forlish.

'Rhiannon!' Their leader, a tall, unshaven man, was smiling broadly. 'I remember seeing you at Cridianton. You dance well — the things you can do with your legs ...'

Rhiannon had no intention of hanging around to hear the rest of the man's filth.

'Help!' she shouted at the top of her voice, then sprang up and raced back for the top of the cutting, where she knew Huw and Sendatsu were. She would even be glad to see the elf at this moment.

For a heartbeat she thought she had surprised them and her long legs ate up the ground. But the Forlish reacted swiftly, racing up to cut her off.

She saw quickly that they would close the angle, so she turned and tore back downhill, off into the Velsh countryside. She did not know what she was running towards — but it had to be better than what was behind her. Again, her quick reactions surprised them and she opened up a sizeable lead. She risked a quick look over her shoulder and saw them spreading out into a half-circle, running hard with swords in hands.

'Rhiannon! Stop! We're going to take you to your father!' the leader shouted. 'He wants to talk to you!'

Anger spurted through her. She would only see and talk to her father again after death — he was boasting he wanted to kill her too! Saying those words with a sword in your hand could mean nothing else. She stopped looking back over her shoulder and concentrated on picking her way over the unbroken ground.

'Sarge, we should have waited until Hector got here!' one of the Forlish gasped.

'How was I to know the silly bitch would run? He told us she was being held against her will!' Sergeant Edric growled.

'Maybe we should put away our swords ...'

'Don't be an idiot! Have you ever tried to run with a scabbarded sword? It'll trip you before you've gone fifty paces! No, lads, she won't get far. She's just a girl.'

* * *

'You go and find her. She doesn't want to see me,' Sendatsu said dully. 'And she is right to want to stay away from me. I would.'

'We don't have time to wallow in pity — she could be in trouble and need our help,' Huw snapped.

'She's probably just angry. And I don't blame her. Go and find her, go and comfort her. You two deserve each other. I will just get in the way,' Sendatsu sighed, thinking of Asami and Gaibun as he said that.

'But what if she's in trouble?' Huw demanded.

'There's nobody around here. We would have seen a Forlish band long before now. Go! She will need someone like you now. She deserves someone like you.' Sendatsu pushed Huw away.

Huw hesitated a moment longer. He was worried about Rhiannon but the opportunity this presented was too good to ignore. Not only was she in need of a shoulder, but Sendatsu had encouraged him.

'All right — but come looking for us after the count of two hundred, if we have not returned,' he suggested.

'Just go!' Sendatsu waved him away, wanting to be alone with his misery.

Huw hurried across to the horses and quickly grabbed his mount. Not only would it help with looking for her but he thought she might like a ride back and the thought of sharing a saddle with her was definitely a warming one.

He headed towards where she had gone, wondering how far she might have reached. He was only a little worried — if she had run into trouble, she would be racing back towards them and there was no sign of that as yet.

Instead he found himself thinking about how upset she would be, and how she needed comforting. Her dream of performing for the elves had been dashed and he was the best person to sympathise about that. It was too soon to try anything. But just the chance to sit and talk, perhaps to hold her, was enough to get his mind leaping ahead ...

The land around here was creased, like an old tunic thrown carelessly on the floor, with endless little ridges and valleys going in all directions. There was no sign of her.

'Rhiannon!' he shouted, hoping she would reply and give him some clue as to where she was.

A faint shout from his left made him turn and peer across the land — to see a group of men running hard, swords in hands. He could not see who they were chasing but the answer was obvious.

Without thinking, he kicked his horse in the ribs and raced after them, fumbling desperately for the crossbow behind his saddle.

Rhiannon paused at the top of a short rise, her lungs heaving and her legs shaking, not just from the fear. She had thought herself fit but racing up and down hills had her gasping for air. The good news was the Forlish warriors were still behind her. The bad news was they had halved the gap, and she feared she had exhausted herself.

'Wait! Rhiannon! We mean no harm!' the Forlish leader shouted, his own voice puffing for air.

She heard that and it gave her a little surge of hope, although she had no intention of obeying them. Meant her no harm! Why, then, were they running after her with swords in hands?

The short pause had given her a little breath back. She hawked and spat, clearing her throat, then set off again, trying to eat up the distance with long paces and hoping that Huw and Sendatsu would bring her a horse before the Forlish got much closer.

But the little valley that she was running through dog-legged to the left and, when she rounded the corner, she discovered it finished in a rock slope steeper than anything she had tried before. She threw herself at it, scrambling up. If she could make it to the top, perhaps she could use some of the loose stones, drive the Forlish back — or at least put some distance between herself and her pursuers, maybe even find a hiding place.

The footing was treacherous and she had to use her arms as much as her legs to pull herself upwards. As she got further up, she slowed down, being forced to pick her way carefully.

'Give it up! You cannot get up there! Come down, for pity's sake — we're just going to take you back to your father, and the king!'

She wanted to scream at them, call them liars, tell them they were murderers, but she did not have the breath — she had to save it for the climb. Then she reached a huge boulder that blocked her progress, its smooth surface proving an impossibility. She tried to scramble up it but just slipped back down.

'Give it up! You can get no further! Look, we are putting our swords away — just come with us and you'll be with your father before day's end!'

She shook her head violently, searching for a way around the boulder. Below, a pair of the Forlish had sheathed their swords and were now scrambling up after her.

'Leave her alone!'

Everyone turned, to see Huw on his horse, dragging it to a stop as he rounded the bend in the valley.

Rhiannon was delighted to see him — but terrified as well. He had his elven crossbow but there were too many Forlish for him.

'Leave the girl,' the Forlish leader snapped. 'She won't be going anywhere.'

Drawing their swords again, the five of them spread out and slowly advanced at Huw.

'Keep back — I warn you!' Huw threatened.

'That's a crossbow, laddie — it's got one shot and then it's done,' the leader said grimly.

'Not this one,' Huw said defiantly. 'As you shall discover if you take one more step!'

The Forlish leader stopped and, for a moment, Huw and Rhiannon both dared to hope the threat had been believed.

'That's the bard,' the leader exclaimed. 'The king will be almost as happy to see him as he will be to get his hands on the girl. Take his crossbow but don't kill him!'

Huw levelled his crossbow and worked the lever, shooting out crossbow bolts as fast as he could. The Forlish ducked and jumped about as bolts flickered towards them — but they were spread wide apart and quick to drop to the ground, or dive to one side as the crossbow swung around to point at them.

When Huw had finished, one of the Forlish was swearing at a bolt deep in his thigh, while the leader was nursing a grazed shoulder — but the rest of the bolts had been wasted on the grass.

'That was a pretty trick. The king will be most interested to see that when we bring it back.' The leader examined his torn tunic wryly, then turned back to where Huw was frantically trying to load more bolts into his crossbow.

'Get him! Alive — but no need to be gentle about it!'

Four of them rushed at the bard and Rhiannon wanted to yell at Huw to get away, save himself.

Then the front Forlishman was knocked sideways, tumbling onto the grass, where he lay unmoving. Everyone stopped cold, staring at the body — and the arrow jutting from its side. As if compelled, every head turned and looked up, to where Sendatsu stood high above, bow in hand.

Rhiannon had never thought she would be glad to see him again — but his arrival was perfectly timed. He even had a sense of style about it. He did not yell, did not threaten, just stood there with bow in hand, another arrow on the string.

'Get the bard — use the horse as cover!' the Forlish leader shouted — then choked as an arrow sank deep into his chest.

The two still on their feet hesitated, while the one with the bolt in his leg hauled himself to his feet and tried to hop away.

They only waited for a few heartbeats — but even that was too long. Huw finished loading his crossbow and worked the lever again, peppering them with the vicious little spikes of wood — and another arrow reached out to claim the wounded Forlishman. The last pair ducked and covered as they were hit by several bolts; one was struck by another arrow and Huw kept loosing at the last man, his teeth gritted as he sent one after another into him, until he finally collapsed and lay writhing.

Rhiannon glanced up as Sendatsu slid down the slope, coming to a stop just near her.

He had heard Huw's call, seen him break into a mad gallop and quickly followed, taking a different route. If Rhiannon had made it to the top, he could have got her away — as it was, the high ground proved to be the deciding factor. Aiming downhill was more difficult but the Forlish were little more than fifty yards away, making them easy targets. He had been almost delighted at the chance to save them both. He needed to do something to make up for what he had done to Rhiannon and what better way than saving her life?

'Do you need help to get down?' he asked awkwardly, trying not to look at her.

'I don't need anything from you,' she told him coldly.

He nodded jerkily, then slid down the rest of the way, hurrying over to where the Forlish lay — all of them moving weakly.

'Are you all right?' Sendatsu called, drawing his sword and looking at Huw.

'Fine,' Huw said shortly, trying not to look at where the Forlish bled and moaned and cried.

Sendatsu finished four of them off with swift cuts to the throat. None would have lived for long anyway — the one struck by Huw's crossbow bolts was slowly bleeding to death. The ones hit by his arrows were in a far worse way and close to death. The only one he left was the leader.

'What were you doing here? Answer me and I can ease your passing,' he said shortly, flipping the man over. The Forlishman had a blood-stained arrowhead protruding from the middle of his chest and, from the bloody froth around his lips, not long to live.

'The girl's father wants her back. We just sought to reunite them,' the Forlishman hissed, his breath coming fast and painful.

Sendatsu looked up at Huw and glanced back to Rhiannon. They had said Rhiannon's father was dead ...

'I thought Hector was dead?' He leaned down slightly.

'Not dead. As alive as you or I,' the Forlishman gasped. 'He is not ten miles from here.'

Sendatsu took a step back. If Rhiannon's father was still alive, then most, if not all, of what Huw had told her was a lie ... His first instinct was to call Rhiannon over, get her to talk to the man — but she was not ready to hear this. Coming on top of what he had done to her, believing Huw had lied to her might destroy her. And Hector was in the pay of King Ward, given these were his men. He needed to talk to Huw.

'What is he saying?' Huw asked, edging his horse nearer.

Sendatsu woke from his reverie and stepped forwards, killing the Forlish leader with a quick thrust.

He glanced over his shoulder to see Rhiannon making her way carefully down the slope. He hurried to Huw's side.

'He was sent to bring you back to Ward. But he was talking about Rhiannon's father — Hector. He said Hector is both alive and near here. But I thought he was dead?' Sendatsu asked carefully, urgently, softly.

Huw felt his heart stop for a moment in sheer terror. He gazed down at Sendatsu and saw a knowing look in the elf's eyes.

'He is alive, isn't he?' Sendatsu murmured. 'You did not tell Rhiannon the truth about why you had to leave Cridianton ...'

'We had to go, I promise you! Hector was going to sell her to Ward,' Huw said quickly. 'I'll tell you it all — just not now! Rhiannon cannot know ...'

'You need to tell her,' Sendatsu warned. 'Trust me, lying does not help anything. She will find out one day ...'

'I know!' Huw stared over at her in terror. 'Just give me time!'

'Don't take too long,' Sendatsu said quietly, glancing back to see Rhiannon was almost at the bottom of the slope. 'If I say nothing, will you help me find my answers?' he asked swiftly.

Huw hesitated. He was grateful, more than grateful, for Sendatsu coming along and saving them. Sitting there with the Forlish closing in had been terrifying, easily the equal of that nasty little fight in the woods. But he needed Sendatsu still. And telling the truth to Rhiannon, on top of Sendatsu's betrayal ... That fear was topped by the worry her father was obviously searching for her. The diversion to Browns Brook must have delayed Hector but he had finally caught up — and if he had soldiers of the king with him, it meant Ward had not finished with either of them yet.

'Decide quickly,' Sendatsu hissed.

Huw gulped. 'I have another plan. A better one, that will serve us both,' he said hurriedly. 'Trust me and I shall explain it all later. Say nothing yet — it will hurt Rhiannon too much.'

'Agreed,' he said, stepping backwards slightly as Rhiannon walked hesitantly over towards them.

She tried not to look at Sendatsu. 'Thank you,' she forced herself to say, the words almost burning her throat.

'I know what those words must have cost you,' he said haltingly. 'All I can say is how sorry I am ...'

She held up her hand. 'I don't want to hear it! I cannot talk to you now.'

Sendatsu glanced over at Huw, still sitting stiffly on the horse, then stepped away. He wondered what Huw's new plan could be. He would exchange his silence for the bard's help — for a while. But Rhiannon needed to know her father was still alive. She had to confront her father to break the hold he had on her — a meeting Sendatsu could only dream about, himself. He looked over to where Huw and Rhiannon were deep in conversation and wondered if he should interrupt.

'Are you all right?' Huw asked awkwardly.

'I'm not hurt.' She half smiled. 'A few scratches and scrapes maybe, but nothing much.'

'And ...' Huw began carefully.

'Sendatsu? I'm still ready to carve his elfhood off with a sharp knife. He tricked me beautifully, said all the things I wanted to hear. He knew how to use me. Literally,' she finished bitterly.

'But he did save us,' Huw pointed out.

'Yes, I know! But how can I feel grateful to him, after what he has done to me? I cannot bear to look at him ...' she trailed off. Talking about Sendatsu had her very close to tears, which was strange, because she had faced the Forlish without flinching. 'We should leave. Go our own way. We can hire a couple of Velshmen to protect us ...'

'We still need him,' Huw said firmly.

'What? I never expected to hear you take his part in this! Do you mean you agree with what he did?' she snapped.

'Of course not!' Huw jumped down from the horse, to be at the same level as her. 'But I talked to him when you were away. He is truly sorry for what he did …'

'A bit late now!'

'Agreed. What he did to you was unforgivable. But my people still need his knowledge, the help that only an elf can provide.'

'Do you think he deserves to be with us after what he did?'

'No!' Huw said heatedly. He felt only too keenly the injustice of the situation, where he had to argue Sendatsu's case to Rhiannon, angering her instead of sympathising with her. 'Look,' he continued, in a softer tone of voice. 'What he did to you was disgusting — and he deserves to pay for it. But there are other things at stake here. He might be a hunted exile, but he is still an elf. He gets the attention of the villages the way we never could. He knows about war and defences — and he is the perfect protection out here. He just saved us for the second time. I'm not saying you have to like him. You don't even have to talk to him. But we know King Ward is hunting for us and the raiders know our names …'

Rhiannon waved him to silence. 'Leaving aside Sendatsu, that reminds me — those raiders kept shouting about my father, telling me I was going to join him! Do you think they were here to hunt for us?'

Huw could not say anything for a moment, for fear of betraying himself … the way she was feeling, she would put him in the same category as Sendatsu.

'They must have been sent up here specially to find us,' Huw said through dry lips. 'They probably only just arrived because they were looking for us down in Browns Brook, the town I pretended was my birthplace.'

'But why were they talking about my father?'

'Maybe they were some of the guards who killed your father,' he suggested, wincing inwardly at the lie and hoping she would never discover the truth.

But Rhiannon gasped in horror at the thought. 'They must have been!' she cried. 'The way they were talking about him ... it was as if they had known him!'

Huw grimaced, not trusting himself to speak.

'If only they were still alive — I would have liked to make them suffer,' she spat.

Huw thanked his lucky stars none had survived.

'But you have to admit, knowing there are groups out there deliberately hunting for us — it makes sense to keep Sendatsu around,' he ventured.

'They are dead,' she pointed out.

'Well, I'm sure Ward would not have just sent these few. True, they would have been enough, had we been by ourselves — but there will be more out there.'

Rhiannon looked away, glancing at where Sendatsu stood, watching them.

'He is truly sorry for what he did,' Huw continued, seeing where her gaze fell. 'And can you imagine what he has been going through — separated from his children, fearing for his life at every turn?'

'No,' Rhiannon admitted, feeling herself weakening — and hating it. She wanted to keep her anger.

'If he comes along with us, I don't want him to talk to me,' she said finally. 'If he tries to talk to me, I shall cut out his tongue and then cut off his staff — I swear it!'

'You won't regret this,' Huw said thankfully.

'I already am,' Rhiannon said sourly. 'The only reason I am doing this is for the Velsh people who would otherwise suffer — and to make Ward pay for what he did to my father.'

'I'll keep Sendatsu away from you,' Huw promised, feeling cold sweat sliding down his back.

She smiled a little at that.

'Well, I am also doing it for you. You are my only friend. You saved me in Cridianton, you have only ever tried to help me and give me good advice — you don't know how much it means to me, having you around.'

Huw felt both excitement and fear at her words and tried to keep both from his face.

'So what is your new plan?' Sendatsu asked as they sat around the fire.

Rhiannon had made her own fire, a good ten paces away, and sat with her back to them. Huw had taken her some food but, while she had agreed to keep travelling with them, she would not exchange a word with Sendatsu. She had made him ride twenty paces ahead and her expression told Huw she was not ready to talk with him either. It was uncomfortable; Huw could not see how it could continue for as long as they needed to keep Sendatsu around — but it was better than seeing her ride away. Rhiannon sensed their distress — but had no sympathy. They deserved to suffer. Well, perhaps not Huw as much but he needed to pay the price for making her accept Sendatsu back.

'Wait,' Huw said. 'I need to talk to Rhiannon as well, although that's a bit difficult at the moment ...'

'I know,' Sendatsu said gloomily. 'I should never have let anything happen between us. My true love still waits for me back in Dokuzen.'

'Your true love? I thought you said your wife was dead?' Huw asked suspiciously.

'My wife died but I never loved her. I had to marry because she was the one my father chose and the marriage brought new power to my clan. No, my true love is Asami.'

'Well, marry her when you return!'

'I cannot — she is married to my best friend.'

'I don't think I will ever understand you elves!' Huw grunted.

Sendatsu sat awkwardly for a moment. 'Look, I know how you feel about her — and what I did must make you hate me ...'

'I did,' Huw admitted.

'I deserved that. But I shall try and make it up — make it up to both of you. And one of the things I intend to do is see the two of you get together.'

Huw snorted. 'I appreciate the offer, but I fear you will do more harm than good!'

Sendatsu shook his head. 'Not now. But I will help you. You need all the help you can get.'

'And what does that mean?'

'Well, you should have pounced long before I came onto the scene. You rescued her from death — or a fate just as bad — at the hands of King Ward and brought her north, to your homeland. You were going to take her to see your father. You can't tell me there wasn't a chance on the way. I know how naïve she was, how impressionable. Otherwise she would not have fallen for me,' he said dryly. 'Don't tell me you weren't tempted.'

Huw wriggled in embarrassment and glanced over to Rhiannon, but she still had her back to them, and showed no sign of being able to hear what they were saying.

'You are right, I did have the chance. She was almost dependent on me for the first few days she was away from her father. He had controlled every aspect of her life — she was used to being told what to do. I could have pressed my suit with her and she probably would have thought it was all her idea.'

'So why didn't you?'

'I wanted her to come to my bed because she chose to — not because she felt grateful!'

'And because you didn't really save her from death,' Sendatsu said gently.

Huw gulped and looked again at Rhiannon. 'Yes,' he admitted. 'I felt guilty. I forced her to run, forced her to come north with me. I could not force her to my bed.'

'So what happened? Why did you run? It obviously wasn't just to get the girl, otherwise you would not have been stopped by a guilty conscience.'

So Huw explained it carefully. How he had heard Hector selling Rhiannon to Ward, in order to make his own fortune. How Hector had promised to persuade his daughter to enthusiastically embrace Ward. How, in return, Hector would get fame and gold to follow.

'That is monstrous,' Sendatsu admitted. 'And I thought my father was bad.'

Huw nodded. 'She thinks her father sacrificed everything for her, gave up his life to make hers a success, when it was the other way around. He spent her whole life carefully planning to use her to restore his fortune. Afterwards, he would have discarded her like a dirty rag.'

'I can see why you didn't tell her back in Cridianton. But why have you not told her still? She needs to know! If she ever meets her father again, it will make today's bitter lesson look like a pleasant memory.'

'I know! I know all that — but now I have left it so long, it makes it hard to say anything. I always intended to but things just kept happening ...'

'And now I have broken her heart, you cannot risk telling her.' Sendatsu nodded. 'You have backed yourself into an unpleasant corner — and there is no easy way out.'

'Don't I know it,' Huw grumbled.

'Well, you will need to tell her. Maybe not tomorrow — but soon. In the meantime, I shall do what I can to help you. The two of you should be together — she will see that, eventually. Now I have hurt her, the appeal of a dependable, kind man will be far greater than that of an elf.'

'Thanks — I think,' Huw said.

Sendatsu grinned. 'Well, you know what I mean. Women love a warrior, a hero, or an elf. They measure it against the farmers and shopkeepers and miners — and bards — and they long for what they do not have.'

'Know a lot about Velsh women, do you? Popular topic in Dokuzen, is it?' Huw sniffed.

'Not exactly. But I have seen women here are much like those in Dokuzen. Women like to dream. But when they find the dream is a nightmare, they are happy to have something real, like you.'

Huw regarded the elf with disbelief. 'Well, thank you very much for that wonderful advice,' he said coldly.

'It is good advice,' Sendatsu insisted. 'Even if it didn't quite sound right. You'll see — the two of you shall be together, I promise. At least one of us should be happy. And as my love is in Dokuzen and might as well be a star in the sky, it had better be you!'

Huw heard the pain in Sendatsu's voice and stopped himself from making another cutting comment.

'If you can help me, I shall be grateful,' he admitted.

'And I did not mean you are not strong, or brave — for you are both,' Sendatsu said softly. 'Just because you cannot defeat five Forlish warriors with the sword does not make you less of a man. In fact, you are more of one than I — given I am an elf!'

They smiled at that and looked over at Rhiannon, who was still pointedly ignoring them. They watched as she rolled herself into a blanket and settled down to sleep.

'I don't think we had better ask her to take a watch tonight,' Huw grunted.

'I'll take it. I don't think I can sleep tonight anyway,' Sendatsu sighed.

'I'll sit with you for a while,' Huw offered, feeling closer to the elf than ever before. 'Tell me of your love back in Dokuzen.'

'Her name is Asami,' he said heavily. 'We have been friends since we were children. She is far smarter than I, brilliant at magic and a genius at herbs. There truly is much you Velsh could learn from her, if only she could be here.'

'Still, smarter than you — not too hard, is it?' Huw nudged the elf. 'What of your children?'

'They would make you smile as soon as you saw them,' Sendatsu said fondly. 'Mai is five and loves animals and plants. She has the brightest smile and to see her dance ... Cheijun is three, fearless when it comes to picking up insects but scared the gaijin humans will come for him in the night. I would like him to meet you, to learn he does not have to be afraid, hear his laugh set a room alight. I close my eyes and I can see them. If only I could hold them once more ...'

The utter misery in his voice touched Huw.

'I'm sure you will see them again,' Huw said slowly. 'I know why those toys mean so much to you now.'

Sendatsu took them out. 'I will have to wash them before I can give them back to Mai and Cheijun,' he said sorrowfully. 'Look at my hands — look at my clothes. Everything is dirty, everything smells.'

'Well, we can find a stream tomorrow ...' Huw offered.

'I want a bath. I want to soak in hot water and wear clean clothes,' Sendatsu said softly. 'But I know there'll be no bath until I return. But these toys deserve more.' He held them in his hand, concentrated for a few moments and reached into the magic.

Huw watched in amazement as the toys began to gently steam, the dirt and grime disappearing from them.

'I don't have much magic but I can do small things to amuse.' Sendatsu smiled.

'What is going on?' Rhiannon called.

The moment was lost and they both looked up.

'Nothing,' Huw replied, casting a glance at Sendatsu. 'Were we making a noise?'

Rhiannon rolled back over. She had not heard anything, but she had felt something. Again, the world had come alive around her, seemingly ready to do her bidding. All she had to do was ask. It was most strange ...

'No. But can you do whatever it is without disturbing me next time?'

Huw and Sendatsu exchanged looks.

'I don't think she has quite forgiven me yet,' Sendatsu said wryly.

'Nothing is ever hopeless,' Huw told him. 'Wake me later. I'm going to get some sleep.'

# 22

*One person tried to warn me. A young warrior from the Tadayoshi clan and Moratsune family approached me one day while I was wandering around my garden. He was polite yet determined and managed to get past my guards. He tried to tell me what was happening, how his family had lived among the Velsh to the west before being ordered out of their home and back to Dokuzen. What he had seen on the way back east had outraged him and he tried to communicate that to me. Sadly, I did not listen.*

*My guards did, however, and reported back to Naibun that word was reaching my ears.*

Broyle looked at yet another walled Velsh village and spat in disgust.

'They're staying ahead of us, sarge. And even if we get them in the end, the Velsh are going to be safe behind their walls,' someone said nervously.

Without looking, Broyle knew it was Ricbert, who had been voicing his concerns with increasing regularity. He was speaking to the others when Broyle was not around, suggesting they would be better returning to Forland to warn the king — or even going back to their unit, rather than chasing around Vales after an elf, a bard and a woman. Broyle knew he could handle Ricbert, could handle them all if it came to it. But he needed them. In fact, he needed more of them.

'You are right,' he said, turning around suddenly.

The other men, who had been exchanging meaningful looks, looked startled, both by Broyle's words and actions.

'This is not working. We need to try something else.'

'Like going home?' Ricbert ventured.

'No!' Broyle barked. 'Like taking one of those villages.'

He could see the doubt in their eyes. They all remembered what had happened the last time — how the clouds of crossbow bolts had covered the men and horses, killing both.

'Not just us!' Broyle growled and they visibly relaxed. 'Look at that village. The wall might be enough to slow horsemen but, if we were back with the regiment, would we be afraid of taking that?'

Dutifully they looked as he pointed at the crude wooden palisade and he could see their confidence return, a little.

'We'd smash that down in a day. We just need to prepare for it. We cannot catch our prey, for they are faster than we are. So we make them come to us. We'll gather up as many men as we can — try to get at least two hundred, maybe even more. And we'll take our time, build battering rams, make shields. When we attack, we'll do it the right way, smash our way inside and teach the Velsh that no pissing little wall is going to stop us! Once they see their fancy crossbows and wooden walls are no defence, once that elf and bard are being dragged feet-first back to Cridianton, they'll give up quick smart.'

'But sarge, how will we know which village they'll be in, which is the right one to attack?'

'We'll tell them,' Broyle said with relish. 'We'll let it slip that we're about to crush the first one we attacked. That's where they're from, so they won't be able to help themselves. They'll rush back, thinking they can protect it — and then they'll be trapped. And they'll finally get to see how the Forlish army really fights!'

'But how will we let them know where we are going to attack?'

'Not sure yet,' Broyle admitted, thinking he might have to sacrifice Ricbert for that task if he could not come up with a better idea. 'But we'll find a way — and return to Cridianton as heroes!'

He could see the grins on the faces of his men now, even Ricbert was looking happy.

'Come on. We need to find more men.' Broyle signalled, and they began marching again, this time with a spring in their step.


Hector was furious with Sergeant Edric. Years of training the girl had not left him well equipped for spending days in the saddle, sleeping rough and eating cold food. He needed a little luxury — or as much as Vales could supply. Obviously he could not just ride into a Velsh village with a squad of armed men behind him — not only would word get around but he might find himself in the middle of a fight. So he sent Edric and half of the men away to look for signs of his stupid daughter, while he took the rest into a village with the ridiculous name of Brynmawr for the chance to at least eat some hot food. He would have liked a soft bed, a warm bath and a softer woman as well but you couldn't expect to find such things in a barbarian place like Vales. He considered it a good bargain if he was able to ride out again without fleas and lice.

He had a reasonable meal — not great but better than whatever Edric's men cooked over a wood fire at night. But Edric was not at the meeting point and he had to waste several turns of the hourglass looking for the man. He was about ready to explode, although, of course, he needed Edric more than the sergeant knew. He silently promised himself the man would suffer on their return to Cridianton, however.

But all his elaborate plans for revenge were wiped out when they found the bodies.

It was almost nightfall and he found himself looking around worriedly, afraid not just that they would not return with Rhiannon but they might not return at all.

'Who did this to them?' Edric's corporal John, a stolid man with little imagination, gasped as they went from body to body, inspecting the wounds.

'I'd say it wasn't a bard,' Hector sniffed. Inside, his mind was racing. Keeping these men in line was going to be difficult without Edric. And how was he going to capture the bard and get Rhiannon back, if Edric and four men had obviously tried — and been slaughtered.

'What now, sir?' John asked.

Hector did not answer right away, for he was trying to come up with an idea.

'Bury them,' he said at last, to give himself time to think.

They had no spades, and the five dead men's swords had been taken from them, so John and the rest of the men had to use their blades to carefully cut away the grass and soil. It was difficult, and instead of a deep grave, they basically scratched out a hollow and then covered the bodies with a thin layer of turf. Hector suspected animals would be at them before the night's end — but that was the least of his problems.

'We still have the king's seal,' he announced. 'That counts for a great deal. All around Vales there are Forlish warriors, loyal and brave, trying to carry out the king's wishes. All we need to do is find a few more — and then we shall be ready to finish the king's orders.' Hector hoped that would be true.


'We are getting closer,' Hanto announced.

Jin and Taigo said nothing, but they exchanged a long look behind Hanto's back. What had seemed to be an easy mission at first had dragged on for almost a moon. These lands were infested with bands of armed humans, while the villages were now arming themselves as well. Hanto had even considered returning to Dokuzen with this news. Jaken needed to know the humans would not be the easy conquest he imagined. But he had decided returning without Sendatsu would not be the wisest course. Besides, even protected villages would not stand up to the might of the elves — and their Magic-weavers.

Still, the progress of the villages was making it easier to track Sendatsu. Every one with a wall around it knew of the strange elf.

'Why is he helping the gaijin? What is the point?' Taigo had asked.

'He is mad,' Hanto replied simply.

The distances they had to cover meant they had taken horses from humans and now rode. It was an unusual experience for the three of them but Jin and Taigo were enjoying not having aching feet at the end of the day. All of them felt filthy and hungry, unable to find proper food or have a bath, and all were longing to finish this task and get home.

Now they had come across a village without a wall, which a traveller told them was called Brynmawr.

'They have been heading steadily west. Soon they will arrive here and, when they do, we shall catch them,' Hanto said. 'We just need to find an ideal spot for an ambush.'

'What is your plan now?' Sendatsu asked as they rode towards the next village, Brynmawr.

'You mean now we cannot tell them the elves are coming to save them?' Rhiannon called back over her shoulder. She was riding ahead of them, so she did not have to look at Sendatsu.

'Yes, that is what I meant,' he agreed.

'I think we need to turn Vales into a country,' Huw voiced the thought that had popped into his head when he had been talking to Sendatsu.

'What do you mean?' Rhiannon turned around, slowing her horse, although making sure she kept Huw between herself and Sendatsu.

'At the moment it's just a collection of villages. There is some trade between them, but only when one has something the other needs. Some villages are so poor they are almost sinking in the mud, while others are rich enough to buy elven-built houses off the others, because they are lucky enough to have coal or tin or iron ore they can mine. Normally there's no way they could be brought together, for the rich are not going to give up what they have, and traditional rivals like Patcham and Crumlin won't work together. But this Forlish attack is not normal. We would not want, nor need a ruler like a king. Instead, we would have a council of leaders, get each village to vote for a headman and for them to come together, get them to agree on the best way forwards for the Velsh. So a loose alliance but an alliance nevertheless. Together there is much we could achieve. We might even have a chance of holding back the Forlish, should they come …'

Huw trailed off, aware he had been caught up in his vision. Well, not really his vision. His father had talked about it often enough, how the Velsh should work together, rather than work against each other, the way they did now.

'It is a brave idea,' Rhiannon declared. 'But there's no reason why it can't work. Everyone can surely see how it is in their best interests to band together …'

'They won't,' Huw sighed. 'I know that already. But we have to try. And what we are doing is the perfect way to begin. We are meeting so many villagers, getting to know the men in charge of each village — saving some of them, even. It is the first step.'

'And we can achieve all this in one moon?' Sendatsu asked doubtfully.

'Yes, we can. And we need to, because time is running out for Vales. But, once we do, it will be simplicity itself to get you the answers you seek.'

Sendatsu said nothing. He could not see it being that simple. He needed to think what to do — use the threat of Rhiannon on Huw or try something else entirely.


'Down!' Broyle hissed, and the others ducked obediently.

His plan had begun well — within a day they had come across a group of dispirited Forlish, who had been beaten away from an attack on a village called Harlech. Just sixteen strong now, they were all that were left of a two-score group that had been terrorising the biggest village in Gwent — only for the rabbits to suddenly grow fangs.

'We had them at our mercy,' they told him. All their sergeants and corporals were dead, so they were happy to follow his orders.

'We were slaughtering the Velsh like sheep. Then this elf joined in — no one could stop him.'

'I know — I saw him in action,' Broyle agreed.

'And they had these strange crossbows — able to loose bolt after bolt into us,' another man remembered.

'Then the whole village came at us — hundreds of them! We could not stand against them,' another mumbled.

'Well, follow me and I promise you there will be revenge,' Broyle vowed, explaining his plan.

They loved the idea, and followed him eagerly. He now had horsemen, enough so they did not have to live off the land, but could start thinking about raiding isolated farms and even unprotected villages for everything they needed.

Then his last scout spotted three figures riding towards them and Broyle could not resist the opportunity. The villages were not going anywhere and the chance to get his revenge on the elf, the bard and the dancer was too good to pass up.

'Ambush!' he ordered.

After what happened last time, he was not going to play around and try to be complicated. He was just going to swamp them.


'Where to now, sir?'

Hector plastered a look of confidence over his face.

'As before, corporal,' he said pompously. 'We shall follow them, while searching for more brave Forlish fighting men who might be in the area. After all, we have the king's seal, so they are bound to help us. Another dozen men and the recapture of my daughter will be easy.'

They had spent the last night in Brynmawr and were now riding east.

'They have not been out here, so we need to search elsewhere,' Hector said.

'Shall we ride around?'

Hector looked at where the corporal was pointing, to a patch of broken ground and thick woodland.

'We'd never ride through there in Balia, sir. Too obvious a place for an ambush.'

'Don't be a fool, man! We're Forlish! We want to find our own men! Besides, as soon as they hear our voices, they will know who we are.'

'Yes, sir.'

'You ride first,' Hector added hastily.


'Here they come,' Broyle whispered. 'Pass the word.' He had walked the track himself, tried to spot his men — and ordered extra cover cut for some, while moving others until they were invisible, yet close to the road. Not even an elf could spot them, he concluded with satisfaction.

'Remember the orders — take them but we want them alive!'

Three riders were now approaching slowly. Broyle could hear them but could not see them — that was too risky — and so needed to judge carefully the right time to strike. The horses were moving slowly and he had to curb his impatience. The time for revenge was so close!

'This looks like the perfect spot,' a strange voice said.

Broyle did not understand what it meant but feared it signalled one of his men had been seen. He dared not wait any longer.

'Now!' he roared, leaping up and out of cover, a thick branch in his hands. He had ordered all swords kept sheathed, for he did not want any of the three dead. Yet.

As he burst out of the bushes his first thought was joy, as he saw the shock on the closest face — then he almost stopped in surprise himself for this trio was not the one he wanted. There was no bard or dancer — although there seemed to be three elves, all of whom were drawing swords and preparing to fight back.


Hanto saw the broken ground and recognised its ambush potential instantly.

'We'll ride into the middle, find the ideal place,' he told the other two who, as always, nodded agreement.

The long, fruitless chase and the hope of finishing it at last made him careless. Normally he would have sent Taigo riding ahead as a scout but Hanto was sure he was the hunter, not the hunted. Besides, nothing he had seen from the gaijin had made him fear them. He was sure they did not have his experience or talents — how could they?

He scanned the bushes on either side to find a place to ambush Sendatsu. After their earlier attempt, he had a healthy respect for Sendatsu's abilities. He had to take Jaken's son out immediately. The humans would be easy to kill afterwards.

'This looks like the perfect spot,' he announced, surveying the thick undergrowth with satisfaction.

He turned to see what Jin and Taigo thought — and then the bushes exploded around them, dozens of humans leaping out, clutching thick clubs.

Hanto reacted without thought. His sword leaped into his hand and he cut down the first human who came near him, the sharpened steel slicing open the human's neck and into his chest. He had a space and took it, spurring his horse through. Behind him, though, Jin and Taigo were slower to react. Jin fell, a thrown club knocking him off his horse, while Taigo was swarmed over by humans, who beat him to the ground.

Hanto screamed with fury and nearly turned his horse to take revenge — except sense and training reasserted itself. He was almost clear and he should not waste that. A lone human tried to chase him but he cut back viciously, feeling his blade strike home and seeing the blood spurt as the human reeled away. Hanto slammed his heels into the horse's sides and felt it break into a gallop — just as another group of horsemen came around the corner of the trail, swords drawn. Beyond reason, Hanto charged into them. The first he overpowered with several swift strikes, a dragon-tail stroke taking the man's head. But the trail was too small and he could not get past the others easily. He blocked a sword coming for his head with ease, looked for a chance to get past — and then fell from his horse as a thrown club crunched into the back of his head.

'Nice throw, sarge!' Ricbert exclaimed.

Broyle ignored him. He was more concerned about the three elves he had brought down — and just what they were doing here.

'Who are you?' an educated Forlish voice demanded — the sort of voice that belonged to an officer. Broyle glanced up at the small party of horsemen who had arrived at just the right moment to trap the third elf — although it had cost their lead rider. For a moment he was about to order his men to attack, then the Forlish accent hit home.

'Greetings!' He forced a smile. 'I am Sergeant Broyle of the king's Third Regiment. I know you are also Forlish from your voices — but these are dangerous times for Forlish to be riding in small numbers. Who are you?'

'I am Hector of Hamtun, on a mission from King Ward himself,' the man blustered, fumbling in a pouch at his belt.

'So you're not an officer then?'

'No, although I have the honour to command these king's guards.' Hector produced a king's seal and flourished it triumphantly. 'I have need of your men, sergeant. Whatever your orders, my mission is more important,' Hector said proudly.

For a moment only, Broyle felt a flicker of fear, then he shook his head. 'No,' he said simply. 'Instead, I shall take the seal and your men.'

'But this is the king's seal! You must obey it!' Hector squawked.

'Only in Forland,' Broyle said grimly. 'And we are not in Forland.'

Hector looked around desperately but he had only a handful of men. More ominously, he had the feeling mere numbers would not stop this man. Besides, his corporal had just died and he doubted whether his remaining men would obey him.

'But you don't understand how important this is! I am chasing a runaway the king himself wants back ... a dancer, who is travelling with a bard and an elf!' he cried.

Broyle, who had been walking forwards to take the king's seal out of the fool's hand, stopped.

'What did you say?' he demanded.

'My daughter was promised to King Ward himself. But she has been stolen by a bard, helped by an elf and they are now travelling around Vales ...'

Broyle waved the man to silence, a chill rippling up his back.

'Your daughter, you say?'

'Indeed!'

Broyle nodded. 'I think we might be on the same path,' he said thoughtfully. 'I am chasing an elf, a bard and a dancer, who are travelling from village to village, showing these Velsh how to protect themselves with walls and strange crossbows ...'

'That's them!' Hector said excitedly.

'This trap was supposed to catch them. Instead we have found something else, something even stranger.' Broyle signalled and his men dragged the three unconscious elves over, making sure their hands were tied tight. 'I think we need to work together.'

'Good.' Hector felt relief flood through him. 'Then you will follow me and help me catch them ...'

'No.' Broyle shook his head. He could see a clear way forwards now, made easier by the king's seal. 'You will come with me and help me set up a trap for them.'

Hector listened, mouth open, as Broyle outlined his plan to lure Rhiannon, Huw and the elf back to Patcham.

'And you shall set up the trap. My men cannot enter a Velsh village and be believed but you can. Tell the story often enough and it will reach your daughter's and her friends' ears. They will come running to protect Patcham and fall into our trap.'

Hector gulped. 'And you are sure you will be able to break their defences?'

Broyle smiled wickedly. 'I saw those walls up close. They are only there to slow us down enough for their damned crossbows to cut us to pieces. But we shall be shielded from them, have no fear of that. All we need is enough men — and now we have your king's seal and the promise this is a mission from King Ward himself, we shall have no problem in persuading raiding parties to join us.'

'And what if I disagree with your plan? What if I think it too risky and refuse to force Forlish officers to serve under you, a mere sergeant?' Hector challenged. He liked the idea — but not so much the part where he told every Forlishman within a quarter-moon's ride what he was doing, given he had no such orders from the king.

'Well, then I shall kill you and pretend the king's seal was given to me,' Broyle stated simply.

Hector gazed at him for just a moment before smiling broadly and holding out his hand.

'Then I say we have a deal,' he said pompously.

'Excellent.' Broyle ignored the hand. 'Do you know anything about elves?'

'Well of course! Why, I am as versed in elven lore as stories of our own fair Forland ...'

'Good. Your first job will be speaking to these elves. First one appears, then these three. I want to know why.'

'Do you think these were the ones who killed Cenred and the others?' Ricbert asked.

'If they are, they will wish they hadn't,' Broyle promised.


'What was that noise?' Sendatsu asked.

'Probably just a fox taking a rabbit,' Huw dismissed.

'I don't think so. It was men's voices, and the sound of steel on steel,' Rhiannon said dubiously.

Sendatsu looked at the trail, how it wound through cuttings and woods, and pointed off to the north.

'I think we'll take the long way round,' he suggested.

'Are you sure? We won't get there until noon, at least,' Huw grumbled.

'Going in there is a bad idea. Trust me — I am not making up what I heard. You will hear no more lies from me ...'

'I'll believe that when next I see pigs circling overhead, looking for a tall tree to nest in,' Rhiannon commented.

Huw began to laugh, then trailed off when he saw the expression on Sendatsu's face.

'Enjoy your joke but I think we should still ride the long way round.'

'Let's go then,' Huw agreed.

Rhiannon said nothing. She had lain awake last night for ages. Not because she was listening to Huw and Sendatsu talk — she could not hear what they were saying. She had strained to hear them at one point then decided she could trust Huw. He wanted the elf to help protect his people, which was understandable. But he would not do anything to hurt her, trick her or lie to her. She knew it deep inside. No, what kept her awake was a feeling she had. It had been as if the woods around her had woken up and were calling for her attention. For a few moments she could feel everything around her — from the insects in the grass to the birds in the trees and the animals in the bushes, as well as every plant. She would have been sure it was some sort of strange dream — except her eyes had been wide open.

So she had lain there, trying to recapture that feeling. It was better than dancing, far better than singing, even better than having a room full of people cheering and applauding her. But although she strained, although she tried to reach out with her mind to the woods around her, nothing happened. Her sleep had been haunted by dreams of strange creatures. But not just any creatures — by dragons. She knew them for what they were, although she had never really enjoyed the tales of dragons. They were all through the various elven stories, even claiming they were friends of the elves, but she had found them boring. They were just big lizards really, and she did not like the small ones she used to find in the thatch at home, so the idea of one as big as a house did not excite her. She would much rather hear about beautiful elven princesses, about huge elven parties — dancing and singing. She had usually dozed off, or thought about something else when dragons came up.

But when they swooped through your dreams, it was much harder to ignore them. Especially when they looked nothing like their pictures! These dragons were brighter, stronger and far more beautiful than the pictures she remembered. They moved with a grace that could never be captured on a scraped lambskin. And they had taken her flying. It should have been terrifying but soaring through the air had been pure joy. How she could have conjured such amazing creatures into a dream, when she had never liked them and never thought about them before was bewildering. But she hoped she could dream of them again. Just thinking of them now made it harder to stay angry at Sendatsu. They did not seem to want to share her mind with anger and frustration.

'Wake up, elf!'

Hanto opened his eyes to see himself surrounded by armed humans. He tried to rise, only to find he was tied tight, while his head ached abominably.

'Release me, gaijin!' he snarled.

'What did he call me?' the human leader turned to an older, plumper human at his side.

'I think it's an insult.'

Broyle sighed. 'I'd worked that out for myself. Listen, elf — what are you doing here?'

'Let us go or you shall suffer the consequences! You do not know what I am capable of!'

'What if he uses magic on us?' Hector whispered.

'We've got men with swords right behind them. The moment they try anything, they will lose their heads.' Broyle waved Hector away. 'Try and talk some sense into the elf. I want answers. If he won't give them, then we'll have to make him scream.'

Hector nervously kneeled before Hanto.

'Honourable elf. We seek answers. Tell us what we need to know and we promise to let you go unharmed.'

Broyle opened his mouth to say he would promise no such thing but decided to leave Hector to it.

Hanto was both insulted and infuriated that mere humans had dared attack him and tie him up — but he was also very aware he was at their mercy. Once out of his bonds he had no doubt he could escape but he needed to use darkness, and magic, to achieve that. Perhaps he should play along until then.

'What do you need to know?' he asked, forcing himself to sound polite.

'What are you doing here? Are you helping the Velsh?'

Hanto snorted. 'Help humans? Are you mad? I am here to recapture a fugitive, a murderer, and bring him back to justice.'

Hector glanced back at Broyle, who signalled him closer.

'Do you think he is lying?'

'Elves don't lie. It is impossible for them to do so,' Hector said with all his authority.

'So are they after the same elf we are?' Broyle asked.

'Probably. If they are, do you think they could help us?'

'No!' Broyle said scornfully. 'We have to take the elf back to King Ward. We're not handing him over to these three.'

'But they could defeat the elf we're after and then we can take him from them ...'

Broyle shook his head. 'Too risky. But we need to find out more about this elf we are chasing, as well as what he is doing here — does this mean the elves think they can just roam around Vales at will?'

'Do you want me to ask them more questions?'

'Not right now. The three we're after could be along any moment — we'll tie them to a tree, prepare the ambush again, and wait.'


'I'll try to do all the talking but Rhiannon, I shall need you to demonstrate the crossbow,' Huw said, as they rode into Brynmawr.

'Fine. I have the perfect target in mind. It is small but I shall enjoy trying to shoot it off anyway,' she declared, staring at Sendatsu for the first time that day.

He kept his mouth shut.

Three riders were enough to excite interest, especially when one was an elf, but Huw and Rhiannon were well versed in calming the people down enough so they heard the message.

'We have heard strange stories. Of raiders around Vales, striking in the night,' the village headman, Aled, said darkly. 'We have seen nothing ourselves, although several lambs and pigs have gone missing, more than the wolves and foxes could possibly have taken.'

'Well, we are here to tell you the stories are true. There are raiders loose in Vales. They are Forlish, sent here by their king to terrify us, so that we beg for his protection and give up our freedom in exchange for peace,' Huw said grimly.

'Forlish? We had a merchant here last night, as well as his guards ...'

'Yes, well these ones come in the night with swords and fire — they don't offer to trade.'

'So how can we stop them?' Aled groaned.

'I can show you a way. We have been around to many villages and showed them how to stay safe, how they can live without fear,' Huw declared. 'With this!' He held up his elven crossbow.

The villagers listened, fearfully, as he explained how a wall of earth or wood, or both, around their village would stop the horsemen — and then the crossbows would kill them. They watched as Rhiannon peppered a small straw target with crossbow bolts.

They were impressed but not convinced. So, finally, Huw had to go to Sendatsu.

'And here to help you is an elf — a real elf from Dokuzen, here to help us defeat the evil Forlish plan!'

Now the people reacted again, villagers pushing forwards once more around Sendatsu.

'Use some magic! Show us how you'll protect us!'

'Are the elves coming to save us?'

Huw and Rhiannon worked to clear a space around Sendatsu.

'I cannot save you with magic. It does not work like that. And do not pin your hopes on elves saving you either. You must save yourselves,' Sendatsu told them.

There was plenty of muttering at that.

'Well, what can you do?' Aled finally asked.

Sendatsu strung his bow, produced an arrow and swiftly drew and loosed, making the target full of Rhiannon's crossbow bolts explode in a shower of straw.

'I can show you how to help yourselves, not just to stop the Forlish raiders, but to live better,' he offered. 'The wisdom and strength of Dokuzen. All you have to do is ask for it.'

There was a quick discussion among Aled and several of the older Velsh, then they turned back to the waiting trio.

'Tell us what we need to do,' Aled said simply.


Nightfall told Broyle he had failed again. So close and all he had achieved was losing two more men. Still, he had replaced them with three others, plus picked up a fool and a king's seal, as well as captured three elves, so it was not a total loss.

'Get a fire going. We'll heat up a few swords and then put some real questions to those elves,' Broyle ordered.

'Food as well? I'm — I mean the men are starving,' Ricbert said.

'Questions first, food afterwards,' Broyle said coldly.

He pushed back through the undergrowth, stretching muscles made sore from crouching in the bushes all day.

'Sarge! They're gone!'

He raced over to where Ricbert stood, shocked. Instead of three elves tied to a tree, the ropes were empty, the two guards he had placed there both dead, their throats slit.

'Get the men together — we're going after those bastards,' Broyle swore.

'And the food ...?'

'Move!'


Brynmawr spent the next couple of days working on an earthen barrier around the village, its front strengthened by rocks, the back face with a step cut into it so that men — and women — could stand there and loose crossbows down on any attackers while leaving one way into the village, an opening that could be blocked by a pair of old carts, outer sides covered with sharp wooden spikes. Meanwhile, the carpenters in the village worked on the crossbows.

Sendatsu wandered around the village, trying to see if anyone knew magic, or remembered anything useful from ancient times.

He stopped to watch the children play — some sort of game where they used short wooden poles with a scoop on the end to throw a rough leather ball from one to another and then between two tall sticks stuck into the ground.

It brought a smile to his face for the first time in a moon and he wandered on, watching others play a game where you had to form your hand into a shape of a knife, stone or cloth to defeat your opponent's choice.

'Anyone have the knowledge you seek?' Aled asked him as he sat watching the children play.

'No,' Sendatsu grunted. It was one more disappointment lost in a sea of them.

'I am sorry. But perhaps you can help us with the knowledge you hold?'

'I suppose I can,' Sendatsu agreed.

Aled disappeared, returning with a group of villagers, which Sendatsu found slightly alarming.

'How do you live so long?' Aled asked eagerly.

So Sendatsu talked about food, different plants to look for, which could be cultivated and grown, from wild onions to nettles.

'A diet heavy in bread, meat and milk might fill a man's belly but it is not good for you. You need to eat more greenery, as much fruit as you can,' he suggested.

'You would have us grub at the grass like so many sheep?' Aled sniffed.

'I wouldn't eat grass. But we eat mainly vegetables and fish in Dokuzen. It is one of the reasons we live so much longer than you Velsh.' Sendatsu shrugged. 'If you planted blackberry seeds, as well as pear seeds, you should be able to create orchards. And the turnips and swedes you feed to your pigs — you would do better to eat them yourselves, and less bacon instead ...'

'If you ask me, the elves don't live that long. It just seems that way, being forced to chew on bark and leaves and pig food, instead of good red meat,' Aled said disgustedly.

Sendatsu sighed. 'I can only tell you the information. It is up to you if you want to use it.'

'No, no, keep going,' Aled insisted.

Sendatsu shrugged and tried suggesting they wash more often, as well as cleaning out their homes, not sharing them with goats and sheep, right down to not using the same knife to cut up raw and cooked meat. The doubtful faces told him he needed to try a different approach.

'What is the one thing that kills villagers more than anything?' he asked.

'Probably childbirth,' Aled said after a moment's thought, a response that had the others nodding. 'Women die, babies die — they both die. How do you elves deal with that?'

Sendatsu sighed again. 'We have priests of Aroaril who can save mothers and babies,' he said sadly.

'That's not going to help us then, is it?'

Sendatsu shook his head. 'I am sorry.'

'Still, we can try some of the other things. Imagine if they all work and we can all live as long and as well as elves!'

They drifted away, leaving him to think about what his people had done to the humans and, for the first time, feel deeply ashamed he was an elf. He was even more disturbed by what Aled had said. If the humans did have the knowledge of the elves, they would live as long and as well. He had learned so much about them in the past few moons, how there was really little difference between them. Except, of course, for magic. And that was slipping away from the elves. The words of the first Sendatsu on that fateful scroll came back to him. What if elves and humans were closer than everyone said? Could elves just be humans who had learned to use magic? Was the truth he sought hidden by even bigger lies than he imagined?

Huw felt the usual satisfaction of helping another village — and finally the thought he had about how the Velsh could save themselves had taken shape in his mind, much like the way the wall was growing around the village.

'Aled, do you have much to do with the nearby villages?' he asked.

The village headman sniffed. 'If we have a good crop of something, we'll often trade it with them,' he finally admitted. 'Now and again a young lass or lad from one or the other will meet and marry — but it doesn't happen too often. Every year a few of the boys leave to find farms of their own, the ones who have got too many brothers to make a living and keep a family on the land we have. Other than that we keep to ourselves, and that's the best way of it.'

'But what if you could all work together? What if we were to stop being a collection of villages and turn ourselves into a proper country — so you could call yourself a Velshman first and a Brynmawr second, not the other way around?'

Aled just stared at the young bard. 'Do you mean bend the knee to that Forlish bastard Ward? Because I wish you had told us before you had us all digging from dawn to dusk ...'

'No! Ruled by ourselves. No kings, no princes, just a collection of village headmen, like yourself, all getting together to meet and talk about their problems, agreeing to help each other. So if a village is rich in iron, or tin, or coal, they can help out those who have nothing — or have had poor harvests. A few men from each village would also join together, to help keep the peace and protect Vales.'

'An army, you mean?'

'Something like that. But they would never go outside of Vales — they would just stay here ...'

Aled sighed. 'Huw, I am a simple man. I am also too old to want to be inspired by the fiery words of a young fellow like you. Ask what you want and I shall put it to my village.'

Huw smiled. 'I want to take a few of your young men. No more than five or six, the younger sons of farmers, who would go elsewhere anyway, searching for their fortune, as you said.'

'The start of this army of yours?'

'That's right. And watch for their return, for they shall bring both tidings and warnings and a way to train the rest of the men,' Huw said, feeling the excitement rising in him.

Aled shrugged. 'I shall send a group to you and you can talk to them. I will not order a youngster to do this but no doubt they will be happy to do something crazy. For me, eating some of the elven recipes is adventure enough!'

Sendatsu and Rhiannon were alternately horrified and excited by Huw's plan.

'You could have spoken with me! Are we to drag a motley band across the countryside? How are we to arm them, feed them, allow them to travel? And do you know how many we shall need to face the Forlish? Thousands of them!' Sendatsu argued.

'It is a brilliant plan,' Rhiannon enthused. 'We can visit Harlech again, even Patcham, get the Forlish swords and horses we have taken. Imagine if we took five or ten men from each village — soon we would have a large force!'

'That's right. And Sendatsu can train them every day. After a moon of that, they will be ready to come back to their villages and train others ...'

'Wait a moment! Are we talking about one or two extra moons? This is pointless, you will need hundreds, if not thousands of swords and axes and spears, as well as shields and armour ...'

'We have to do something,' Huw stopped Sendatsu in mid-flow. 'This is the best way forwards. We shall bring together men from all different villages, get them thinking like Velshmen. And imagine if we had a thousand men, all trained to fight in the elven way. With the crossbows as well, it might be enough to hold back the Forlish ...'

'Huw, you are talking about leading those men to their deaths! You need more time, more everything! I will not be around to see this through ...'

'We have no other choice. And to do this is better than doing nothing,' Huw insisted. 'Besides, this is the best way to help you. If we create a whole country, then it will be simple to find out what all know about the elves. And you can go back to Dokuzen without us, knowing you will not leave Velsh children to be slaughtered by the Forlish.'

Sendatsu shook his head. 'You are too tricky by far,' he growled.

'If you want answers, this is the fastest way. Remember, once I have united Vales, I can make people help you. And the men you train can carry on your work when you are back in Dokuzen.'

Sendatsu groaned. But then he remembered the children of Rheged — and Mai and Cheijun, trusting him to return to them. Perhaps this was a way to serve them both.

'All right. But one moon only. No more.'

'No more,' Huw agreed.

'And I cannot lie to them,' he said hoarsely. 'If they go to their deaths, they must know what they are facing.'

'I know.' Huw patted his shoulder. 'But it is also true that confidence means much to an army. It is why the Forlish are so strong. They know they cannot be defeated. But we shall throw some doubt into them up here — and we shall inspire the Velsh. If they think they are as good as elves, they will try to be. But I shall not ask you to tell them a lie. Just teach them to fight and that will be enough.'

Sendatsu sighed. 'I will do what I can,' he said finally.

'We need a banner. A rallying point, to say we are Velsh, not tied to any village. Anything elven that springs to mind?'

'A dragon,' Rhiannon said instantly. They had been in her dreams every night now.

'A dragon?' Huw pondered.

'A red one,' Rhiannon added.

'It says magic without saying elf,' Sendatsu offered.

'I like it! Imagine it — the symbol of Vales, a red dragon! I think it will catch on.' Huw grinned. 'Now, if I could just give them their own language as well, bring them all together ...'

'You are playing a dangerous game,' Sendatsu warned gently.

'What do you mean?' Rhiannon was even quicker than Huw.

'You are setting yourself up to be the first king of Vales,' Sendatsu pointed out. 'You are visiting every village, getting every headman to acknowledge you; now you are forming an army and will give them a banner and a symbol to march underneath.'

Huw paused for a moment. 'I had not thought of that,' he admitted. 'And it is not something I would take on. I would have no man or woman bow the knee in Vales, to anyone. They can all have a say, always. I shall never take a crown nor seek to rule others.'

Sendatsu chuckled. 'You kept saying I was the hero the Velsh needed. But maybe it is you!'

'Please — no more of that,' Huw pleaded.

Rhiannon watched Huw and wondered how she had not seen the strength in him earlier. True, he had not acted like this when they first met. But he seemed to have grown up, to have taken on an authority his age did not deserve. He was a man who knew what he had to do and was determined to achieve it, no matter the cost. She had always liked his gentleness, his kindness, but now that was allied with a little of the steel that had been in Sendatsu.

'I shall say no more. But, as you said — actions speak louder than words,' Sendatsu said.

'The people will see the truth,' Rhiannon said, inspired both by her anger at Sendatsu and her admiration for Huw.

# 23

*Whenever I left my villa — and that was not often, admittedly — I was accompanied by a swarm of guards. At first I appreciated this gesture, thinking it was to ensure my safety. But it meant none could get near me to speak, and I only heard the reports Naibun wanted me to hear.*

*I did not hear of it then but the young warrior who had bravely talked his way into my garden was found dead, apparently the victim of humans.*

*As yet this did not worry me, although after seeing the way the guards dealt with another young warrior who wanted to speak to me, I did ask Naibun to reduce the guards around me. As ever, he was happy to agree with whatever I said.*

As Aled predicted, and Huw hoped, there was no shortage of young men wanting to come along with the elf and learn how to be soldiers, to fight for their country. Third or even fourth sons of families, they would normally have headed north, to Powys, the area of Vales with almost all of the mines, which always needed men. The land around Brynmawr was rich and fertile, but there were only so many families it could support. If they were lucky, they might meet and marry a woman from another village who would inherit some land. But, more likely, they would have to strike out on their own, become crofters, grub a living from some rough land. That or go north and earn enough to come back and buy themselves some land to work. Often such men ended up on the outskirts of Vales, in Rheged, where life was hard and the land sour.

More than a dozen wanted to join Huw but he would only take ten, the older and stronger ones. All were sixteen or seventeen, all already thinking of leaving the village for something better.

'Why do the boys leave? Why are there more men than women in your villages?' Sendatsu wanted to know.

'The problem is women dying from childbirth,' Rhiannon said sharply. 'It is the same in Forland. Giving birth can be as dangerous as battle. Women die, babies die, both die. There are men and women who live to old age together but maybe as many as one in six women don't make it through the childbirth years, while many children die before their first birthday.'

Sendatsu winced. Aled had spoken about that and he should have made the connection. 'I know. My wife, Kayiko, died giving birth to my son, Cheijun. But that was rare. We have women trained in childbirth, herbs — even priests of Aroaril ...'

'We have women who know what to do. But if the baby has turned, there is nothing anyone can do. And the men do nothing to help either. Beyond trying to fill their wives' bellies, that is,' she snapped, glaring at him.

'This is another reason why we need to restore the worship of Aroaril to these lands,' Sendatsu said hastily. 'Meanwhile, I'd better go and see our new recruits.'

'You do that,' Rhiannon told him. 'And next time you think of bedding a woman, imagine her screaming in agony as the child you gave her rips her in two.'

Sendatsu fled, Huw just a pace behind.


At long last it was the night of the Festival of Summer, to mark the season passing. Asami had been chafing at the way the days seemed to drag. She was nervous about trying to break into the tombs of the forefathers but the festival was also the last day of the full moon. For the past few days she had opened a gateway through the trees for Sendatsu to return — but there was still no sign of him. She was sick with the thought he might have been killed. And if he was safe, why had he not returned? Was the knowledge they sought not there? Did the humans not know about magic and Aroaril? There was so much to worry about and nobody to confide in. It made her crazy decision to rob the tombs seem more sensible. If Sendatsu could not find what they needed, then she would have to.

At the back of her room was a long rack of robes. Flowing and graceful, the everyday robe was made from cotton; the ceremonial from silk. But nestled in there were other outfits; the hakama and half-kimono that all elves wore while training to fight.

Hers was in dark green, which helped her fade into the shadows. She bound up her hair and pulled on a black cotton hood that covered her head and most of her face. The rest of her face she blackened with a mixture of charcoal and body oil. Her sword went into a sheath across her back, while she slung a large, sturdy cotton bag across her shoulders. Into that went a tinder box and candle and then she was ready.

She walked out — and into Gaibun, who was dressed exactly the same.

'Ready for the tombs of our forefathers?' Gaibun asked.

'You don't have to come along,' she said firmly.

Gaibun looked at her. 'Please, Asami. Give me a chance to make things up to you. Let me help you.'

'But this is going to be dangerous ...'

'Of course it is! Sumiko wants you to bring the books to her so she can overthrow the Council. Jaken wants me to bring the books to him so he can use their information to both break the Magic-weavers and overthrow Daichi. But if we work together, lie to them both, we can get ourselves in a position to bargain for Sendatsu.'

'Go on,' Asami said carefully.

'We get the books out and offer to hand them back to whoever returns Sendatsu. Jaken wants to destroy the Magic-weavers. If we offer him evidence of their plotting, he'll pay any price for it. And I think Sumiko will do anything to be able to overthrow the

Council. Both sides think they can trust us, so we speak to them both, get the best deal we can and then we pick which side we want to go with,' he said.

'And you think we can trust them to honour a deal?'

'No, but I think if we make them give us Sendatsu first, they have no choice.'

'What is in it for you?' she blurted.

'I want to know the truth. And I want to return Sendatsu. It is the honourable thing and that is all that is important. My father taught me that. He raised me to live by his rules — even though that saw him lose the clan leadership to Jaken. And yet Jaken thinks to tempt me away from that, to bribe me. No doubt he thinks it amusing to corrupt the son of the elf he betrayed for political power. Well, if Jaken falls, then my father will lead clan Tadayoshi.'

'But you have to lie to make that happen, you have to deceive to do the honourable thing ...'

'I know!' Gaibun said fiercely. 'I shall find a new path to take, I don't have to make all the same mistakes as my father.'

Asami reached out to touch Gaibun's arm — the muscles there were tense, jumpy. Gaibun held her hand.

'Being so close to you and yet so far apart has been tearing me in two. I have not been myself but now I see clearly again. I will help you, you will see I have changed. Do you think there is a future for us?'

'We shall always be friends,' she told him.

He squeezed her hand hard and grimaced at the same time.

'But first we have the tombs waiting for us and time trickling away ...'

'Fine. I deserve little more,' he sighed.

'Gaibun ...'

He let go of her hand. 'Are we going to do this or not?'

She nodded and they ran silently down the street, keeping to the shadows.

* * *

Apart from the constant tension between Sendatsu and Rhiannon, this was a golden time for Huw. Every village had a few young men who were going to leave anyway — and jumped at the chance to train with an elf; become protectors of Vales. Harlech handed over the weapons they had taken, as well as a dozen horses, which meant they could carry supplies and let the recruits practise riding.

Rhiannon, with help from some village women, had sewn a dragon on a white square of linen. It was not quite the sort of dragon Huw had imagined from his childhood stories, it seemed shorter and chunkier, but it was unmistakeably powerful.

Usually they kept it furled, strapped to a saddle, but when they got close to a village it was brought out, tied to a long, straight branch they had found for the purpose and carried proudly. Word began to spread and they were often greeted with cheering children, as well as young men carrying axes and the like, begging to join the 'Dragon Warriors'. It was a fierce name and one Huw was happy to see adopted.

Village headmen liked the idea of having an elven-trained army that would ride Vales and rid it of the Forlish menace, although Huw was careful not to say too much about what would happen after that. The Forlish armies were far to the south — and he fervently hoped they would stay there for as long as possible, to give Sendatsu time to turn the Dragon Warriors into something that might stand a chance against the Forlish.

Sendatsu was still doubtful but he was careful to hide that and instead concentrated on training the young Velshmen. They were fit and strong, used to working long hours — but he made them wish they were back on their farms within days. Straight away they were made to cut bow shafts for themselves from nearby yew trees and, on the rare times when they were not training, had to make shafts for themselves.

Every day they had to use the bow, until their arms, shoulders and backs were screaming. Then they picked up swords. To begin with, Sendatsu had them use wooden swords, carved from sticks, rather than real blades. But while they used the wooden swords for practice fights, they had to master the three basic blocks and nine basic strokes as they walked or rode to the next village, using the real swords to mimic those until they could barely lift their arms.

Then they were made to do it all over again.

Sendatsu thought some would leave, just disappear in the night. But none did. Part of that was undoubtedly pride, wanting to show an elf they were tough enough. Part of that was also Huw and Rhiannon. Each night they would play and sing for the young Velsh. No longer were they performing elven tales and songs, now these were stories of old Velsh heroes, songs of farming, of the girls left behind as young men went off to find their fortune.

Huw and Rhiannon worked on those as they rode together, while Sendatsu yelled at the recruits behind. Often they were writing the songs from scratch, working off short tales Huw's father had told him years ago. Rhiannon discovered she had a talent for writing tunes, coming up with the melodies for Huw's lyre, using her pure, clean voice to give him the notes to follow.

Also, they were the ones working on the villages they visited. Some of these were quick and easy — ones like Catsfield and Pigstrood that they had helped before. All they needed from there was food, men and horses, if any could be spared. But there were still many others they had not yet visited, which not only needed to be warned and helped, but persuaded to become part of Huw's plans.

While Sendatsu worked his young warriors, it was Huw and Rhiannon who spoke to the village headmen, showed them the crossbows and helped build watchtowers and protective walls, patrolled with dogs at night. With all the young dragons, walls could be thrown up in no time at all. Huw was writing down all the headmen's names now, keeping a long list of villages and the ones who would be eager to join a greater Vales, others who were unsure but would probably go along — and the ones who mistrusted the very idea.

When he had left Vales, such a thing would have seemed impossible. But the Forlish raiders had changed Vales. Every village had been affected by them in one way or another and even the most stubbornly independent could see the value in working together and having strength in numbers. It was easy to bring these isolated villages in, sell them on the idea of a united Vales. Sendatsu was seemingly content to teach the young dragons — but Huw's greatest problem was with Rhiannon. Working on the songs, performing for everyone each night — it was hard not to think of themselves as a couple, not just a duet. Once or twice he thought he should act, lean in and kiss her, or at least take her hand. But he could not. After what happened with Sendatsu, he did not think she would appreciate it. Then there was his natural nervousness around her and the fear she would reject him. But most of all there was his conscience. He had lied to her. It might have been for the right reasons but he did not think she would see it like that. Especially as she had said, on more than one occasion, she could trust him. Of course, if he did not act before he told her the truth, then it would be all right. He told himself that anyway. It was the one bad habit he could not break.

And none of that was helped by Sendatsu. The elf would always ask if Huw had come clean with Rhiannon.

'You have to tell her. She has to know. Not only for the two of you — but also for her. Hanging over her all the time is the legacy of her father. It was one of the reasons she was able to believe me, the lies I told her,' Sendatsu admitted. 'She was used to being ordered around, used as a piece in her father's game. We both know what the result of that game was going to be — she needs to know as well. At the moment she still holds to his memory, still thinks everything he did was for her. Learning the truth about me was painful for her but it was also valuable ...'

'Really?' Huw could not help but ask.

Sendatsu grimaced. 'Not for me,' he agreed. 'And she wouldn't see it like that just yet. But it has changed her. She is stronger in herself, more confident. She has more of her own opinion — and certainly doesn't agree with me all the time any more.'

'I'm sure she'll thank you one day,' Huw said dryly.

'Well, she won't thank you if you don't tell her the truth — and soon! Sit her down and explain everything. She will be angry but she will also understand. What she will never forgive is if we run into her father. Seeing as you told her he was dead, who do you think she will believe?'

'I will tell her. I just have to find the right time,' Huw insisted.

'There is no right time. Just tell her!'

But he could not bring himself to say it. There was always a really good reason — usually because he had seen her rip Sendatsu apart, then turn back to him with a smile. He could not bear the thought of her leaving, of never seeing her again.

*I just have to get her to fall in love with me, then she will listen,* he told himself.

And that did not seem too far-fetched a prospect.

Rhiannon found herself thinking about Huw, more and more. When she had first known him, he had been a friend — but she had never imagined it being anything more. She had seen the way he looked at her, read the way he acted around her but she had always been confident there would never be anything between them.

After Sendatsu, she had not wanted to be involved with anyone. She never missed a chance to remind Sendatsu of what he had done, although he always refused to fight back. The sign of a guilty conscience, she told herself. But she could not help comparing Sendatsu with Huw. She had thought the elf was everything Huw was not — strong, powerful, confident, a warrior, as well as exotically good-looking.

But Huw had never lied to her.

And since he had come up with the idea of the Dragon Warriors, he had shown his strength, his courage and confidence. The way he dealt with the various village chiefs had been impressive. He used persuasion, conviction and inspiration to get them to come along with his dream of a free, united Vales. Watching the recruits sit around a fire, spellbound, as he told them of his dreams, watching village chiefs shake his hand and declare he was the man to lead Vales — it was stirring.

Yet he was still the gentle, kind Huw she had first grown to know in Cridianton. Singing and performing with him, she had been able to put Sendatsu out of her mind. Once or twice she thought Huw might have tried to kiss her, indeed at one point their heads had almost been touching — but then he moved away.

She wondered if he was thinking of Sendatsu, and her reaction to the elf's lies and betrayal. And she wondered if she might be better off making the first move. It was strange, as she had been sure she had wanted nothing more to do with men and their lies and their lust, but time softened that stance, slowly. And she could see the village women looking at Huw differently. When they rode in, their eyes always went to Sendatsu. But when they rode out, it was to Huw that they looked.

Not that Huw noticed. But perhaps, if she left it too long, he might ...

For now it was safe enough but she resolved to keep an eye on the young bard.

With almost all of Gwent protected they headed north, into Powys, the part of Vales with the mines and the riches. Here they found the Forlish raiders again, looking for the gold that followed the precious metals being dug out of the ground. The big mining villages had been hit and hit again, usually when most of the men were underground. Here the people had become desperate. Miners did not want to leave homes and families unprotected, so production from the mines had dropped right away. People were scared and more than scared. Families were leaving, looking for somewhere safer, and the village chiefs were at their wits' end.

When Huw arrived, riding at the head of more than a hundred men, he was the answer to their desperate prayers. At first, of course, he nearly caused a panic. Nobody recognised the dragon banner and the mere sight of so many armed men had women and children running, screaming. They were met with a grim-faced mob of miners, faces and hands streaked with dirt but the picks, axes and shovels in their hands were clean and well cared for. It took some quick talking — mainly to hear the Velsh accents — before they were accepted.

The presence of so many miners, as well as huge piles of spoil from the pits, made protecting these villages fast and easy.

Even though Forlish raiders could arrive at any day, between the dragons and miners, earthen walls were thrown up in a day, while in another day there were enough elven crossbows to leave it well protected. There were always men willing to join the Dragon Warriors rather than dig for a living, although Huw could promise them no money, just food and a great deal of pain at Sendatsu's hands. The pits also used small horses, ponies really, to drag carts of soil and ore around and Huw used almost all of his remaining Forlish gold to buy the small, tough horses, as well as pay smiths to make hundreds of arrowheads.

They had quite a force now, an impressive sight, even if most of them were mounted on pit ponies rather than battle chargers, and there was not one of them over twenty summers.

But they believed. They believed in Huw when he told them about a free Vales, where all would help each other. They wept when he sang them the song he and Rhiannon had written for them and for Vales itself. Huw called it 'Land of My Fathers' and they clamoured to learn the words, the lilting Velsh voices joining together each night to shout them to the skies. They sang it when they rode into a new village, to announce their presence and prove they were Velsh.

They even sung it when they trained, although they only just had the breath for it. Sendatsu was ruthless with them, holding nothing back when it came to improving them.

'Better take your punishment here, rather than when you meet the Forlish,' he told them.

He did not know whether he was teaching them the right way to fight, for the Forlish did not battle man to man but stood shoulder to shoulder in the shield wall. But it was all he knew — for now, it would have to do. They were changing every day, getting stronger, faster, more skilful.

Sendatsu had had many sensei during his years of training, as well as his father's methods, and he tried to take something from all of them. As for his father, Jaken's way was his inspiration — to do exactly the opposite.

At first he praised the recruits grudgingly but when some of them began to hold their own against him, force him to fully exert himself to beat them, the praise came naturally.

Initially he tried to stay apart from them. After all, soon he would be returning to Dokuzen. But, even in Powys, the same old stories about the elves had been spread far and wide and the answers he sought were as elusive as ever.

It was doubly frustrating. At every mining village, or farming village or fishing village they stopped at, there were elven buildings. Most were beautiful, some were wrecks and some had been crudely rebuilt, but all were poignant reminders of home. Or was it still home? With each passing day, Dokuzen seemed further away, both literally and figuratively. Try as he might, he could not stop himself from becoming involved with the Velsh struggle.

He missed his children, an ache so deep it physically hurt, but now he was imagining a different way to get them back. More and more, the temptation was there to take them, get Asami and leave behind Dokuzen, live out here. The days were passing swiftly and Huw's plan was coming to fruition — there was a real chance of making a whole country out of Vales. If that happened, then they could search for magical humans much more easily.

But, if Huw was planning to trick him once more, he had a new plan. At the next full moon he would talk to Asami, get her help to get his children and bring them all out of Dokuzen. His young dragons might not be as good as the elves just yet but, with more training, they would be the match of a Council Guard. If he could but march into Jaken's villa with a score of them at his back, then he would hold his children in his arms once more ... it was a thought to give him hope, at least. No matter what, there would be an end to his torment out here.

The recruits fell asleep each day, completely exhausted by the endless marching and training. At first the only ones awake barely an hour after dusk were usually Sendatsu, Huw and Rhiannon. Sendatsu left the other two to talk and instead wrapped himself in a blanket and dreamed of his children.

But the recruits thrived under his training and soon he sat with the best of them, talking about many things. He liked their company, which was something he had never imagined — although it had the bonus of not having Rhiannon make endless sharp comments about him.

The tombs of their forefathers were nestled beside a stream that fed the lake at Dokuzen's heart and supplied water for much of the city. So making their way out to the tombs was easy enough. But, as they saw instantly, getting inside was going to be difficult.

Torches burned at every corner of the building, while a squad of guards patrolled, or sat in the shadows of the ornate front entrance.

'It looks like Jaken has left plenty of guards here still, despite the festival — almost as if he knew someone might be coming,' Asami said, looking hard at Gaibun.

His face was partly obscured but it did not seem to change.

'It was an obvious precaution. I am sure he knows much of what the Magic-weavers plan,' he said coolly. 'Are you sure you want to go ahead with this?'

'What choice do we have, if we want to get Sendatsu back?'

'Well, are you doing it for the right reasons?'

'What do you mean? If you are not here to help me, then you can go any time ...'

'That's not what I said,' he interrupted. 'But are you trying to get Sendatsu back to help him or to salve the guilt you are feeling for helping Sumiko send him away? I will help you either way but you should be certain in your own mind which it is.'

'It is to help him,' she said immediately.

Gaibun smiled. 'Well then, we only have the guards to worry about.'

Asami ground her teeth in frustration. 'Sumiko knew guards would not stop me, where they would give any other Magic-weaver pause,' she spat.

'Then we shall just have to get in there without being seen,' Gaibun said lightly.

Asami studied the area carefully. Once this had been beautiful gardens but they had been allowed to grow out of control over the past century. Now, however, someone had cut most of them down, clearing an open space for twenty paces in any direction around the building. But they had forgotten about the branches of the closest trees, which stretched almost to the roof.

'I'll need you to cause a diversion at the front, lead as many of them away as you can and keep them looking in that direction while I go in from the back.'

'They will expect something like that,' Gaibun warned.

'Not like this, they won't,' Asami promised.

Sendatsu's dragons had their first real test outside the large mining village of Merthyr. This village was set up high, giving it a perfect view of the surrounding countryside. They had only arrived the night before and work had barely begun on defences, let alone building enough crossbows for the villagers. But the lookouts they posted had seen a band of Forlish approaching.

'There're nearly forty of them,' Sendatsu reported. 'They will be here by noon — not enough time for us to make crossbows, let alone a wall.'

'Then we must ride out and meet them,' Huw said calmly. 'After all, we outnumber them more than three to one.'

'What? These boys aren't ready to take on that number of Forlish!' Sendatsu growled. 'We could lose half of them.'

'Then you tell me a way to defeat those Forlish without seeing fighting inside the village,' Huw demanded.

'Huw, we're not ready yet — I don't want to lose these boys,' Sendatsu pleaded.

Huw smiled, a little. 'What's this? Not only did you tell me we can't save everyone, but then you were walking around, praying to find Forlish to kill in your lust for revenge, after Rheged. Now you tell me you don't want to fight or risk anyone!'

Sendatsu was about to argue, then realised the truth. 'I don't want to see them die,' he admitted. 'I would rather they stay alive than see the Forlish punished.'

'Then find a way to win,' Huw said forcefully.

Sendatsu sighed and looked at the huge piles of spoil that marked the way into the village.

'All right,' he said thoughtfully.

'Good. I'll go and talk to the headman, make sure he knows what we are about to do — and that he needs to be grateful,' Huw said grimly.

Asami half wondered if Gaibun was really going to help her — or betray her. It was one of the reasons she had sent him away to make the first move on the tombs. She waited, trying to keep the nerves at bay, eyes struggling to pierce the darkness and see Gaibun in action. She told herself there was nothing to worry about. They may not have a marriage of love but they were still close. He was a man of honour, he had always been so. It had cost him, several times, in competitions against Sendatsu — just as it had cost his father against Jaken.

Still, as time dragged on and nothing happened, it became harder to convince herself. Just when she feared he was not going to act, the two torches at the front of the building were snuffed out by a sudden wind. Asami felt the breath of the magic and nodded approvingly.

The guards reacted instantly, some rushing to relight the torches, the others clustering together to watch the shadows, swords in hand.

As the torches spluttered back to life, a stone flew out of the night and struck one guard on the temple. Before the elf had even hit the ground, Asami — and the guards — saw a shape at the edge of the trees in the torchlight.

'After him!' someone ordered.

Four guards raced out into the night as the figure vanished once more. But that still left five elves out the front of the only entrance to the building.

Still, that was half of them gone, she reflected. Instantly she turned towards the back and reached out into the magic, bringing the trees alive.

The guards shouted as tree limbs suddenly sprouted longer, reached the roof and began to rip the tiles away, opening it up to the night sky.

'Stop them!'

Three of the guards raced around the back, where they began fighting the trees not with their swords but with magic. Asami could feel their attempts to drive her back and ruthlessly pressed forwards, overwhelming their limited magic abilities with her superior strength.

'Help!' one cried as they were driven to their knees.

The remaining two bent their concentration to the task of helping their comrades — and instantly Asami stopped the flow of magic, instead racing across the open ground. Distracted by the effort of using magic, their whole bodies directed towards the trees at the rear, they did not react quickly. Asami jumped high and took one out with a kick, then landed and struck the second across the back of the neck with the rigid edge of her hand. They fell, while the three at the back were already sprawled on the ground, stunned by her magical assault. She reached into the magic and forced open the chains on the door then, with a quick glance around her, stepped into the tombs.

Captain Leofric watched the village cautiously. He had been in Vales for the past month now, and what had at first seemed like a ridiculously easy task had been growing progressively harder. The Velsh villages had been easy to raid. A quick charge inside, fire a couple of houses, kill anyone who tried to stop them and grab food, valuables and women. It had been almost too easy. The Velsh had no weapons, no organisation and no defences. But then he had begun to come across villages fortified by walls. To a man used to smashing through the stone walls of Balian towns, the earthen or wooden walls looked small and flimsy. But he quickly learned he had neither the equipment nor the numbers to get through even these pitiful defences. Far from being slumbering sheep, these Velsh villages had teeth. They always had guards on and big dogs who barked warnings. Any attacks

400

were met with a stinging hail of small crossbow bolts. These may not be big enough to punch through shields but were deadly to his unarmoured men. One might not kill you, but they came in swarms. After losing six men in one attack, he learned to steer clear of these villages and strike only at the undefended ones.

But there were fewer of these around and his men were getting hungry — and restless. They had taken little plunder and were a long way from any taverns or whores. So Leofric had brought them into the northern province in the hopes of finding both more undefended villages and richer pickings.

'No wall around this one, sir — but they might have seen us coming,' his scout reported.

Leofric spat as he looked up at the village. He could tell it was there from the smoke, and while he could glimpse huts in among the mining spoil, there was little movement. He chewed his lip as he contemplated moving on in search of yet another village. He glanced over his shoulder at his men, who were eating the last of their food and trying to fix broken saddles and tack. Already a handful had horses that were going lame. They needed a rich haul.

'We go in. Fast. If they have seen us, why aren't they running?' he decided.

'Maybe they are planning a trap, sir,' his scout suggested.

'Velsh? A trap? With what? They have no army, no flag, no weapons — nothing. They won't be able to stop us,' Leofric snorted.

And so it seemed as they rode swiftly up the rutted path into the village. It was not too steep, for both animals and carts had to make the trip safely, which meant it did not travel in a straight line but instead zigzagged up the hillside. Nobody was running, there was no sign of alarm — it was just as he hoped, just as it had been when they had first come to Vales.

The horses, blowing hard from the long ride and then the gallop up the path, slowed down as they reached the top and began to thread their way through the piles of mine spoil. Ahead, Leofric could see both the village and a handful of people running away. He relaxed.

Then an arrow flew down and tore out his throat.

The shocked Forlish watched as their captain flew backwards out of his saddle and crashed into the ground, a white-feathered arrow sticking out of the bloody mess that had been his neck. But they had no time to react.

Men appeared on the top of the spoil piles now, men cheering and singing, standing beneath a flag of a red dragon. Men who held strange bows. These were not the crossbows that loosed small bolts no thicker than a finger or much longer than a foot. These unleashed arrows the length of a man's arm, tipped with a wicked steel head. Many of these missed but those that hit sent men and horses tumbling to the ground. And the Forlish were packed together, making them an easier target.

'Off the horses! At them!'

The sergeants jumped down from the horses, which could never hope to make it up the slopes of loose earth and rock, and led a rush at their tormentors. But the slopes were almost impossible to climb, especially while holding swords. Men needed to use both hands to steady themselves and, even then, many slipped and fell, rolling back down and often bringing others down with them. All the time the arrows snapped at them, often missing but also striking and hurling men over. Then, just as the first Forlish were getting close to their prey, one of the bowmen threw down his bow and drew his sword.

'At them!' he bellowed and lunged down the slope.

Bows clattered to the ground, swords were drawn and the Forlish were astonished to see the bowmen run at them.


The tombs were even darker and dustier than Asami remembered. She had a picture of it in her mind, and an idea where the books would be waiting at the back, but it was too hard to see, even though moonlight was shining into the tombs from the cracks she had opened in the roof and back wall. She could have used the dust that lay thickly on every surface, ignited it into a fiery ball — but she feared she would need all her energy for magic before this night was out. Besides, she had placed a candle in her pack for a reason.

She lit it swiftly and then hurried forwards, dodging past the actual tombs to where she remembered the cabinet of books stood.

They were right where she expected them to be — a huge case pressed against a wall. Swiftly she scanned it for a lock, not really paying attention to the books inside. Once she had access to them she could scan them properly, find the ones she needed. She planned to smash open the weapons cabinet afterwards, take some of those items as well. With a little luck, she could take just one or two books, lock up the book cabinet again and nobody would know these had been her real target.

The lock was tucked underneath and she reached for the magic, using it to heat the metal inside the lock, allow it to spring open. With a reluctant squeal, it clicked back and she could throw open the doors. She had expected the books to smell stale and musty but there was nothing like that. No matter, Sendatsu's return was within her grasp. She reached out a hand and touched one, feeling its slightly rough cover ...

Next moment the whole building shook, like a tree in a gale. She snatched her hand back instinctively before she realised it could not be her.

'Come out! We have the building surrounded! Don't make us come in there!' a magically enhanced voice boomed through the tombs.

Asami glanced up in horror. It sounded much like Jaken's voice. And if he was here, then she had been betrayed. She would be lucky to escape with mere banishment ... If she sealed up the cabinet now, pretended this had all been a joke, she might just escape. But if she left without the precious books, then Sendatsu would be lost forever. There would be no second chance at this.

Even as she thought that, she reached in to grab a handful of books — only for another hand to haul her back and away.

Sendatsu had hidden on the rear slope of the spoil with half the dragons. It had been a hard wait but he kept his fears to himself. He needed to set an example. Several of the men had slipped down to the bottom to empty their bowels — only the fact they were so young and thought they were invincible thanks to their elven training stopped even more signs of fear. So he smiled and tried to look relaxed, although inside he was worrying about keeping them safe. The thought of seeing them die had his insides knotting themselves ever tighter.

As the Forlish slowed at the top of the slope he rolled to his feet and stood, sighting on their officer. He willed the arrow to strike home — and let out a huge breath of relief when it tore out the man's throat, although he had been aiming for the chest. It was the signal and the dragons surged to their feet and began pouring arrows down. Most of these missed — but any that hit were deadly, while Sendatsu picked off man after man. He glanced left and right and the dragons were all standing strong. He looked down at the Forlish, struggling to climb up the piles of spoil to get to his boys, and dropped his bow. He had planned to just loose arrows at them but too many were missing. He would have to take them on. While he quailed at the thought, his dragons were taking so much heart from the simple act of singing that he drew his sword and pointed it at the Forlish.

'At them!' he bellowed and led the charge down the slope.

The leading Forlish looked up in surprise, for they had been concentrating just on staying on their feet. They were also tired, breathing hard from the climb — and Sendatsu and the dragons had all the momentum. Too much momentum, for once they began, it was impossible to stop. Sendatsu unleashed a massive cut that the first Forlishman could not block. His sword crashed through a despairing parry and sank deep into the man's chest. Sendatsu twisted his blade, ripping it clear, but could not recover in time to strike the next man. No matter. He swivelled and shoulder-charged the Forlishman, sending him flying and giving himself the time to use the tiger-claw stroke, which split apart a Forlish head.

Behind him his dragons flooded into the gap he had created, hacking and slashing with more enthusiasm than skill but using numbers and the advantage of speed and height to drive their veteran foes downhill. Above them was the flag bearer, the only dragon who had not charged, who instead waved the dragon flag from side to side.

From inside the village, Huw and Rhiannon saw the signal and led the rest of the dragons out, charging down the path into the Forlish who were falling back in disarray. It was too much for even troops as good as the Forlish, who turned and ran, grabbing their horses if they could, just sprinting for it if they could not get near a horse.

'Chase them! Get every horse, every sword you can!' Huw worked his crossbow, aiming at their legs to bring down as many Forlish as he could. A man might not die but neither could he run with one or more bolts in his legs.

The dragons responded, overtaking the runners, until only a dozen mounted Forlish were able to get away. The others, seeing themselves trapped, turned and fought back to back, surrounded by knots of dragons who brought them down one by one, like dogs flinging themselves on a bear.

Sendatsu seemed to be everywhere, his sword flashing red wherever he went, and he always seemed to be where a dragon was in danger, until there were no more Forlish standing, only those lying flat, hands on their heads, or flopping around in agony.

'We did it!' Huw reined in his horse by Sendatsu, who was covered with Forlish blood.

'This was nothing,' Sendatsu growled, looking to where two of his dragons were trying to help a dying third.

'Wrong. This was the start. Now the people will see we are just as good as the Forlish,' Huw corrected.


'Time to go,' Gaibun said firmly.

'But the books — Jaken — what are you doing here?' Asami cried.

'Trying to save your life. Jaken is out there with half the Border Patrol and in no mood to take prisoners. I saw them coming and doubled back here — most are still flooding through the woods but if we don't go now, they will have the place surrounded. I gave them conflicting orders, sent most of them off in the wrong directions, but, while they recognised my voice, they will also recognise we are not in the area I sent them unless we hurry.'

'But the books ... Sendatsu ...'

'Quickly then! Time is running out!'

Asami saw the ones with blue covers, as Sumiko had said, and grabbed a handful at random. She stuffed them into her bag and turned to go.

'This way.' Gaibun pulled her towards the back of the building, not towards the front. 'Jaken's own archers are out there. To go out the front is death.'

'But there is no other way out!'

'You made one when you used the trees. How else did you think I got here?'

They hurried to the far end, where the stone wall had split and made an opening wide enough for one person to squeeze through.

'Wait!' Asami held Gaibun back. 'First let me use the trees to clear our path.'

She closed her eyes and reached into the magic, feeling the trees come alive around her, the branches sweeping across the open ground in all directions. Elves were trying to fight her, to stop the trees, but she pushed through the opposition, although she could feel her strength draining.

The wooden doors at the front of the building blew in, clattering and smashing their way into the stone tombs. It broke her concentration and both she and Gaibun ducked instinctively.

Next moment the dark interior was ablaze with light — literally ablaze as a dozen lanterns were hurled inside, smashing and spreading pools of burning oil.

'Time to go.' Gaibun squeezed through the gap and held back a hand for her. She slipped through, turning sideways, panting for breath, her legs wobbly after what she had done with the magic. The old stone was unbelievably thick and rough and she felt her clothing catch and snag on it as she squeezed through. Gaibun held her left hand, pulling her out, while her right was clasped around the top of the bag of books.

'We're clear, the elves out here are all down — but not for long. Move!' Gaibun pulled on her hand but the bag was stuck. Desperately she pulled at it with her remaining strength — and it ripped and tore, the books spilling out back into the building. She stared at it in shocked surprise, trying to think but struggling with the magic fatigue. She could have sworn that bag could not have ripped. The tear had appeared as if by magic ...

'Come on!' Gaibun hauled her away and she could not fight him.

'Wait!' She dropped to the ground, the only way to get him to stop. 'The books — they fell out ...' She held up the torn bag as evidence.

'We cannot go back,' Gaibun told her grimly.

She opened her mouth to protest but an arrow zipped between them before she could speak.

'Move!' Gaibun yanked her to her feet and she found new strength to run, while arrows whistled past them. Only the dark, and their dark clothing, saved them.

Once in the trees, they stopped, looked back. Not only were Border Patrol pouring around the building, spreading out and searching for them, but smoke was pouring out of the old tombs. And none were making any move to fight the spreading fire, even though the stream was right beside it.

'They're going to let it burn,' Gaibun said, confirming what she was already thinking.

'We can't ... we have to do something,' Asami moaned.

'We have to get away. That is all we can do.' Gaibun began guiding her away. She did not have the strength, nor the will to stop him.

'But Sendatsu ...'

'Will have to find his own way home,' Gaibun said coldly.

Almost blinded by tears of frustration, her mind a whirl of exhaustion and despair, Asami stumbled along beside him.

Although they had lost three of their dragons, with another eight wounded, it made a dramatic difference. Not only had the survivors gained a swagger but the villagers had seen other Velshmen drive away the Forlish. Their losses were made up in a day, with more than a score of young men eager to sign up, while 'Land of My Fathers' was being sung around fires every night.

And the headman was completely won over. Merthyr was a rich village, even able to afford to buy elven buildings from poorer villages, ship them up to Merthyr and then rebuild them there. The tin that came out of Merthyr was much in demand to make brass and Huw had suspected the headman, Griff, would be less than impressed at the prospect of becoming part of Vales if it meant handing over some of his riches. But, after seeing the dragon flag drive back the Forlish, he was caught up in the mood of excitement.

'I never thought we could do that but if your boyos can keep the Forlish away from us, I'd be happy to be part of your Vales,' he said.

'It's not going to be my Vales ...' Huw began.

'Come now! Who else is it going to be? It's you who's making this all come true,' Griff declared.

Huw was pleased to have the man's support — although the rest of the meeting left him feeling discomfited. The richest villagers, as well as their wives and families, had all gathered inside an elven-built hall. While he wanted to tell them about a united Vales, they had other things in mind. Once they discovered he was unmarried, some of the women had almost thrown their daughters at him. He had never seen that before. Usually it was Sendatsu who got all the attention but the elf wanted to stay with his wounded dragons. At first Huw found the attention flattering but he was soon making excuses to get out of the meeting, as well as Merthyr, as fast as possible.

Rhiannon had also seen that, and made her think. She had been enjoying her relationship with Huw, the time they spent together working on songs and plans for Vales. The thought of him accepting one of the young women being propelled towards him, of losing him, began to haunt her. And not just because of their singing and music. She realised, with a jolt, the thought of Huw with another woman was too painful to imagine.

So, that night, while Sendatsu worked with the new dragons, she sat down with Huw.

'We had plenty of success at Merthyr. What are your plans for the next one?' she asked.

'Well, we need to head to the coast, visit some of the shipping villages, where our goods are bought and shipped south to Forland and beyond. Along the way, I need your help,' he admitted. 'When I began asking these headmen and village chiefs to join my idea of a united Vales, I did not think it would be me they would want as their leader.'

'Well, who else would they choose? You have the dream, you have the dragons, you have given them a flag, a song, pride. It is natural,' Rhiannon said. 'Sendatsu was right. You are the hero they need.'

Huw shook his head. 'We all are. We all bring something that the people need. By ourselves we would be nothing — only together can we help them.'

Rhiannon just smiled. Spending so much time with Huw told her he was not merely dissembling. He truly did not see himself as others saw him now. Gone was the uncertain bard, the man with doubt in every line of his face and body. Here was a confident man with a compelling voice and certainty he was doing the right thing for his people. The villagers, the dragons, the headmen — they could all see his vision when he sang it for them and knew only through him could it become reality.

She wished she had seen this Huw earlier.

'It is not enough to spin a tale of a united Vales. We must have a real plan for how it could work, how we could truly make a country from these scattered villages.'

'Me?' Rhiannon laughed. 'I don't know about making a country …'

'Do you think I do? But we must have something ready. Please, help me.'

Rhiannon looked into his eyes and realised he could have asked anything of her at that point and she would have agreed. But, unlike Sendatsu, he was not about to pounce, which made him all the more attractive.

They had a bundle of lambskins to write on, as well as ink, but it was too precious to waste with foolish ideas — they had to talk and think before putting the new Vales down in writing.

'The main thing has to be sharing some of the wealth around. But it can't be too much, or we shall put off all the richer villages in Powys,' Huw grumbled.

'Maybe each village has to put in a tenth of their goods — and then all of it is shared around equally,' Rhiannon suggested. 'Not too much to upset the big villages but enough to make a difference to the smaller.'

They worked on villages sending their chief to a central meeting, where all could decide important matters.

'But we can't have it that we need to get everyone's agreement. Two-thirds should be the figure. Otherwise we'd never agree to anything,' Huw reckoned.

'You need to negotiate on behalf of Vales with the Forlish and Balians and Landish. Now, each village is competing against each other, so the buyers can go from one to the next, can beat your prices down,' Rhiannon pointed out.

And so they went on, trying to come up with a country where life would be fair, where all could live well.

'Sendatsu can show us how to eat better, live better — live longer,' Huw said, then moved on hastily when he saw the expression on her face at the mere mention of Sendatsu's name. 'I'll have to give up command of the dragons — they should be independent. Otherwise people will do things out of fear of the dragons, not because it is best for Vales.'

'But you will need them. People don't do things because it is right. Often only greed or self-interest or fear will make them,' she warned.

'Then perhaps you should command the dragons.' He grinned.

'I would do a good job. After all, I am a better fighter than you.' Rhiannon smiled back.

'Oh, really? Is this the same girl who froze on stage in front of King Ward, and had to be saved by me playing the "Song of Elves"?' Huw teased.

'I'll show you!' Rhiannon laughed, leaning across to try to push him over.

Moons of riding and days of wielding shovels to help villages build defensive walls had added muscle to Huw but she caught him by surprise and he went over backwards; he flailed his hand, trying to stop himself, and only succeeded in bringing her down as well. Next moment they were lying down, side by side, just inches away from each other.

Huw's laugh died as he realised just how close they were. Her thigh lay across his, while her tunic was rucked tight around her breasts, which were almost touching his chest. He looked into her eyes and wanted so much to kiss her. And more than kiss her.

But then he found himself thinking about her father, perhaps out in Vales this very night. And the lies he had told to get her up here — and he could not.

'I am sorry. I did not mean to …' he said hurriedly, then rolled to his feet and strode away, trying to control himself — and stop himself from going back.

Rhiannon lay there, bewildered. She had been sure Huw had been about to kiss her — she had seen it in his eyes. She was tempted to go after him but could see him walking over to where Sendatsu and the new dragons still worked by firelight.

'Here's Huw now! Will you give us a song to ease these brave lads' sleep?' Sendatsu called.

Huw forced a smile. 'Of course. And then I need to talk to you.'

Sendatsu nodded. He sat and listened, watching the faces of his dragons as Huw sang to them, and realised he loved them. He had given them his knowledge but they had also given him something as well. Huw was the leader here but he could not just sit back and avoid responsibility any longer. He had run away from things all his life — now he felt the temptation to make changes to his own life, even to Dokuzen. With a force like this, he could make a difference.

'Sleep well — you'll need it for the morrow,' Huw told them. 'If you are to march and fight with the dragons!'

They cheered him, but Sendatsu could see there was something wrong with Huw, and willingly followed the bard away from the new dragons.

'What is it?' he asked urgently.

'Rhiannon — we were about to kiss!' Huw said desperately.

'So? Isn't that what you wanted? Why not kiss her?' Sendatsu grunted, trying not to think of Rhiannon's long, slim legs …

'But I haven't told her about her father yet!'

Sendatsu groaned. 'What did I say? It is going to come back to bite you. You have to tell her, and tell her now. Why have you left it so long?'

'Well, I wanted to make sure she would listen to what I had to say and not think I was a liar like …'

'Like me,' Sendatsu finished grimly.

Huw shrugged. 'Sorry.'

'No matter. Look, you have to do it now, or she will be asking questions. If you were so close, she will want to know why you did not kiss her.'

Huw nodded shakily. 'I shall.'

'Do it! Explain what happened but don't say her father is loose in Vales. Not yet anyway. Let her digest that he is a bastard who was about to sell her to Ward for gold. When she accepts that, then let her know he is up here looking for her, trying to drag her back to Cridianton and Ward's bed.'

Huw nodded again. 'I shall,' he declared.

'Good man! You two should be together. Just don't tell me what happens afterwards.' Sendatsu clapped him on the back.

Huw threw back his shoulders and strode towards where he had left Rhiannon. He would tell her. It was time to get it off his chest, he resolved. Then they could have a real future together.

But Rhiannon was not by the fire, where he had left her. He looked around, suddenly afraid, to see her beckon to him from the shadows, then walk away, down into a hollow, far from where Sendatsu and the dragons were around other fires.

Feeling his stomach swooping around, Huw hurried over, trying to stop his hands shaking and his mouth drying out. He was more nervous now than he had been before performing for Ward at Cridianton. But he had to get it out. They could not have a life together until she knew the truth.

'Rhiannon, there is something very important I need to tell you,' he began as he walked down into the grassy hollow, trying, unsuccessfully, to see in the darkness.

But he did not get the chance to say anything else. Rhiannon took his hand and pulled hard, yanking him down to the ground. She leaned in and kissed him on the lips for what seemed like forever and no time at all.

All other thought fled from his mind and he helped her to rip his clothes off.

# 24

*I can remember only too well what snapped me out of my melancholic mist. I was visiting my wife's grave and kneeling beside her gravestone, wishing she was there with me, when a pair of young elves attacked. How they did not kill me I do not know. I heard a whisper of movement behind me and, even in my grief, still retained enough of my skills to roll to my left, so the sword struck the top of my wife's gravestone, rather than the top of my head.*

*I always carried a sword and it was in my hand when I rolled to my feet. My eyes cleared for the first time in moons and I recognised my young attackers — both Council Guards and members of my own clan. Too late I remembered that Naibun had removed my guard detail, at my request.*

*'What are you doing?' I demanded.*

*'You must die, traitor!' one roared and then they were both rushing at me. But although my hands had held tears rather than swords since my wife's death, the old moves came back to me. My first attacker lost his head, the second could not move with my sword deep in his lungs.*

*'Who sent you? Why did you do this?' I demanded of the dying youth. 'Answer me and I shall ease your passing.'*

*His only answer was to spit in my face.*

*I finished him off and wiped my face clean. Now I knew I was in danger — but I still did not realise the direction.*

'Work harder!' Broyle ordered.

Sweating men cursed him under their breath but redoubled their efforts.

After a day of fruitlessly searching for the elves who had escaped from him, he had discovered his prey had slipped past him and were now fortifying the village of Brynmawr. He was tempted to launch an attack but he had too few men — and the business with the elves escaping had shaken his men's confidence. Better to stick to his original plan, he reasoned.

He found a pair of farms nestled in an isolated valley, surrounded by thick woods. And once the families living there were buried deep, it became the perfect base. He had men out hunting, others raiding villages for items they needed — sometimes he even sent Hector into a village to buy something they would have struggled to find in a night-time raid — and always he rode the trails, searching for more men. He had put together nearly two hundred now, not quite as many as he wanted but probably sufficient for the task. Through much trial and error, he had managed to create a crude catapult and was now working on another. Men had slaved to build it and now to master it, able to hurl a boulder several hundred yards. It was nothing like the huge trebuchets and ballistae down with the army in Balia but he hoped it was easily enough for a walled village.

With that was a huge ram, an entire tree trunk with its roots trimmed to make a fearsome club head. Just getting it to the village was going to be a feat in itself. Once there, he planned to build a wheeled base for it, shielded, where twenty men could push it in close in relative safety and then smash a hole in the walls.

The men had also been working with axes, building huge, heavy shields, which covered not just the chest but the whole body. Any advance would be slow but completely protected. His whole battle plan called for getting as many men as possible inside the walls. There they would be like foxes in a hen house.

He planned to kill everyone and everything, save perhaps one person, who could then tell the tale of the fools who tried to defy the might of the Forlish!

'Are we ready?' Hector asked impatiently. Sitting here, having little to do, had grated on his nerves but he recognised Broyle's drive and vision and was not prepared to defy him.

'Yes,' Broyle said finally. 'It will take us until the next full moon to get everything across to Patcham. And hopefully we can find a few more men on the way. Go into every village we come across. Spend some money and leave the message for the elf and bard with your daughter. We want them to reach the village before we do. If they arrive afterwards, they might be too scared or too clever to go inside.'

'What if they don't take the bait?' Hector demanded. 'I did this because you promised me my daughter back!'

'If they fail to save Patcham, it will destroy their plans. They have to try and save the village,' Broyle dismissed. 'If they do not, they will betray everything they have done. I hope they are too afraid! It will make the rest of the country easy pickings. They will run and nowhere will be safe for them.'

'But what if they bring in extra men?' Hector pressed.

'Let them. They won't stand against us,' Broyle boasted. 'One last thing — don't let anyone know it is your daughter. If word gets back to them, they will know it is a trap for sure and might do something clever, like emptying the village. And we can't let that happen. We have to make an example of them, show the Velsh they cannot hope to stand against us.'

Hector looked at the busy camp and nodded. There was no way a pack of ragged-arse sheep-shaggers could stand against these men.

'We move at dawn! Move or I'll strap you to the front of the ram and wheel you out for the Velsh bows myself!' Broyle roared.

Nothing grew in Sumiko's garden. The earth was bare, hard and smooth, revealing nothing. It had been two days since the tombs were destroyed, although that knowledge had been kept from most of Dokuzen's residents. As few had ever visited — and all had been discouraged over the last few years — Sumiko doubted it would ever become wide knowledge. She had raged around her garden, wiping out everything when she heard — although she had had time to think since, to try to see how she could drag something out of this disaster.

'Jaken suspects my hand in this but, seeing as I and the rest of the Magic-weavers were sitting with Daichi and the Council while you were at the tombs, there is nothing he can prove,' she said. 'Does he suspect you?'

Asami smiled wanly. 'Of course — but he can prove nothing. Gaibun got me away from there safely before returning and joining the search, to cover himself.'

'But did he betray you from the start? Did he guide Jaken to you?'

Asami shook her head defiantly. She had lain awake, worrying that very thing, but could not force herself to believe it. 'He is an honourable elf. He would not do such a thing. Besides, he did not have the time. I barely had time to get into the tombs before the Border Patrol were on us. No doubt Jaken was ready for us.'

'And the books were destroyed — you are sure of that?'

Asami hesitated. The race away through the woods had been a blur. She had been so tired, so drained by the magic and failure that she expected to be caught at any moment. Yet the dozens of Border Patrol had missed her. 'The tombs were ablaze when we left and I dared not wait and see. But nobody was making any move to fight the fire.'

Sumiko sighed. 'And you were not even identified?'

'I do not believe so.'

'It seems too convenient you were able to get in there, see the books, yet not be able to take them away — and still be able to escape,' she said absently.

'I know, sensei. It seemed to me that Jaken had it all planned. He wants us to think the books have been destroyed. I should have got at least some of them out — I am sure magic was used to keep them all in there,' Asami agreed.

Sumiko kneeled down, let a handful of dirt trickle through her fingers. She straightened back up and the first shoots began to push through the ground, easing their way back into patterns.

'We shall let Jaken enjoy his victory for a little while,' she mused. 'The books have not been destroyed. I did not think Jaken would have left such power waiting for anyone to steal. You proved it. His first response was to burn the tombs, not capture the thieves. He even let you get away with the tale of the fire. Surely it would have been easier for the vaunted Border Patrol to grab you than it was to let you go. So we know he must have the books and it has cost us nothing.'

'So what now?'

'Now it gets difficult. It all depends on whether Jaken told the Council everything or whether he plays his own game. If he told them, it is within their chambers. But, if I know Jaken, he will hide it from the Council. I think they are in his villa somewhere.'

'So how do we get them out?'

'I do not know yet,' Sumiko admitted. 'Give me time to think on our next move. Jaken is a cunning and dangerous opponent. He has been a step ahead of us. We must not only catch up but overtake him.'

'As you wish, sensei. My apologies for not succeeding.'

Sumiko nodded briefly, let Asami walk away before turning back to her plants. She let them grow while her mind wandered.

'Sensei — can I help?' Oroku asked gently.

'No, this is something I need to do,' Sumiko replied absently. 'We have learned something of value — Jaken underestimates us, and he also knows the value of what is in those books. Best of all, it did not even cost us the girl to discover it. We can still use her.'

'Do you think she begins to suspect our motives?'

'She has no choice but to trust us.' Sumiko smiled. 'She has to cling to hope, for it is all she has left.'

'Has Asami said anything about the Magic-weavers' plans?'

Gaibun shook his head. It was a treacherous path he was walking but he knew the prize at the end was worth it.

'No, sir. Today is the first time she has gone back to see Sumiko.'

Jaken chuckled. 'The fools! They think I will forget about them! They might be gifted with magic but they failed the test when it comes to thinking.'

'Sir?'

'They know the books have not been destroyed. I will give them that, at least. But to imagine I would be so crude as to see this as my final victory — do they think me human?'

'I wouldn't know, sir.'

Jaken looked Gaibun up and down critically. 'You would be wondering why I didn't destroy the books. Or at least I hope you are — or I have sadly misjudged you as my heir apparent.'

'I have wondered about it, sir,' Gaibun admitted.

'Good. So I shall tell you. But breathe a word of this to another soul and you shall wish for Sendatsu's fate.'

Gaibun nodded hastily.

'There are many lies in the books. But there is also a great truth. A truth I discovered. We did not seal ourselves away from the humans because we were afraid of them.' Jaken paused, relished the anticipation the young elf could not keep from his face. 'It was the other way around. Our forefathers wanted to seal us away to protect the humans. They feared we would rule the humans, treat them like slaves. With our knowledge and magic, we could fashion an empire across this continent. And, once I control the Council, that is what we shall do.'

He smiled at the shock on Gaibun's face. 'I have kept the books under close guard since I discovered what lay in there. Until now I could not act, because I needed to control the Council. That is within our grasp. Once Daichi is out of the way, I shall rule and bend the Magic-weavers to me. With their help, we shall break out of the magic barrier around Dokuzen and rule this pitiful continent from sea to sea. I shall be the emperor and you will be my right hand.'

Gaibun bowed low.

'I long to see the day,' he said hoarsely.

'It will come soon,' Jaken said complacently. 'Once the Magic-weavers think I have been lulled into stupidity, they will try to take the books. I shall stop them and use that as my reason to take control of the Council.'

'You honour me today, sir.' Gaibun bowed again.

'I treat you like a son,' Jaken corrected. 'One I can be proud of.'


Even the youngest dragons could tell something had changed in camp. They woke to hear Huw singing — a deep, rumbling joyful greeting to the dawn. The smile their leader wore was infectious and many of them, particularly the ones who had been with them from the start, grinned at each other and winked at the sight of Huw and Rhiannon together.

'You are a lucky man.' Sendatsu nudged him.

'What do you mean?'

'You look like the cat that has swallowed the cream!'

Huw flushed a little.

'You two deserve each other,' Sendatsu told him solemnly. Part of him felt a pang. If only he and Asami could be together ... He put that thought away and tried to concentrate on Huw's happiness instead. 'See, I told you there was nothing to worry about.' He slapped Huw on the arm. 'You told her the truth and look what happened!'

For the first time that morning, Huw's smile faltered.

'What?' Sendatsu stopped in horror. 'You didn't tell her!'

'I meant to. I started to, but then things got distracted ...' Huw said helplessly.

'You idiot!' Sendatsu groaned. 'How could you bed her without telling her the truth first?'

'Well, when she's not wearing anything, and grabs hold of you, it's bloody hard to stop!' Huw flared.

Sendatsu opened his mouth, then nodded his agreement. 'All right. But how do we get out of this mess? If you tell her now, she is just going to think you tricked her into bed — even though you didn't get anywhere near a bed — just the same way I did.'

'Well, perhaps when we have made everything official, sworn our love to one another and Walked The Tree at Midwinter, she will listen then?' Huw said hopefully.

'That's assuming we can keep it a secret as long as then,' Sendatsu said darkly.

Huw thought about that for a moment.

'Well, maybe I should go and talk to her now. Sit her down and explain everything? I mean, she seduced me, not the other way around.'

Sendatsu's face showed his struggle.

'I know I'm the one who's been telling you to be honest but now I have some truth for you. If you tell her the morning after, you have to be prepared for her to walk away. She might have been the one who seduced you but that was a huge decision for her. After what I did, for her to make that commitment to you was enormous. She placed her trust in you. If you throw it back in her face the next morning, she might walk away and never come back.'

'I don't want that to happen! I don't know what I would do then,' Huw moaned.

'But she needs the truth. She deserves it. If you truly love her, you have to give her the truth and trust her — and hope.'

Huw's face twisted in an agony of indecision.

'Do you think she will really walk away, after last night?' he ventured.

Sendatsu sighed. 'You have to be prepared for it. I hurt her badly. All this time she has seen you as the trustworthy one. In a way, that makes your lies even worse.'

Huw looked away. He wanted to be honest with Rhiannon. After all, he had saved her back in Cridianton — just not from quite the same fate as he had described. But the thought of being without her ... If the night where he had sat in his father's chair, listening to Sendatsu and Rhiannon, had been the worst of his life, last night had been the best. Losing her now, in the moment of winning her ...

'I can't do it,' he confessed.

'Man, you have to!' Sendatsu urged. 'If you don't tell her, she will find out somehow. The lie between you will sour and poison everything you have.'

Still Huw agonised.

'What are you two talking about?' Rhiannon greeted warmly.

They both jumped, guiltily, but she did not notice, as she was too caught up in her own happiness. Last night Huw had sworn his love for her, had promised they would Walk The Tree together at Midwinter. She had believed him utterly. It all made sense now. She had been foolish, naïve when she fell into bed with Sendatsu. Her head had been full of dreams about Dokuzen, as well as her own ambitions. But Sendatsu's betrayal, while bitter, had at least opened her eyes to what was right in front of her. Without that, she might still be ignoring Huw and his obvious love for her — something real and not the product of a fairy tale.

'About the training,' Huw answered quickly and although Sendatsu gave him a warning look, he said nothing.

'Well, hadn't we better begin? The day is getting away from us,' Rhiannon pointed out.

'Of course!' Huw raced off instantly.


He was silent, thinking, as they rode towards the next village.

'Is there something the matter? Are you regretting last night?' Rhiannon asked finally, after they had ridden for several miles without saying a word.

Huw turned and his smile was instantly genuine. 'I could never regret last night. And I meant every word that I said,' he said hoarsely.

Rhiannon laughed. 'Good! I was getting worried there — thought you might be thinking of that big-breasted blonde back at Merthyr. What is a blonde doing in a Velsh village anyway? Must be some Forlish blood there!'

'No — of course not!' Huw snorted. 'I hardly noticed her anyway!'

'So you did notice her then?' Rhiannon teased.

Huw fumbled and flustered for a moment, until Sendatsu came to his rescue.

'How about a song to ease the march?' he called.

Huw gratefully eased his lyre out and the two of them began to play and sing.

Sendatsu watched them, worried for Huw — and for Rhiannon when she found out the truth.

'Pick up your feet! And I want to see any riders drawing their bows. You never know when we could meet more Forlish!' he shouted at the dragons.

He found Huw was even more sensitive to the knowledge he held, and the danger the truth posed to his relationship with Rhiannon. So they headed back east, through Gwent and towards the tree outside Pontypridd, where he could again see Asami. Sendatsu was barely even bothering to ask people about what happened when the elves left, magic, or Aroaril now. His plan to seize his children and escape with Asami was forming, day by day. He had no intention of telling Huw he planned to take two squads of his best dragons into Dokuzen and escape with his children and Asami. This dream was beginning to consume his thoughts. Even though he could not find the answers Sumiko wanted, this would ensure he would see his children again. Keeping this from Huw was a warm glow inside, enabled him to get through each day.

And these began to blur. On and on they went, from village to village. Spreading the word until it began to spread before them. Now they rode into villages to be greeted by home-made dragon flags, as well as young men eager to become dragons. It began to take on a life of its own, with even the most doubting village chief forced to hand over men, food, horses and any weapons and agree to the idea of a united Vales in the face of such excitement among his people. And, with the numbers and knowledge of the young dragons, they could now throw up a wall around a village in a day, then ride on, the job done. From the northern coast, where Forlish, Landish and Balian boats were filled with iron, tin and coal, to the mining villages that dug the raw materials out of the ground, back into the farming villages of Gwent they spread the word. Many of these villages had suffered from the raids, had been living in fear — and Huw gave them back hope. He gave them a symbol to unite behind, a song to rally them and the knowledge one of their own had defeated the Forlish three times now. He even had an elf following him!

Sendatsu was also trying to spread his knowledge around these villages. After all, if he was to find a home somewhere quiet out here, he should make sure the people were happy to have him as a neighbour — and he might need their help as well. Every day he was noticing things being done by the Velsh that could be easily changed, make them healthier and let them live longer. Sensible things like ensuring the water was clean and boiled before drinking, cleaning their knives between chopping up raw meat and carving cooked joints. Not pissing inside their own homes and making sure their dung pits were far enough away from where they slept. He had tried to talk to them about the importance of cleaning as well, but there was only so much the humans were willing to take in. It was enough of a struggle to try to get clean clothes for himself, as well as take a bath more than every few days. But he was determined the dragons would not get sick and he made every effort to see they kept clean, had their latrine pits a long way from their campsites and boiled everything from food to water. Even so, at every village, one or two went down with stomach troubles and there was little that could be done to help.

Certainly there was a woman or two in every village who had some skill with herbs — but that did not always do the trick. And, as for the rest of the Velsh, herbs were of no use if a tree had crushed your legs.

Once again he wished he knew how to bring back the worship of Aroaril here or, better yet, find new evidence of it.

They did not want to leave anyone behind, so the sick were carried on the backs of horses until they recovered. Never staying in the one place more than a day seemed to help — although the dragons grumbled at being asked to make new camps and dig new pits every day.

Their crowning moment was when they ran across a small group of Forlish, no more than a score — and destroyed them. The dragons now numbered over three hundred and the raiders stood no chance.

Villages were now repelling other raiders — two attacks had been turned back by the massed crossbows — and reports of bands of raiders were few and far between. Smoke was no longer staining the sky. The Velsh were beginning to talk about the peace afterwards.

It was a heady time for Huw, between the acceptance of the villages, the feeling they were really making progress in protecting the people, the development of the dragons and, most importantly of all, Rhiannon.

He had not told her the full story about what had happened back in Cridianton but he was almost ready to. He was nearly confident enough she would listen to the truth.

He was worried about Sendatsu leaving them, for he could sense the elf's desire to see his children again far outweighed his willingness to help the Velsh. It was tempered, somewhat, by the knowledge many of the young dragons were almost ready to pass on his knowledge and in fact were even now helping out the new recruits.

Once they had gone back through Gwent it would also be time to travel again into the most southerly province, Rheged. After their earlier experience there, Huw was dreading it. With so many dragons behind them, he knew it would be very different this time but no doubt it had been devastated. There were few raiders around Powys and Gwent was well protected, which meant they had to be all down there.

Sometimes Sendatsu hoped this westward march would give him something he could offer to Sumiko and Asami. He also wondered if Asami had lived up to her promise and found another way to bring him home. If not, he would take in his dragons. They weren't actually his, more Huw's, but he was confident the dragons were loyal enough that they would follow him wherever he went.

He admired Huw for what he was doing. The young bard had been nobody, had no training and his father had been a farmer. Yet he was bending the whole of Vales to his vision of a united country. He had not only seized responsibility, he had embraced it. Sendatsu admired him for it — but did not want to copy him. No, he wanted a quiet life, with his children.

If only Huw would take his advice and be truthful with Rhiannon ...


'Maybe we shouldn't do anything,' Gaibun suggested. 'If the Magic-weavers try anything, Jaken plans to seize control of the Council and then summon the clans and use them to crush the humans. When he does that, he will end the barrier. We can use the confusion to bring Sendatsu back.'

Asami gaped at him. She had listened to his words with growing horror. 'And having Jaken as Elder Elf, watching him ride out of Dokuzen and crush the humans, turn them into our slaves will be a good thing?' she finally gasped.

'What choice do we have? To put our faith in the Magic-weavers is a mistake. Jaken knows they plan to come after him — he wants them to do it. He will use it as his excuse to take control of the Council, tell everyone that Daichi was not strong enough to keep the Magic-weavers in line.'

'But this is wrong. So wrong. The humans will welcome us with open arms — and we shall destroy their lives. I can't be a part of that.'

'So what do you suggest? If we join with Sumiko, we doom ourselves. Jaken is a step ahead of the Magic-weavers.'

'I don't know, but I cannot help Jaken turn himself into an emperor. Our forefathers would be turning in their tombs.'

'If only we could get word to Sendatsu,' Gaibun pondered.

Asami sighed. 'Thank you for telling me this. I know Jaken's offer must be tempting and I can give you nothing in return.'

'I told you I would show you I have changed,' Gaibun said stoutly. 'You mean so much more to me than a promise from Jaken. He tricked and betrayed my father, insulted his honour.

Does he really think I will turn my back on everything my family taught me for personal gain?'

'He believes everyone thinks as he does,' Asami said bitterly. 'But you are right when you say the Magic-weavers are not prepared for him. I'll talk to Sumiko. Carefully. We have to do something, find a way to stop Jaken's plans. I fear time is running out for Sendatsu.' She touched Gaibun's arm. 'Thank you again. Your actions are proving you have changed. I don't know what the future holds for us but I am willing to forget the past.'

'That's all I ask.' Gaibun smiled, holding her hand again.


The news of the dragons was sweeping through Vales and they were being hailed from village to village. Any Forlish they saw — and there were few of them — just ran. The dragons were now a small army and one both proud and confident.

Then they rode into Catsfield once more, and everything changed.

At first it seemed the same. The village wall had been strengthened since they had left, while cheering people welcomed them inside and young men demanded to know what they had to do to become a dragon.

But Llewellyn, the dour village chief, looked even more sour when they joined him and his wife in their large hut.

'Don't tell me you are unsure about a united Vales?' Huw asked him, ready to deal with him as he had many a doubting chief in Powys.

'No, boyo — nothing like that,' Llewellyn sniffed. 'I am all for it! No, we have heard dire news.'

'What?' Huw smiled, sure it was nothing that he could not handle.

'We received a visit from a stranger. He was Forlish but obviously no warrior. Might have been a merchant once — he sounded like one, ready to sell us anything. Claimed he had been driven out of Forland, like so many others, and was just looking for somewhere safe to live. Course we told him here was perfect — only he refused. Said a village with a wall was less safe than one without.'

The three of them looked at each other.

'Had he been drinking?' Rhiannon laughed.

'Nay. He was serious. Claimed to have come from the west, where he had nearly run into a large band of Forlish. Said he only escaped through luck — had hidden under a bush while they camped. Anyway, he told us the Forlish were angry. Sick of being defeated and turned back by our walls and crossbows. Reckoned they had scraped together enough men so they could go from walled village to walled village, burning them to the ground and killing all inside, so we'd be so scared we'd pull down our own walls and make a bonfire out of our crossbows.'

'What?' Huw gasped. 'Where is this man now?'

'Did he say anything else?' Sendatsu asked.

Llewellyn shrugged. 'He wouldn't stay here. He left two days ago, riding hard. Never said where he was going, just where he wouldn't go.'

'And where's that?'

'Patcham.'

Everyone looked at Huw, who had gone very white.

'Patcham? Tell me everything he said!' he demanded.

'I have! He heard the Forlish were going to teach us a lesson and would start with Patcham. He wanted to know where it was, so there was no chance he could get caught in there ...'

Llewellyn trailed off as Huw stood and staggered outside, leaning on the rough wooden wall and sucking in huge gasps of air.

'It's going to be all right,' Rhiannon told him, rubbing his back.

'I don't know if it is,' Huw moaned. 'Here I was, thinking I was saving lives — all I have done is anger the Forlish. They are going to bring their army north and we can't stop them ...'

'That is a fear for another day,' Rhiannon said crisply. 'This isn't the real army. This is the raiders we have driven out coming together. But we have a new weapon now — the dragons Sendatsu has trained.'

Huw straightened up. 'You are right,' he breathed. 'They think all we have are walls and crossbows. But we have the dragons. We can go there and defeat them — drive them out and save Patcham at the same time!'

'Wait!' Sendatsu snapped.

They turned in surprise.

'This is a mistake. It smells like a trap,' he warned. 'A strange man comes into this village, tells them he heard Patcham is about to be attacked by a huge force, then he runs elsewhere? It stinks worse than my dragons after a day of training!'

'What, do you think they meant for us to hear that? Why?' Huw asked.

'To draw us in, trap us and destroy us. If they get you, the dream of an independent Vales is gone,' Sendatsu said simply. *And my plan for getting back to my children is also gone ...*

'And the man? Llewellyn said he was not a warrior,' Rhiannon pointed out.

'He's probably a Forlish merchant they paid to spread that message. There would be enough of them over the border — and they have had time aplenty to get one up here since we started to defeat them,' Sendatsu dismissed.

'But we cannot leave Patcham. They are sure to attack — and if we do not stop it, then my village will be destroyed,' Huw said in anguish.

'Which proves it is a trap. They must have found out who you are,' Rhiannon reasoned.

'Perhaps — or maybe they chose Patcham because it was the first one we helped,' Sendatsu suggested. 'Either way, we would be better off sending a couple of dragons on fast horses with a message from you, telling the people to leave. If they get out now, they will be safe.'

'And we shall be safe as well,' Rhiannon agreed.

'But the village will be burned and the Forlish will have their victory,' Huw said slowly.

They paused.

'If we let them burn Patcham, it sends a message to every village in Vales. We lied. Walls and crossbows cannot save you. At the moment we have the people on our side but if they think we cannot help them, that we lied to them about helping them, the dream of a real Vales goes up in smoke. People will do what the Forlish want — pull down their walls, burn their crossbows and put their hands up to accept Ward's rule.'

'Surely not!' Rhiannon exclaimed.

'They might — if they felt it was the only way their family would survive,' Huw said.

'That may or may not be true. But the real issue is we cannot stick our heads into this trap,' Sendatsu pointed out.

'But I think we must,' Huw sighed. 'It is the only way. We have to take our best men, go there and defeat the Forlish, turn them back once more.'

'Perhaps it is not such a risk. If we bring every dragon with us, plus the men in the village, we will have so many men the Forlish cannot hope to win,' Rhiannon suggested.

'No! We cannot take everyone,' Huw said instantly. 'We have to make them attack Patcham.'

Sendatsu carefully stuck his finger in his ear. 'I know my ears are not exactly the same as yours but I swear I heard you say you wanted them to attack Patcham!'

'Well, I don't want them to attack Patcham. But I want them to attack where we want. If we march in there with three hundred dragons, they are going to walk a few miles west and sack Crumlin instead. It will not have the same impact on me but it will have the same effect on Vales. It will destroy everything we have done these past moons.'

'If they bring their army north, they will be able to do that anyway,' Sendatsu grunted.

'But by then we shall have a united Vales and meet them with five thousand dragons,' Huw said calmly. 'We shall empty Rheged and even Gwent, send everyone north but our fighters. We shall sting them and draw them in, use our land to hit them time and again. They shall find no food, we shall lead them a merry dance through hills and valleys, taking a slice at a time, until they give up. They will discover we are more trouble than we are worth. Don't forget we are the source of much of their iron ore and coal, which feed their war machine. If we take that away, even for a few months, they will face uprisings from the Landish and Balians. Especially when we travel south to meet the leaders of those nations, to talk about uniting to put an end to the Forlish threat.'

They gaped at him.

'Well, if the elves are not going to help us, then it seems other men must.' Huw shrugged.

'All right,' Sendatsu said slowly. 'But what if this is not just about defeating the Velsh resistance. What if they want us — want you? I mean, there are easier villages, smaller villages than Patcham. But that is your home. Making it their target seems a little personal ...'

Rhiannon chuckled. 'But that's ridiculous! Who among the Forlish has a grudge against us? Who is hunting us and wants revenge on Huw?'

Huw's and Sendatsu's eyes met for a moment and the same thought flashed between them: Rhiannon's father, Hector.

'Well, there was that group of Forlish that tried to grab us earlier, when we left Crumlin,' Huw said quickly, to end the possibility that Sendatsu might let something slip.

'It could be them. They might have been left over from the ones we sent running at Patcham,' Rhiannon mused.

'This is getting us nowhere. We cannot let Patcham be destroyed. How many dragons should we take with us? We need enough to secure victory but not so many it scares the Forlish off.' Huw changed the subject swiftly.

'We should only take the best ones — the ones who can use both bow and sword well,' Sendatsu said immediately. 'Probably a hundred of them. Any less and we risk death.'

'Can you start organising them? We shall need to take all the horses, as well as the weapons. The others can follow as best they can. Rhiannon, you can lead them ...'

'What?' Rhiannon spat.

'I don't want you in Patcham. It is too dangerous. What if something was to go wrong ...' Huw began reasonably but her eyes flashed dangerously and he trailed off.

'If you think I am going to stay here while you ride into danger, you are very much mistaken, Huw ap Earwen!' she snapped. 'Or is there some big-breasted wench you would rather have by your side?'

'Of course not!'

'Then do you have another reason for me not to see these Forlish?'

'No — what possible reason could I have?' Huw asked weakly.

'You don't have a chance, man, give in now while you can still retain a shred of dignity,' Sendatsu said, forcing a grin to make it seem like a joke.

Huw spread his hands. 'I am sorry. You shall share a fast ride into danger and death with us.'

'Good! And I don't want to hear anything ridiculous like me staying in safety ever again!'

'I'll go and start sorting out the dragons. There are a couple of wounded and sick, ones who have been with us for longer, who can look after the new recruits.' Sendatsu half-smiled.

He stared hard at Huw. Of course Huw had wanted her to stay here, away from the possibility of meeting her father. Huw had to tell her the truth. Now.

But Huw could not bring himself to say it. When we are in Patcham, when she cannot ride away — that will be the time, he told himself.

Sendatsu wondered whether he should try harder to avoid this, take two squads of dragons and ride off in the night. But it was nothing more than a passing thought. He could not leave his friends, leave the dragons — and leave the children of Patcham — to the mercy of the Forlish. He simply could not do it. He could not live with himself. In a way, he was one of them. Or were they the same as him? The lines were all blurred. He ate almost the same food as they did, dressed as they did and had given up on the bathing, although, funnily enough, the smell seemed to have gone away now. He had never wanted responsibility before, but now he discovered he preferred it to running away.

Hanto's visible wounds had healed but his pride stung. Jin and Taigo had been battered around and were of little use. And although they had been able to steal new horses, they were no closer to finishing their mission. Far from being able to catch Sendatsu and his two companions alone, the cursed son of Jaken was now surrounded by hundreds of warriors and slept each night in either a walled village or an armed camp patrolled by vigilant guards.

'He is teaching them how we fight,' Jin muttered angrily, as they watched Sendatsu leading scores of human warriors through exercises that looked horribly familiar.

'We need to get him,' Hanto brooded.

But there was no chance they saw, although they shadowed the war band as it moved south and west.

'Does he plan to use them against the Council?' Taigo wondered.

'Even several hundred humans would be no match for us,' Hanto snorted. 'Humans cannot fight like we do.'

Jin and Taigo exchanged looks and compared fading bruises from the last time they had encountered humans.

'We shall continue following them. They will make a mistake and we shall strike.'

Jin and Taigo rolled eyes at each other. They had heard this all before — and were no closer to getting Sendatsu. At least they were travelling east, towards home.

Glyn was delighted to see them again, and the whole village turned out to cheer the dragons as they rode in beneath the huge flag, singing the new Velsh anthem. It had taken longer to ride in, because the villagers wanted to show Huw what they had done since he was away, expanding the defences, so now there were two walls around the village, although the new ditch around the outside had not been finished.

'It's not just for defence — the first wall didn't give us enough room for the animals inside the village,' Glyn pointed out proudly. 'Took us bloody ages to fill in all the holes we dug, though!'

'You've done well,' Huw applauded.

'As have you — look at the banner — and the men riding with you! Velsh dragons — a fine sight! Ah, it is good to see you again. I suppose you are here to get some of our youngsters to join up — and secure our promise to be in a united Vales!'

'No — I am here to save your lives, and the very existence of Vales,' Huw said grimly.

The smile faded rapidly from Glyn's face.

'We need to talk to everyone. Now,' Huw warned.

It took some time to calm the village down but, finally, they gathered around to hear Huw, as they had done just a few months ago. He was reminded of that as he looked out over the village.

'People of Patcham. We have come to you in a time of great danger. The Forlish are planning to launch a massive attack on this village. I have ridden here to save the village. But there is no point in risking lives. I need the women, the children and the elderly to pack food and clothes and get over to Crumlin.'

While the people had listened to his news about the Forlish in silence — albeit shocked silence — this caused more reaction.

'Dafyd has promised to open doors to us. I know only too well of the traditional rivalry with Crumlin. But this is a time to put aside petty feuds. We are all Velsh, and they will help us in our time of need!' Huw shouted. He had stopped to visit with Dafyd on the way in and extracted such a promise from him — another thing that would have seemed inconceivable just a moon or two ago.

'Any men who want to stay are welcome. But we fear these Forlish have prepared for the crossbows — and will be carrying shields or the like.'

'How long have we got?' Glyn asked.

'We don't know,' Huw admitted. 'They could be here at any time. So we need to get the women and children to safety now ...'

'Forlish! Forlish in the trees!'

434

The shout from above stopped everything, made everyone turn and look.

As well as the extra wall, Kelyn and his helpers had built a lookout tower, a perfect post to provide plenty of warning of anyone approaching. The usual watchers were down on the ground but a handful of boys had climbed up there, to get a better view of the excitement going on below — and now they yelled and pointed.

'Let me see.' Sendatsu exploded into action, sprinting across to the ladder propped against the house wall. He went up the rungs swiftly, hands and feet pumping, then swung up onto the small platform, which swayed a little under his weight and the weight of the four boys already up here.

'Over there, Mr Elf!' one cried.

Sendatsu looked out to the tree line and saw the Forlish emerging, dragging strange machines with them. Others carried huge shields but he tried to ignore those, instead concentrating on numbers. He divided the line in half, then half again, then tried to count that quarter. It was not easy, because they were not advancing in line but rather as a mass. He climbed down the ladder much slower.

'What is it?' Huw asked anxiously.

'Nobody is going anywhere,' Sendatsu said grimly. 'They were waiting for us. They must have been watching. We must stay here, for good or ill.'


'We have waited centuries for the right time to act,' Sumiko said reflectively. 'The magic had to fade in the people, the barrier begin to break down. Finally our time was coming but our best chance was lost. And now you tell me Sendatsu has still not made contact with you.'

Her garden had grown again, but filled with plants the likes of which Asami had never seen before. Tall, spiky, with vicious thorns, they loomed over the paths.

'Yes, sensei.'

'Do you think he is dead?'

Asami gulped. With each phase of the moon that passed, and no contact on the other side, that very fear was growing. 'I am sure he is alive,' she said defiantly.

'Then what is he doing? I thought he doted on those children? It seemed natural that he would turn the human world upside down to get the answers we wanted, the proof we needed?'

'I don't know, sensei. But if there are answers out there, he will find them.'

Sumiko turned abruptly. 'We cannot wait forever! Jaken grows ever stronger with each passing day. And our plans have advanced too far to call a halt. My Magic-weavers have been spreading the word among the people that the magic is dying and the Council has no idea how to stop it, that the barrier will soon fail, exposing us to the hordes of gaijin outside. The people are ready; the esemono are terrified and even the middle classes and merchants are fearful. They can see the barrier coming down and thousands of gaijin humans rushing in to swamp us. They believe only the Magic-weavers can save them. But if we do not act soon, the Council will crack down. For now they see it as silly rumours — but that happy state of affairs cannot continue too long.'

'Sensei, we must beware Jaken. He seeks to use us to further his own aims. If we act, he is ready and will seize control, claiming Daichi and the rest of the Council could not control us. Once he has Dokuzen, his next step will be the human lands, it is a horrible idea of having human slaves ...'

'I don't care what happens to them!' Sumiko interrupted.

'Sensei, give Sendatsu more time. He will find what we need!'

Sumiko paused, while new plants burst into life, slicing and shoving others aside to gain space for themselves. 'We shall give him half a moon. We cannot afford any more. Be ready when I send for you,' she said finally. 'If Sendatsu cannot help us, we shall have to kill the Council and seize power ourselves.'

Asami struggled to keep her face impassive.

'With the clans left leaderless, we can gain the books and use them to show the people we had no choice. Would the likes of your father support us then?'

'Perhaps,' Asami hedged.

Plants sliced each other apart behind her.

'Find out. Carefully. And then tell me.'

'Yes, sensei.'

Sumiko parted the plants, allowing Asami to leave the garden safely, and watched the girl walk away until she was out of sight.

'Can we really kill Jaken?' Oroku broke the silence.

'Let us pray to Aroaril that it does not come to that.'

'And Sendatsu?'

'He is either dead or as good as. We must plan to take over without his help. We have half a moon to be ready before we strike.'

It could have been a panic. It nearly was a panic. In no time at all, everyone could see just how many Forlish were out there — and what they were bringing with them. There were more than two hundred of them, all carrying shields or helping wheel three huge machines closer to the village. The catapults were obvious enough, while the giant battering ram's intent was all too clear.

'Calm down! Everyone keep calm!' Huw had to use every bit of his voice to bring things under control. 'Now, we need women and children to head home and stay inside. Those catapults are to damage and bring down the walls, as is the ram. But we don't just have crossbows this time — we have elven bows. And we don't just have one elven warrior, we have scores of elven-trained warriors!'

With the help of Glyn and Kelyn, they managed to move the women and children to houses at the far side of the village, further away from the catapults.

'They're setting up camp directly opposite the main gate,' Glyn reported. 'Where we don't yet have a ditch.'

'Perhaps we could try and get the women and children clear — put them on the horses and send them out the back,' Huw suggested.

'And by the time we get them through the ditch and holes we have dug, the Forlish will be upon them,' Sendatsu pointed out.

'Should we send out a parley, seek to get safe passage for the women and children?' Rhiannon wondered.

'I'm sure they would agree. And then as soon as the women and children were out there, they'd be killed,' Sendatsu spat. 'Remember what they did to the women and children in Rheged?'

'What do you think they will try — and how will we stop them?' Huw asked.

Sendatsu sighed. 'It seems obvious. They will use the catapults to damage the inside wall, try and bring down as much as possible. Then they will advance behind shields, push that ram right up, carve a huge hole in the first wall then flood through. It's a good strategy and I don't think we can stop it. There is nothing we can do to keep the catapults far enough away from the wall — and they will have made shields strong enough to withstand the elven crossbows.'

'So that's it then?' Glyn asked dispiritedly.

'Not at all.' Huw clapped his hands. 'We plan for them getting in — and counter that. We'll use the space between the walls, hit them from either side. The elven crossbows will sting them, the bows of the dragons will hurt them. But we also need to plan for them getting inside. We'll block off the spaces between huts, create another wall there. The village still has all the Forlish weapons from the first attack. We'll be able to arm enough men with swords as well as crossbows, so we can meet them on equal terms, at least.'

'Let them inside?' Glyn asked in horror.

'Well, we shall try to keep them out. But we have to plan for them doing enough damage to the walls to get past,' Huw said.

'Then what good are walls? Why did we spend so long trying to build the blessed things?' Glyn snorted.

Huw hesitated. 'The wall was never going to hold back the Forlish forever,' he finally admitted. 'It is perfect for small groups of bandits and raiders. But the Forlish are too used to breaking through walls of wood and stone. Our only hope is to use a wall of men to keep them back — the dragons.'

'Nice to know that now,' Glyn grumbled.

'Well, that wall saved your life before. And it might just do so again — for they will not be able to see what we are doing behind it,' Rhiannon reminded him.

'When will they attack?' Kelyn asked.

'Tomorrow. They'll want to give us some time to worry, to let fear eat away at us,' Sendatsu predicted.

'So it looks like a busy afternoon and night,' Glyn said with forced cheerfulness.


'What I would have given to see their reaction when we walked out,' Broyle gloated.

'Why didn't we strike when we saw them riding? We could have taken them!' Hector muttered. He had been forced to see his daughter ride into that filthy Velsh village. What if a catapult hit her? What if some lust-filled soldier grabbed her?

'They would have escaped. There were too many of them and we don't have many horses,' Broyle dismissed him. 'Besides, we want to destroy the village. We want the Velsh to know their new warriors and flag and weapons won't save them.'

Hector said nothing. Broyle's desire for revenge was dangerously close to obsession. But if it meant the return of his daughter — and she was not too soiled — then he was willing to tolerate the madman. After all, Broyle had managed to bring together this little army from beaten remnants. And they acknowledged him — a mere sergeant — without question. Of course the king's seal had helped but mostly it was pure Broyle.

'Get the catapults in position — and start bringing up the stones!' Broyle waved.

Hector could only stand back and admire the organisation of the Forlish warriors. Men prepared the camp, dug defensive trenches in case the villagers tried to sally out, or dug latrines further back, while others began fires and more prepared the catapults.

'I don't think they are going to attack us — I should be so lucky — they won't be mad enough to. But there is no reason not to take them seriously, rather than just a bunch of farm boys led by an elf,' Broyle confided.

'So you are confident of getting in?' Hector asked nervously. He was only too aware of how long it had been since the king had sent him off. Would Ward have forgotten about them by now? Would he have found a new favourite? Would he welcome their return with open arms or with a horrible punishment?

'By about the third or fourth cast, we'll have the stones landing on the wall,' Broyle said confidently. 'Catapults are tricky things — not bothered much by the wind, of course, but the weight of the stone can affect the range dramatically. We try to find stones all about the same shape but there is no such thing. So we'll damage a good hundred yards of the inside wall and then send in the ram, with the men around it. Once we have smashed a hole in the first wall and can get inside, then all their building work becomes our friend — for they cannot get out. We hunt them like rats!'

'But no women are to be killed — my daughter cannot be harmed,' Hector said hurriedly.

'I know. The men will have their orders. No women dead — and no fun until you have been reunited with your daughter.'

'The king wants her for himself — so tell them it is King Ward they will answer to if she is harmed,' Hector insisted.

'I'll tell them. But I do wonder if the king will still want that filly, after she's been ridden by half of Vales.'

'How dare you!' Hector snarled, going purple in his anger. 'She will be the consort of the king himself — and it is he you insult, as much as her!'

'Seems strange to champion her virtue on one hand, when you plan to sell her to the king with the other,' Broyle said calmly.

'Have a care, Broyle — you go too far!' Hector threatened.

Broyle stepped in close and Hector subsided.

'You're not so big a fool as to threaten me,' Broyle said softly. 'And if my men hear you trying to order me about one more time, I shall see you hung from a tree with a noose made from your own guts. Understand?'

Hector nodded swiftly.

'Good. Now stay clear and let the real men go to work. I'll send for you when we have the village in our hands and you can get your daughter again in yours.'

Hector shook with rage as Broyle walked away. How dare the man! Once they were safely back in Cridianton, he would speak to the king about the sergeant's attitude. Well, probably.

The gap between the two walls took advantage of the natural upward slope and Glyn and Kelyn had made sure the two gates were not facing each other, which would force any attacker who got inside the first wall to cross the open ground and run around before attacking the second, inner gate to get access into the village itself.

'This is clever work,' Sendatsu approved, standing on one of the fighting platforms and looking down. 'The only problem is, they may not come in here.'

'Well, they have to tell us where they plan to break in,' Huw said with a confidence he did not entirely feel.

'Really?' Sendatsu smiled.

'The catapults,' Glyn breathed. 'Where they breach the inner wall will show us where they will attack.'

'Their arrogance is also their weakness,' Huw predicted.

'Well, we shall see,' was all Sendatsu said.

Meanwhile, both dragons and villagers tore down fighting platforms and used the timber to block the spaces between huts, to create a final position.

'I hope we never have to use this,' Rhiannon commented, as she helped organise the women.

'We shall do everything we can to hold them at the walls. But they have spent a moon getting ready for this — they will not be easy to stop. We have to break them apart, give the dragons a chance to use their skills. The huts will help do that — and then we have our best trick as well,' Huw said loudly. There was plenty of fear in the village. Apart from battle, there was the sense of being trapped. Huw had never felt sympathy when hunting rats in a granary before — but now he could imagine the sensation of having no escape from the doom coming for you.

He was trying to inspire the people, although, like trapped rats, they would have no choice but to fight. And they knew their fate should the Forlish win.

'This is all a huge risk,' he whispered to Sendatsu. 'Have we made a mistake?'

'Ask me in two days,' Sendatsu grunted. 'I would have been happier had we got the women and children to safety. I would have been far happier to have the rest of the dragons here. It was always their plan to attack here. Which means Rhiannon's father must be out there, driving them. You need to tell her.'

'Not now,' Huw said worriedly. 'We have to concentrate on winning this battle. Rhiannon is doing a wonderful job with the women ...'

'You keep finding excuses to not tell her. You need to find a way to say something,' Sendatsu said bluntly.

'But I have a far better idea,' Huw claimed. 'Once we have won here, I shall tell her that I do not want to wait for Midwinter to Walk The Tree with her. Instead we shall go out there and become married — and then I can tell her.'

Sendatsu whistled softly. 'Well, she won't run then, it is true. But I should prepare myself for many nights sleeping out in the kitchen, rather than in bed with her.'

'I have it all worked out,' Huw insisted.

Sendatsu just shook his head.

'Look,' Huw said gently. 'This could be our last night together. I don't want to spend it apart, in anger and fear and hurt. If we get through the next day, then I have all the time in the world to tell her.'

Sendatsu looked at him, then nodded reluctantly.

'Go then,' he said. 'Enjoy your night. But don't let anyone else hear you talking like that!'

# 25

*Naturally I ordered Naibun to investigate what happened, why two Council Guards of my own clan tried to kill me. Naturally, as he was the one who had ordered it, he was unable to tell me anything useful.*

*But the failed attempt on my life snapped me out of my grief. I began reviewing all the plans for the final withdrawal back into Dokuzen. At first these seemed to be ordinary enough but, as I read further, I began discovering strange details, odd discrepancies and events that seemed impossible. It became quickly clear that things had not been going as planned. I went to speak to old friends and allies — and found them almost all missing, dead or withdrawn from public life. Too late, I listened to all the stories being spread, heard of all the human deaths. Even then, in the face of the mounting evidence, I wanted to believe Naibun.*

*Only days remained before the barrier went up and I tried to confront Naibun with my concerns — only to find he had journeyed into Vales. Determined to confront him and discover the truth, I hurried after him. But first, just in case, I spoke to the Magic-weavers.*

The next morning was dull and cloudy, the promise of rain on the air. To those inside the village, fearing it was the last day they would see, the dark clouds matched their mood perfectly.

To the Forlish, it was just another day. They had spent too many days and nights before battle to be worried about a small village with a couple of flimsy walls. They expected to have a hard morning reducing the walls, then a short fight followed by plenty of plunder, drink and women — not necessarily in that order. Besides, Broyle had them primed for revenge, thirsting to pay back these impudent Velsh who had defied the might of Forland, used trickery to kill their friends in the night.

Once the light was enough to judge the cast of stones, Broyle signalled to his catapult crews.

'Loose!'

The first two stones landed short, one sinking into the turf outside the outer wall, the other landing somewhere in between.

'Ten yards closer, and smaller rocks,' the catapult captains called.

Many hands moved the catapults closer, while others greased the wood with lard. They had cut the wood only a moon ago, tried to let it season as much as possible — but it was still dangerously green and, they feared, ripe for cracking. None wanted to be near one when that happened.

Broyle had wanted to use the catapults to crush every hut in the village, to spread fear and pain long before his soldiers broke through the wall. He had been bitterly disappointed when the catapult captains had warned him the machines would be lucky to last long enough to do sufficient damage to the wall. The stones they were loosing were as small as they dared to use, little larger than a man's head. But even that weight put huge stress on the throwing arms.

They wound the catapults back and then stood well away for their second cast.

'First was close!' the spotter, high up in a nearby tree, called. 'Second hit the wall!'

The Forlish cheered lustily as the catapults were adjusted, more grease applied — and slightly heavier stones chosen this time.

'Loose!'

'Both hit!'

The crews on the catapults slaved hard, stripped to the waist, taking it in turns to wind and load.

Broyle watched grimly, not allowing even a small smile on his face. His men were watching for his reaction and he would give them nothing yet. But when they saw the first section of the inner palisade tumble down, hit by a second stone in a row, he allowed a quick grin at the crew of that catapult.

The catapults gnawed away at the inner wall, bringing down one or two or more logs with every hit. But then the main beam snapped on the first catapult, the wood breaking under the strain, sending thick splinters in all directions, making men duck for cover and leaving one of the crew screaming out his last.

'Keep going. Every stone that hits is worth it,' Broyle ordered curtly.

So the remaining catapult worked on, flinging stones into the damaged inner wall, knocking more logs askew, snapping others and causing damage even when it bounced in front and then sprang up. Broyle was just beginning to relax when everything stopped.

'What is it?' Broyle stormed down there, to see the men gathered around the catapult.

'Cracked through. It just couldn't take that much strain.' The crew captain shrugged. 'Nothing we could do.'

Broyle resisted the temptation to have the machine try to hurl the man at the village.

'Shields! We assault now!' He signalled.

The men gathered around the battering ram, forming up to protect the men who would be wheeling it forwards. Broyle had built two types of shields — the usual sort, which could be held with one hand, as well as bigger ones, which would cover men from head to toe. These were massively heavy, difficult to drag across rough ground — but they would get his men safely to the wall. Once there, they could be discarded and the normal shields would come into their own. He wished they had body armour but he had neither the tools, materials nor the time to make that. Besides, once inside the wall those damned crossbows would lose most of their effect.

Broyle took his place in the middle of the men, near the ram, and hefted a shield. They would ensure this would be a slow advance but a safe one. They had the giant ones at the front, then men in the second and third ranks carried the smaller shields, which could be held up high to stop anything falling from above.

He wanted a simple attack route, rather than anything fancy. The damned shields were too heavy to try anything else. The track to the village led not to a gate but to solid wall. But that was fine by him. He had the catapults demolish chunks of the inner wall behind, now the ram was pointed at the part of the outer wall shielding that breach.

'Forwards!' he called and grunted with the effort of lifting the heavy wooden shield.

Huw, Sendatsu and Glyn watched the Forlish begin their slow advance.

'At least the catapults have stopped,' Sendatsu observed.

'Not in time to save the inner wall.' Glyn looked at the wreckage mournfully. It was still a barrier — but nothing substantial enough to protect a man.

The inner palisade was wrecked for a good fifty paces, a massive gap towards which the Forlish were aiming their advance. Rocks, broken logs and chunks of wood were scattered around. Logs hung at crazy angles off surrounding parts of the wall, while others stood, the top half snapped off, like broken teeth. It was still an obstacle. Men would not be able to keep tight ranks and get through and over this. But it was not enough.

'We knew that would go.' Huw waved it off. 'And at least we know they are going to come right at us.'

'They don't need to play around. They have plenty of men,' Glyn muttered.

'So we'll thin them out. Does everybody know their place?'

Heads nodded and Huw smiled, trying to keep his fear from showing. They had prepared as best they could but the mass of Forlish, advancing behind their huge wooden shields, was a daunting sight. So many things could go wrong … he did not know how Ward could find war so thrilling. He would be far happier if he could put aside the crossbow forever and take up the lyre instead.

'Sendatsu, give them something to think about,' he managed to say without his voice shaking.

Sendatsu waved to the waiting dragons and eased to the front of the fighting platform, one of just two they had not demolished to use elsewhere. Of the dragons he had brought to Patcham, half had some skills with the bow — nothing like elves, of course; it took years of training before a bowman could hit what he was aiming at. Luckily the mass of Forlish was a big enough target that even these boys should be able to strike it.

He strung his bow, watching the young men around him.

'Take your time. Don't hurry,' he called, seeing several of them struggle, more out of nerves than anything else. 'We're going to loose six arrows. No more until they get close!'

He was nervous, more nervous than he had ever been in his life. This could end very badly — and not just for him. Mai and Cheijun were in his thoughts all the time and he was determined to get through this for them. But what of the others? He had grown close to many of these humans. The thought of losing them to the Forlish was frightening. Then there was the way everyone thought his elven skills were going to prove the difference. Victory or defeat would be on him. But he kept all that hidden. He had to. He looked at the Forlish. They were little more than a hundred yards away but advancing slowly, very slowly.

'Draw and loose!' he called, laying an arrow on the string and drawing back, feeling the strain as he did so.

'Arrows!' someone called and Broyle instinctively ducked, before cursing himself. Those crossbows could not reach this far! He straightened, only for something to strike his shield with a crash, making the shield shake and pushing him back as though he had run into a wall. A steel point appeared through the wood, sticking out a finger's breadth through the oak. He stared at it in astonishment.

Next moment the whole line shook as more struck home with explosive sounds, while a pair of men went down screaming in the second rank, where they had not been holding their shields over their heads. One had an arrow through his eye and fell quickly, while the second had one jutting from his neck and his screams and blood sprayed around the tight group of Forlish.

'Keep those shields up!' Broyle barked. He could almost understand men not wanting to march with heavy shields held high overhead — but now they were paying for their stupidity. Worse, their deaths were having an effect on the men, naturally slowing them down.

'What are those things? I thought their crossbows didn't have any power?' Ricbert muttered.

Broyle lifted his shield across, giving him a slight opening to peer through. Next moment he dropped it back with a curse, as an arrow thumped into it.

'Those aren't crossbows,' he snarled. 'The elf has trained some of the Velsh to use his bow.'

Instantly he regretted speaking aloud, for he could feel the line slow down further.

'The shields are too good for them!' he shouted. 'We are safe here!'

And it did seem to be true. Shields shook with the impact of the arrows — and although some punched part of the way through, none of the men were hurt. Men holding shields high in the second and third ranks were also safe, although a couple took cuts to the wrist or forearm as points stuck through.

'Stay together. Give them nothing,' Broyle ordered.

He was sweating now, not from the thought of what awaited him but from the effort of using the heavy shields. Each pace forwards meant they had to be part lifted, part pushed. They stuck on clumps of grass, or small rocks, forcing swearing men to lift them high to get them forwards. Arms and shoulders were soon burning with the effort, while the men in the rear ranks were changing shields from arm to arm as their shoulders cramped from the effort of holding the heavy wood high.

448

Now the arrows made the advance even more miserable. Any gap seemed to invite an arrow, while each strike made the shields shake and the men curse.

'Not far now!' Broyle shouted, more in hope than anything.

Then, blessedly, the arrows stopped. He risked a quick look, to see the village but fifty paces away.

'They must be out of arrows,' Broyle declared. 'At the double now, lads!'

Sweating men gasped as they pushed and manhandled the hefty shields forwards. Broyle had another quick look at the village and then ducked behind the shield again.

'Those damned crossbows!' he called.

Instantly the Forlish progress stopped as men instinctively cowered behind the shields. But, unlike the loud thump that announced the strike of an arrow, this was more like the pattering of rain. Dozens of bolts bounced off shields, or stuck in the thick timber. Men knocked shields together, obsessing about not leaving any gap, while those behind clustered forwards, all seeking shelter.

Broyle glanced left and right and grinned as he saw his shields were working. A handful of men were cursing as bolts sneaked through, finding gaps in the wall of wood — but only enough to annoy, not enough to kill.

'Keep moving!'

He was a little concerned they were using up too much energy just getting to the village but reassured himself that, once inside, they could discard the wooden protection and hunt the Velsh down.

'We got a couple,' Sendatsu reported. 'But their shields are too big. The bolts aren't able to get through either.'

'We knew that would be the case. Glyn, call the villagers back. We'll hurt them here.' Huw clapped him on the shoulder, trying to smile.

'Is everyone ready?' Rhiannon asked.

'Who knows?' Huw muttered. 'But we have to hope they are.'

'The men will fight. They have to. They know their families are behind them,' Rhiannon said softly. 'The Forlish think they have us trapped but they have made a big mistake — it will just force everyone to fight harder.'

The three of them looked at each other for a few moments longer, knowing this could well be the last time they were together.

'Good luck,' Sendatsu said awkwardly.

'Be lucky yourself,' Huw said heavily.

'Elves don't need luck.' Sendatsu grinned. 'We're too good for it.'

He glanced over at Cadel, one of his young dragon squad leaders. 'Keep them both alive,' he said shortly.

Cadel nodded grimly and Sendatsu smiled at him. Cadel was easily his best pupil, and his squad had all fought at Merthyr. They had also declared themselves ready to die to keep Huw and Rhiannon alive. That had embarrassed Huw but Sendatsu expected no less. It was what an elf would have done. Cadel was the first dragon he would have liked to take into Dokuzen. He hesitated a moment longer, wanting to say more, but there was no time and he did not have the words. He raced off to join his group of dragons, while Huw and Rhiannon waited with the villagers. They were spread out by the remnants of the inner wall. The Patchamers were almost all armed, thanks to the weapons they had taken from the very first attack they had defeated. But nobody, least of all themselves, knew how they would stand against the Forlish.

'Here they come,' Rhiannon said.

'They? You are Forlish too.' Huw tried to smile at her.

'Don't count me as one of them,' Rhiannon sniffed, hefting her elven crossbow. 'They are not my people.'

Huw laughed. 'Then let's hear you sing "Land of My Fathers".'

She smiled, then threw back her head and began to sing. A moment later Huw joined in and then the dragons a breath behind them, then the Patchamers, until the whole village was singing together.

Huw felt the hair come up on the back of his neck. The song never ceased to amaze him, how they took strength from it. Even the men who had been ducking away to drop their trews and empty their bowels a moment earlier were standing tall and joining in. Let the Forlish come, he thought.

Broyle was sweating and breathing hard as they came to the outer wall. The slope had made the last few yards seem like miles and he could see he was not the only man struggling. The heavy shields were hard to keep moving and keep together — the only good thing was that storm of crossbow bolts had been blessedly brief and had now dried up. He did not care why. As a sergeant he was used to worrying only about what was in front of him, rather than the entire battle. That habit was hard to break and he had to force himself to think about his next move.

'The ram!' he called.

The Forlish lines paused, the men at the front leaning against the shields, everyone else holding shields high while the ram crew moved forwards. They were also sweating, having hauled the heavy ram across soft grass, and the ram did not quite race at the palisade with the pace Broyle had imagined. But it still struck home with a crash, sending logs flying in all directions. Sweating and swearing, the ram crew dragged it back and ran in again, widening the gap. This time the ram was caught on the wreckage of the palisade and they struggled to free it.

Now arrows came in, snapping in flat, making the ram crew duck and cower and spinning several of them round as they struck. Men screamed and bled and died or cursed and clutched at shafts sticking out of their arms and legs. One man had a shaft through his chest which pinned him to the ram itself and he gasped, blood bubbling out of his mouth, writhing helplessly against the thick trunk.

'More shields!' Broyle called angrily.

The heavy shields were dragged across, while other men tried to provide cover. The depleted ram crew was joined by fresh hands and the ram was dragged clear, then shoved forwards again, the dying man pinned to the wood jerking and moaning, other men trying to ignore his painful death.

Again it crashed into the palisade, again more logs were knocked clear, giving them a view inside. The inner wall was also wrecked and all that waited for them was a crowd of Velsh peasants. They were singing something but Broyle had no interest in listening to that, any more than he would pleas for mercy.

'Not long now,' Broyle told those nearest to him. 'Make ready!'

He decided everything was working well. He was used to battles going exactly to plan and saw no reason to question things now.

One more effort and the ram crashed home with force enough to dislodge the dying man pinned to the side, where his body was crushed by one of the heavy wheels.

'That's enough,' Broyle judged. 'Second and third lines — forwards!'

The men in the front rank leaned against the shields gratefully, their ordeal over, their effort made. All they had to do was tilt the shields around and let the next two ranks, the ones with the smaller shields, race inside. Or so they thought.


'Wait! Wait for it!' Huw shouted.

The temptation to start loosing bolts was almost too much. But he wanted the Forlish in the open, and away from their big shields. Loosing too early would have been a waste. He had let Cadel and his squad loose a few arrows each through the gaps now appearing in the outer wall but nothing more. He knew it was the right thing but it was still terrifying to watch the Forlish knock a hole in the wall and then swarm inside, shields held high. But by waiting the Velsh saw their chance. The Forlish could not hold their tight lines. At some places they had to climb over the broken stumps of the wall, at others they rushed straight in. In an instant there were gaps everywhere and the shields they carried, only big enough to cover the torso, were held low by arms tired of holding them high on the slow advance.

'Loose!' Huw shouted.

A cloud of bolts followed his order and he worked his own crossbow feverishly, pumping them out at the mass of Forlish. All around him the villagers used their crossbows, while Cadel and his group of dragons bent their longbows.

The Forlish covered up as best they could. While the sheer number of bolts meant some were striking home in legs and hands and arms, the Forlish clustered together, shields close, to protect anything vital. Only a handful were down, although far more were being wounded, especially in the legs. That did not slow the villagers, however, who worked their crossbows as if the Forlish could be turned back by the sheer number of bolts alone. Huw reloaded swiftly and guessed every Forlish shield had at least two bolts stuck in them, while many had far more — and not counting the ones that had hit and bounced off.

The advance was still coming, more and more Forlish creeping forwards past the first wall and inching towards their tormentors. Huw loosed one more bolt and cursed as he watched it sink harmlessly into a shield. He hesitated nervously. He could see the Forlish edging closer, worried they would get too close and could take waiting no longer. He turned and waved to Kelyn, atop the watchtower. He, in turn, waved a sheet of red linen.

Huw counted slowly to ten.

'Stop! Hold!' he bellowed, his voice cutting through the shouts and cries.

A few more bolts whistled out before the message was passed on but Huw was relieved to see almost all were listening to him and they were not lost in the fear and adrenalin.

The Forlish peered out from behind the shields, wary of a trap, but when they saw the villagers merely standing there quietly, weapons in hands, the Forlish straightened and began to run forwards, eager to take the fight to their tormentors.

And then Sendatsu struck.


Sendatsu and his dragons had waited, hidden by the curve of the inner wall, for the signal. He had more than eighty dragons, the best fighters bar the ones with Huw and Cadel. Almost all had fought the Forlish outside Merthyr and while he would have preferred the same number of elves, he was proud to lead them. All were eager to follow, to show him how good they were — which was a fear in itself. He had told them many a time what had to be done — whether they could hold to that was another matter.

He could hear the noise of the Forlish attack, the shouts and screams, but he was fixed on Kelyn, in the watchtower above.

'The red, we have the red!' he shouted.

Instantly they kicked their horses into the charge — or as much of a charge as pit ponies could manage. Sendatsu and the leading riders all had spears — if not real hunting spears then at least long shafts of sharpened wood, while the rest would draw swords. Sendatsu's fear was being caught up in the mass of Forlish, dragged down and his dragons killed by their superior numbers but, if the dragons could time this right, there was a chance to scour the area between the two walls clean of Forlish. If that worked, then Sendatsu would signal to Huw and the villagers could join the attack, turn the Forlish back then and there. If not, then it was on to the reserve plan.

'Stay close, hold together!' he bellowed as he spurred his horse on. 'Keep to my left!'

The dragons tried to obey but few had ridden a horse before joining the dragons and gaps were already opening up between them as they went wide around the corner. Sendatsu could not spare the time to stop and reform, he just hoped and rode on, tearing around the angle of the wall to where the Forlish were rushing towards the villagers. He saw instantly they had timed their charge well — the Forlish were up and running, strung out more than they would have been, had the bolts still been flying. He aimed for the midpoint between the two walls, hoping his dragons stayed to his left, closer to the villagers than the heart of the Forlish, then forgot about that as he picked out one at the front, a bearded warrior with a long sword and a shield that bristled with crossbow bolts.

The Forlishman turned at the sound of the hooves but wasted precious moments staring in shock at the sudden appearance of this strange cavalry. Sendatsu guided his horse with a touch of his heels, then leaned forwards, putting his weight behind a lunge of the spear. It was a boar-hunting spear, eight feet of solid wood topped with a heavy iron head, and only Sendatsu's huge strength enabled him to hold the point steady and pick out his spot. As the Forlishman raised his shield in a despairing effort, Sendatsu thrust home, feeling the shock as the iron head punched into the Forlishman's belly, bursting through his back in a spray of blood. He let go of the handle as the man screamed in agony, folding over the blade that was now trapped inside him, the weight of man and spear too much for even Sendatsu to try to hold. Instead he reached back and drew his sword from where it was hanging between his shoulder blades and brought it down in a vicious cut that sliced a man's head almost from his shoulders, throwing blood across the horse's side.

Now things got harder, for the ground was littered with rocks and broken timbers, each one with the potential to throw him out of the saddle — and once he was on the ground, the Forlish would pounce.

He swerved around a log, aimed at a third Forlishman, who ducked down low but Sendatsu nudged his horse and it dropped its shoulder into the warrior, knocking him backwards. Sendatsu leaned across his horse and slashed upwards, ripping open another Forlishman's back, hearing the bubbling scream of his target as he regained the centre of the saddle in time to urge his horse to leap over a log lying in the grass. Then he was through to the other side and turning his horse, trying to see what was happening.

His dragons swept after him, the lead riders using spears to thrust down at the Forlish. These had some slight warning and a few were able to raise their shields, the wooden spears splintering in the impact, although the force was enough to hurl the Forlish backwards. Others were not so lucky. Spears found their targets in chests and stomachs, sending men flying in all directions. Other dragons hacked down with swords, opening up huge wounds in heads and shoulders as they rode through.

Yet several dragons had ridden out too close to the outer wall, to where the Forlish were a solid mass. These young Velshmen hacked and slashed furiously but their horses lost momentum in the press of bodies, the pit ponies not big enough or strong enough to carve their way through. Once they stopped, they were swiftly hamstrung by veteran warriors and the Velsh dragged down and cut to pieces by vengeful Forlish.

'Around!' Sendatsu gestured furiously, flinging blood from his blade, furious at the sight of his men dying. The dragons tried to obey but while they moved closer to the inner wall, it enabled Forlish to scamper to safety. Isolated Forlish were helpless; trying to block one blow, they opened themselves up to a second. But there were not enough of those and many of the dragons at the back rode clear through without even swinging their swords.

Sendatsu cleaned his blade on his horse's mane and knew they had not done enough damage. Too many Forlish remained. He had let his concern for the dragons blind him to what needed to be done. He felt a pang at the thought but there was no time for regrets. He waved to his dragons, who were reforming again.

'What now?' one of his other squad leaders, Tadd, cried. Almost as good a swordsman as Cadel, he was another of Sendatsu's favourites.

Sendatsu looked grimly at where the Forlish were locking shields. Those warriors had fought cavalry often enough to know how to counter them. More than two dozen Forlish were down, dead and hideously wounded from the first charge — but they would not be caught like that this time.

'Off the horses!' Sendatsu decided.

His dragons obeyed without question, turning the beasts and sending them running back, away from the Forlish.

'Form up together,' Sendatsu ordered.

'And what then?' Tadd asked.

'Wait to see who they attack,' Sendatsu stated, glancing towards where Huw and the others stood. He hoped the Forlish would advance towards them, opening up their flank to his attack. But he had the horrible feeling they would choose to march towards Sendatsu and the dragons. What would Huw do then? Attack? Sendatsu hoped not.

Broyle cursed as the Velsh charge struck home, cutting down his lead men. If only he had spears, he could have turned that charge into a massacre. But there were many things he did not have and he ignored them, concentrating instead on what he did have. Plenty of men for a start. And shields as well.

'Form up! Tight formation!' he bellowed. He had to do two things — firstly stop another one of those charges and then make sure the two groups of Velsh did not join together.

Instantly the mass of Forlish shuffled together, linking shields.

He was about to order some of the big shields to be dragged in, to help break up another cavalry charge, when the mounted Velsh dismounted, forming up on foot instead.

Almost instantly, the bolts from the elven crossbows began to swamp his front rank, forcing them to duck and cover, the constant noise of the bolts thudding into shields making it hard to think.

'They want to hit us in the flank when we go for the villagers,' Ricbert said nervously. 'What do we do?'

Broyle nearly hit him. Those damned bolts were driving him mad and the last thing he felt like doing was discussing tactics with anyone, let alone Ricbert. Grimly he forced himself to come up with something.

'You take command of that flank. Keep a double line there. They'll never be able to break that. Once we have set the villagers running, we'll turn and deal with them properly,' he growled.

Huw had cheered Sendatsu's charge, delighted to see the leading Forlish ridden over — but swiftly realised they had not done enough. Instead of striking through the heart of the Forlish, they had merely taken out the front rank. He cursed the elf. His desire to save as many as possible might well have had the opposite effect.

'Crossbows!' he called, to give himself time to think.

'We need to make them do something stupid,' Rhiannon said.

'You're right.' He nodded and they locked eyes, knowing what that meant.

'Back! Fall back!' he shouted.

The villagers stopped loosing crossbows, turned and ran. With a roar, the Forlish flooded after them.

# 26



Sendatsu breathed a sigh of relief that Huw did not try something really foolish, although it left him with a difficult task that could cost the lives of many of his dragons. He waited a few moments, until many of the Forlish were moving, racing after the villagers.

'Attack!' Sendatsu waved his sword and raced in, followed by the rest of the dragons, all of them shouting and cheering.

The Forlish closest to him slowed at once, orders were shouted and a shield wall was made to face him.

He knew how dangerous this was. Each of his men needed at least four feet of space around them, so they did not accidentally cut one of their comrades. But the Forlish stood shoulder to shoulder, their short swords bristling in between the thick wood, needing only half that. If he tried to meet them in a line, each one of his men would be running down a corridor that ended with two men waiting for him in the first rank, another two behind. And good as his dragons were becoming, they were not good enough to beat four Forlish. Only he was. And that seemed to be the answer. Instead of following him in a line, they bunched up close behind him, in more of a wedge shape. Tadd and another squad leader, Bowen, were at his shoulders, the others spreading out from there.

Sendatsu picked his spot, aiming at where a tall warrior stood next to a much shorter man, so their shields were not quite at the same level. He had practised this move a few times with the dragons — this would be the first time for real. But he was not thinking about what could go wrong, about what was happening elsewhere — his total attention was on what he was doing. It was the most valuable lesson he had gained from his father.

He could see the Forlish line bracing for him, the sharp swords eager to cleave his flesh if he made the slightest mistake. The two closest to him had crouched slightly, tilting their shields to throw him off. Perfect. Gathering himself, he leaped high, his foot landing on the shorter man's shield and driving him down, while allowing Sendatsu to push up and thrust over the top of the taller man's shield, the blade slicing through tunic and neck, ripping the throat open and sending the dying Forlishman staggering back into his fellows.

Sendatsu landed in the space he had created and cut to his right in the classic thunder-strike stroke. The Forlish had their shields in their left arms, meaning the Forlishman on that side was unprotected and Sendatsu's sword sliced through tunic and ribs and stomach, sending intestines puddling out. The man's agonised screaming had only just begun when Sendatsu recovered and slashed back to his left, to where the shorter warrior was just regaining his balance. He had no more time, for Sendatsu scythed the blade around in the tiger-claw stroke, took his head and flipped it over onto the rear ranks, while the rest of the body slowly collapsed, fountaining blood.

The Forlish had seen death and destruction every day but this still gave them a pause — and then Bowen and Tadd were beside Sendatsu, their blades hacking and cutting. Unlike the Forlish, they held the swords two-handed and could change the point of attack in a heartbeat. If a shield was raised the blade cut low, if the shield stayed low then the head was the target. The Forlish to the left and right of the gap Sendatsu had made, now unprotected on one of their sides, instinctively turned to cover themselves. But that only made the line more disrupted, gave the following Velsh dragons more of a chance.

A dozen Forlish went down and every one that died or lay screaming in his own blood made the rest of the line that much weaker.

For a moment Sendatsu thought they might even throw the whole Forlish line into panic — but these warriors had fought too much to give up that easily. The second line held, locking shields and pushing back at the Velsh, trying to get close, to give the dragons no room to use their swords in extravagant blows. The closer they got, the more the advantage swung to the Forlish, with their shields and short swords, which were deadly at close range.

Sendatsu tried to create space by dropping to one knee and sweeping his sword out, slicing into legs. The elven steel cut through flesh and bone; with the Forlish wearing nothing more than woollen trews it was easy to bring down a pair of men, and they would probably never walk again. But, by the time he had stood, more Forlish in the rear ranks had pushed into the gaps. It was time to go, before there was no time at all, he judged.

'Back!' he cried, and the dragons responded instantly, as he had told them to, turning and running. He waited but a heartbeat before following them.

The Forlish saw them running and could not stop themselves. They raced after Sendatsu and the dragons, desperate to avenge the losses they had suffered. Sendatsu smiled to himself as he ran. More than fifty of the Forlish were chasing him, rather than taking on Huw and the villagers. Just what he wanted.

Broyle followed the mass of villagers through the wreckage of the inner wall. Ricbert had held off the attack of the elf and his Velsh warriors; now Broyle's men were chasing the fleeing Velsh. This was all going to plan. A short fight and now the Velsh were running — just like everyone who tried to face the Forlish ran.

Huw looked back and almost quailed to see the mass of Forlish boil over the inner wall and race into the village. There were more than a hundred of them — and he could expect no help from Sendatsu for some time. But they had talked about this — it was the only way.

'Hold at the barricade!' Huw called as the villagers ran back among the first huts.

Getting everyone to stop, to get past the instinct to keep running was hard but two things helped — first there was nowhere to really run to, secondly the barricade they had built forced men to come to a halt.

'Wait for them!' Huw shouted, which was easier said than done.

Once among the huts, there were only glimpses of the pursuing Forlish and having to hold there was hugely difficult. Huw could sense the fear among the villagers — he was terrified himself. He gripped his crossbow tight and knew he should say something, but did not trust his voice.

'Steady! Wait for them!' Rhiannon called and he looked up at her gratefully.

Moments later the Forlish rushed into view, the fastest of them having drawn ahead of their fellows while the two dozen carrying crossbow bolts in their legs limped, further back.

Huw did not even need to say anything — as soon as the first Forlishman raced into sight, every man with an elven crossbow loosed bolts — and kept going, triggering their weapon time and time again.

The lead Forlish were engulfed in a cloud of bolts and collapsed, struck on all sides, from all directions by the wicked little bolts. Men ran forwards, holding up their shields in forlorn hope, only to shudder and stumble as the bolts struck. Onwards they came, some of them almost to the feet of the villagers, but each strike made them jerk and shout, until they finally fell, twitching, some of them pierced in more than a dozen places.

For a few moments Huw dared to hope they could hold the Forlish off like this — but more were attacking all the time, and these came in a thicker mass, able to link shields and use them to make it across the dead ground and the dead bodies littering it to where the villagers waited. In moments, there was fighting across the line and Velsh threw down crossbows to draw swords to protect themselves. And every crossbow that hit the ground meant fewer bolts reaching out, making it easier for the Forlish to come to grips with the Velsh.

Glyn gripped his sword tight as a howling Forlishman raced at him. He had worked his crossbow like a demon, only to see the last of his bolts wasted on the shields many of these Forlish carried. He had practised with this sword every day for the past moon, after the elf Sendatsu had taught them all a handful of basic strokes. It was a polished piece of metal the length of his forearm and he had spent a turn of the hourglass sharpening it last night. He wanted to run but had nowhere to run to — and no way of protecting his family if he did not stand now. He looked at the sword and knew he had to steel himself. The first time the Forlish had come to his village he had stayed in his hut, listened in terror to the shouts and cries as friends were killed and dragged off, while his wife and children wailed around him. He tried to use that memory now to make himself stand. The fear was thick in his belly and his legs seemed frozen but he made himself step forwards to meet the charge. Move your feet, keep them light, he told himself, following the things Sendatsu had taught them. Shouting something, a wordless cry, he slashed furiously at the Forlishman's sword arm. The blade bit deep, grating on bone, and he heard the man's bellow of pain. A feeble lunge came back, aimed at Glyn's eyes, but he swung the blade in a high block, flicking blood onto himself. Ignoring that he moved smoothly into position, his body remembering what he had learned, then cut down at the neck. This one also bit deep and he saw the Forlishman's eyes open wide in horror as his lifeblood spurted out. The man had a rough beard and cruel eyes but Glyn could only see pain and fear in them now. Choking, the Forlishman fell and lay writhing. Glyn did not know whether to finish him off or leave him there. He even had the urge to help the man try to staunch the wounds he had inflicted. But a shout from his left told him there was no time. Swinging around, he parried a blow without thinking, his hand ringing from the force. He brought the blade up in time to deflect another slash but then a young dragon came to his aid, driving his sword deep into the Forlishman's side.

Breathing hard, Glyn gripped his sword again and faced the Forlish, the fear thick within him. But he could not go, he could not let his family down, his village down. Not again.


Huw watched as a Forlishman ran at him, sword drawn back for the death blow. He loosed twice, seeing them wasted in the Forlish shield, and dropped the bow to fumble desperately for his sword, knowing he did not stand a chance.

'Face me!' Cadel leaped in front of him, sword held in both hands.

'Prepare to die, boy!' the Forlishman roared. He was six feet tall, with broad shoulders and a barrel chest. Cadel was just as tall but he was slim where the Forlishman was solid, his legs were scarce as thick as the Forlishman's arms. But he was fast — Huw had seen him in action.

The Forlishman swung his sword in a massive cut that Huw knew he could never have hoped to block. But Cadel threw up his own sword almost nonchalantly, deflecting the blow over his shoulder, then he went on the attack, raining blows at the Forlishman, using the cross and figure-eight styles Sendatsu had taught him.

The Forlishman blocked one with shield, the second with his sword, then they came too fast for him. One sliced open his ribs, the next his shoulder then, as his shield dropped, the last took his head.

'Stay behind me!' Cadel told Huw, who nodded vigorously.

The Forlishmen seemed to be clustering around Huw now, perhaps sensing he was the leader, and Cadel's squad fought furiously to protect the bard. Huw watched, feeling both delighted and useless as the young dragons worked as one, their superior skills too much for the Forlish to break.

Feeling safe now, as Cadel's bloodied sword ripped apart the last Forlishman near him, Huw glanced around quickly. Men fought over the dead, slipping and sliding on blood and shit and entrails. Wounded screamed as their wounds were stepped on, as their lifeblood pumped into the ground. Forlish stabbed and swung at the Velsh, who tried to match their speed and new-found skills against the implacable Forlish advance. The villagers fought grimly, knowing it was not just their lives but the lives of their families at stake here. The men who had hidden from a handful of Forlish just a few months ago, when Huw's father had been cut down, now stood toe to toe, swinging unfamiliar weapons and refusing to back down.

He glanced to his left and saw a Forlishman writhing on a hunting spear, the heavy iron head sticking out between his shoulder blades. To his right the village tanner was whirling a long hoe around his head, while a Forlishman reeled away, his eyes lost to the rusting iron blade, his face a mask of blood. But, to either side, other Velsh struggled desperately, or lay screaming in puddles of gore and brains. The smell was revolting, the sounds horrifying. They could not last.

'Over the barricade!' Huw bellowed.

It was the last refuge, their last hope. Several villagers were caught and hacked down as they turned to escape but most tumbled over the low barricade and then began thrusting swords and spears and hoes at the following Forlish.

'Rhiannon!' Huw shouted with all his might.

In answer, she stood.

She and many of the women were on the roofs of the huts that weaved in and out of the barricade — and all of them had elven crossbows in their hands. They worked the weapons furiously, sending down a new rain of bolts. Attacked from in front and above, the Forlish were easy targets and a dozen fell in the first few moments.

But the Forlish were grim opponents, used to victory. Some began to pull apart the barricade to reach the men, while others scrambled up onto the low roofs to attack the women, seeking an easier target.

A pair chose the hut Rhiannon and half a dozen other women were using.

'Get them!' She pointed and they converged their aim on the two Forlish as they tried to clamber up the roof, which bowed under their weight. One of them was struck repeatedly by bolts but the second kept coming, a bolt jutting from his upper arm and a bloodied sword in his hand. The women began looking backwards, to the dubious safety of the ground and the huts beyond, but Rhiannon knew they could not leave. Let one Forlish through here and a dozen could follow — and the children were in the huts behind. She loosed her last pair of bolts but one missed and the second, while striking his chest, did not seem to slow him. Rhiannon dropped her crossbow and leaped at him, kicking out as if she was performing a dance. Her leather shoe slammed into the side of his head and tumbled him over backwards and off the roof. She landed awkwardly on the thatch and nearly followed him off the roof, while the rafters groaned under the weight of her fall. She clung to the roof for a long moment before scrambling back up to the top. She accepted her crossbow back and loaded it with shaking hands.

'I did that move for their king — but it works better here!' she called to her companions, trying to make light of the fear she could feel coursing through her veins. More Forlish were threatening them, while others were hacking and cutting at the menfolk across the barricade.

'Sendatsu, we need you now,' she murmured to herself, amazed she could even speak those words, hidden as they were by shouts, screams, the ringing sound of steel on steel, as well as the deeper sound of steel on wood and the sickening sound of steel in flesh.

* * *

Broyle had not been overly concerned by finding a new barricade, or even by more Velsh resistance. His men had taken losses but were still churning forwards and it was only a matter of time before the enemy broke — for good this time. He did not have to do anything. There was no need in a fight like this. His men would keep attacking until they had killed everyone. It was the way of things. Certainly the Velsh were fighting better than he had expected — they were using their swords in a completely different way to anything he had seen before. Most warriors used a combination of strength and speed to batter down their opponents. There was no need for finesse. But these Velsh were different. A blow aimed at a head suddenly became a body cut, getting underneath a shield hastily raised, while parries turned into lunges and cuts seemingly without any effort. But it was not enough to stop his men.

Then he heard singing and turned. And felt fear for the first time in many a day.

Sendatsu ran easily, well within himself, making sure he stayed at the back of the dragons, who in turn stayed ahead of the leading Forlish.

'Stand and fight, you gutless sheep!' a Forlishman yelled and Sendatsu marked the owner of that voice, a tall warrior with a long moustache.

The ground was soft and sloping and he could feel it in his legs — and knew the Forlish, already tired from their exertions and carrying shields, had to be feeling it more. He led them on.

'Cowards! We'll get you!' the lead Forlishman shouted, his voice catching from the exertion.

Sendatsu glanced over his shoulder and saw the Forlish were ragged now, men dropping out the back, their tight lines in disarray.

'Close up!' he called and the lead dragons slowed a little, turning them into a solid mass.

'Sheep-shagging scum!' the Forlishman shouted but Sendatsu ignored him, judging instead his own men.

'Now!' he roared and turned, running as fast as he could back at the Forlish.

The lead chaser, the man with the insults, only had enough time to look surprised before Sendatsu was upon him. One slash of the sword and the Forlishman reeled back, trying and failing to keep his guts inside his body.

The other dragons were only half a step behind Sendatsu and were among the Forlish, dealing death with every blow a heartbeat later.

The Forlish thought they were the hunters — they never got the time to realise they had fallen into a trap. By the time they raised heavy shields on weary arms, the faster dragons were upon them, swords reaching out for throats and chests and bellies. The Forlish tried to stop, tried to form a new line but they were scattered and tired.

Sendatsu rampaged through their lines. A cut to the left opened up a man's chest, a slice to his right slashed open a throat as he used the cross pattern, the floating cloud and the figure-eight. These were not men to him — they were just straw targets in an exercise.

The Forlish, veterans though they were, were tired and scattered and could not stand against the dragons, much less Sendatsu. They turned and ran, throwing down swords and shields and racing for the hole in the outer fence.

'Let them go!' Sendatsu barked and the handful of dragons that had begun to pursue slowed to a reluctant stop. 'We stick to the plan!'

He left three of them to help their wounded comrades, then led the rest around a little further, to where they had made another gate into the village last night. Inside, they could see the battle raging, where the Forlish were threatening to overwhelm the villagers.

'We hit their right flank and we don't stop until the last Forlishman is dead. And sing — let them hear you coming!' Sendatsu shouted.

He had little more than sixty dragons left but the Forlish had suffered badly as well and their numbers were far reduced.

Roaring out 'Land of My Fathers', the Velsh dragons followed him in a charge across the village.

The Forlish heard them coming — but could do nothing about it. Those who tried to turn and form a new line just exposed themselves to the relentless crossbows, while the dragons ripped into their right flank and, with Sendatsu at their head, began rolling it up.

Broyle tried to impose some order, to organise a force to hold off this attack that was crumbling his right flank but he did not know how to rally the men. He had never faced anything like this — none of the Forlish really had. Defeat and reverses were what happened to the other side, not them. Without any training, without a group of sergeants on who he could depend, Broyle shouted useless orders that were lost in the confusion and watched in frustration as his men were felled.

And all the time a cloud of vicious little bolts descended on them.

'Back! Get out of here! Run for your lives!' a Forlish voice shouted.

Broyle stopped in horror. 'Who said that?' he demanded angrily. But few could hear him and even those that could were not listening to him.

Huw had clambered onto a roof, where he could see what was happening. The Forlish were almost ready to run, they just needed one more thing to tip them over the edge. He summoned his best Forlish accent and yelled down at them: 'Back! Get out of here! Run for your lives!'

The time spent in Ward's court in Cridianton served him well. The Forlish nearby could spot who was doing the shouting but others, unable to see him, only heard a voice of authority.

'Flee! Run!' Huw shouted in his best Forlish voice, using his training to make it as loud as possible.

It was enough. Assailed on all sides, without any direction from their own officers — indeed without any officers — the

Forlish heard the fake orders and chose to obey them. First one, then a handful, then a stream of them raced for the gap in the wall and freedom.

'After them! Don't let them get away!' Huw yelled in his normal voice, sliding down from the roof to join in the pursuit.

The temptation was to let them go, to preserve the lives of the villagers and the dragons — but over that was the thought this group of Forlish had come together to hunt him down. They had to be wiped out, or at least sent running back to Forland.

The villagers responded instantly. They had seen their village attacked three times now, their friends and family killed — and these were the men responsible. They hacked and slashed at the running Forlish, while others pumped crossbow bolts into legs and backs, bringing the runners down. Even the women joined in, groups of them isolating and slaughtering the Forlish as they discarded shields, swords, anything that would slow them down.

Wounded Forlish begged for their mates to help them, pleaded for mercy — and received neither.

Broyle tried to rally his men at the outer wall, to give others the time to get away — or perhaps to snatch victory from defeat. He brought his sword down viciously at a shouting villager — and was shocked to see the man throw his blade up in a parry. The force of the blow drove the villager down and Broyle confidently swung again, thinking to despatch the man. But another parry was followed by a lunge that Broyle had to work hard to avoid. Furious, ignoring what was going on around him, he stepped in close and locked blades with the villager. Still the man resisted, farm-bred strength holding Broyle at bay until the Forlishman smashed a head-butt into the man's face and finally thrust his sword into the helpless villager's chest. He roared his triumph and looked around, hoping he had inspired more of his men. But although a handful joined him, a cloud of elven crossbow bolts made such a task impossible.

Broyle was the only one with a shield and, while he ducked behind its protection, the rest of his men were struck and went down howling. He was alone. He could not believe he had to run — to be driven back by a pack of farm boys and soft villagers! How could this have happened? He burned with the shame of it. His plan to trap and destroy them had been turned upon itself. If only he'd had proper armour and weapons, things might have been different …

'Come on, sarge, let's get out of here while we can!' Ricbert grabbed his arm and tugged him away from the village.

'Where did you come from? I thought you'd killed that elf?' he asked numbly.

'He killed us. I ran to live — and now you need to run too.'

Stumbling blindly after the man, he allowed himself to be led away from the defeat, from the piteous cries of the wounded and the howls of the Velsh as they savaged the slow and the hurt, any that they could reach.

'We have to get back to Forland, we have to tell them what happened. We thought the Velsh were just sheep waiting to be sheared, but they have grown teeth. If we don't bring the real army up here soon, we'll have a worse problem than the Balians,' Ricbert yelled into Broyle's ear.

But Broyle could not imagine returning to Cridianton in disgrace, telling King Ward his finest warriors had been defeated by a pack of villagers.

Gazing around, he could see only a few score of his men still alive, and more were being dragged down and butchered every step of the way.

'The king has to know,' Ricbert cried. 'We have to warn him!'

Broyle's head cleared a little and he nodded, began lengthening his stride and drawing clear of slower runners and the limping wounded.

Hector watched from the trees as the Forlish marched forwards. It had been a slow enough advance that he had plenty of time to worry about what was going to happen to Rhiannon in there. Would she try to resist — would she fall victim to the lust of the victors? He did not trust Broyle to keep his soldiers on a tight leash but dared not speak to the man again. He bit his nails and paced as the Forlish crawled their way into the village.

The sounds of fighting drifted back to where Hector waited and he shuddered at the thought of Broyle's brutal men hunting through those tight streets inside the village. Surely the village had to surrender and beg for mercy soon. But the noises went on and on, and he wondered what was happening in there. He began to walk out, hoping to see something and yet afraid of what he might witness.

Then the Forlish broke and began flooding back towards him.

For a long moment he stared in disbelief, then saw the first Velsh appear out through their smashed wall, loose crossbows at running men, hack down the slow and the wounded, and he turned and fled, blundering through the trees, no thought beyond saving himself.

But, after he nearly ran headlong into a tree, he forced himself to stop and breathe, try to think a little. Obviously Broyle's plan, his confidence in the Forlish fighting man, had been drastically misplaced. These men would run or die. But what of him and his need to find Rhiannon, return with her to Cridianton? What was going to become of that?

He had sacrificed too much, invested too much time and effort to give up, even now. He could not return to Cridianton without Rhiannon and the king's seal and hope to escape with his skin intact. He needed both — and preferably the elf and bard as well. He had to find Broyle. Hector turned around and walked back, into the first soldiers, who ran past him, wanting to get one of the few horses.

'Where is Sergeant Broyle?' Hector demanded, grabbing one of the fleeing men.

'Dead, probably! Like we all will be if we stay here!' the man gibbered.

Hector released him with distaste and walked on. He pushed through more men, shoving them aside as he searched for a familiar face. He had almost given up — and the bloodthirsty shouts of the victorious Velsh were getting uncomfortably close — when he saw Broyle running, like the others.

'Broyle!' he bellowed, cutting across to intercept the sergeant.

Broyle did not slow down but Hector would not be denied. He thrust out an arm and grabbed the sergeant by his sweaty, blood-spattered tunic.

'Where are you going?' he shouted, his fear of the man lost in his anger.

'Let go of me!' Broyle snarled.

But Hector had had enough. 'Where will you run? If you go back to Cridianton, Ward will have you executed for this failure. Is that what you want?'

'If we stay here, the Velsh will get us!' Ricbert cried, trying to free Broyle from Hector's vicelike grip.

'There is another way! If we get my daughter, the bard and the elf, then we can return in triumph,' Hector insisted.

'You're mad — we have lost! We were slaughtered out there,' Ricbert insisted.

'Is this how you want to be remembered? As the man who led the Forlish to defeat, who showed the Velsh we could be beaten?' Hector asked, ignoring the corporal and focusing only on Broyle.

Broyle felt as though he was coming back from a distant place. 'No,' he admitted.

'Then come with me now. Obey me and we can return as heroes.'

'Are you going to listen to this? It's madness,' Ricbert spat.

'You go back to Cridianton. I shall stay,' Broyle said, his voice getting stronger. He straightened and Hector released his grip at last.

'Good. Gather some men and we shall head west. They have won today but might just let their guard down. We shall be ready,' Hector promised.

'Cridianton is death for any that return like this. We have to give the king something or he shall show us no mercy,' Broyle told Ricbert.

For a moment more the corporal looked as though he would argue, then he nodded.

'I'll get as many as I can before they all scatter to the four winds,' he finally agreed.

Huw halted the Velsh at the tree line. They had caught and killed two dozen more Forlish on the way down from the village and to keep going was pointless. They might track down a handful more but they risked more than they would gain. These Forlish would keep running and, if they had any sense, would go nowhere near King Ward. Or at least Huw hoped so.

'We did it!'

Villagers and dragons embraced one another, laughed and cheered, or sank to the ground in tears, overcome by what they had faced.

Huw knew they had to help the wounded, as well as gather up as many swords as they could find — but first he wanted to hold Rhiannon. He had brought down a pair of running Forlish with his crossbow, men who had been butchered by vengeful villagers, but he had not fought with the sword at all. Still, he had been close enough and the reaction had him shaking. The village had been turned into a charnel house and he dreaded to think of what he might find there, of the men who had died or been crippled, ones he had persuaded to fight for him. Glancing around, he saw Sendatsu cleaning his sword off on a handful of leaves, although his face, arms and chest were covered in blood.

'Are you hurt?' Huw hurried over.

'It's not mine,' Sendatsu assured him tiredly, then forced a smile. 'Well, we beat them, we saved the village — this is another tale that will grow with the telling around Vales.'

'We shall make sure all know of your part in it,' Huw assured him. 'We would not be here without you.'

'I don't want fame, or to be in a song. I just want to hold my children again,' Sendatsu declared. 'Besides, it was the dragons who were the difference.'

'Who would not have survived, would not exist without you. We have proved that Velsh can fight and beat the Forlish ...'

'Not quite. They were badly led, and not wearing any armour or in numbers much greater than ours ...'

'Oh, we should enjoy the victory while we can. By the time we have finished with it, there will be a thousand Forlish, all wearing armour and riding on winged steeds against us,' Rhiannon interrupted. But her smile was too bright, her eyes too wet to put much weight in her words.

'Are you all right?' Huw asked.

'I never want to see that again.' She shuddered. 'Why do men love war so much, spend so much time preparing for it? How could you want to do something so terrible?'

Sendatsu nodded agreement. At times during the past few moons, he had found himself almost in love with battle. The thrill of defeating others, of standing triumphant over your foe, had been intoxicating. But now, however, he would be happy never to fight again.

'You were wonderful. The women were the difference, helped us hold on long enough.' Huw dropped the crossbow and enfolded Rhiannon in his arms.

Sendatsu wanted to get out his children's toys, wanted to kiss them and promise them he would never again do anything so foolish — but he could not get the blood off his hands.

'I don't want to talk about it. Or think about it,' she declared.

'Then think about this. Why don't we Walk The Tree tomorrow?'

She leaned away from him. 'Are you serious?'

'As I can be,' Huw vowed.

Instantly she leaned in and kissed him, while around them, many of the dragons and villagers cheered and clapped.

Sendatsu walked slowly away. He would watch that then ride east. He would speak to Asami. If she did not have any hope for him, then he would travel back to Dokuzen with Cadel, Bowen, Tadd and a score of his dragons. He would be reunited with his children, one way or another.

# 27

I found Naibun at a small human church of Aroaril, accompanied by what looked like the entire Council Guard, and many Border Patrol as well. He greeted me warmly and invited me to eat with them but I could see a shadow behind his eyes.

Calmly, I outlined my suspicions and what I had learned.

'You have been killing our people, killing their people, spreading stories among our people and the various other tribes — and were you behind the attempt on my life?' I finished.

For a long time he did not answer and I dared to hope he would have an explanation for it all.

Finally he spoke. 'Yes. You are not fit to lead the elves ...'

'We are not elves! We are humans, just like everyone else!' I raged.

'No, we are special. But you would deny it, deny our birthright and our powers. I shall take control of the elven people and lead them to their true destiny,' he told me.

I had had enough. 'You shall do nothing of the kind. You will be arrested and tried for your crimes against the people of this continent ...'

'Wrong. It is you who will be punished. You will be killed here, the victim of a human attack. The people will mourn your passing but not for long. Your death will be the excuse I need to stop this ridiculous idea of a magic barrier around Dokuzen.

*We shall take control of the humans, make them our slaves and rule — as we were meant to!'*

*I went for my sword but the Council Guards, who I thought loyal to me — stopped me.*

*'You shall die tomorrow,' he told me, with a smile on his face, which I could no longer recognise, 'die with every human with magic. We have invited them all here to give them a gift, under the shelter of Aroaril. And then we shall kill them, so there will be nothing to stop us.'*


'You have a victory, your majesty!'

Cheering crowds filled the streets around the castle at Cridianton and Ward stood high on the wall, waving to his people, unable to keep the smile from his face.

At long last the Landish had surrendered. And, in the same quarter-moon, the siege of Pevensey had finished with the city elders begging for mercy — and being impaled for their troubles. Balia was at his mercy now, while the far southern countries of Demetia and Crolland were within his grasp. Already they had envoys waiting to see him, to offer terms to stop the Forlish armies rolling over their fields and towns. His vision was coming true.

'Captain Edmund,' Ward beckoned one of his war captains to his side.

'Sire?'

'The news from the south is all good. But I have not heard anything from the north for almost a full moon. Find out what is going on there.'

'I should think the Velsh are about ready to bend the knee to your majesty,' Edmund rumbled. 'I have one of my best sergeants up there and he'll be making sure there are tears in every Velsh village.'

'I hope so,' Ward agreed. 'Send me news within the next quarter-moon. I want to know the Velsh are mine before I decide whether to use my fleet to invade the Skilly Isles, or pay the Velsh a visit they will never forget.'

* * *

'Will your father lead clan Tadayoshi and support the Magic-weavers?' Sumiko demanded.

'Sensei, I cannot say for sure. Perhaps we would be better speaking to Gaibun's father. After all, he was Jaken's rival ...'

Asami had spent the previous few days arguing with Gaibun over this very thing. Gaibun was sure neither of their fathers would do such a thing, the shame of being appointed by Magic-weavers too much for them to bear. Asami wanted to believe her father would do what was necessary for the good of Dokuzen — but reluctantly agreed with Gaibun.

She found herself doing that more and more of late — agreeing with Gaibun. They had been talking as much as they ever did in those long-ago days when they were teenagers and had not a care in the world. At last they had found a common purpose.

'Then we shall have to rule without the clans,' Sumiko interrupted. 'Sendatsu has another few days to contact us or we shall have to act without him. Either we shall overthrow the Council and rule the elves, or die in the attempt.'

'The Magic-weavers have not tried anything. I have spent the last moon waiting every night but they fear to act,' Jaken said scornfully.

'I do not know what they plan,' Gaibun admitted. 'But I know they fear you and believe you have a trap set for them. They want to contact either my father or Asami's father and see if they are willing to rule the elves as their puppet.'

Jaken chuckled. 'They are so predictable! The only question is whether we let them make their attempt and then act, or act first. The first has the appeal of having them do the work for me — once Daichi and his supporters are dead, it will be child's play to step in. But that means Daichi will die without knowing I am the architect of his doom.'

'Surely, lord, to step in and save Dokuzen from the Magic-weavers is the best course, the honourable thing to do ...'

'But nowhere near as much fun,' Jaken mused. 'Have we heard from Hanto at all?'

'No, lord.'

'Then we can assume he has failed. A pity. Now the responsibility falls to you. No doubt they will make one last attempt to contact my son. If Sendatsu returns, then the Magic-weavers will act. We will be prepared, of course, but advance notice of even one turn of the hourglass will be perfect.'

Gaibun felt Jaken's eyes burn into him and drew himself to attention.

'Yes, lord,' he promised.


The day after the battle brought only hard work and tears. Walls needed to be rebuilt, weapons collected and cleaned, wounded tended and graves dug. The Forlish dead were dragged out into a huge pile, where the smashed wood from the old palisade was stacked around them and the corpses burned. It had to be done fast — crows and ravens were flying in from all over Vales to fight over the bodies, while several that had died by the woods looked like they had been mauled by foxes and wolves. The smell of death and blood hung over the village.

It had been a victory but everyone had suffered. There were few men who did not have some sort of wound, while a dozen were badly wounded and unlikely to recover. Sendatsu had showed them how to deal with cuts: clean them with honey mead, stuff the gap with cobwebs and then crudely stitch shut, before bandaging with washed strips of linen, adding a herbal poultice. For those who had lost a hand or more of a limb, they sealed it with pitch — but there was nothing to be done for those with wounds to the chest and stomach. Sendatsu watched them struggle to make these dying men comfortable — some of them his young dragons — and he burned with shame. In Dokuzen, the priest of Aroaril would have come around, blessed them and healed the most grievous, while women and men would have used a mixture of herbs and their own magic to aid those with light wounds.

With his help, some of the wounded would recover, although the village was filled with crying rather than rejoicing because of the number of dead and wounded. Families had lost fathers, sons, brothers, cousins and friends — while two women had been killed in the chase of the Forlish, leaving children howling for both mother and father.

Huw and Sendatsu went around the dragons, speaking to all of them, spending time with the wounded and trying to make their pain easier. Out of the hundred who had ridden into the village, a dozen were dead and twice that many wounded, many of those unlikely to ever fight again.

'A high price to pay,' Sendatsu sighed.

'We had no choice,' Huw said sadly. 'But their sacrifice will not be forgotten. Men shall sing of this day — the whole Vales will know what we did!'

Sendatsu tried to smile but could not. 'And when Ward travels north with his full army? What will happen then? How will you stand against them? They will be armoured, armed with spear and sword, locked in tight ranks, disciplined and led well.'

Huw leaned against a wall. 'I notice you said "you", not "we",' he said slowly.

'I cannot stay here. I need to get back to my children. I am all they have, do you understand?'

Huw wanted to argue with Sendatsu, but the blood and violence of the previous day seemed to have washed that out of him. Besides, he could not deny the elf had already helped them immensely.

'I know,' he said tiredly. 'As for the Forlish, what else can we do? The elves are not going to come to our aid — we must stand or fall on our own. We shall pull everyone as far back into Vales as we can, then hit and run and hide — hope that he loses patience, hope the Landish and Balians rise as well, so he is forced to send his men home. All we have is hope.'

Sendatsu wanted to ask more but was afraid it would give Huw the chance to persuade him to stay longer.

'What about Rhiannon?' he asked, changing the subject. 'Have you told her the truth yet?'

Huw pushed himself up off the wall and looked over his shoulder.

'Not yet,' he admitted. 'I shall tell her after we have Walked The Tree.'

'And that will make all the difference?' Sendatsu asked cynically. 'Do you think she will be happier you admit you lied only after you are married?'

'I don't think she will be any happier but at least she will not leave me then,' Huw said defensively.

'Trust in her. Trust in yourself!' Sendatsu urged. 'You can't expect to last together if you don't believe that what you have is strong enough to withstand the truth. You can't build a life on a lie.'

Huw looked at him. 'You seem able to preach to others but ignore such advice when it comes to your own life,' he said wryly.

'What do you mean?'

'You have all these abilities, all this knowledge, and all you want to do is hide them.'

'I have a responsibility to my children ...'

'You use them as an excuse,' Huw accused. 'You don't want to be a leader. You could go back to Dokuzen and change everything there, if you but had the will.'

'You don't understand it. You have never been there. You don't know what that would take!'

'I know I am changing Vales,' Huw fired back. 'Nobody would have said that was possible even three moons ago but look at us now. And I didn't begin with half of what you have!'

Sendatsu heard the words but had no intention of getting into this debate. He would get his children back and then put this whole nightmare behind him, somehow.

'Don't change the subject,' he said, changing the subject. 'You must tell Rhiannon. She deserves to know. Her father is still out there.'

'Fine. Run from my words, as you run from all responsibility. But one day it will catch up to you. If there is one thing I have learned, it is that life will find out your deepest fear — and make it come true. How you deal with that is the mark of who you are.'

'Rhiannon?' Sendatsu prompted, shutting his ears to the bard's words. 'Her father?'

'You thought he was behind the Forlish attack,' Huw pointed out, with a sigh.

'So I was wrong there. But he is not going to give up and go home. You don't want to meet him when she doesn't know the full truth ...'

'I shall tell her today,' Huw promised. 'Now, when we Walk The Tree, we need two witnesses to tell our families. Usually it is the two fathers who watch the ceremony but, for obvious reasons, that won't happen with us. I would like you to be there.'

Sendatsu was surprised by how much that meant to him.

'What about Rhiannon? Would she want me there?'

'She does. We have been through so much together, we three. It seems right that you should be there.'

'It feels strange, given our history. But I shall be glad to — honoured.' Sendatsu smiled. 'Who is the other?'

'Rhiannon is asking Glyn. We need to be escorted to the tree from separate directions, then make our vows together and walk once around, sunwise.'

'A strange ceremony,' Sendatsu commented. 'Are you sure there is nothing in the history of Vales about worshipping Aroaril? Did the elves not try to show you God?'

'Nothing I have heard.' Huw shrugged. 'Of course, we do not have a written history. Our knowledge of those times is hidden in myth and mystery.'

Sendatsu nodded. Perhaps he should find some good men and women and simply try to get them to talk to Aroaril ...

'Are you having second thoughts about witnessing for me?' Huw asked.

'Of course not!' Sendatsu assured him. 'But should we not take some of the dragons with us? Where is this oak tree?'

'It is not far outside the village. There is no need to take the dragons. They are needed to help rebuild here.' Huw waved it off.

'But the Forlish ...'

'Are still running. Besides, we shall have you there. There is no finer swordsman in Vales!'

'Flattery does not change the need for having more men there. What if there are a couple of Forlish out there waiting for us? Why not let another dozen witness this ceremony?'

'I doubt that there are any Forlish left within ten miles of this village.' Huw smiled. 'And Walking The Tree is an old and sacred ritual. To perform it in front of a score of armed men would forever spoil the day for Rhiannon ...'

'And you are going to spoil it enough for her by revealing your lie afterwards,' Sendatsu finished for him.

'Indeed,' Huw admitted.

'Then I shall respect your wishes.'

'It will be all fine, you'll see,' Huw insisted.

Sendatsu smiled but another worry nagged at him. Hanto was still out there somewhere. He had not been seen or heard of for a moon or more but he was not the sort of elf to give up easily.

Glyn was delighted to agree to be a witness. He had been unsure about the break in tradition but, after what they had all been through, he recognised that waiting until Midwinter was not always possible.

'I shall be able to tell the grandkids about this.' He grinned. He had come through the battle with a slight wound to the left arm, dressed and bandaged in the way Sendatsu had shown them. 'I wasn't sure about this way of treating wounds — normally we just wrap a rag around it and put a lucky elfbolt in there to help it heal. But none of the wounds have gone green and runny yet.'

'Thank you for that thought — right before I eat!' Rhiannon told him.

Glyn patted her arm. 'I am honoured to stand in for your father on this day — and happy you are marrying Huw. The two of you together — it gives me hope, it does!'

Rhiannon laughed. She was excited about the day, although it was not exactly as she had imagined it. She had always thought her father would be there, for one. And, if she was honest, a scruffy bard with an unusual face had not been even close to the daydreams.

But that was who she had fallen for and, after all, there were unexpected benefits. For a start there would be an elf there — and she had always wanted elves at her wedding. The big difference was the number of people who would be there. In the Forlish tradition, the whole village would watch and celebrate with the couples being married. The Velsh married with just the two fathers present, or at least one witness from each family, then returned to the village for all to celebrate. Often the nearest oak tree was far away and making the whole village journey for a day or more would not work. In Forlish villages, the oak tree was usually at the centre of the village but the Velsh climate was not quite the same. Patcham was just lucky enough to have one only a few miles away. She did not like the Velsh tradition as much but, seeing as she would be living among them as one of their leaders, she wanted to show them she admired their ways. She wanted to be more Velsh than the Velsh, so had insisted they stick strictly to the Velsh tradition, rather than taking a squad of dragons along.

She did not have a proper wedding dress, which should be made of white linen, but she still had a few of her dancing dresses, so chose her favourite.

Busy though they were, heartbroken though many were, most of the village still rallied to wave them goodbye as they rode out to the oak — the remaining dragons forming a guard of honour.

'There's still time to tell her the truth before we go ahead with the wedding,' Sendatsu murmured as they rode away.

Huw ignored him. Nothing would spoil the happiness of this day, he decided.

They rode gently west, towards the woods that split Crumlin from Patcham, talking and laughing as they went.

Glyn told stories of Huw's childhood and how the village had thought Earwen's son had his head stuffed full of fleece.

'He always wanted to sing, to play,' Glyn reminisced. 'Nobody thought he would amount to anything and now look at him. This boyo will become the leader of a united Vales!'

'I only ever wanted to be a bard,' Huw corrected. 'Now we do what we must to protect Vales. I do no more than Rhiannon and Sendatsu — and oftimes I do less.'

'Well, the people know the truth of it. It is a Velshman who has given us the courage to stand with you. I often thought your father was a fool for not beating the nonsense out of you and making a proper farmer. But I now thank the stars above he ignored me.'

Huw sought to change the subject, uncomfortable with the praise, while Rhiannon and Sendatsu could see much hilarity in these memories.

'So what was he like as a child?' Rhiannon teased. 'Was he as dirty and dressed as badly as he is now?'

'Oh, worse,' Glyn assured them. 'You should have seen him singing to the sheep. They thought it was the craziest dog they had ever come across!'

'I can just imagine him as a boy, singing to the animals. Did they ever join in?' Rhiannon laughed.

'They made a better audience than some I have performed to,' Huw admitted with a smile.

'Aroaril knows what he was like as a boy — I had to just about fight to get him to take a bath in honour of the day.' Sendatsu smiled.

'Here now — you won't be making everyone take baths when you rule Vales, will you?' Glyn asked nervously. 'I don't hold with that!'

They laughed as they rode. Huw looked at Rhiannon and was so happy he was almost afraid.


'This is our chance,' Hanto snapped. 'We kill the others, grab Sendatsu and be back in Dokuzen before nightfall. We may not get another opportunity, so we cannot make another mistake.'

Jin and Taigo wanted to go back, more than anything. Their wounds had not really healed properly, while they were filthy and hungry, struggling to find enough to fill their bellies. Hanto, on the other hand, was driven by something more. His eyes still burned with the desire for revenge.

They had watched the battle the day before with a mixture of fear and excitement, worrying that Sendatsu would be killed but hoping to find an opening in the chaos that followed. They had stalked through the woods but been unable to get close enough. Now, as if responding to their prayers, four riders had left the village — including Sendatsu.

'No mercy. I want him dead rather than escape me again.'

His two companions nodded dully, willing to do anything if it meant a return to the comforts of Dokuzen.


'Here we are!' Glyn pointed out the oak, sitting alone in a small clearing, a well-trodden path to it, and around it.

'So what now? Do we sit here while you walk around it?' Sendatsu asked. He had relaxed; they were still close to the village, so close they could see the lookout tower and the wall, and the laughter had eased his fears.

'Not at all. You stay with Huw here, while I take Rhiannon across to the west. Then we both approach, one from the east, one from the west; the fathers — that's us — step back and the two of them take their hands, exchange vows and Walk The Tree together.'

'And what are the vows?'

'Well, to love, honour and obey, of course.' Huw grinned. 'Although I doubt the obey part will ever come true.'

'Nor should it.' Rhiannon winked at him. Her hair had been braided elaborately by Glyn's wife, Wendi, while she wore a long cloak over the dress she had chosen for the wedding.

'They promise to take no other, to raise their children well, to always be faithful and to work together, to look after each other as long as there is breath in their body,' Glyn added.

'A vow for the whole of Vales,' Sendatsu said softly, thinking of the weddings he had been to at Dokuzen, the two elves before a priest of Aroaril, swearing to God they would never be apart. Sometimes it worked but often one or both took other lovers, like Gaibun with Asami. Then there was his marriage — they had been polite to each other but there had been no love there.

It was typical of many marriages in Dokuzen. Life went on whether families were together or fighting. In fact, there were feuds that had been going for generations, clans who actively sought to destroy another. There were elves that would have drawn swords if not for the culture of exquisite politeness. Instead they devoted their lives to secretly undermining the opposing clan. It was one of the things that kept Jaken so busy. The simplicity and the selflessness of Vales seemed to be a far better way of living.

'Give us a short while to get ready, then begin to walk,' Glyn instructed as he and Rhiannon kept riding, while Huw and Sendatsu got down from their horses, tying the reins around the low-flung branch.

'It is traditional to keep the man waiting for a little while — to make him think about what he will miss if he does not marry the woman of his dreams,' Glyn whispered as they rode on into the woods.

'But not too long.' Rhiannon smiled as they climbed down from the horses, tying them to a tree.

'Let him sweat a little. He does not know how lucky he is.' Glyn chuckled.

'We are both lucky,' Rhiannon corrected. She made her way around the horses so both were between her and Glyn and then slipped off her cloak and laid it over the saddle.

'Did your wife make you wait?'

'Too long!' Glyn laughed.

'Well, there we are then. Does my dress look fine? Is it too crushed?'

But Glyn did not answer, just made a strange sort of choking noise.

Rhiannon wondered if that was some sort of compliment, or perhaps the man needed a drink of water. She stepped around the horses, twirling her dress as she did so.

'Are you all right …?' she began, then stopped in horror.

Glyn stood facing her, but there was blood at his mouth and a sword point was sticking out of the middle of his chest. He gave her a last, agonised look, then his eyes rolled up and he collapsed onto the ground. Rhiannon watched his slow-motion fall in terror and then looked up to see a Forlish warrior leering at her.

She took a pace backwards, opened her mouth to shout a warning, only to have a large, dirty hand clamped across her mouth.

'Don't want you to let them know the surprise we have for them.' The warrior who had killed Glyn grinned viciously. 'Come on, down the path.'

She kicked out, determined to alert Huw and Sendatsu, but a powerful punch into her kidneys left her agonised, temporarily paralysed with the pain. A strong arm grabbed her wrist, twisted it high behind her back, while the rough hand smothered her attempts to call out. She tried to dig her feet in but she was helpless against her captor's greater strength. She was hustled down the path towards the tree.

'Well, you are getting what you want here — but don't blame me if it comes back to bite you when you tell Rhiannon the truth,' Sendatsu muttered.

'I shall tell her. Once we are married,' Huw insisted.

'It may be your marriage but might also be your funeral,' Sendatsu grumbled.

'Nobody asked you to stay here,' Huw said tartly.

'Well, actually you did,' Sendatsu reminded him. 'You've been trying to get me to stay here for longer than I wanted since we met!'

'Well, after today you can do what you want, go where you will,' Huw said absently. 'Do you think she's taking a long time down there?'

Sendatsu looked down the path and tapped Huw on the shoulder. 'Here they come!'

Huw straightened his shoulders, closed his eyes and took a deep breath — then shouted in shock and surprise as he saw, not Glyn escorting Rhiannon to the tree, but a struggling Rhiannon being hustled down the path by a Forlish warrior.

'Let her go, unless you want to spend the rest of your life

screaming in agony,' Sendatsu vowed, his sword leaping into his hand.

'Drop the sword, elf! And you drop any weapons you have, bard!' the warrior shouted. 'Drop them or she dies!'

To emphasise his words, another three of them appeared out of the shadows, swords in hands, all of them pointing at Rhiannon.

Sendatsu and Huw exchanged helpless looks. They were a good ten yards away from the little group and it was impossible to cross that distance before one or more of the Forlish killed Rhiannon.

'If we drop our swords, we are dead anyway,' Sendatsu murmured.

'Quick now, my patience is running out!' the Forlishman snarled.

Rhiannon struggled anew. She had seen Sendatsu in action often enough to know four Forlish warriors were not beyond his ability. But he could not act if they held her. She hated that. It was just like those stories they performed. The helpless heroine. Well, she would not be a part of that. She stamped down on her captor's calf, raking her heel down the muscle, then bit down on the hand over her mouth — trying not to think what it tasted like — heard the howl of pain and snapped her head back for good measure, trying to hit his nose, feeling solid contact but not the satisfying squish that indicated she had struck her target.

It half worked. She was free for a moment, jumped forwards and opened her mouth to shout, 'We're all dead anyway — kill them!' before another blow in the ribs dropped her to her knees.

Sendatsu and Huw both started forwards as she threw off the first Forlishman but two others converged on her, one slamming his fist into her side, the other grabbing her arms and twisting them back.

'No closer! No closer or I swear she dies!' Her original captor, blood streaming from his hand and his cheekbone swelling red, held his sword close to her neck.

Rhiannon could feel the cold steel, the edge rough from all the sharpening, and went very still. It was all very well sitting around a warm fire, talking about how death was better than being dragged before Ward — but it was hard to embrace it when it was a hair's breadth from your throat.

Sendatsu was torn. Everything he had learned told him to take his chances and attack. But he cared too much for Rhiannon to risk her life.

'Enough! Drop your swords!' The Forlishman grabbed Rhiannon's hair, pulled her head back to expose her throat.

'Sendatsu! Drop your sword!' Huw cried, agonised, hurling his own knife to the ground. His crossbow was still on his saddle and too far away to be of any use.

'I can't! If they get us, there is no way out,' Sendatsu hissed. 'They won't hurt her — they want to bring her back to Ward unharmed.'

Huw looked back and, in response, the Forlishman jerked his hand in Rhiannon's hair, making her cry out. But she stared at them, her eyes telling them not to give in.

'Do you bet her life on it?' Huw muttered.

'I count to three and then I strike! King Ward wants you alive but he'd rather have you dead than not at all. I have my orders — you have your choice. One, two ...'

Sendatsu tensed himself to leap across the distance, praying that Rhiannon's soul would forgive him if he was wrong.

'No!' Huw grabbed Sendatsu, held him back.

'What are you doing?' Sendatsu gasped. 'They will kill us — if not now then later. And you are the only man who can unite Vales. The people need you!'

'The dragons! They will search for us, they will follow us and free us,' Huw whispered urgently. 'Please, I cannot save Vales knowing she died for me — I could not live like that!'

Sendatsu looked into his eyes and, although his head told him otherwise, his heart knew he could not sacrifice Asami if the roles had been reversed. His hand opened nervelessly and his sword fell to the ground.

'About time!' the Forlishman rasped. 'On your knees, hands behind your heads! Move and she dies. Tie them.'

Two of the Forlish sheathed swords and produced coils of rope, while the third rushed across and grabbed both Sendatsu's sword and Huw's knife. Sendatsu itched to strike, to attack them — but the sword was still right at Rhiannon's throat and Huw's eyes implored him not to do anything.

One at a time, Sendatsu and Huw had their hands bound, then they were dragged to their feet and pushed back against the oak tree, tied to it around the waist, then their bound hands tied to a branch overhead. They were not gentle about it, hauling Huw's and Sendatsu's arms up high, stretching their shoulders, while tightening rope coils around chests and stomachs so they bit into flesh.

'I thought we were being taken back to Ward,' Huw grunted, as the rope dug into his chest and his arms ached from being hauled up high.

'Oh, you will be,' the Forlishman assured, dragging Rhiannon to her feet.

'Why aren't you tying me up?' Rhiannon blazed. 'Don't you think a woman is dangerous?'

'Not at all. But before you meet King Ward, I thought you would like to meet an old friend first.' The Forlishman touched his swollen cheek with a still-bleeding hand gingerly. He spoke to one of his men, who raced back down the trail. 'And then you can tell me what an elf is doing here, what you are doing with the Velsh and your new way of fighting. King Ward will reward me well for those answers.'

'Listen to me,' Huw said urgently. 'I know Ward. He will not reward you for failure. You lost too many men — he will take your knowledge and your only reward will be death! You can't go back but there is another way. Stay here with us. Work for me. Here in Vales you can make a new life ...'

The Forlishman strode across the clearing as Huw tried to give his words every last bit of his skill and persuasion.

'Live here? Betray my king? Here is my answer!'

And the Forlishman drove his fist into Huw's stomach. Held by the ropes, Huw could not move and gasped as the air was driven out of his lungs. Winded, he hung in his bonds.

'Bastard!' Rhiannon raced at the Forlishman but the other two warriors grabbed her arms, held her as she kicked and screamed threats.

'Quite her father's daughter,' the Forlishman observed.

Even as he twisted in pain, the words cut through to Huw and he glanced across at Sendatsu, to his left, who also looked at him.

'Were you one of the ones who killed him? I swear I'll make you pay!' Rhiannon vowed.

'Shut up!' the Forlishman shouted. 'You know nothing. I am going to give you a gift, you little fool!'

'I want nothing from you,' Rhiannon spat.

'We shall see.' The Forlishman smiled and turned to Huw and Sendatsu. 'I have dreamed of this day for a long time,' he told them. 'I attacked your village, killed an old man and took four women, only for someone to slaughter half my men and take them back. I think that was you.'

Huw gasped, but not from pain. Was this the man who killed his father?

'I have hunted you ever since,' the Forlishman continued. 'I have many questions to ask you. But first I want you to all meet someone very important. It seems you were about to Walk The Tree together. Well, we may be in the barbarian Vales but even here, isn't the father invited?'

'Both our fathers are dead, thanks to you and your kind!' Rhiannon hissed.

The Forlishman only smiled. 'Really? Then who is that behind you?'

The men holding her let go of her arms and, against her will, Rhiannon turned.

'Hello my darling,' Hector said, a broad smile on his face as he walked into the clearing.

# 28

*'You have failed,' I told Naibun.*

*He laughed in my face. 'You always had a rich sense of humour, Sendatsu! This is my triumph and there is nobody to stop me ...'*

*'I have already. Before I came here I set the Magic-weavers working on the barrier. They are building it now, even as we speak. In another turn of the sun it will be complete and nobody will be able to get in or out of Dokuzen for at least a hundred years. And you know the process. Once started, it cannot be stopped.'*

*Naibun knew instantly I was not lying, and his fury was terrible to see. When he calmed down, I was lying on the ground in a pool of my own blood and he had smashed everything else in sight.*

*'I shall still rule Dokuzen,' he hissed. 'You shall die, along with the other humans who dared to challenge the might of the elves. You shall die at dawn and then we shall return to Dokuzen.'*

*It did not feel like a victory as they dragged me away, but at least it did not feel like an utter defeat.*

Rhiannon stared in shock as her father strode over and enfolded her in his arms. She stayed rigid, looking at his familiar — and yet forgotten — face with incredulity.

'Father? Is it really you? Are you really alive?' she gabbled, tentatively touching his cheek.

'Of course it is me,' Hector said with just a touch of asperity, then relaxed a little. 'I am safe and well, as I always have been.'

'But how did you get here — are you a prisoner also — what is going on?' Rhiannon's last words were a desperate plea.

Since she had seen Hector's ring in Huw's hand, she believed her father was dead and her world had completely changed. Now everything was thrown into the air.

'A prisoner?' Hector threw back his head and laughed heartily. 'Quite the opposite! No, Sergeant Broyle here is under my command.'

The three of them looked at the Forlishman with the swollen face, who glowered back.

'But he killed my friend Glyn, he and his men grabbed me, hit me, threatened to kill me ...'

'No!' Hector exclaimed. 'They were told to do whatever was necessary to free you but they were under strict instructions not to hurt you.'

'Well, that did not happen,' Rhiannon declared, feeling where her ribs were bruised. 'Are you sure this is not all some trick ...?'

'Look!' Hector produced the king's seal and flourished it for her benefit. 'I am here by the command of King Ward, to rescue you and return you home.'

'Rescue me? Bring me home?' Rhiannon repeated stupidly. She could make no sense of what was happening, it was all too much.

Hector embraced her once more and kissed her gently on the forehead.

'There is much to tell you, much to explain. You have been lied to by your so-called friends over there and it will take some time to show you the truth.'

He glanced over to where the bard and elf hung in their bonds and could not restrain his smile of triumph. He had waited so patiently for this moment, watching the village and avoiding the Velsh patrols, until the time came to pounce. That they seemed to be ready to Walk The Tree was disturbing, although it had split Rhiannon away from her protectors. But it meant he had to go carefully here. He wanted to storm in and slap the little bitch silly.

Did she have any idea of the trouble she had caused him? Even now it was going to take some fast talking and the information Broyle could wring out of the bard and elf to get back into Ward's good graces. And to get her to jump willingly into Ward's bed was going to take some clever work. Indulging his natural inclination to take out his anger and frustration on her could spoil everything.

'Why don't you sit down?' he suggested gently.

Huw's arms were burning but the pain was nothing to the kick in the guts he had taken when Hector had walked into the clearing. He knew he had to find the words to fight against the tale Hector was about to spin, he had to tell the whole truth — but all he could think of was Rhiannon's expression when Sendatsu had revealed his lies and the sick feeling inside at the thought of her walking away with Hector and into Ward's arms.

Sendatsu could see no good way out of this — and he was also cursing Huw for stopping him. The Forlish would never have killed Rhiannon. It had all been a bluff. But Rhiannon was also their hope, given she was the only one still free.

'Rhiannon! Don't listen to him! He's a liar! Tell her, Huw!' he yelled.

'Sergeant!' Hector barked and Broyle raced to where Huw and Sendatsu hung.

Both Huw and Sendatsu tried to protest, to call out to Rhiannon, but Broyle winded Huw with another huge punch, then ripped a strip off his tunic, balled it up and stuffed it in his mouth as a gag. As for Sendatsu, when the elf tried to clench his jaw shut, to defeat the gag, Broyle just held his nose until the elf was forced to breathe.

'What if the elf uses magic to get himself free, like those other ones did?' Ricbert suggested, drawing his dagger and holding it above Sendatsu's heart.

'Just stand by him and if he tries anything, slit his throat,' Broyle said casually.

Sendatsu spent less time thinking about that than he did the news these Forlish had captured Hanto — although they'd obviously lost him once more. Had Hanto told him anything?

'We need him alive,' Hector suggested. 'I doubt we will be able to get all the information we need about Dokuzen and the elven plans from this revolting Velshman.'

'Fine. But if he tries anything, he dies,' Broyle said harshly.

'Just gag him for now,' Hector advised, then turned back to a still-stunned Rhiannon. 'Now, my dear, you can see that I am not just alive but perfectly healthy and in the good graces of our lord the king, otherwise he would not have given me both his soldiers and his seal. So what lies did that filthy Velsh bard tell you to make you leave Cridianton and come and live here among the scum of the earth? What did he say to trick you into satisfying his lust?'

Sendatsu knew they had to do something to get through to Rhiannon. He grunted at Huw, trying to work the cloth out of his mouth, although Ricbert's dagger was dangerously close. Huw, for his part, was staring at Rhiannon, his eyes liquid pools of terror. This was his nightmare sprung to life and, just like a bad dream, he could do nothing to stop it.

'He said you were dead and that if I did not come with him, then I would be next. That Ward wanted me to be his mistress,' Rhiannon said dully.

Hector gave her his broadest laugh. 'And you can see the truth of that in front of you! No, the real story is much more sordid than that. He heard how the king thought you were far better than him, how the king was thinking of sending him away, back to stinking Vales. So, in his jealousy and insane lust, he tricked you into following him away from there, away from me and all who loved you!'

Rhiannon shook her head slowly.

'But he had your ring! You never take off your ring!' she protested.

'I had taken it off because the king was going to give me another, as thanks for bringing you into his court.' Hector shrugged. 'He must have stolen it from my room, breaking in the same way he stole into your rooms.'

Something was niggling at Rhiannon, something was not quite

right — but she dismissed that for the much bigger issue: Huw had lied to her. That blacked out everything else.

She jumped to her feet and stormed over to him.

'How could you?' she screamed. 'How could you do that to me? I thought you were my friend — I thought you were helping me! I cried because I was so sorry I had kept you in Cridianton too long for you to get back and save your father! I stayed awake at nights thinking about that — and all the time you were lying! You knew how much being at court meant to me — but you just had to have me for yourself, didn't you! Was it all lies? Did you get your elven friend to bed me and trick me so that I would fall into your arms? Was anything you said to me the truth?'

Both Huw and Sendatsu were trying to speak now, trying to protest her accusations — although of course nothing understandable was coming out of their mouths.

Hector sat back, satisfied. It was all proceeding as planned. He would let her rant and rave at them some more, then take her a little way away while Broyle worked on them, got them in the right mood to confess to anything. Nothing that would kill them, of course, but enough to make them babble his version of events to save themselves from more pain — and get them ready to tell all about the elves and their plans for a free Vales.

'You bastard! I was going to Walk The Tree with you! I thought I loved you!'

Rhiannon had been certain she could never feel as bad as when Sendatsu had admitted his lies to her. But this was so much worse. With Sendatsu, she had contributed to her own downfall. With Huw, she thought herself wiser. She thought she knew what she was getting into. This was not some flight of fancy, some little girl's dream. This was the real thing. She had seduced him. She was going to Walk The Tree with him — they were going to have a life together. To find it was all based on a lie was almost too much for her. Her insides alternately felt as though they were filled with ice, then boiled with rage that she had been fooled — again!

'You bastard! How could you? How *could* you?' she screamed, beating her fists against his chest.

'I'll never forgive you for this. *Never!*'

Hector nodded. Excellent. Just what he wanted to hear from her. Soon she would be amenable to suggestion herself — he planned to tell her that getting into Ward's bed was her only way back to court. While it seemed unlikely she was still untouched, he was confident she had the acting ability to fool Ward on the first night. He was imagining what he needed to say to her when it all took an unexpected turn.

Rhiannon stopped hitting Huw and looked at him. 'Why?' she pleaded. She had been so sure. He had been there from the start, her only friend — had it all been an act? She was just a foot away from Huw, trying to read his expression. Tears were rolling down his cheeks and he was shaking his head desperately, obviously trying to say something.

She leaned in and ripped the gag out of his mouth.

'Tell me the truth!' she commanded.

'Yes, I lied to you about your father!' Huw cried, agonised, and she turned away, stricken. 'But only to protect you!'

'What?' Rhiannon turned back, tears rolling down her face as well. Huw's admission of a lie was the final dagger into her heart. She did not know whether to howl or vomit. 'How can you imagine that was protecting me?'

Hector signalled to Broyle, who ran in to cut Huw off.

'Your father was selling you off to Ward! Hector promised you would go to Ward with open arms and legs — his price for that was riches and fame!' Huw yelled as fast as he could.

'No!' Rhiannon and Hector exclaimed, but for completely different reasons.

Broyle was there a moment later to cut off Huw's words with another blow to the stomach, then stem the flow by stuffing the gag back in his mouth.

'Wait!' Rhiannon said angrily. 'I still wanted to talk to him — I had not finished!'

'He said all you needed to hear when he admitted his treachery in his first breath. Why do you want to hurt yourself further by hearing more lies from his foul mouth?' Hector said consolingly.

He drew Rhiannon into a gentle embrace and let her tears spill out. 'After all I have done for you, all I have sacrificed for you, do you really think I would betray you?'

'No,' Rhiannon admitted, her face still buried in his shoulder.

'It's like I always told you. Men only want you for your body. You should have listened to me. This evil Velshman tried to twist your mind against me. He showed his true background and breeding with the way he behaved. Now, why don't you come away with me. We shall have something to eat and drink, let you clean yourself up, then we can come back and hear the truth from these two. Sergeant Broyle shall have them ready to talk when we return. Come with me. I am your father, only I know what is best for you. You do believe that, don't you?'

'Y-yes,' Rhiannon sobbed.

'I have been searching for you up here all this time — only I have what is best for you in my heart and mind. Now come away with me and we shall talk about what we need to do to get back into the king's favour when we return to Cridianton.'

Hector nodded to Broyle, who drew his knife and eased closer to Sendatsu.

'I'm going to enjoy this, elfy,' he sneered. 'I'm going to make you look like a human. And then you're going to beg to tell me everything you know about Dokuzen and what an elf is doing here.'

Sendatsu just glared at him.

'Don't worry, miss. I'll make them pay for what they did to you! They'll be singing soon enough — but not a tune they wanted to make!'

Rhiannon looked up at Hector.

'There's no need to do that to them,' she said haltingly. 'I can tell you everything about their plans.'

Hector smiled at her. 'I am sure you will. But we need to be sure. We can't have the elf using magic on us! Now come with me. Everything will be fine. Everything will be as it was. This will all seem like some bad dream.'

Huw saw her in Hector's arms and could not stop the tears streaming down his face. How could he have been so stupid?

Sendatsu had told him time and again that he had to tell Rhiannon the whole truth, explain to her about her father and trust she would understand. Now she had heard the lies from Hector's mouth and not only would she hate him, but Hector would use her for his own foul purposes. Huw thought nothing could be worse than sitting in his father's chair, listening to Sendatsu make love to Rhiannon in his father's bed. But seeing Hector's gloating face and Rhiannon's tears made that feel like a pleasant experience. He could still see the anguish in her eyes, the expression on her face when she declared she would never forgive him. His own peril and impending torture seemed like nothing in comparison.

Sendatsu watched Rhiannon cry noisily and Huw sob silently but, as much as he felt sorry for them, he was worried about himself. Was this to be the end of everything? He had to stay alive for his children; no matter what they did to him, a priest of Aroaril could fix it, if he could but get back to Dokuzen. If they thought him broken, if they left him alone, then he could use magic to free himself and get away. He told himself that but he could imagine the coming pain and his mind shrank away from it.

'What are they doing?' Rhiannon pointed to where two of Broyle's men were stoking a fire, heating the tips of their swords inside the flames.

'We need the truth out of them. After what they did to you, you'd probably like to take the knife to them yourself.' Broyle chortled.

That gave Rhiannon pause. As much as she wanted to lash out at Huw and Sendatsu, as much as she felt betrayed, the idea of torturing them made her feel even more sick.

'What are you going to do to them?' she demanded.

'I don't think you need to worry yourself about that. Sergeant Broyle and his men know what they are doing. Don't concern your little head about it. Come with me now.' Hector's grip on her arm was firm and he began tugging her away.

But as much as Rhiannon was delighted to see her father, his declaration that all would go back to the way it was, he would make the past months seem like a bad dream, did not sit well. For all the wrong Sendatsu and Huw had done her, they had also shown her she was a strong woman, able to make decisions on her own, able to take action. Whatever else had happened, she did not want to go back to being a little ornament, totally dependent on her father. Now she had tasted freedom, she would not walk so easily back into the cage he offered.

'Wait! Father, listen to me,' she said sharply. 'Trust me, please! I told you I know everything about their plans, about them. I can tell you and King Ward everything you need to know.'

Hector smiled thinly. 'I am sure you can. But he does not want to hear it from you. We shall leave now ...'

'Aren't you listening to me?' Rhiannon cried, fighting back against his pull. 'Father, none of this is necessary ...'

'Get her out of here, Hector. We need to go to work,' Broyle grumbled, holding up a sword with a glowing tip. 'I've been waiting a long time to get my hands on these two.'

'Come on, dear.' Hector began pulling Rhiannon away but she dug her heels in and ripped her arm free of his grasp.

'Who is in charge here?' she demanded. 'Father, if these men are truly under your control, then order them to stand down. I will tell you now about Sendatsu and why he is here ...'

'Of course they are under my control!' Hector blustered. He glanced over at Broyle, who was staring flatly at him, flanked by his men, all of them holding swords. 'And I am instructing them to get the knowledge from this filthy Velshman and his elven accomplice!'

'So you won't even listen to me?' Rhiannon gasped. 'I have a voice here. I thought this was all about rescuing me?'

'And it is!' Hector snapped. 'But I know what is best for you and you need to obey me now!'

He reached for her again but she stepped back, knocking his hand away.

'No,' she said.

'What?' Hector asked dangerously.

'I will not obey! I am trying to tell you everything you need to know and you won't listen to me. Why can't you see that ...'

'Enough!' Hector roared, swelling up. He had tried to be patient with her, tried to be kind, but the frustrations of the last few months bubbled over. 'I see you have been in this dirty little country too long! You will learn your place again. I spend months looking for you and when I finally rescue you, this is all the thanks I get!' He loomed over her, sure she would crumble and fall down, beg forgiveness, as she had always done in the past. He added the final threat, the trick that had always worked on her. 'Your mother would be ashamed of your behaviour!'

But that was a different Rhiannon.

She felt the habits of a lifetime urge her to give in, to obey whatever her father told her. Then she ignored them, as her mind sifted through what he had been saying.

'But if you have been looking for me all this time, why did you not simply ride up to the village by yourself? I would have seen you and come running out!'

Hector paused for a moment, thrown by her question. 'Well, that elf would have spitted me on an arrow before I got close! Anyway, what has that got to do with anything? I am ordering you to follow me now. I should have known this would happen — I knew he was trouble from the start. The Velsh have a smell about them, you can tell them right away,' he snarled at her, towered over her.

Rhiannon looked at him anew. Perhaps he did fear that Sendatsu would kill him from a distance if he had ridden in, although that did not quite seem right. But there was another point there.

'You've said it again,' she said slowly. 'That you knew Huw was Velsh. But I was the only one who knew. You thought he was from Forland, from Browns Brook.'

'I found out — I have ways and means ...' Hector defended but she interrupted him now.

'No. You would have denounced him. You did not know he was Velsh but you just lied to me and told me you did. Why did you lie?'

Her voice was calm but inside all was boiling. Could no man she loved tell her the truth?

That was too much for Hector. 'You dare accuse me of lying?' he screamed at her. 'You will regret that!'

'So it was a lie,' Rhiannon said flatly. 'And if you were lying about that, what else have you been lying about?'

'How dare you?' Hector's voice shook with anger. 'After all I have done for you, this is how you repay me? You should fall on your knees and beg forgiveness! No other man would have looked after you like I did, would have devoted themselves to your dream ...'

Once, Rhiannon would have fallen on her knees and apologised. Once she would have accepted what her father said without question. But that time had passed.

'Was it my dream — or was it yours?' she asked. 'Tell me — was what Huw said the truth? Were you planning to sell me to Ward?'

Hector goggled at her defiance. He had never imagined such a thing could happen. She had been under his thumb for so long, to see her stand up to him was impossible to believe. On top of what she had already put him through, his anger surged out of control. He backhanded her across the face, sending her to the ground.

Both Huw and Sendatsu surged forwards — or tried to — their bonds held them in place.

Hector glared down at Rhiannon, who lay on her stomach.

'That was for your own good,' he told her. 'You asked for that. Now stand up and follow me and we can discuss what is going to happen next.'

Rhiannon pushed herself to her knees and wiped away a trail of blood from her mouth, where her lip was split.

'Now I can believe those men were under your command,' she said bitterly. 'But I do not know what else to believe.'

'Believe the evidence of your eyes! That Velsh bard said I was dead and I stand before you, ready to accept you back, ready to forgive your mistakes.' Hector held out his arms, restraining himself from hitting the insolence out of her.

'But was that his only lie? Or were you really planning to whore me to King Ward? For I shall not be sold off to any man.

I will never trust another man enough to get into bed with him.'
Rhiannon forced herself to her feet.

For a moment Hector thought about trying to come up with a
convincing story to persuade her but then he saw the look on her
face and lost control. His dreams, his plans, everything was built
around getting her to walk willingly into Ward's bedchamber.
There was no chance of that now. Everything was turning to
ashes, because the stupid little bitch had run away. Well, if she
could not be persuaded, she would be taught her place.

He stormed forwards. Rhiannon stood her ground. She did not
believe he would hit her again. He had never raised a hand to her
before; his domination had always been through persuasion and
guilt.

But he was past all restraint. He struck her again, this time
with his fist, sending her crashing to the ground.

Rhiannon lay there for a long moment, her head a whirl of
pain, trying to come to terms with what was happening. She
could feel her cheek and eye swelling already as she pushed
herself to her knees.

'You will never hit me again,' she stated flatly. 'And you can
forget about me doing anything else you want. I shall make my
own life ...'

'Seize her!' Hector ordered, driven beyond the borders of
reason.

Broyle and one of his men dropped their swords and grabbed
her arms, hauling her roughly to her feet.

'You think you have a choice here?' Hector raved. 'You will
do what I tell you, one way or another! You are too valuable for
me to give away. Do you know how much I have had to put up
with over the years? I spent my whole life developing you for the
court, so you would restore my fortune after your stupid bitch of
a mother ruined everything for me. I listened to your idiotic fears,
put up with your whining, I pretended to enjoy your company
while I trained you and changed you from useless to useful. After
all I have done, you don't have the right to do anything other
than what I tell you. You will return with me and you will bring

us back into the king's good fortunes in his bed — or you will be beaten every day until you beg to do what I want!'

Even Huw and Sendatsu stopped struggling as they listened to Hector snarl at Rhiannon.

Rhiannon stared at her father. His words cut deep inside, hurting more than the blows he had given her. But she would not let him know that.

'Thank you, Father, for finally telling me the truth,' she said carefully. 'Now I know where we both stand.'

'So are you going to listen to reason or do I turn you over to Sergeant Broyle here?' Hector snapped.

For answer, Rhiannon collected the blood still running into her mouth from her cut lip and spat it into his face.

'You little bitch! You are even worse than your mother!' Hector howled. 'Tie her up!'

'We don't have enough rope,' Broyle warned.

'Then use the reins from their horses! I don't care what you do but I will not tolerate that!' Hector wiped away the bloody spittle.

Broyle held Rhiannon, twisting her arms tight behind her back as his men collected reins, then tied her hands together, lashing the other end to a branch, forcing her arms up high.

'Who do we start on first?' Broyle asked eagerly.

'I'll take the bard, you work on the elf?' Ricbert offered.

'No need for gags any more,' Broyle agreed. 'But we had better hurry. Some of their friends might decide to come looking for them if we tarry here too long.'

'Father, listen to me. There is no need to do this,' Rhiannon said desperately. 'I can still tell you all you need to know ...'

'But I don't think we can quite trust you, missy.' Broyle leered.

He pulled the gags out of Sendatsu's and Huw's mouths.

'Why don't you try and hit a man, instead of your daughter, you fat bastard?' Sendatsu shouted at Hector.

'Oh, I plan to,' Hector said conversationally, stepping up to Huw.

Huw glared at him, hating him for what he had done to Rhiannon as well as what he had done to them both.

Hector stared back at him with loathing. This was the man who had wrecked his careful plan, who had turned his own daughter against him. He let his rage build up to the level where he could not stop it and then unleashed a series of punches, hitting Huw in the face and body, not stopping until he was puffing and barely able to throw another fist, and blood was running from Huw's mouth and nose and his eyes were swelling shut.

'Is that all you have, you bastard?' Huw spat out blood and tried to look defiant. He had been able to roll his head with most of the blows but enough had struck to leave his head ringing like a bell.

'I shall be back, after Corporal Ricbert has finished,' Hector promised.

Rhiannon had tried to close her eyes and ears to the beating but the sound of fists on flesh, as well as Huw's grunts of pain, had been too much.

Sendatsu had watched Huw being hit and knew his own turn was next. Broyle was heating up swords in the fire and grinning at him. He tried to tense himself, prepare himself for the pain, tell himself that it would not be that bad — but he was still deathly afraid.

Working briskly, Ricbert tore open both Sendatsu's and Huw's tunics.

'Look at the elf — he's covered in scars as it is,' Ricbert declared.

'Let us go now, or suffer the consequences,' Sendatsu told them defiantly.

The Forlish roared with laughter.

'Let's add a few more scars.' Broyle withdrew a sword, its tip glowing, and walked over, pressing it against Sendatsu's ribs.

The smell of burning flesh was thick, Sendatsu's scream was terrible to hear but the worst thing for Rhiannon was the sizzling sound.

Huw tried to dodge his blade but there was no way he could move in his bonds. The sight and sound of what had happened to Sendatsu made the anticipation even harder — and it was as bad as he feared, a searing agony that whipped through his body. Although he tried not to, he screamed, part of him hoping that might even carry to the village, have his dragons hear and come to their rescue.

'That was too loud. I think we should put the gags back in before the next one,' Hector suggested.

'I thought you were going to question them?' Rhiannon said raggedly.

'That can come later. Now we are just giving them a lesson. The Forlish are not to be defied. This will pay them back for all the good men they killed,' Broyle said with relish.

Two more swords were brought from the fire and the hot tips drawn down and across Sendatsu's and Huw's torsos, leaving ridged red burns behind. The pain of the second one was, if possible, even worse than the first, which still flamed. The pair of them bucked and shrieked at the agony of it, their cries muffled by cloth.

'What about the girl? Do we give her a blade also?' Ricbert asked.

'No — her skin must not be broken, only her spirit,' Hector ruled. 'If she is damaged goods anyway, perhaps you need to use a different sort of blade on her to bring her to heel …'

Broyle's throaty laugh made Rhiannon's skin crawl.

'Leave her alone!' Huw screamed around his gag, trying to use anger and hatred to block out the agony from his side.

'Do you want to watch? You know, that might hurt him more than a hot blade,' Broyle mused.

'Father! You can't be serious!' Rhiannon cried.

'You brought this upon yourself,' Hector said coldly. 'It is your fault. You pushed me to this. You must learn to obey me without question.'

Huw had never wanted anything as much as he wanted to rip himself free of his bonds, revenge himself on the Forlish and save Rhiannon. To watch her being raped — Broyle was right, it would be even more painful than the hot blades. How could Hector allow this, let alone be the one who suggested it? The gorge rose in his throat and he strained to free himself. Surely the dragons would come, surely this could not really be happening ...

'Struggle all you like, there's no way you'll get free,' Broyle told him, stepping close so he could whisper in Huw's ear. 'You planned to Walk The Tree with this girl. Now you're going to see me and my mates take her and ...'

Huw shut his ears to Broyle's filth and wrenched at the ropes with all of his strength. It was not enough.

Rhiannon felt like her heart was a bird, trying to escape her ribcage, it was beating so fast.

'Don't do this! Father, you can't do this,' she begged.

But Hector just stared at her.

'You whored yourself to the elf and Velsh. What is the difference?' he growled.

'Every difference in the world! Daddy, you were the one who raised me, protected me, who taught me about men, who braided my hair and picked my dresses ... you can't let this happen ...' She put everything she had into her plea, while she strained at the thin leather holding her prisoner.

'I hated every moment of it,' Hector spat. 'I did it because it was the only way to restore my fortune. I made you into what you are because that is what I needed. Now you are no good to me. I need you to do whatever Ward wants and, until I am sure you will act that way, you are nothing to me.'

His words drained the strength out of her and she hung there, an empty husk. Everything — *everything* — she had believed in, all she had known, had been brought down around her today. Whatever they did to her body would be nothing compared to what Huw and Hector had done to her spirit — especially Hector. He had been her whole world, he had been all she had known. And now he said that meant *nothing*? It was too much even for tears.

Broyle and Ricbert cut the reins hanging from the branch, freeing her hands. She did not fight back, she just hung limply in their arms as they dragged her around the tree, right in front of where Huw was tied. She was vaguely aware of Huw fighting against his bonds and making desperate noises behind his gag. But everything seemed to be encased in ice, or locked away behind an invisible wall, at a distance from her. All she could see was Hector's angry face, not a scrap of pity or remorse or sympathy there.

'Are you really going to let us do this?' Broyle hesitated and everyone looked to Hector.

Rhiannon appealed to him with her eyes, silently begging him to prove his words were just anger and all they had shared, all he had done for her was not a lie.

Hector glared at her.

'Yes,' he spat.

That was the final straw. She went beyond anger, beyond tears. This could not be happening — *this would not happen.*

And the world came alive around her.

# 29

*I was flung into an old church of Aroaril, along with scores of humans. The last remnants of the lists the Magic-weavers had compiled, now rounded up or tricked by Naibun into coming here. With their passing, the Velsh, the Forlish, the Breconians, the Landish ... all the people of this land would be greatly reduced. In here was magic, knowledge, light and goodness. Soon to be destroyed. Men and women from every country across the land prayed together, knowing that was all they had left. I gave them one flicker of hope, explained how the elves would be sealed off from the rest of the world until their magic was almost done, that the rest of the lands would be protected from elven conquest. It provided little cheer, although I found some myself in seeing the way men from Landia kneeled beside those from Forland, embraced Balians and wept with Skillian Islanders. Given something to unite them, these men had put aside their petty differences. Perhaps it could happen again.*

*As for me, I wrote this account in the old language, Nipponese, and used my limited magic to protect it, hide it behind the Aroaril stone in this human church. Now my story is done. I hope it provides some guidance, some truth for those who follow me. For the barrier will decay over time and humans will again meet so-called elves. I shall be long dead, my memory wiped from history's pages.*

*Once again I pray a better Sendatsu can be found at that time.*

* * *

'No!' Rhiannon told her father.

She took a deep breath, and inhaled everything around her. She could feel the energy from the plants, sense the birds in the air, the animals deep in the trees and the insects on the ground. They were all there for her. For a long moment she did nothing, just exulted in the feeling. It fizzed through her blood, smoothed away the pain of her father's blows.

Everything seemed to call out to her, ready to do her bidding. Broyle and Ricbert grabbed her arms, prepared to hurl her to the ground.

She spoke to the trees around, told them what she needed, and they did the rest.

Branches scores of years old and weighed down with time swept across, suddenly given the springy whip of the newest twigs. They smashed into the two Forlishmen, sending them flying.

'Skies above! The elf must be using magic!' Hector roared.

The other two Forlish guards ran at Sendatsu, swords at the ready, rushing past Rhiannon without a second glance. It was a fatal mistake. The old oak came to life and blasted them into the air, to be caught and hammered by other trees, until they fell limply to the ground.

'Stop him!' Hector bleated.

Broyle and Ricbert came to their feet once more but she pointed at them and they were engulfed in insects. Ants and spiders swarmed over their legs, bees and wasps covered their heads and shoulders, more and more dropping out of trees, flying in or racing out of the grass around them. Broyle and Ricbert screamed in pain and terror as they were bitten and stung but their mouths only filled with their attackers, every opening of their bodies filled with tiny vengeance. Arms flailing, they tried to scrape their insect attackers away but hundreds more replaced every handful they managed to remove. They tried to run but could go nowhere — they fell to the ground and thrashed under huge mounds, until the only movement was the writing of the insects as they fed.

Hector turned and ran, fast as his legs would carry him.

'Stop!' Rhiannon shouted.

A branch broke free of a nearby tree, thick as a man's leg and twice as long, fell and then accelerated across the clearing. At first it aimed at Hector's legs but then she jerked her hand up and, at the last moment, the branch swerved upwards and drove deep into Hector's back, slamming through the chest and throwing him forwards, where he rested grotesquely, slumped over the broken branch, his blood draining into the soil.

Rhiannon looked around but nobody was moving. Sendatsu shrank back as he saw the fire, the fury and the magic bubbling in her eyes — and then they closed and she fell limply.

Sendatsu reached into the magic himself, changed the fibres of the ropes holding he and Huw tight and they fell away. He tore out his gag but the effort of using even that much magic, on top of what the Forlish had done to him, left him exhausted. His ribs were really hurting and his vision was beginning to swim, so he fell to his knees.

Huw ripped the gag out of his mouth and rushed to Sendatsu's side.

'You saved us — you saved us with magic!' he gasped.

'No. Rhiannon,' Sendatsu tried to explain. The ground seemed soft and he decided to lie down, just for a little while.

Although Huw was in agony, his face and body on fire with pain, he needed no second invitation. He glanced over to where all the insects bar the ants were leaving what remained of Broyle and Ricbert, then raced over to where Rhiannon lay, unmoving.

'Rhiannon! Are you all right?' He picked her up in his arms, brushed her face.

Her eyes fluttered open and took a moment to focus on him. He smiled nervously at her — then she shrank away from his touch, pushed him away. 'Get away from me!'

Huw felt a little part of him die inside.

'Let me help you,' he said softly, helplessly.

'I don't want to talk to you, I don't even want to see you right now!' she cried.

She felt as though she was about to fly apart. The shocks had piled up on each other, one after another — her father's return, Huw's lies, Hector's lies, then his admission of betrayal ... then the magic. The plants and animals and insects had been somehow connected to her. It had been both exciting and terrifying and, even now, she was not entirely sure it had really happened.

How could she do magic? She was a human! But she had destroyed the Forlish — and killed her father. *She had killed her father.*

He had lied to her. And Huw had lied to her, everyone she loved had lied to her.

'You lied! You lied to me!' she screamed at Huw, and at Hector, who lay behind him. She wanted to rage at her father, to tell him she was a strong, proud woman, not a plaything. That a daughter was not a man's property and certainly not to blame for the mistakes made in his life. But he could not listen, so she had to shout at Huw instead.

'I know, I am sorry.' Huw held out his hands, knowing it was doing no good but hoping she could forgive him, offer him a second chance.

'I trusted you, I believed in you — and you betrayed me!'

Again, Huw could only agree.

'You say it was for my own benefit, you were protecting me — but it was really all for you. Did you even love my mother?'

'What?' Huw stared at her, then glanced over his shoulder to where Hector lay.

'Don't mistake me for him,' he said, heat coming into his voice now. 'I take responsibility for my lie but I truly thought it was for the best. It was wrong and I am sorry. I know it does no good but I was going to tell you, today ...'

'That makes it even worse! How do you think I would feel, having Walked The Tree with you, for you to turn around and tell me that?' she screamed.

'I am sorry!' Huw yelled back. 'I was scared of losing you ...'

'Well, you are half right then! After what happened with Sendatsu, I can't believe you tricked me, lied to me. Did he know as well?'

'Sendatsu said I should tell you, he warned me I needed to be honest,' Huw admitted. 'He has nothing to do with this ...'

'This gets better and better! Were the two of you laughing at me behind my back — had you both planned everything from the start?'

'No!' Huw shouted back, the memory of when Rhiannon was with Sendatsu too painful to let go lightly. 'That was Hector's lie. What happened between us was real ...'

'Don't mention his name! I never want to hear it again!' Rhiannon bellowed.

'I am sorry — sorry for everything. But you must understand that I did it all to protect you. You heard what your father was planning to do to you. I had to get you out of there and I knew explaining all that would take too long ...'

'I deserved the truth! If nothing else, before we Walked The Tree!' she screamed.

'Hey, you two — enough!' Sendatsu staggered to his feet and towards them both.

'What?' They both rounded on him.

'We are alive — we should be happy for that.'

'Happy? You think I can be happy after this? What have I got to be happy about?' Rhiannon asked bitterly.

Huw, who could see Rhiannon slipping away from him with every word, did not speak but his battered face said it all.

By contrast, Sendatsu's mind was whirling and happiness was bubbling through him. Rhiannon could do magic. A human could do magic. This was not one of the answers he sought but it was exactly what Sumiko wanted. This would change everything in Dokuzen. This was his ticket home ... was this also proof that there was no difference between humans and elves?

'You can do magic now. You can come back to Dokuzen with me. You can get the elves to save Vales, you can change everything!' He struggled to convey the enormity of it all to the pair of them.

'What?' Rhiannon's head was spinning and she could not think straight.

'You are the first human to do magic — you are the most important person in the world now!'

Rhiannon gaped at him, as did Huw.

'I don't feel important,' she groaned, wanting to disappear down a deep hole, leave all this far behind.

'Don't you understand? You are the one person who can bring elves and humans together. You are the one these lands have been waiting for the last three hundred years!'

Silence greeted Sendatsu's words as Huw and Rhiannon stared at him in shock.

Sendatsu smiled encouragingly at her, his heart singing. He had his answers, he had everything he ever dreamed of! He could go home, he could see his children, he could feel Mai's and Cheijun's arms around him even now and tears pricked his eyes as he imagined their reaction. Part of him was warning that Rhiannon's life would be in terrible danger the moment she revealed her magic to the elves — but all he could think about was his children.

'It's not going to be like that at all,' a harsh voice interrupted.

Sendatsu spun, Rhiannon and Huw turned also, to see Hanto walk into the clearing, Jin and Taigo at his shoulders. All three had their bows bent, the arrows pointed at them.

'You really should learn how to stay hidden in woodlands. All that screaming and shouting led us right to you.' Hanto smiled wolfishly. 'I can't begin to tell you how much I've been looking forward to this.' He glanced at his companions. 'Kill the humans.'

He kept his drawn bow pointed at Sendatsu, while the other two instantly loosed, sending arrows leaping across the clearing.

The story continues in

# VALLEY OF SHIELDS

EMPIRE OF BONES, BOOK TWO

# Author's Note

Many of the place names in *Bridge of Swords*, indeed the whole series, are real names, to be found in the pages of history or even on today's maps. However, the fictional towns and villages named in this series bear no relation to their real counterparts.

There are also several historical hints and notes, from the Chinese repeating crossbow to the Welsh flag and anthem. Again, there is no intention to make this, or them, real.

This is not only a work of fiction, it is a work of fantasy.

# Acknowledgements

A book does not end up on the shelves without a great deal of work by a great many people. I need to thank my beta reader Belinda Lay, agent Sophie Hamley, publisher Stephanie Smith, editor Kate Burnitt, copy-editor Abigail Nathan, proofreader Ron Buck and designer Darren Holt. Without their help, advice and eagle eyes, *Bridge of Swords* would not be the same book. My name is on the cover yet they all helped to make it better and stronger, as well as hide flaws, correct mistakes and eliminate my talent for repeating key words and phrases.

www.ingramcontent.com/pod-product-compliance
Lightning Source LLC
Chambersburg PA
CBHW020239120726
47904CB00001B/30